BLOOD SPORT
&
SHATTERED

DICK FRANCIS wrote more than forty international best-sellers and was widely acclaimed as one of the world's finest thriller writers. His awards included the Crime Writers' Association's Cartier Diamond Dagger for his outstanding contribution to the genre, and an honorary Doctorate of Humane Letters from Tufts University of Boston. In 1996 Dick Francis was made a Mystery Writers of America Grand Master for a lifetime's achievement and in 2000 he was awarded the CBE in the Queen's Birthday Honours list. Sadly he died in 2010.

Dick Francis

BLOOD SPORT
&
SHATTERED

PAN BOOKS

Blood Sport first published 1967 by Michel Joseph
First published in paperback 1968 by Pan Books
Shattered first published 2000 by the Penguin Group
First published in paperback 2001 by Pan Books

This omnibus first published 2011 by Pan Books
an imprint of Pan Macmillan, a division of Macmillan Publishers Limited
Pan Macmillan, 20 New Wharf Road, London N1 9RR
Basingstoke and Oxford
Associated companies throughout the world
www.panmacmillan.com

ISBN 978-0-330-54546-4

1 3 5 7 9 8 6 4 2

A CIP catalogue record for this book is available from
the British Library.

Typeset by SetSystems Ltd, Saffron Walden, Essex
Printed in the UK by CPI Mackays, Chatham ME5 8TD

Visit **www.panmacmillan.com** to read more about all our books
and to buy them. You will also find features, author interviews and
news of any author events, and you can sign up for e-newsletters
so that you're always first to hear about our new releases.

BLOOD SPORT

CHAPTER ONE

I awoke with foreboding. My hand closed in a reflex on the Luger under the pillow. I listened, acutely attentive. No sound. No quick surreptitious slither, no rub of cloth on cloth, no half-controlled pulse-driven breath. No enemy hovering. Slowly, relaxing, I turned half over and squinted at the room. A quiet, empty, ugly room. One-third of what for want of a less cosy word I called home.

Bright sunshine by-passed the thin pink curtains, spilling a gold slash on the faded brown Wilton. I didn't like pink. Also I didn't have the energy it would take to argue the landlord into changing to blue. After eight months I knew he never renewed anything until it had fallen to bits.

In spite of the prevailing calm the feeling of foreboding deepened and then identified itself and dissolved into a less threatening, more general state of gloom. Sunday morning, June 20th. The beginning of three weeks' leave.

I rolled back on to my stomach and shut my eyes

1

against the sun, and took my hand six inches from the Luger, which was far enough, and wondered how long a man could sleep if he really put his mind to it. Even a man who never slept soundly to start with. Three weeks, the three obligatory overdue weeks could be got through more easily asleep.

Three millenniums of sleep lay under the pillow. The nine-millimetre equalizer, my inseparable friend. It went with me everywhere, to beaches, to bathrooms, to beds other than my own. It was there to save my life. Not to take it. I had lived through a lot of temptations, and I lived with that too.

The telephone bell put paid to the three weeks before they had gone half an hour.

''Lo,' I said blearily, balancing the receiver on the pillow.

'Gene?'

'Uh huh.'

'You haven't gone away then.' There was relief in the voice, the voice of my boss. I looked at my watch. Ten o'clock.

'No,' I said unnecessarily. He knew I wasn't going away. I didn't understand his relief. It was missing when he spoke again.

'How about a day on the river?'

He had a motor cruiser somewhere on the upper Thames. I'd never seen it. Hadn't been asked before.

'Invitation or order?' I said, yawning.

He hesitated. 'Whichever you'll accept.'

2

What a man. You did more for him than you believed you would, every time.

'Where do I go, and when?'

'My daughter will fetch you,' he said. 'She'll be there in about half an hour. Family party. Boating clothes. Come as you are.'

'Sure,' I said. Complete with stubble, Luger, and shorts. A riot. I never wore pyjamas. They slowed you up too much.

Boating clothes, I decided, were greyish brown cotton trousers and an olive green nylon jersey shirt. I carried the Luger with me in the left hand pocket when the doorbell rang. One never really knew. But a look through the wide-angled spyhole showed it was only Keeble's daughter, as arranged. I opened up.

'Mr Hawkins?' she said hesitantly, looking from me to the dingy brass six screwed on to the solid dark stained wood.

'That's right,' I smiled. 'Come in.'

She walked past me and I shut the door, interested to notice that four flights of stairs hadn't left her breathless, as they did most visitors. I lived high up for that purpose.

'I was just finishing my coffee,' I said. 'Would you like some?'

'It's very kind of you, but Daddy said not to waste time, he wants to be off up river as soon as possible.'

Keeble's daughter was just like her photograph on Daddy's desk. Half woman, still at school. Short bouncy dark hair, and watchful dark eyes, a rounded body slimming down, a self-possessed touch-me-not expression, and an endearing gaucheness in her present situation.

She looked cautiously round the sitting room, which neither she nor I nor anyone else would have classed as elegant living. The landlord's furniture was junk-shop stuff and I had made no effort to improve it. My total contributions to the scene were two rows of books on the shelves and in one corner a tin trunk of oddments which I had never bothered to unpack. A drawn back curtain revealed the kitchen alcove and its entire contents: cupboard, refrigerator, sink, and cooker, all of them showing their age.

One went through the sitting room to the bedroom, through the bedroom to the bathroom, and through the bathroom to the fire escape. The flat had everything but a drawbridge and a moat, and it had taken me weeks to find it. Only the tiny spyglass had been lacking, and the landlord had been furious when he finally noticed I had installed it. It had cost me three months' rent in advance to convince him it wasn't there for the sole purpose of being out when he came.

I watched Keeble's daughter search for something nice to say about my living quarters and give up the struggle with a defeated shake of her young head. I could have told her that I had once had a better flat, a spacious comfortable first-floor front with a balcony overlooking a tree-dotted square. It had proved too

4

accessible to unwanted guests. I had vacated it on a stretcher.

'I'll fetch my jacket,' I said, finishing the coffee. 'And then we'll go.'

She nodded, looking relieved, oppressed already by the emptiness of my home life. Five minutes of it had been enough, for her.

I went into the bedroom, picked the jacket off the bed, and transferred the Luger from my trousers into its built-in under-arm holster, fastening it there with a press stud on a strap. Then, coat over arm, I dumped the dirty coffee cup in the sink, pulled the curtain across the kitchen, opened the front door, and let myself and Miss Keeble out.

Four uneventful storeys down we emerged into the quiet sunlit Putney street, and she looked back and up at the solid old converted house. It needed paint and oozed respectability, exactly like its row of neighbours.

'I wasn't sure I'd come to the right place. Daddy just said the fourth house along.'

'He gives me a lift home, sometimes.'

'Yes, he said so.' She turned to the white Austin standing at the kerb and paused with the key in her hand. 'Do you mind if I drive?'

'Of course not.'

She smiled for the first time since she'd arrived, a quick flashing affair which verged on friendliness. She unlocked her door, climbed in, and reached over to unlatch the opposite one for me. The first thing I noticed as I bent to get in were the L plates lying on the back seat.

'When did you pass the test?' I said mildly.

'Well . . .' the smile lingered, 'as a matter of fact, yesterday.'

For all that, she drove very well, careful but confident, quiet with the gears though a bit heavy with the hand signals. She crept somewhat tentatively around the Chiswick roundabout and up the slope to the M4. The big blue motorway sign said no L drivers, and her nose twitched mischievously as we passed it.

'Did you come this way to fetch me?' I asked idly.

She edged into the slow lane and hit forty.

'Er, no. I live in a hostel with about sixty other girls in South Ken. Daddy just rang me and said as I'd got the car up in London this weekend I could collect you and meet him in Henley. Sort of spur of the moment thing.'

'I see.'

We came to the end of the fifty mile an hour limit and her foot went down with determination.

'Do I scare you?' The needle quivered on sixty-five.

I smiled wryly. 'No.'

'Actually . . .' Her hands gripped the wheel with the tension of inexperience. 'Actually, you don't look as if you'd scare easily.'

I glanced at her in surprise. I look ordinary. Quiet and ordinary. And very useful it is, too.

'Anyway,' she went on frankly, 'I asked Daddy about coming this way, and he said he guessed your nerves would stand it. He seemed to find it very funny, for some reason or other.'

'He has his own brand of humour.'

'Mm.' She drove on for several miles in silence, concentrating on the road. The speed dropped slowly down to fifty again, and I guessed she was finding the motorway not such pure fun as she'd imagined. The usual number of Sunday Jim Clarks were showing off in the fast lane and family outings with Grandma driving from the back seat were bumbling about in the slow. We went down the centre and pulled out bravely now and then to pass an airport bus.

Eventually, in thinner traffic after Windsor, she said, doubtfully, 'You do . . . er . . . work for Daddy?'

'Yes. Why not?'

'Well, no reason why not. I mean,' she looked embarrassed, 'I mean, I can't remember him ever asking anyone from work . . . well, he just doesn't usually, that's all.' She looked as if she wished she hadn't started.

'A kind thought,' I suggested; and wondered what he wanted. Not just to give me a sunny day out. As his daughter said, he didn't do that sort of thing.

We made it to Henley with the paint intact, and she parked neatly in a large gravelled enclosure by the railway station. Her hands trembled slightly as she locked the doors, and I realized that it must have been her longest drive, as well as her fastest.

'You drove beautifully,' I said sincerely. 'Like a veteran.'

'Oh.' She gave a laugh which was half a cough, and looked relieved and pleased. 'Well, thank you.' She would be more relaxed, I knew, on the way back, and less strung up when she got there. To give and to remove confidence were tools of my trade, and there was no union to say I couldn't use them on Sundays.

'*Flying Linnet* . . . that's our boat . . . will be somewhere along the bank,' she said. 'It isn't far.' She smiled again and gestured, 'That way.'

We walked down to the river and along the neatly built broad tarmac towpath, where half the town seemed to be out feeding the ducks. The sun sparkled on the dark green water and there was a queue at the boatyard for rowing boats and punts. There were gardens and lawns and seats, and a bowling green, and a playground with a slide and swings, all of them sprinkled with sunny Sunday faces and murmuring summer voices. Families and couples and groups: few alone. Three weeks alone, I thought bleakly. I could spend them beside the deep green river feeding ducks, and just jump in when I couldn't stand any more of it.

'There's Daddy,' said Keeble's daughter, pointing. The sun lay along her light brown arm and shifted in burnt toffee shadows on the curves of her orange tan dress. Too young for me, I thought inconsequentially.

Or rather, I was too old. Aeons too old. Forty still lay a couple of years ahead, but I could have told Methuselah a thing or two.

Keeble had stepped ashore from one of the boats moored top to tail along the towpath and was walking towards us, hand outstretched, welcoming smile in face. My boss, except for an open-necked shirt, looked his usual weekday self, a short slightly chubby man with a mild manner and a faintly anxious expression. The light blue-grey eyes blinked freely as usual behind the unimpressive spectacles and as usual he had missed a patch while shaving. Premature baldness had made him look fifty at thirty-five, but far from regretting this, he believed it was the cause of his rapid promotion over well-thatched contemporaries. He may have been right. He looked harmless, cautious, unambitious, one of nature's safest plodders. It was eight years since he had inherited me along with the rest of the setup, and to discern the cutting brain behind the waffle had taken me two minutes flat.

'Gene,' he said. 'Glad you could come.' He pumped my hand up and down perfunctorily, the social gesture as meaningless to him as to me, and we exchanged smiles to match. For his daughter the warmth came from the heart. She kissed him affectionately on the cheek and his eyes held a glimmering pride I had never seen in him before.

'Well, Lynnie my love, you got here safely. Or did you let Gene do the driving?'

'Do me a favour,' she said. 'He didn't even flinch.'

Keeble flicked me an amused glance, and I repeated the compliment to her skill, with her father nodding his thanks to me over her head, knowing exactly why I said it.

They turned and began to walk back along the path, gesturing to me to come. Keeble's boat, the one they stopped at, was a graceful neat-looking fibre-glass cruiser with a cabin forward and a large open cockpit at the back, the decks spotless and the chromium shining. Sitting casually side by side on the pale blue plastic upholstery were a man and a woman, both of whom raised smiling faces at our approach and neither of whom got up.

Lynnie jumped down into the boat and kissed the woman, and Keeble stepped carefully after.

'Come aboard,' he said to me, and again in his tone there was a choice. An invitation or an order, whichever I would accept. I opted for the invitation, and embarked on more than the *Flying Linnet*.

'My wife Joan,' said Keeble, stretching a hand to the seated woman. 'Gene Hawkins, honey.'

Joan Keeble was a frail birdlike woman with a coyness of manner left over from the time when she was pretty. She twinkled her eyes at me, inviting admiration. I scraped some up, and exchanged the necessary platitudes about weather, boating and driving daughters. Keeble waded into this with a wave towards the man sitting beside her.

'You two haven't met . . .' he hesitated a fraction. 'Dave . . . Gene, this is Dave Teller.'

Teller stood up, shook hands economically, and said he was glad to know me. He wore a sloppy wrinkled pale blue shirt hanging out over patched cotton trousers, battered plimsolls on his feet, and a dirty old baseball cap on his head. American, well educated, prosperous, assured: the categories clicked over from habit in my assessing mind. Also he was a lean man nearing fifty, with a strong beaky nose, straightforward eyes, and a marvellous dentist.

Keeble offered no information beyond that bald introduction, but bustled about getting his ship ready to put to sea. His yell into the cabin for a certain Peter to come and help produced no results. I stuck my head through the door and saw a boy of about twelve engrossed in fitting a new roll of film into a small simple camera.

'Peter,' his father yelled.

Peter heaved a martyred sigh, scrambled the back of the camera shut, and went out past me with his eyes down and his fingers winding the knob. Sure-footed, he stepped without looking on to the narrow side of the boat and from there to the towpath.

'He'll fall in one day,' Lynnie said to the world in general. Her brother didn't even hear. Still concentrating on his camera with one hand he was slowly untying the rope from the mooring ring with the other, crouching down on the tarmac in his clean black jeans and getting up with two large dusty patches on the knees. Pointing his viewfinder at a passing formation of ducks he clicked the shutter and with a serious, absorbed expression wound on the film.

Farther up the path Keeble and Teller were undoing the bow rope, talking amicably in the sun. Lynnie and her mother straightened the cushions and coiled the ropes and fussed around over a lot of nothing, chatting trivialities. I wondered what the hell I was doing there and felt out of contact with everything around me. Not a new feeling, but recurring more often. The two levels of living were growing farther apart. The day-to-day social level had lost all meaning, and underneath, where there should have been rock, had opened a void of shrivelling loneliness. It was getting worse. The present was bad enough: the future an abyss. Only work brought my splintering self into any sort of whole, and I knew well enough that it was the work itself which had started the process. That and Caroline. Or, to be more accurate, Caroline's husband.

'I say, hold this rope, will you?' Peter said. I took the wet snake he offered. 'Hi,' he added, seeing me properly for the first time, 'Who are you?'

'Anybody's guess,' I said with more truth than sense, and his mother stared at me with astonishment and told him my name.

Keeble came back on board and started the engine. Teller stood up on the small forward deck and cast off the bow rope when Keeble told him, and Peter left it until almost too late to leap on board with the stern. The camera bounced on the cord round his neck. 'Birthday present from Gran,' he said to Lynnie with pride. 'Super, isn't it.'

'You'll drop it in the river, if you aren't careful.'

'This is only my second film. I used the first one up on the boys at school. Do you think those ducks will come out all right?'

'I expect you had your finger over the shutter.'

'I've got a book in there.' He nodded to the cabin, expertly sifting out the affection behind her sarcasm and showing no resentment. 'It tells you about exposures and focuses. I think I'll just check what it says about sunny days. It was cloudy dull all week at school.'

I don't belong here, I thought. I wished I were asleep.

The *Flying Linnet* nosed upstream through a scatter of row-boats, Keeble at the wheel, Teller sitting forward still on the cabin roof, and Peter trying to get past Lynnie teasing him in the cabin doorway. Joan Keeble sat down on the wide seat across the back and patted the place next to her for me to join her. With an effort I did so, but after a minute or two, in the middle of apparently idle hostessy chat, she pulled me back to attention by trying delicately to find out who I was and why I had been invited, while not wanting to have me realize that she didn't know.

I could play that sort of game for ever. Inference

on inference. I didn't know the answer to why was I there, but that she needed to ask it, that indeed she had asked it, told me a great deal about non-contact between Keeble and his wife, and opened new doors on to Keeble himself. I knew then why he'd never before asked me home. It was one thing to employ a microscope, but another to put oneself under the lens. I thought it all the odder that he'd done it now.

As if he could feel my mind on the back of his neck he turned round and said, 'The lock's just ahead.' I stood up and joined him, and Peter gave up his struggle and went back to his duty with the stern rope.

'Marsh Lock,' Lynnie said, standing beside me and looking forward through the windscreen. 'Not an easy one, from this side, going upstream.'

When we got nearer I saw what she meant. The broad stretch of river narrowed abruptly to the lock gates on the left and the weir on the right, alongside. Baby whirlpools and trails of bubbles met us fifty yards away, with larger eddies and convolutions bubbling up as we went on. The boat tended to swing sideways under their power, and Keeble spun the wheel rapidly to keep her straight. Ahead of us water in tons tumbled over the weir, green and brown and splashing white, thundering down in great curving leaps, smelling of mustiness and mud.

A low wooden wall divided the lock approach from the turbulent weir water, and to the calm side of the barrier Keeble neatly steered his boat. Teller standing at the bow threw his rope over the hook on a mooring post there, and Peter slung a loop over a bollard at the stern.

I looked idly over the side of the boat, over the wall, up to the weir. Bouncing, tumbling, foaming, sweeping away back into the width of the river, the rough water looked superb in the sun. I felt the warmth and the fine spray mixed on my face and wondered whether if someone fell in there, he would ever come up.

The lock gates opened, the downcoming boats chugged out, and the *Flying Linnet* went in. Teller and Peter did their stuff mooring us to the side and Peter took a photograph of the boat in the lock. Water surged through the sluices in the upper gates, lifting us up, and in ten minutes we were going out of the lock on to another broad calm stretch of river, six feet higher than the one below.

'There are fifty locks on the Thames,' Keeble said. 'Lechlade is as far up as you can go except in a rowing boat, and that's about 300 feet above sea level.'

'Quite a staircase,' I commented.

'The Victorians,' he nodded, 'were a brilliant lot. They built them.'

Teller stood up on the foredeck holding the coil of rope, the peak of his baseball cap pointing forward like an attentive bird. I watched him, speculating, and Keeble followed the direction of my eyes and gave me only silence to work on.

Less than half a mile upstream from the lock we made an obviously pre-arranged stop at a riverside pub, Teller jumping ashore with his rope and fending the boat off the concrete edges as we drifted towards it. He and Peter tied expert knots, and everyone followed them ashore.

We drank sitting on a ring of uncomfortable metal chairs round a table with a sun umbrella spiked through its centre. Lynnie and Peter had Cokes and without consultation Keeble bought Scotch for the rest of us. Joan sipped hers with a pursed mouth and screwed eyes, as if it were a mite too strong for fragile little her, but I noticed she finished a long way first. Teller left his untouched for several minutes and then tossed it back in kingsized gulps. Keeble drank in pauses, revolving his glass in his hands and squinting through it at the sun. They were talking about the river, and other days on it, and other weather. On either side of us, round more umbrellas, sat more family parties much the same; Sunday morning drinks, Sunday lunch, Sunday snooze, *Sunday Express*, Sunday supper, *Sunday Night at the London Palladium* . . . safe little families in a sheltered routine, well-intentioned and more or less content. Even Keeble fitted in. Whereas I . . . was apart.

'Drink,' Keeble said. 'You're on holiday.'

Faced with instant sharp curiosity from the rest of his family I meekly picked up my glass, still full when theirs were empty. It felt wrong to drink in the morning; it raised sub-conscious bells of alarm. I liked the taste of alcohol all right, but couldn't afford its effects. Alcohol encouraged you to put your trust in luck, and I was better off trusting a clear head. Consequently I sometimes didn't touch the stuff for weeks on end, and on that morning had had none for nearly a month.

Keeble watched me swallow the whisky, as vivid and familiar as a long-lost friend. The extent to which I was ever on holiday lay in the jacket across my knees, a pound of deadly mechanism in an under-arm holster; but it did seem most unlikely that I would need it on the Thames. When Teller ordered a refill, I drank that too. And then, since it was my turn, a third.

Peter lasted the course to three Cokes, and then wandered away with his camera poised, looking for excuses to use it. Next door a boatyard, like the one at Henley, was doing a roaring trade in punts. Four of the pub's more enthusiastic customers were having trouble stepping aboard, and Teller said chuckling, 'What's the fine for punting under the influence . . .?'

'A soaking,' Lynnie said. 'Silly nits.'

The punt pole waved recklessly as they set off, but the four men didn't fall in. The punt skidded ten feet up the river and hit the pub's landing stage with a thump that tumbled them into a leg-waving heap. I tried to laugh with everyone else and only succeeded in feeling more remote than ever.

We finished the drinks, re-embarked, and went up through the next lock, Harbour, to an unpopulated green-pasture stretch of river, where we moored for lunch. Peter swam, jumping off the boat repeatedly in glittering splashes, and Lynnie helped her mother in the cabin, preparing the food. Teller sprawled lazily on the back seat, and Keeble sat down with a Sunday newspaper and unfolded it, and I wearily began to wonder just when he would come to the point.

The point, however, was the newspaper. We had arrived.

'Read that,' he said, tapping a small paragraph on an inside page.

I read it.

'There is still no sign of Chrysalis, free in Kentucky, US, since Tuesday. Anxiety mounts for the safety of the £500,000 stallion, sire of this year's Derby winner, Moth.'

'Is this what you mean?' I asked, puzzled, making sure I'd read the right section. I had. He nodded vigorously.

'Didn't you know about it?' he asked.

'That Chrysalis had got lost? Yes, I suppose so. It was on all the news bulletins on Wednesday.'

'And it didn't mean a damn thing to you,' Teller said, with a trace of controlled and civilized bitterness under his smile.

'Well . . .'

'I have a share in that horse,' Teller said. 'A one-eighth share, 200,000 dollars worth.'

'Wow,' I said blankly. It seemed a lot of money to invest in one-eighth of a horse.

'What is more,' he said, sighing, 'I have spent all of last month negotiating the sale, and was lucky to beat out another syndicate that was bidding for him. And now as soon as he gets over there, this has to happen.'

'I'm sorry,' I said, conventionally polite.

'I can't expect you to understand.' He shook his head, excusingly. 'It isn't the money which matters, it's the horse. He's irreplaceable.'

'They'll find him.' I had no doubts of it, and I didn't care one way or the other.

'I am not so sure,' he said. 'And I would like you to get out there and look for him.'

For five seconds no one twitched a muscle, least of all me. Then Teller turned his head to Keeble and smiled his glossy smile. 'I wouldn't play poker with him,' he said. 'OK, I'll buy what you say about him being all that good.'

I glanced at Keeble and he gave me raised eyebrows, a tiny shrug, and a slightly embarrassed expression. I wondered just how complete his testimonial had been.

Teller turned back to me. 'Sim here and I, we were in the same business, way back in World War II.'

'I see,' I said. And I did see. Quite a lot.

'It was just a war job for me, though,' he said. 'I got out of the Army in '47 and went back home to Pappy, and a couple of years later he died and left me his racehorses and a few bucks on the side.' The beautiful teeth flashed.

I waited. The story had hardly begun.

After a pause he said, 'I'll pay your fare and expenses, of course, and a fee.'

'I don't hunt horses,' I protested mildly.

'I can guess what you hunt.' He glanced again at Keeble. 'Sim says you're on vacation.'

I didn't need reminding.

'Chrysalis', he said, 'is the third stallion of international status to have disappeared in the last ten years.'

CHAPTER TWO

They tried pretty hard in their subtle way, but it seemed ridiculous to me.

'You know about horses,' Keeble said. 'Your father trained them for racing.'

'There's the police,' I pointed out. 'Also the insurance company. Also every man, woman, and child with an eye for a horse in the state of Kentucky. And I presume there's a reward?'

Teller nodded.

'So why me?'

'No one found the other two.'

'There's a lot of land in America,' I said. 'They're both probably free on a prairie somewhere having a high old time siring herds of wild horses.'

Teller said grudgingly, 'The first one was found dead in a gully two years after he disappeared.'

'That's it, then.'

'But the second one ... I bought that one too. I had a one tenth share. This is second time around for me.'

I stared at him. 'Were any of the circumstances the same?'

Reluctantly he shook his head. 'No ... except that they both got free. Allyx was never found. That's why I want something special done about Chrysalis.'

I was silent.

Keeble stirred. 'You've got nothing else to do, Gene. Why not take your holiday in the States? What will you do with yourself, if you stay in Putney?'

His eyes had stopped blinking, as they always did when he was intent. It was the surest guide I had to the complex calculations which sometimes lay beneath his most casual remarks. He couldn't have guessed, I thought in alarm. He was a manipulator but not clairvoyant. I shrugged and answered him on the surface.

'Walk round Kew Gardens and smell the orchids.'

'They have no scent,' said Teller, pointing out the obvious.

'He knows that.' Keeble nodded, still unblinking. 'Any fruitless way of passing the time, is what he meant.'

'I guess you two operate on your own private wave-length,' Teller said with a sigh. 'But I'd like you to come back with me, Gene, and at least take a look. What's the harm in that?'

'And what's the good in it? It's not my sort of job.' I looked away, down into the green water. 'And ... I'm tired.'

They hadn't a quick answer to that. I thought it would have been simple if all that was the matter with me was the straightforward tiredness of overwork, not the deadly fatigue of a struggle I wasn't sure I could win. Chasing some crazy colt over a thousand square miles didn't look like any sort of a cure.

Joan came out of the cabin into their defeated silence with a bowl of salad and a string of bright fussing chatter. A folding table was erected and the dishes put on to it, and we sat around in the sun eating cold chicken and hot french bread. There was a pleasant pink wine to drink and strawberries and cream afterwards, and Peter, still in wet bathing trunks despite orders from his mother, took mouthfuls and photographs by turn. Lynnie, sitting beside me, told Dave Teller an amusing story about the finishing school she attended, her warm bare arm brushing unselfconsciously against mine. I should have enjoyed that placid Sunday picnic on the river. I tried to. I smiled and answered when I was spoken to and concentrated carefully on the taste and texture of what I was eating, and all that happened was that the fat black slug of depression flexed its muscles and swelled another notch.

At four o'clock, after dishwashing and dozing, we started back towards Henley. My refusal to go to America hadn't basically disturbed Teller or Keeble an ounce. I concluded that whatever had prompted the suggestion it wasn't a burning conviction that I and only I could find the missing horse. I put the whole thing out of my mind. It wasn't hard.

There was a punt in difficulties at the approach to Harbour Lock. Teller, again standing up on the bow with rope at the ready, shouted back to Keeble and pointed ahead. We looked, all of us, following his finger.

Where the river divided, going slowly into the left fork round the bend to the lock and fast on the right straight to the weir, a sturdy post in mid-stream bore a large notice, a single word: DANGER.

A girl, lying flat half in and half out of the punt with her arms round the post, was trying to tie up to it by passing a rope from one hand to the other, and making a poor job of it. On the stern, watching anxiously, punt pole in hand, stood a young man in a red-and-yellow shirt. He waved his arms when he saw us coming, and as Keeble throttled back and drifted near, he shouted across the water.

'Could you help us, sir?'

Since the punt was full in the weir stream with only the girl's slender arms keeping it from floating straight to destruction, he seemed remarkably cool. Keeble cursed about ignorant nitwits and edged nearer with his engine in slow reverse. The *Flying Linnet*, unlike the punt, was too big to go through this particular weir, a long row of separately openable gates; but the summer current was quite strong enough to crash her nastily against the thick concrete supports and pin her there for someone else humiliatingly to rescue.

Keeble shouted to the girl that we would tow them away, and to hand the mooring rope to me or Lynnie, whichever she could reach, as soon as we were nearer. The girl nodded, her arms still stretched forward round the big post, her long fair hair nearly brushing the water, her body quivering with the strain.

'Hold on,' Lynnie shouted urgently. 'Oh do hold on. Just a little longer, that's all.' She leaned over the side as if trying to shorten the few yards of water which still lay between, her worry and fright growing as we drew nearer. With the engine doing little more than tick over, the noise of the water on the far side of the weir began to fill our ears with its threat, but Keeble at any rate remained calm and sure of himself, an easy master of his boat and the situation. With six feet still to go the girl took one arm off the post and held out the rope towards Lynnie's groping hand. Then, disastrously she dropped it. Crying out, beating in big splashes on the water, she struggled to get her arm back round the post. Lynnie yelled to her to get hold of the rope again, it was fastened to the punt under her chest, to get hold of it again and hand it over. But the girl was now far too frightened either to listen or to let go of the post again, and the panic was rising to screams in her voice.

Out of the side of my vision I saw the young man start forward to help her, apparently at last realizing that their position was serious. The punt pole swung awkwardly in his hands, curved through the air in a clumsy arc, and hit Dave Teller on the head. With buckling knees the American fell forward off the bows and straight into the water.

I was up on the cabin roof, out of my shoes and into the river after him almost before any of the others realized what had happened. I heard Keeble's despairing voice shouting 'Gene' in the second before I went under, but I was thinking simply that speed was the only chance of finding Teller, since anything that sank in a river the size of the Thames was instantly out of sight. Algae made the water opaque.

Diving in as near to where he had gone as I could judge, I kicked downwards, arms wide. I was going faster than Teller, I had to be. I had a strong impression that the punt pole had knocked him out, that he was on a slow one-way trip to the bottom.

About eight feet down my fingers hooked almost immediately into cloth. Even with my eyes open I could see nothing and with my right hand I felt for his face while I tried to kick us both to the surface. I found his face, clamped his nose between my fingers and the heel of my hand on his mouth, and turned him so that I held his head against my chest. He didn't struggle; couldn't feel.

From that point on the rescue operation failed to go as per scheduled. I couldn't get back to the surface. The current underneath was much stronger, very cold, sweeping us downwards, clinging round our bodies with irresistible force. I thought; we'll hit the weir and be pinned there down deep, and that will be that. For a treacherous instant I didn't even care. It would solve all my problems. It was what I wanted. But not really with another life in my arms, for which I was literally the only hope.

My chest began hurting with the lack of air. When we hit the weir, I thought, I would climb my way up it. Its face might not be slippery smooth. It had to be possible . . .

There was a sudden tug as if some fisherman had us hooked. I felt us change direction slightly and then a tug again, stronger and continuing and stronger still. No miraculous rescue. It was the water had us, gripping tighter, sucking us fast, inexorably, into the weir. The sheer overwhelming weight and power of it made nonsense of human strength, reduced my efforts to the fluttering of a moth in a whirlwind. The seizing speed suddenly accelerated further still, and we hit. Or rather, Teller hit, with a jar which nearly wrenched him away from me. We spun in the current and my shoulder crashed into concrete and we spun again and crashed, and I couldn't get hold of any surface with my free hand. The tumbling and crashing went on, and the pain in my chest went deeper, and I knew I wasn't going to be climbing up any weir, I could only find it when it hit me, and when I reached for it it hit me somewhere else.

The crashing stopped, but the tumbling went on. My ears were roaring to bursting point. There was a sword embedded in my chest. The searing temptation came back more strongly just to open my mouth and be finished with it. But by my own peculiar rules I couldn't do that, not with someone else involved, not when what I was doing was in a way what I'd been trained for. Some other time, I thought lightheadedly, some other time I'd drown myself. This time I'll just wait until my brain packs up from lack of oxygen, which won't be long now, and if I haven't any choice in the matter, then I haven't any guilt either.

The tumbling suddenly died away and the clutching current relaxed and loosened and finally unlocked itself. I was only seconds this side of blackout and at first it didn't register: then I gave a feeble kick with legs half entwined round Teller and we shot upward as if on springs. My head broke the surface into the sun and air went down into the cramp of my lungs like silver fire.

The weir, the killing weir, was fifty yards away. Fifty yards *upstream*. We had come right through it under the water.

I took my freezing, stiffened fingers off Teller's face, and held his head up to mine, and blew into his flaccid mouth. The current, gentle again and comparatively warm, carried us slowly along, frothy bubbles bursting with little winks against our necks. I trod water with my legs, and held Teller up, and went on pushing into him all my used-up breath. He showed no response. It would be exceedingly inconsiderate of him, I thought resignedly, if he had died right at the beginning and I had gone to all that trouble for nothing.

There were shouts from the banks suddenly and people pointing, and someone came after us in a dinghy with an outboard motor. It puttered noisily by my ear and hands stretched over the side to grasp.

I shook my head. 'A rope,' I said, and breathed into Teller. 'Give me a rope. And pull slowly.'

One of the two men argued, but the other did as I asked. I wound the rope round my arm twice and held it, and when I nodded they let the boat drift away until we were a safe distance from its propeller and slowly began to pull us towards the bank. Teller got ten more of my ex-breaths on the way. They didn't seem to be doing him a bit of good.

The dinghy towed us out of the weir stream side of the river and landed on the same side as the lock. People appeared in a cluster to help, and there was little doubt it was needed, but even so I was loth to part with Teller until one large calm man lay on his stomach on the grass and stretched his arms down under the American's armpits.

'Don't worry,' he said. 'We'll go straight on with the breathing.'

I nodded, took my mouth away from Teller's and transferred his weight into the stranger's arms. He began to pull him out of the water as fast as he could.

I put a steadying hand on Teller's chest and felt it heave suddenly under the clinging blue shirt. I hadn't enough breath left myself to tell the man who was lifting him, and while I was still trying to, Teller, half out, gave a choking cough and opened his eyes. There was some water in his lungs, racking him. The stranger pulled him even more quickly out on to the grass, and as his ankles bumped over the edge his returning consciousness flooded into a stark sort of awareness which had nothing to do with a release from drowning. Somewhere between a cough and a groan he said 'Jesus,' and again went completely limp.

Another couple of strong wrists hauled me up on to the bank in his wake, and I knelt there beside him feeling the reassuringly small swelling on the side of his head but anxiously listening to the dragging breath bubbling in his throat.

'Roll him over,' I said. 'Carefully ... just so his tongue isn't choking him.'

We put him on his side and his breathing eased immediately, but I wouldn't let them pick him up and carry him up to the lock. Almost any injury was bound to be made worse by moving, and he'd been moved too much already. The calm man agreed and went briskly off to fetch a doctor.

The lock-keeper arrived along the towpath, followed at a rush by Keeble and all his family. Their faces were all strained with shock, and Lynnie had been crying.

'Thank God,' Keeble said, crouching beside me. 'You're both all right.' His voice held almost more incredulity than relief.

I shook my head. 'He's hurt, somewhere.'

'Badly?'

'Don't know ... He crashed into the weir.'

'We didn't see you go over. We were watching ...'

'They must have gone under,' said the lock-keeper. 'Through one of the gates. Those gates wind upwards, same as a sash window. We've got two of them a couple of feet open at the bottom today, with the river a bit full after all that rain.'

I nodded. 'Under.'

Dave Teller choked and woke up again, coughing uncontrollably through the puddle in his lungs, every cough jerking him visibly into agony. From his fluttering gesture it was clear where the trouble lay.

'His leg,' Keeble said. 'He's not bleeding ... could he have broken it?'

The jar when he had hit the weir had been enough. I said so. 'We can't do anything for him,' said Keeble, watching him helplessly.

The crowd around us waited, murmuring in sympathy but enjoying the disaster, listening to Teller coughing, watching him clutch handfuls of grass in rigid fingers. Not a scrap of use begging them to go away.

'What happened to the punt?' I asked Keeble.

'We towed it ashore. Lynnie got hold of the rope.

Those kids were terribly shocked.' He looked round for them vaguely, but they weren't in the crowd. 'I suppose they've stayed back at the lock. The girl was nearly hysterical when you and Dave didn't come up.' A remembering bleakness came into his face. 'We towed them into the lock cut and moored there. Then we ran along to the lock to get the lock-keeper... and he was already down here.' He looked up across the river to the pretty weir. 'How long were you under the water?'

'A couple of centuries.'

'Seriously.'

'Can't tell. Maybe three minutes.'

'Long enough.'

'Mm.'

He looked me over objectively, boss to employee. One shoulder of my green jersey shirt was ripped in a jagged tear.

'Bruised,' he said matter-of-factly.

'The weir,' I agreed, 'has knobs on.'

'It's like a flight of steps under there,' said the lock-keeper solemnly. 'Going down from the top level to this one, you see. The current would have rolled you right down those steps, I reckon. In fact, it's a bleeding miracle you ever came up, if you ask me. There's some every year fall in this river and never get seen again. Current takes them along the bottom all the way to the sea.'

'Charming,' Keeble said under his breath.

Dave Teller stopped coughing, rolled slightly on to his back, and put his wrist to his mouth. His strong beaky nose stuck uncompromisingly up to the sky, and the wetness on his face wasn't from the Thames. After a while he moved his hand and asked Keeble what had happened. Keeble briefly explained, and the screwed-up eyes slid round to me.

'Lucky you were with us,' he said weakly, the smile in his voice making no progress on his face. He moved his hand apprehensively behind his ear, and winced when it reached the bump. 'I don't remember a thing.'

'Do you remember asking me to look for your horse?'

He nodded a fraction, slowly. 'Yuh. You said no.'

'I've changed my mind,' I said. 'I'll go.'

In the cabin of the *Flying Linnet* Keeble watched me slowly strip off my sodden clothes. I had never, as far as I remembered, felt so weak. I'd left half my muscles under the weir. Buttons would no longer come out of their holes.

'You heard what the man said,' Keeble remarked. 'It was lucky you were with us.'

I didn't answer.

'Make a note of it,' Keeble said. 'Stick around. You never know when you'll be needed.'

'Sure,' I said, refusing to acknowledge that I understood what he was talking about.

He wouldn't be deterred. 'You're like Dave's horse. Irreplaceable.'

My lips twitched. That was the crunch, all right. His job would be a little harder if he lost his head cook and bottle-washer. Personal regard didn't come into it.

I struggled out of my jersey. He handed me a towel, glancing non-committally at the marks of this and previous campaigns.

'I'm serious, Gene.'

'Yeah,' I sighed. 'Well . . . I'm still here.'

It was too much of an admission, but at least it seemed to reassure him enough to change the subject.

'Why are you going to the States?'

'Maybe I owe it to him.'

'Who? Dave?'

I nodded.

'I don't follow,' he said, frowning. 'Surely he owes you? If anyone owes anything.'

'No. If I'd been quicker, he wouldn't have gone in, wouldn't now have a smashed thigh. Too much whisky and wine and sleeping in the sun. I was much too slow. Abysmally, shamefully slow.'

He made a gesture of impatience. 'Don't be ridiculous, Gene. No speed on earth could have prevented an accident like that.'

I put the towel round my neck and started to take off my trousers.

'That accident', I said briefly, 'was attempted murder.'

He gazed at me, eyes blinking slowly behind the mild spectacles. Then he turned, opened the cabin door, and stepped up into the cockpit. I heard him shouting to Peter.

'Get out of that punt at once, there's a good chap. And don't let anyone else get in it. It's important.'

'Not even Lynnie?'

'Not even Lynnie.'

'I don't want to,' said Lynnie's voice in a wail from the cockpit. 'I never want to go in a punt again.'

She wasn't much her father's daughter. His mind was as tough as old boots. The chubby body which contained it came back into the cabin and shut the door.

'Convince me,' he said.

'The boy and girl have scarpered.'

He raised his eyebrows and protested. 'They were frightened.'

'They didn't stop to answer questions. They may quite possibly think Dave and I are dead, because they didn't even wait to make sure. I should say they never even intended to appear at any inquest.'

He was silent, thinking about it. The boy and girl had gone from the lock when we had eventually returned to it: gone unnoticed, leaving the punt behind. No one had given them a thought until after the doctor had splinted Teller's leg and seen him carried on a stretcher a hundred yards to an ambulance.

When the doctor asked how the accident happened, the causes of it weren't around.

'We don't know,' Keeble said. 'They may very likely have come down the towpath and seen you were all right, and they might have dozens of personal reasons for not wanting to stay.'

I finished kicking my legs out of the clammy cotton trousers and peeled off my socks.

'The boy stood on the stern too long. He should have been helping with the rope.'

Keeble frowned. 'Certainly he seemed unconcerned, but I don't think he realized quite what a jam they were in. Not like the girl did.'

'The first time he moved, he hit Dave straight on the head.'

'Punt poles are clumsy if you aren't careful . . . and he couldn't have counted on Dave standing in so vulnerable a spot.'

'He'd been standing there most of the way, seeing to the bow rope.'

'The boy and girl couldn't know that.'

'He was certainly standing there when we approached the punt.'

'And,' Keeble said in a demolishing voice, 'no one would deliberately put themselves into so much danger just to bait a trap.'

I dried my legs and wondered what to do about my underpants.

Keeble sighed down his nose and fluttered his fingers. 'No one except you.'

He reached into a locker and produced a bundle of clothes.

'Emergency falling-in kit,' he explained, giving them to me. 'I don't suppose anything will fit.'

As there was a mixture of his own cast-offs, which were too wide, and Lynnie's, which were too narrow, he was right. Everything, besides, was too short.

'In addition,' he went on, 'how did the boy and girl know we were on the river at all and would be coming down through Harbour Lock? How long did you expect them to wait there clinging to the post? How did they know exactly which boat to hail, and how did they avoid being rescued by any other boat?'

'The best accidents always look as if they couldn't possibly be anything else.'

'I grant you that,' he said, nodding. 'I just think that this one literally couldn't be set up.'

'Yes, it could. With a safe getout, in that if it didn't work according to plan, if for instance Peter had been on the bows instead of Dave, they had no need to go into the act of yelling for help, because of course they wanted to make sure it was us before they started.'

'They were in danger,' Keeble protested.

'Maybe. I'd like to take a closer look at that post.'

'And there might have been other boats around, helping. Or watching.'

'If Dave never came within range of the punt pole

they lost nothing but an opportunity. If other boats had been watching there would simply have been more people to cry accident. The girl was screaming and splashing and dramatically dropping her rope when the boy hit Dave. We were all watching her, not him. Any sized audience would have been doing the same.'

'And how could the boy and girl have known where Dave would be this Sunday, in the first place? And why on God's earth should anyone want to kill him?'

I stepped into some aged grey trousers of Keeble's and found them a foot too generous round the waist. My boss wordlessly held out a short striped elastic schoolboy belt, which took care of the problem by gripping like a tourniquet.

'It was a simple accident, Gene. It had to be.'

The trousers ended four inches above my ankles, and the socks I slowly fumbled my way into made no effort to bridge the gap.

'Gene!' said Keeble, exasperated.

I sighed. 'You'll agree I'm a sort of specialist in arranging accidents?'

'Not usually fatal ones,' he protested.

'Not often.' And no more, if I could wriggle out of it. 'Just a general stage managing of events, so the victim believes that what has happened to him is the merest mischance.'

Keeble smiled. 'You've sprung more hares that way . . .'

'So,' I said reasonably, 'I'm apt to spot a rig-up when I see one.'

The smile half faded and changed into speculation.

'And no,' I said, 'I was not concussed in the recent boating party and I haven't got water on the brain.'

'Keep your telepathy to yourself,' he said uncomfortably. 'I just think you are mistaken.'

'OK, then I'll spend my holiday in Putney.'

He said 'No,' so vehemently, so explosively, that there was no subtlety left in the situation. From his naked alarm I saw unmistakably how much he understood of my depressed mental state and how convinced he was that I wouldn't survive three weeks of my own company. Shocked, I realized that his relief when I answered his telephone call had not been at finding me at home, but at finding me alive. He had dug me out on to the river to keep an eye on me and was prepared to send me off on any old wild goose chase so long as it kept me occupied. Then maybe, I supposed, he thought I would snap out of it.

'The blues', I said gently, 'have been with me for a long time.'

'Not like this.'

I had no answer.

After a pause he said persuasively, 'Three world class stallions disappearing ... isn't that also the sort of accident you don't believe in?'

'Yes, it is. Especially when someone tries to get rid of the man who bought two of them.'

He opened his mouth and shut it again. I almost smiled.

'It was a craftsman's accident,' I said. 'It could hardly have been done better. All they didn't bargain for was interference from someone like me.'

He still didn't believe it, but as he was now happy that I should, since it meant that I would go to the States, he raised no more objections. With a shrug and a rueful smile he tossed me a darned brown sweater, which hung round me like a tent; and I picked up my own wet clothes and followed him out into the sunshine.

Peter and Lynnie both giggled at my baggy appearance, the nervous shock still sharp in their voices, especially Lynnie's. I grinned at her and ruffled her hair, and made as if to kick Peter overboard, and some of the tension loosened in their eyes. In another half hour they would have reached the compulsive talking stage and an hour after that they would be back to normal. Nice, ordinary kids, with nice, ordinary reactions.

I climbed wearily up on to the cabin roof and spread out my clothes to dry. My shoes were still there where I had stepped out of them, and absentmindedly I put them on. Then, standing up, I looked across to the weir, and back to the hefty post with its notice; DANGER, and at the innocent empty punt tied up behind the *Flying Linnet*: and I found myself thinking about the legend of the Sirens, the sea nymphs who sat on a rock near a whirlpool and with their pretty voices drew passing sailors towards them, to lure them to their death.

CHAPTER THREE

The punt had the name of the owner screwed on to the stern on a small metal plate. The lock-keeper, consulted, said that it came from a boatyard about a mile down the river, next to a pub; you couldn't miss it.

'That,' I murmured to Keeble, 'is where we had our drinks this morning.'

His eyelids flickered. He said to the lock-keeper, 'I suppose a lot of punts from there come up through your lock?'

'They sure do, on a fine Sunday like this,' he agreed.

'Did you happen to notice this one, with a girl and a young man in it? The girl had long fair hair, white trousers, and a pink shirt, and the boy was wearing tight pale blue jeans and a red-and-yellow check shirt.'

'I should say they came up before my dinner break. I can't remember anyone like that this afternoon.'

The lock-keeper eased the white-topped hat back on his head and eyed the boats lining up to go into the lock. He was a youngish man with an air of long-suffering patience, the occupational result, no doubt, of a life spent watching an endless procession of incompetence. People, he had said matter-of-factly, fell into his lock every day of the week. Near-drownings, however, were of no special interest to him: he too often had to deal with the unsaved.

'Would you know them again?' Keeble asked.

The lock-keeper shook his head decisively. 'Not a chance. And if I don't get back to my lock there'll be a lot of bad tempers coming through the gates and as like as not we'll be fishing out another one . . .'

He gave me a sketchy farewell salute as one of the few who had gone down his weir and walked away, and strolled unhurriedly back to deal with his Sunday going home traffic problem.

'We may as well tow the punt back to the boatyard,' Keeble said thoughtfully. 'We've got to go down past there anyway, and they won't be able to spare anyone to come and fetch it on a busy day like this. And maybe they'll know where the boy and girl came from . . .'

And maybe they wouldn't, I thought: but even the most hopeless questions have to be asked.

'I'd like to look at the post,' I said.

Keeble was agreeable, but Lynnie and Peter and their mother were horrified when they found where we were proposing to go, and said they would wait on the bank. In a row, with anxious faces, they stood guard over the punt, while Keeble neatly manoeuvred the *Flying Linnet* upstream a little way through the downcoming cruisers, and then drifted gently across towards the post. I, standing on the stern seat, caught hold of the crossbar with its emphatic warning and clung on to it while Keeble put the boat into reverse against the drag of the weir stream.

Once the engine was thrusting hard enough to hold its own, so that the tension on my arms slackened, I knelt down on the seat and tried to do what the girl had been doing, to pass a rope round the post from one hand to the other. The tendency of the two-ton *Flying Linnet* to drift away couldn't have been much less to deal with than the weight of the punt, but even allowing also for the fact that my arms were longer and stronger, it was easy. I secured the rope and gave a thumbs up to Keeble, who stopped the engine. Then with one toe wedged and the narrow side of the boat under my pelvis, I shoved up the sleeves of the brown sweater and leaned down and over to inspect the scenery.

'For God's sake be careful,' Keeble said, his voice sharp over the noise of the weir.

I turned my head and laughed at him.

'We haven't any more dry clothes,' he pointed out, scowling. 'None that you can get into. If you fall in again you'll have to go home wet.'

Smiling, I turned back to the post. But feel and look how I might, there was nothing out of the ordinary about the square sturdy white-painted baulk of timber set rock-like up on end in the Thames' bed.

Keeble shrugged and said, 'I told you so,' and steered his boat back to the bank.

'How about fingerprinting the punt?' I said.

'You never let up.'

'You should be glad of it.'

The long line of past occasions when not letting up had led to a useful harvest rose up between us, and I saw his conviction waver.

'All right, Gene, if you're sure.'

'Get Raben to do it. He's the best.'

'All right. Tomorrow.'

'How about the police?'

He pursed his lips. 'It's not our usual territory. More theirs I agree. But they're not likely to take your theory seriously, or to act on it, unless we tell them what your job is . . . and impress them with it. No, I'm not in favour of that. We could just go along with this quietly on our own for a little while, I think.'

'So that if nothing turns up, we won't have made bloody fools of ourselves?'

All his facial muscles contracted for a second. 'You are not paid to turn your perceptions on your boss.'

'I probably am.'

'That's a point.'

The boat grounded gently against the bank, and I helped Joan and Lynnie back on board. Peter, on his father's directions, stepped into the punt and handed him up the mooring rope, which Keeble fastened to the cleat on the *Flying Linnet*'s stern. Then, towing the punt, we took our turn into the lock, explained what we were doing to the lock-keeper, and cruised downstream to the pub and its next door boatyard.

A flustered middle-aged boatman there was trying to cope with returning family picnic parties and a bunch of youths and girls who wanted to fill in the half hour before the pub opened at seven o'clock. The late afternoon shone redly on his big sweating face and his freckled bald head, and we had to wait while he juggled his customers precariously in and out of skiffs and punts and took their money and warned the young couples that it was an offence to be on the river without lights after dark and that the boatyard closed at nine-thirty anyway.

When Keeble at last had a chance he asked the boatman if he had seen the girl with fair hair and the boy in a red-and-yellow check shirt who had hired a punt that morning.

'Seen 'em? I suppose so, I've been here all day.'

'I mean, do you remember them?' Keeble said patiently.

'Where are they then?' The boatman looked round suspiciously.

'They've gone,' Keeble began.

'Then who's going to settle up?' said the boatman belligerently, this last problem looking to be just one too many for his temper.

'Oh, I will,' said Keeble soothingly. He took his wallet out of his back pocket and unfolded it to show the usual thickish wad. Keeble didn't have to live on Her Majesty's pay and worked from conviction, not need; his beer money represented a week's wage to me, and his boat a year's.

'How much do they owe you?' He handed over what the boatman asked and offered a fiver on top. 'I'd like to hire this punt for this evening and tomorrow,' he said. 'Is that all right?'

The boatman took the money without hesitation and made a few half-hearted efforts to appear cautious.

'Where'll you be taking it?'

'Henley,' Keeble said.

'You won't leave the cushions out if it rains?'

Keeble shook his head.

'All right then.' The boatman had already tucked the notes away. 'And you'll bring it back tomorrow?'

'Tomorrow afternoon,' Keeble agreed. 'Now, about those young people who took it this morning . . .'

Unexpectedly the boatman suddenly leered. 'I remember 'em,' he said, 'come to think of it, they was the two who had no business to be out together.'

'What do you mean?' Keeble asked.

'Well, see, this girl, she said like, what if her old man had put detectives on her, what would they say if she went off all day with him in a punt, and how she'd said she'd only come out as long as it was nothing anyone could use in a divorce. And the fellow in the check shirt turned round and said old money bags, meaning her old man, see, would never find out where they'd been, he was in France on business wasn't he, or somesuch, and then they took note that I was standing there hearing and they sort of nudged each other and shut up. But I reckon as they were off for a bit on the side see, and didn't want no one to catch 'em.'

'Exactly,' said Keeble to me with another touch of I-told-you-so.

'And very nicely done,' I agreed. 'Artistic.'

'You haven't seen them since this morning, I suppose?' Keeble said to the boatman. 'Do you happen to know how they got here?'

'Car,' said the boatman, waving an arm. 'They came from the car park back there.'

'Which car, do you know?'

He gave Keeble a pitying stare. 'Look, there's cars in and out all day, what with the pub and us. And I'm looking at the river, see, with my hands full an' all, and I couldn't tell you no one who's come and gone nor what they came in, but they must have come in a car, because they come in the morning, and there's no buses along here on Sundays before half-two in the afternoon.'

'Thank you anyway,' said Keeble, sighing. 'You've been very helpful.' He added another pound to his overpayment and the boatman's eyes swivelled rapidly from the pub to the clock over the boathouse door.

Still ten minutes until the bar opened. I proceeded to fill them.

'Did the young man, or the girl, or both of them, speak with any special type of accent?' I asked.

Since he spoke broad Berkshire himself, the boatman's hesitation was understandable. 'They talked', he said, considering, 'like they do on the telly.'

'Not much help,' Keeble commented.

'How do you lash the end of your punts' mooring ropes?' I asked.

'Eh?' said the boatman, puzzled.

'Do you lash the end of the ropes to stop them unravelling?'

'Oh, I get you. No, we splice 'em. Turn the ends back and sort of weave them in. Lashing's no good as it comes undone too easily.'

I unwound the punt's mooring rope from the *Flying Linnet*'s stern cleat. 'This one is coming undone, though.'

'Let's see that,' he said suspiciously, and I gave it to him. He twisted the frayed unravelling strands in his strong dirty fingers and hovered in what I guessed to be a fairly usual mixture of fury and resignation.

'These bleeding vandals . . . excuse me, ma'am,' he apologized to Joan. 'These so and sos, they tie up to a tree, see, or something, and come they want to push on, they can't undo the knots if the rope's wet, and they just don't bother, they cut through the rope and off they go.'

'Does that often happen?'

'Every summer, we has this trouble now and then.'
He pulled the rope up straight, measuring its length
with his eye. 'There's a good four or five feet gone off
this one, I shouldn't wonder. We've been talking of
switching to chains, but they can get into holy terrors
of knots, chains can. Here,' he added to Keeble, 'you'd
better have another punt, one with a better rope.'

'This one will be fine,' Keeble said, fastening it on
again. 'We'll see you tomorrow.'

He towed the punt down to Henley and right into
the garage-like boathouse which kept the English
summer off the *Flying Linnet*. The punt was secured
alongside by Peter and his father and everyone disembarked along a narrow boardwalk carrying things like
the remains from lunch, newspapers, bathing towels,
and in my case, wet clothes and a loaded jacket, out
through the boathouse and into Keeble's Rover, which
was parked on a neat square of grass at the back.

Peter's main care was for his precious camera, again
hanging round his neck on its cord.

'I suppose,' I said idly, 'you didn't happen to take
a photograph up there by the weir? You didn't happen
to get a shot of those people in the punt?'

He shook his head, blinking like his father.

'Gosh, no, I didn't. I don't suppose actually I would
have thought of taking one, not when everything was
happening, do you think? I mean, it would have looked

a bit off if you and Mr Teller had been drowning and I was just standing there taking pictures and so on.'

'You'll never be a newspaperman,' I said, grinning at him.

'Wouldn't you have minded, then?'

'I don't think so.'

'But, anyway,' he said mournfully, 'I couldn't, you see, because I finished the film at lunch-time and I didn't have another one, so even if there had been a fire or something I couldn't have taken it.' He looked at his camera thoughtfully. 'I won't finish up any more films in the middle of the day, just in case.'

'A fire,' I agreed seriously, 'would anyway make a much better picture than just people drowning, which they mostly do out of sight.'

Peter nodded, considering me. 'You know, you're quite sensible, aren't you?'

'Peter!' exclaimed his mother in unnecessary apology. 'That's not the way to talk.' And she wasn't much pleased when I said as far as I was concerned he could say what he liked.

Keeble drove round to the station car park, where Lynnie and I transferred to the Austin.

'I'll ring in the morning,' Keeble said, standing half out of his respectable car.

'Right.'

'Take care of Lynnie.'

'I'll do that.'

Lynnie kissed her parents goodbye, but her father

51

more warmly, and made a face at Peter as the Rover rolled away out of the gate. Then she climbed into the Austin, waited until I was sitting beside her, and stretched out her hand to the ignition.

She was trembling again.

'Shall I drive?' I said mildly, making it absolutely her own choice.

She put both her hands in her lap and looked straight out through the windscreen. Her face was pale above the orange dress.

'I thought you were both dead.'

'I know.'

'I still feel churned up. It's silly.'

'It's not silly. And I expect you're fond of Dave Teller.'

'He's sent us presents and things, since we were little.'

'A nice man.'

'Yes.' She sighed deeply and after a pause said calmly, 'I think it would be better, if you really don't mind, if you drive back.'

'Of course I will.'

We changed places, and went back to London with more cars passing us than we passed. At Chiswick roundabout I said I would drive her to her flat and go home by taxi, but with a sideways laughing glance she said no taxi would stop for me in her father's clothes, and that she was feeling better and could quite easily do the last lap herself: so I rolled round the few corners to Putney and stopped outside my own front door.

Summer dusk filled the quiet streets. No one about. Lynnie looked out of her window upwards at the tall house, and shivered.

'You're cold,' I said, concerned for her bare arms.

'No . . . I have a cardigan in the back . . . I was just thinking about your flat.'

'What about it?'

'It's so . . . empty.' She gave a half laugh, shrugging it off. 'Well, I hope you won't have nightmares, after today.'

'No . . .' I collected my things and got out of the car, and she moved over into the driver's seat.

'Will they have saved any dinner for you at the hostel?' I asked.

'Not a hope,' she said cheerfully. 'But I expect there'll be some cake and milk about, there usually is.'

'Would you care to eat with me? Not up there,' I added hastily, seeing the beginnings of well-brought-up suspicion. 'In a restaurant, I mean.'

'I've my mother to thank for my beastly mind,' she said unexpectedly. 'I really am rather hungry, and I don't see at all why I shouldn't have supper in your flat, if you've got any food.' And without more ado she got out of the car and locked it, and stood expectantly beside me on the pavement.

'There are some tins,' I said, reflecting. 'Wait here

just a second, would you. I just want to have a look round the back.'

'Round the back?'

'For burglars,' I said sardonically. But I went to look, as usual, at the powder-coated bottom flight of the fire escape. No one had been up or down all day.

Lynnie climbed the stairs to the fourth floor as easily as before, and having checked via a well-placed paper clip that my door hadn't been opened since I had shut it that morning, I put the key in the lock and let us in.

The green plastic lampshade in my sitting room scattered its uncosy glare over the tidy room, switching the soft grey light outside into sudden black, and evoking the forlornness of institution buildings on winter afternoons. It wouldn't be much trouble, I thought, to go out and buy myself a red shade in the morning, and see if it propagated rosy thoughts instead.

'Sit down,' I suggested. 'Are you warm enough? Switch the electric fire on if you'd like it. I think I'll go and change, and then we can decide about going out.'

Lynnie nodded, but took things into her own hands. When I came out of the bedroom she had already investigated my meagre store cupboard and had lined up a packet of soup, some eggs, and a tin of anchovies.

'Soup, and anchovies on scrambled eggs,' she said.

'If you'd really like that,' I said doubtfully.

'I can't cook much else.'

I laughed. 'All right. I'll do the coffee.'

There were burnt specks in the eggs when she had finished, which harmonized nicely with the scraped off over-done toast and the brown anchovy strips, and there had been a slight over-emphasis on pepper.

'No one', she sighed, 'is going to marry me for my cordon bleu.'

There were plenty of other reasons why she'd be fending off suitors knee-deep in a year or two: a curvy figure, delicate neck, baby skin; the touch-me-not expression, the awakening social courage, the quick compassion. No one was going to care if she couldn't cook. But she wasn't secure enough to be told so at that moment.

'When were you seventeen?' I asked.

'The week before last.'

'You didn't waste much time passing the driving test.'

'I've been able to drive since I was eight. Peter can, too.' She finished her eggs and stirred two heaped teaspoonfuls of sugar into her coffee. 'I was hungry. Funny, that.'

'It's a long time since lunch.'

'A terribly long time . . .' She suddenly looked me straight in the face, which she had mostly been avoiding, and with devastating innocence said, 'I'm so glad you're alive.'

I turned a hopeless wince into a laugh. 'I'm so glad Dave Teller is.'

'Both of you,' she said. 'It was the worst thing in my whole life when you didn't come up.'

A child untouched by tragedy, I thought. A pity the world was such a rough place, would catch her by her pretty neck one day and tear her guts apart. No one ever escaped. To have got to seventeen unlacerated was merely a matter of luck.

When we had finished the coffee she insisted on doing the dishes, but when she hung up the tea towel I saw all her mother's warnings pour back, and she glanced at me and quickly away, and stood stiffly in the centre of the room, looking nervous and embarrassed.

'Why don't you have any pictures on your walls?' she said jerkily.

I gestured to the trunk in the corner. 'There are some in there, but I don't like them very much. Not enough to bother with hanging them up ... Do you know it's after ten? I'd better take you home or the hostel will shut you out.'

'Oh yes,' she said in great relief, and then hearing her own voice, added in confusion, 'I mean ... I didn't know if you would think me very rude, dashing off as soon as we'd finished eating.'

'Your mother is quite right to tell you to be cautious,' I said lightly. 'Little Red Riding Hood couldn't tell a wolf from her grandmother ... and you can never rely on a woodcutter turning up in the nick of time.'

The rigidity dissolved like mist. 'You do say some

extraordinary things,' she said. 'As if you could read my mind.'

'I could,' I smiled. 'You'd better put that cardigan on. It will be cold outside.'

'OK.' She pulled a dark brown jersey out of her bucket-shaped holdall and put it on. I bent to pick up a clean folded handkerchief which had fallen out with it, and when she was ready, handed it to her.

'Thanks,' she said, looking at it casually. 'That's the one Peter found in the punt.'

'In the punt?'

'Yes, down a crack between two of the cushions. He gave it to me because it was too small for him, he said. Too cissy.'

'Did he find anything else?'

'I don't think so . . . I mean it isn't stealing or anything, is it, to keep her handkerchief? I'll give it to her of course if she comes back, but by the time Peter was sitting in the punt, they had been gone already for ages.'

'No, it's not stealing,' I reassured her, though technically it was doubtful. 'But may I have a look at it?'

'Of course.'

She gave it back and I unfolded it: a white square of thin gauzy material. In one corner, a stylized bear in a flat straw hat.

'Is that out of Walt Disney?' I asked.

She shook her head and said with surprise at my ignorance, 'Yogi Bear.'

'Who is Yogi Bear?'

'I can't believe it! Well, he's a character in a lot of cartoon films. Like Top Cat and Atom Ant and the Flintstones.'

'I've seen the Flintstones,' I agreed.

'Like them, then. The same people make Yogi Bear.'

'Do you mind if I keep it for a day or two?'

'Of course, if you really want to,' she said, puzzled. 'But it surely hasn't any value.'

Down in the street I said I might as well finish the job and drive her to her hostel.

'I'm really all right now,' she protested. 'You don't need to come.'

'Yes I do. Your father said to look after you, and I'm seeing you safe to your door.'

She raised her eyebrows and gave me a comical look, but compliantly went round to the passenger's seat. I started the car, switched on the lights, and started towards Kensington.

'Do you always do what Daddy tells you?' she asked, smiling.

She was feeling much surer of herself, I thought.

'Yes, when I want to.'

'That's a contradiction in terms.'

'So it is.'

'Well, what do you actually *do*? What does *anyone* do in the Civil Service?'

'I interview people.'

'What sort of people?'

'People who want jobs in Government departments.'

'Oh!' She laughed. 'A sort of Personnel Officer?'

'Sort of.'

'It sounds a bit drizz.'

'The sun shines occasionally.'

'You're pretty quick. We only made up drizz yesterday.'

'A very useful word.'

'Yes, we thought so, too. Covers a lot of things nicely.'

'Like wet boyfriends?'

She laughed. 'Actually, it's pretty drizz to *have* a wet boyfriend.' She pointed. 'The hostel's down there, but we have to drive around and find somewhere to park the car all night. One or two squares down here don't have meters yet.'

The nearest empty space was a good quarter of a mile from the hostel, so I walked her back.

'You don't need to . . .' she began. 'Well . . . don't say it. Daddy said.'

'Right,' I agreed.

She sniffed resignedly and walked beside me out of step, the leather bucket bag swinging and her flat shoes silent on the pavement. At the hostel's glossy black well-lit front door she came to a stop and hovered on one foot, her half anxious uncertain expression saying clearer than words that she wasn't sure how to part from me. I wasn't old enough for uncle terms or young enough for a casual contemporary brush-off. I worked for her father, but wasn't his servant. Lived alone, looked respectable, asked nothing: I didn't fit into any of the categories she had yet learnt how to deal with. I put out my hand and smiled.

'Goodnight, Lynnie.'

Her clasp was brief, warm, relieved.

'Goodnight . . .' There was a pause while she made up her mind to it; and even then it was little more than a breath. '. . . Gene.'

'I wish you,' I said, 'blind traffic wardens and foam rubber bumpers.'

'Goodnight.' The chuckle rolled spontaneously in her throat. 'Goodnight.' She turned on one toe and jumped the two steps up to the door, then looked over her shoulder and waved as she went inside.

Little Lynnie, I thought, whistling to a passing taxi, little Lynnie, right at the beginning of it. Flying half consciously, half unconsciously, the notice-me flags of the pretty young female; and it was no use pretending that she didn't make me hungry; that she wasn't absolutely what I would have liked as an oasis in my too continent life. But if I had learnt anything in thirty-eight years it was who not to go to bed with.

And, more drearily, how not to.

CHAPTER FOUR

The Buttress Life Offices on Thirty-Third Street were high on customer appeal on the sixth floor. On the fifth and seventh they tucked the computers and electric typewriters into functional plasterboard cubicles. I sat three inches deep in black leather and considered that of all American craftsmen, I admired their chair designers most: in no other country in the world could one sit on the same seat for several hours without protest from the sacro-iliac.

I had waited forty pleasantly cool minutes already. Long enough to discover that the rows of pot plants along the low wall dividing the forty-foot-square hall into five smaller bays were made of plastic. Long enough to admire the pinewood walls, the ankle-deep carpet, the carefully lowered ceiling with its inset lights. In each bay there was a large desk, with one large chair behind it, one at the side, one in front. Nearly all occupied. Dividing each bay neatly in two stood a second, smaller desk; for the secretary-receptionist with his back discreetly to his boss. In front of him, in each bay, the long black leather bench for waiting on.

I waited. There was still someone for the big man to see before me. Very sorry, said the secretary apologetically, but the schedule had been crowded even before Mr Teller's cable arrived. Could I possibly wait?

So why not? I had three weeks to spare.

The light was dim, and piped music poured over everything like syrup. That and the built-in deadness of the acoustics made the earnest consultations going on at the five big desks completely inaudible to the waiting benches, while at the same time giving the customers a comforting illusion that they weren't alone in their troubles. Everyone, at the core of things, was alone. Just some more than others.

I hadn't slept all night after leaving Lynnie; but not her fault. It had been one long stupid struggle between a craving for oblivion and conviction that appeasing it wasn't so much morally wrong as a thoroughgoing defeat. I had never learnt to accept defeat. Obstinacy had given me what success I had had in my job, and it alone seemed to be keeping me alive, since all other props were as much use as toothpicks in an avalanche. Enthusiasm for finding Dave Teller's horse burned in me as brightly as wet coal dust: and the nation would hardly collapse if I left its employ.

Caroline had crowded like a flood-tide through my head and down my body. Caroline . . . whom I would have married, had it not been for the husband who would not divorce her.

Caroline had left him to live with me, and had felt guilty about it. A mess. An ordinary, everyday mess. Her fine passion had fretted away over six frustrating years of will-he won't-he; and to the end he wouldn't. Not that he'd ever got her back. In the year since she had left me she had returned to nursing and was working as a sister in a Nairobi hospital, impervious to come-back letters from either of us.

The sharp pain of her departure had dulled to the extent that I no longer felt it through every waking minute: it came stabbing back at longer and longer intervals. But when it did, I remembered her as she'd been at the beginning, and the hunger was pretty well unbearable. It was easy enough to find different girls to talk to, to work with, to take to bed: hard to find a match on all levels: and Caroline had been a match. In the past year, instead of receding, the loneliness had closed in. My work, of its nature, set me apart. And I had no one to go home to, to share with, to care for. The futility and emptiness had gone down to my roots, and nothing seemed to lie ahead but years and years more of what I was already finding intolerable.

The clients at the big desk stood up, shook hands, and left. The secretary ushered the man with the earlier appointment round into the presence. I went on waiting, without impatience. I was accustomed to it.

The punt, investigated in Henley that morning, had produced nothing but ten different sets of smudged fingerprints, of which the topmost and stickiest were Peter's. The Yogi Bear handkerchief was on its way round the manufacturers, in the distant hope that someone could tell where it had been sold. Dave Teller, briefly visited, had said wanly to charge everything to him. The Super VC 10 which lifted off at 3 PM British Summertime from Heathrow had landed at Kennedy at 3.10. Buttress Life closed its doors at 6, which gave it still a half hour to go. And outside in the canyon streets the hundred degree heatwave crept up a notch to a hundred and one.

My turn came round for the big desk. The big man, on his feet behind it, held out a large dry flabby hand and produced the sincere smile of the professional insurance man. Having settled me into the large comfortable chair alongside he sat down himself and picked up the cable discreetly placed to hand by the secretary. A polished chunk of wood sat on the desk between us. On it, neat gold letters facing me said helpfully: Paul M. Zeissen.

'We received this cable from Mr Teller,' he said. A slight, very slight undertone of disapproval.

I nodded. I had sent it myself.

'Our own investigators are experts.' He didn't like me coming: but he wouldn't want to lose the Teller policies. His politeness had effort behind it.

I smoothed him down, more from habit than anything else.

'Of course. Please think of me simply as an auxiliary. Mr Teller persuaded me to come over because he has unfortunately broken a leg in England, and will be immobilized in hospital for a few weeks. He sent me very much on impulse, as a personal friend, to . . . kind of represent him. To see if there was anything I could do. There was no suggestion that he wasn't satisfied with your firm.' I paused delicately. 'If he criticized anyone, it was the police.'

Paul M. Zeissen's smile warmed up a fraction from within: but he hadn't risen to high executive status in his tough profession without disbelieving half that everyone said. That was all right with me. Half of what I'd said was true. Or half true, anyway.

'Mr Teller understands of course,' he said, 'that it is for our own sakes that we are looking for the horse?'

'Naturally,' I agreed. 'Mr Teller is also most anxious that you should succeed, as the horse is irreplaceable. He would infinitely prefer his return to any amount of insurance money.'

'A million and a half,' said Zeissen reverently.

'Worth more on the hoof,' I said.

He glanced at me with a first gleam of real welcome. Once he'd swallowed the firm's affronted pride, it was quite clear that they'd nothing to lose by letting me in.

'One of our best men, Walt Prensela, is in charge of the Chrysalis case,' he said. 'He'll give you the picture. He knows you're coming, I sent him a memo with a copy of the cable.' He pressed the switch on his desk intercom.

'Walt? We have Mr Hawkins from England here. Shall I have him come up to you now?'

The polite question was, as so often in American affairs, an equally polite order. The affirmative duly came. Zeissen flipped the switch and stood up.

'Walt's office is one floor up, number four seven. Anyone will direct you. Would you like to go up now?'

I would; and I went.

I'd expected to have to deal with the same ruffled feathers in four seven, but I didn't, because Walt had done his homework, though I wasn't sure of that at first. He greeted me with business-like casualness, shook hands, waved me to the spare chair, and sat down himself, all in five smooth seconds. Much my age, I judged, but shorter and a good deal thicker. His hands were square and powerful with nails so brief that the fingertips' pads seemed to be boiling over backwards. There were middle European origins in the bone structure of the skull, topped by roughly cropped wiry grey-brown hair, and his deep-socketed brown eyes were set permanently into the I-don't-believe-a-word-of-it expression of his boss downstairs, only more so.

'So, Gene,' he said, neither with nor without much friendliness, 'you've come a long way.'

'Dave Teller's idea, Walt,' I said mildly.

'Looking for horses ... do you do much of that?' His voice was flat; uninformative.

'Practically none. How about you?'

His nostrils twisted. 'If you mean, was it I who didn't find the other two, then no, it wasn't.'

I tried a smile: didn't get one back.

He said: 'Buttress Life had to pay up for Allyx three years ago. One million six hundred and forty-three thousand seven hundred and twenty-nine dollars, give or take a nickel. Showman, the first one, was insured with another company.'

'Accident?' I murmured. 'Or design.'

He rubbed his left thumb over the top of the round-ended fingers, the first of a hundred times I saw that gesture.

'Now that you've come, design. Before, I wasn't sure.'

'I'm officially on holiday,' I protested. 'I came only because Teller asked me. You should read no meaning into it.'

He gave me a level, half sardonic stare.

'I checked you out,' he said, flicking at the copy of the cable, which lay on his desk. 'I wanted to know just what sort of limey busybody was being wished on to me.'

I didn't say anything, and he made a clicking noise at the side of his mouth, expressive of understanding, resignation and acceptance, all in one.

'A screener,' he said. 'How come Teller found you?'

'How come you found me?' I asked instead.

'I mentioned your name in two places,' he said complacently. 'The FBI, and the CIA. And got a positive reaction from both. A couple of useful pals there filled me in. It seems you're a major stumbling block in the way of the planting of spies in certain Government departments and places like biological warfare research laboratories; and you've passed on some useful warnings on that subject to our people at Fort Detrick. They say the other side have tried to deter you, a little roughly, once or twice.' He sighed. 'You have a clean bill with our boys. And how.'

'And with you?'

'They said you didn't like limelight.'

'It's all yours.'

'Just so as I stand in right with Buttress.'

My decisive nod satisfied him. If we found the horse, he was welcome to the handshakes.

'Fill me in, then,' I said. 'How did Chrysalis get lost?'

Walt glanced at his watch and checked it against the electric clock on the wall. The little box-like office had no windows, as the single glass panel faced out on to the corridor; and although it was cool and comfortable enough, it was no place to talk if one didn't have to.

'Five after six,' Walt said. 'Do you have any other engagements?'

'Know any good bars?' I suggested.

'A mind reader.' He raised eyes to heaven. 'There's Dalaney's a block up Broadway.'

We stepped out of the air-conditioning into the sweltering street, up 30 degrees in two paces. With the humidity running also at 98 per cent, walking as little as a hundred yards left one damp to the skin. I never minded it: New York in a heatwave was always preferable to New York in a snowstorm, or anywhere hot to anywhere cold, for that matter. Cold seeped farther than into the bones; numbed the mind, drained the will. If the depression deepened towards winter, defeat would come with the snow.

Dalaney's was spilling out on to the pavement with a business convention let out of school. An oblong name tab sat on each neat Terylene lapel, a confident smile hid the anxiety behind every face; they stretched from the substantial group outside into the deep cool gloom of the bar. Pushing through them looked a problem; conversation in their company an impossibility.

'How about your hotel? Where are you staying?' Walt said.

'The Biltmore.'

Walt's eyebrows rose two clear inches.

'Teller's paying,' I said. 'He has an account there.'

'What did you do then? Save his life?'

'Six times,' I agreed, matching his sarcasm.

'He must really think,' Walt said reflectively, 'that you might get his horse back.'

'We,' I said.

'Nope. You. There's no trail. I've looked.'

A coloured cab driver in rolled-up shirt sleeves took us to the hotel, hot air blowing in gusts through the open window each time he accelerated. The city moved sluggishly under the brazen sun, and there was more rubbish than usual littering the streets.

'This is a filthy town,' said Walt, seeing it through my eyes. 'Give me Chicago.'

'Too cold,' I said automatically. 'Beautiful, but too cold. That freezing wind off the lake . . .'

'Are you guys from Chicago?' said the cab driver. 'I was born there, in the Loop.'

We talked to him about that. I drifted away into the disorientated state of not caring a jot about the cab driver, or Walt, or Dave Teller, or Caroline, or anyone on earth. We went up to my room in the Biltmore and I dragged through the host motions of ringing down for a bottle of Scotch and ice and seeing to heat, light and ashtrays. Walt loosened his tie and took a first appreciative swallow.

'You look pooped,' he said.

'Natural state.'

'I guess it's midnight already, to you.'

'I guess.'

There was a considerable drinking pause. Then he said, shifting his sturdy body in the white leather chair, 'Well, do you want to know about this horse, or don't you?'

'Sure.' The boredom in my answer came over shockingly strong, even to me. He looked faintly startled and then speculative, but when he spoke it was strictly business.

'They were taking him in a horse van from Kennedy Airport to Lexington, Kentucky. He'd spent the compulsory twenty-four hours immigration quarantine in the airport stable, along with six other horses which came over on the same flight. All normal at that time. They loaded Chrysalis and four others into the van, and drove westwards from New York on the Pennsylvania turnpike.'

'Time?' I asked.

'Left Kennedy 4 PM Monday. Last Monday, that is. A week today. Estimated Lexington midday Tuesday. Seven hundred miles.'

'Stops?'

'Yeah,' Walt said. 'Stops. That's where the trouble started.' He swirled the clinking ice round in his glass. 'They took their first meal stop at a diner near Allentown, about eighty-five miles from New York. There were four men in the van, two drivers and two grooms. Drivers in the cab, grooms in back with the cargo. At the first stop they took turns to eat, drivers first, grooms after. The drivers chivvied the grooms, and gave them too short a time to eat a good meal. There was an unfriendly argument.'

'They all say so?'

'Yeah. I've talked to all four, one at a time. They're

71

all trying their hardest to pin the blame on the others. They left the diner and went about two hundred miles to their night stop at Bedford. That was no better. Far from cooling off, they had begun to scuffle.

'They turned off the turnpike on to the interstate highway – seventy – south of Pittsburg, and left that again at Zanesville, taking the south-west fork to Cincinatti. About fifty miles farther on they turned due south to cross the Ohio River into Kentucky, and go on through Paris and down the Paris Pike to Lexington.'

'I'll need to see it on a map,' I said.

He nodded. 'From Zanesville to Paris they took secondary routes, though all paved roads, of course. Right? Now it was in Ohio that the van was hi-jacked, and it was over the state border in Kentucky when it was found, which has caused a couple of arguments here and there.'

'Hi-jacked! That's the first I've heard of that.'

'It was hi-jacked by mistake for a truckful of liquor which was about twenty miles behind it along the road. The vans looked alike, same colour, same size, and neither of them had any large identifying signs.'

'How did it happen?'

'By that time, Tuesday morning, the drivers and grooms were all eating at the same time, though at each end of the lunch counter. They left the horses unguarded for a full quarter hour, and during that time someone simply drove off with the whole works.'

'Surely the drivers locked up, and took the keys, at least?'

'Oh sure. It was an expert job though. A direct wire contact from the battery terminals to the starter motor.'

'So then what?'

'When they found the van gone the drivers called the police but it wasn't until Wednesday morning that the van was found off the road and out of sight around a hill in Kentucky. But – no horses. The ramps were down, and all the horses had been let loose.'

'Deliberately.'

'Sure. Untied. All the halters were still in the van. Those racehorses were all free with no bridle or anything to catch them by. The Kentucky boys reckon the horses were let out to create a diversion, to get the cops off the tails of the hi-jackers by making them chase horses all over.'

'And it worked.'

'Yeah,' said Walt gloomily. 'The owner kicked up stink. All the horses were valuable, not only Chrysalis. But only Chrysalis was insured with Buttress.'

'Did they get all the others back?'

'Yeah. But Chrysalis has as good as disappeared off the face of the earth.'

'How do you know the hi-jackers meant to take the liquor truck?'

'The only thing they left in the cab of the horse van was a screwed-up scrap of paper. It was a note of the time the liquor company's truck made its daily run along that route.'

'Fingerprints?'

'Gloves. Even for writing the note.'

Walt had talked himself dry. I refuelled his glass and felt like sleep.

'What do you think?' he said.

I shrugged. 'It was Chrysalis they really wanted. The timetable note was the blind.'

'But why? Why should anyone want to steal a stallion? That's what's got us all floored. I don't know much about horses, I'm a false claims man really. I just got pitched into this between cripple cases, if you get me. But even I know that it's the stallion's name that brings in the stud fee. Say someone's stolen Chrysalis, what's the point? They can't advertise him for stud, so he isn't worth a dime. We figured someone might be nutty enough to want him all to themselves, like some world famous painting, but you can hide a painting quietly in a cellar, which you can't do with a horse. The whole thing don't make sense.'

I had my own views on that, but I said only, 'What happened to Allyx?'

'I only know about that from the files. I got the case out and looked it up this morning. Allyx was a French horse, apparently one of the best young sires in Europe. He was nine when he came over here, and already his get had won a list of races as long as your arm. Dave Teller was head of the syndicate which bought him; that's why he was insured with us, as we do all the Teller estate work. Allyx was delivered safely to the Teller stud farm. No trouble in transit that time. But he was there only four days. Then there was a fire in the stables one night and they took all the horses out of the barn and turned them loose into a small corral.'

'And when they came to fetch them – no horses?'

He nodded. 'There was a broken rail over the far side, which no one knew about. All the horses had got through it, including Allyx. They caught all the others, though some were free for days. No sign ever of Allyx. The company had to face that he probably got into the foothills of the Appalachian Mountains and maybe broke his neck, and in the end they had to pay up.'

'What about that fire?'

'There was apparently nothing suspicious about it at the time. One of our very best men found no evidence of a fire being set. Still, stable fires can be started so easily . . . a cigarette butt in a pile of straw leaves no trace. This one didn't do much damage before they put it out. No question of kerosene, for instance. The whole chain of events was agreed to be accidental.'

I smiled thinly.

'What about Showman?'

Walt shook his head. 'I don't know how he got loose. But they found *him*. Dead, of course. He'd been dead some time, I think.'

'Where?'

'Oh, in the Appalachians. He came from that area, same as the others. But then Lexington has more stud farms than anywhere else in the States, so there's no significance in that really.'

'You went down to Lexington last week?'

He nodded. 'Flew there Wednesday, when Mrs Teller called us.'

'Mrs Dave Teller?'

'Uh huh.' Something moved obscurely in Walt's face. Dave's wife had made an impression. 'She's English, like you.'

'I'll go down there tomorrow,' I said. I watched him waver and decide not to tell me about her. Instead, he looked at his watch, put down his glass firmly, and stood up.

'Must be off,' he said. 'It's our anniversary, and my wife's fixed something special.'

'Give her my apologies for keeping you.'

'That's all right. It fitted in fine. I go home from Grand Central, right downstairs. A quarter of an hour to train time.'

I walked with him to the door.

'Walt . . . would you be free to come down to Lexington in the morning?' As he hesitated, I added, 'There's no point in my covering all the ground twice. I'd appreciate having you along.'

'Be glad to, Gene,' he said too politely, and I thought to hell with you Walt, to hell with everything on earth, including me, but I'm stuck with this horse nonsense for the next three weeks, and if I say go to Lexington, you go. I hid the violent moment of irritation in turning from him to open the door, and I understood his reluctance anyway, as who likes to be dragged down to do the same piece of work twice, especially under the critical eye of an imported limey busybody? He shook my hand. 'I'll call you in the morning,' he said, his feelings under better control than mine.

'Seven-thirty?'

'All right.' He loosened his jaw muscles into what looked like going to be a smile but didn't quite make it, sketched a salute with the thick-topped fingers, and ambled unhurriedly away down the passage.

I had dinner in the hotel restaurant. A steak. Never eat steak west of Nebraska, they used to say. The beef was bred on the prairie and walked eastwards to the markets: when it got to Nebraska it hit the corn belt and only after that was it fat enough to kill. New York steaks were mostly superb, but I didn't suppose they'd walked in through the New Jersey Tunnel. Long distance haulage took care of that . . . and whoever had removed Allyx and Chrysalis had had a haulage problem too. You couldn't ride a stallion along state highways. For one thing, they no longer took kindly to a saddle after years at stud, even if they had been reasonable to handle in the first place.

Nightclubs attract me like wet Mondays in

Manchester, and apathy kept me from even reading the list of shows. I went straight upstairs after dinner to catch up on a lot of lost sleep and woke again infuriatingly at two, dead tired and with a restless brain.

From habit, the Luger lay under my pillow.

It was another long night.

CHAPTER FIVE

We flew down in the morning, Walt's puffed eyes showing that the anniversary had been duly celebrated, and mine feeling as if they'd been rolled in grit.

The two drivers, reached by telephone, met us by appointment in the entrance hall of a motel near the centre of Lexington, where Walt had stayed on his previous trip. He booked rooms for us both, and we took the drivers up to his, which proved a mile short of Biltmore standards but hot on cleanliness and Kleenex.

Walt switched on the air-conditioning, shuffled chairs around, and promised beer later. The drivers, very much on the defensive, went sullenly through the disastrous tale again, aware beyond any doubt that they should never have left the horses unwatched and were more than likely to lose their jobs. Nothing they said added much to what Walt had already told me.

'Do you know each other well?' I asked.

The thin birdlike one said they did.

'And the grooms. Do you know them? And do they know each other?'

'Seen them around,' said the heavy one. 'The lazy so and sos.'

The thin one said, 'One of them came from the Midway Farm.'

That was Dave Teller's. 'He came specially for Chrysalis. It's him ought to be blamed for the whole thing.'

'Did the boys know each other, before the trip?'

'Sure,' said the heavy one. 'Way they talked they both been in the horse game all their lives.'

Walt sniffed and nodded. He'd checked all this, his resigned face said. Routine.

To the drivers I said, 'I want you to think back, and make a list of all the cars and trucks you can remember seeing on the road, all the way from Kennedy to the place you lost the horses.'

They looked aghast and as if I were crazy.

'Look,' I said, 'on those turnpikes you sometimes see the same cars over and over. The ones going your way, that is. You see them at the rest stops, and maybe you start off first, and then they pass you, and then you see them again maybe stopped at another diner while you go on to the next one, and then they come past you again. Right?'

They nodded.

'So maybe you still remember some of the cars and

trucks you saw on that trip? Especially any you saw on both days.'

They stared at me. The heavy one said, 'It's impossible. It was a week ago.'

'I know. Try, anyway. Think it over. See if you can remember any at all, between you. Then write them down and leave the list here for us, sometime this evening.'

I took out my wallet and tried twenty dollars each for size. It went down well enough. They said they would try.

'Don't invent anything,' I said. 'I'd rather pay for nothing than a lot of hogwash.'

They nodded and went, with the beer postponed to their return.

'What are you looking for?' Walt said curiously.

'Another horse van, I suppose.'

He thought it over. 'They could just have planned to rendezvous where the empty van was found. They didn't need to be seen on the road.'

'I don't think they can have been sure when they would be able to do the hi-jacking. They wouldn't know where the drivers would stop for meals. No good fixing a rendezvous in Kentucky if the opportunity came earlier, up near Wheeling.'

'They wouldn't want to drive too far with a hot truck,' Walt agreed. 'In fact, it was twenty-five miles, mostly back roads. They made straight for the hills, where it would take longest to round up loose horses.'

'Any tracks?'

'No tyre tracks of any use. The nearest road was gravel, dry and dusty this time of year. There were the tracks of the van going off the road round behind a hillock, but on the road itself they were just a jumble. Every car which passed raised a cloud of dust and wiped out all tracks which were there before.'

I grunted. 'Hoof prints?'

'Dozens of those. In all directions.'

'Back on to the gravel road?'

He shook his head resignedly. 'Impossible to tell. None on top of the van's tyre tracks, anyway. But we took a lot of soil samples, on the outside chance something would turn up later.'

'You did it pretty thoroughly.'

The smile almost came. 'A million and a half', he said briefly, 'is a lot of insurance.'

Midway Farm had prosperity printed on its gate posts, and I went through them alone, as Walt had said he felt the onset of a migraine headache.

A middle-aged Hungarian woman opened the door to me and in halting English asked me my business. Diagnosing her accent from long practice I replied in her own language, as it was simpler, and presently, having consulted in the drawing room, she showed me in there.

Dave's wife stood in the centre of a quarter acre of

deep green carpet, surrounded by deep green walls, white paint, and tomato red upholstery. She flicked my card with one thumb and said, 'You're the man who fished Dave out of the river.'

'Yes,' I said, surprised.

'He telephoned to me yesterday,' she explained. 'He says I am to trust you entirely.'

She was a slim small-boned creature with the rounded tight little bottom which comes from riding horses a great deal in early girlhood. Her jawline was delicately square, nose narrow, eyes wide and bright. Grey speckled the mouse-brown springy hair, and if she was wearing cosmetics one would have needed to be nearer than I was to be certain of it. Decisive assurance showed from every crisp gesture, and from her tone I gathered that taking her husband's word for things was not her habit.

'Sit down,' she said, pointing to a tomato chair. 'Drink?' It was two o'clock on a hot afternoon. 'Scotch,' she said without waiting for an answer, making it a statement, not a choice.

I watched her splash the pale golden liquid on to ice cubes in two tall glasses, and add a token drop of water. She came across and held out one of them with a graceful suntanned arm. A heavy gold chain bracelet loaded with fobs and charms clinked from her wrist, and into my nostrils floated a trace of 'Joy'.

I tasted the whisky. Hedges and Butler's Royal, I

thought. Too fine and light for anything else. The flavour from one sip lasted a long time on my tongue.

'Eva says you speak Hungarian,' she said, moving away, picking up her own glass, and taking an adult swallow.

'Mm, yes.'

'She was most impressed.'

'I came about Chrysalis,' I began.

'Do you speak any other languages?' Her voice veered more to American than English and had the abrupt, inconsequential lurch of two drinks too many; but it didn't show in her face.

'German,' I said, raising a dutiful social smile.

The way I'd been taught languages, it took a week for a smattering, three months for fluency, and two years to bring one to the point of recognizing typical speech and thought patterns when one heard them translated back into perfect English. In one period of seven years, in my twenties, I'd been crammed with German, Hungarian, and five Slavonic languages, from Russian and Czech to Serbo-Croat. None of them was likely to come in handy for finding stallions, and in any case they were almost out of date. The new boys were learning Swahili, Arabic, and Chinese.

'And French, I suppose?' she said.

'A little,' I agreed.

'Enough for the necessities of life, I expect.' Her expression and emphasis gave the word necessities a precise meaning, which wasn't food and drink.

'Absolutely,' I agreed, acknowledging her definition.
She laughed. Nothing frail or fine-boned about that.

'Chrysalis,' she said, 'is a right bloody nuisance. He
wouldn't have been my choice in the first place; that
Purple Emperor strain is as soft as an old man's pencil
and he's passing it on, they always do. Moth won the
Derby in a shockingly bad year and if anything had
given him half a race he'd have folded like a wet
sheet.' She took a deep swallow. 'Do you know the
first bloody thing about horses?'

'What *is* the first bloody thing about horses?'

She gave me a startled stare which turned into an
incredulous laugh. 'The first bloody thing about horses
is that they make bloody fools of men.'

I smiled back spontaneously, amused by the contrast
between her robustness of thought and language and
her delicacy of frame.

'I'm going for a swim,' she said. 'Bring your drink.'

She mixed herself a new one in passing, and without
looking back crossed the green carpet, pulled open a
sliding glass door, pushed through the insect screen
outside it, and walked with rock-like steadiness across
a paved terrace and on to a deep green lawn. Sighing,
I got to my feet and followed her. The grass was
thick and resilient, a different species altogether from
English turf, and a sprinkler on one side threw diamond sprays around like water.

She stopped on another paved area round a kidney-
shaped pool and unfastened some clips on her yellow

dress, which came off in one piece, and left two more in view underneath. Her body was slender and well cared for, but not at all a young girl's. Middle to late forties, I thought: and the sort of woman who would have been uninteresting under thirty.

She slipped into the water and floated, and I watched the sun make watered silk ripples over her brown stomach.

'Come on in,' she said. 'There are plenty of swim suits in the hut.'

I smiled and shook my head, and sat down on one of the soft plastic pool-side chairs. She took her time, humming and splashing gently with her hands. The sun was hot, but not like in the city. I took my jacket off and felt heat baking into my skin through the white cotton shirt. Peacefulness gradually seeped in too. I was in no hurry for her to rejoin me, which she presently did, the water drops shining singly on her oiled skin.

'You've hardly touched your drink,' she observed accusingly. 'Surely you're not one of those soft buggers who can't hold their liquor?' She picked up her own glass and went on proving that she, at any rate, wasn't.

'Chrysalis . . .' I began.

She interrupted immediately. 'Do you ride?'

'I can,' I said, 'but I don't.'

'Why not?'

'I haven't a horse. Nor a kingdom to give for one.'

'Drink your whisky,' she said, smiling.

'In a while.'

'Then strip off and get in the pool.'

I shook my head.

'Why not?'

'I like it as I am.' And I had too many bruises, from the weir.

She shrugged, half annoyed. 'Don't you do any bloody thing?'

'How many people knew at what hour Chrysalis would leave Kennedy Airport?'

'God,' she said, 'you're a bloody bore.'

'Don't you want the horse back?'

'No,' she said vehemently, 'as far as I'm concerned, we'd be far better off with the insurance.'

'Two hundred thousand dollars', I agreed, 'is a heck of a gamble. Supposing he never sired another like Moth?'

'There's no stopping Dave, when he's set his mind on something.' She sat on the edge of a full-length chair bed and smoothed cream on to her face from a dusky pink tube. 'And he had meant to sell off a bit of that, when he got back. God knows what will happen now he's strung up in those goddam pulleys.'

'He'll be home in about four weeks.'

'Yeah. So he said.' She lay down flat and closed her eyes. 'I told him to take his time. It's too bloody expensive being ill over here.'

Five quiet minutes passed. A single jet plane flew across, a silver streak so high up one couldn't hear it until it had gone. The air was still. The oiled brown body in the yellow bikini took in a hefty dose of ultra violet and the ice cubes melted in the drinks.

'Take your clothes off, for God's sake,' she said, without opening her eyes. 'Or are you ashamed of that pink-white slug of a body the English usually bring over here?'

'I'd better be going.'

'Do what you damn well like.' She fluttered a lax wrist in a double gesture which said, equally well, stay or goodbye.

I stood up and walked over to the hut, a large beautifully made pinewood structure with a protruding front roof, for shade. Inside were a bathroom and two changing rooms, and in the tiny lobby some shelves in a cupboard held bright coloured towels and swimsuits. I took a pair of blue shorts and put them on. The bruises on my legs very nearly matched. I left my shirt on, picked up a towel for a pillow, and went back and lay down on the next bed to hers.

She merely grunted with her eyes still shut, but after another minute she said, 'If you want to know about the timetable for Chrysalis, you'd better ask Sam Hengelman in Lexington. He fixed the van. He runs a private service from here. Dave called me and told me the date the horse was being shipped over, and I called Sam Hengelman. And he took it from there.'

'Who else did you tell the shipping date to?'

'It wasn't any goddam secret, for God's sake. I

called six or seven of the syndicate to let them know. Dave asked me to. Half Kentucky knew about it, I guess.'

She suddenly sat up straight and opened her eyes.

'Why the hell does it matter how many people knew when Chrysalis was coming? It wasn't him the hijackers wanted. They simply made a balls of it and took the wrong truck.'

'Supposing they got just what they wanted?'

'Were you born yesterday? The blood-line is what breeders pay stud fees for. Chrysalis isn't worth a sou to anyone, if they can't use his pedigree. No one's going to even send a decent mare to a stallion someone just happens to have handy, which has no name in the stud book, no history, and no papers; let alone pay fifteen thousand dollars for the privilege.'

'Buttress Life have been looking for an insurance swindle.'

'They can look till they're blue in the face.' She picked up her glass, swallowed, and grimaced. 'This drink's as warm as that pool and just as sodden. Mix me another, will you?' She held out the glass to me and I unwound myself from the bed and took it and my own back into the house. I mixed her the same size dose as before, concocted a different one for myself, and took them both back, the ice clinking coolly as I walked.

'Thanks.' She sank almost half. 'That's better.'

I stood beside the pool and put one toe in the water. It was blood warm, or more.

'What's the matter with your legs?' she said.

'The same as your husband's, only mine didn't break.'

'What's under the shirt?'

'The sun's too hot. I can do without a sunburn.'

'Yeah.' She lay flat again. 'Pink-white slug.'

Smiling, I sat down on the edge of the pool with my back towards her and dangled my feet in the water. I ought, I supposed, to go away and do something more useful, like interviewing Sam Hengelman. But Walt would no doubt have thought of that, and done it, since his threatening migraine would only have lasted until the car we had rented had taken me out of sight. Walt and Dave's wife hadn't exactly clicked.

'Mr Hawkins,' she said from behind me.

'Mm?'

'What do you do for a living?'

'I'm a civil servant.'

'With this?'

There was a sharp metallic click, the one sound guaranteed to raise the hairs on my neck as if I'd never left the jungle.

'Do you know what you're doing with that thing?' I asked, as conversationally as I could.

'Yes.'

'Then put the safety on.'

She didn't answer, and I stood up and turned round, and looked straight into the barrel of my own gun.

I deserve it, I thought. Slow, careless, and stupid. I was anything one cared to mention.

She was sitting with her legs curled underneath her, the Luger lodged unwaveringly in her fist. The gap between us, five yards at least, was too great for anything constructive in the way of action, so I simply stood still.

'You're a cool bastard, I'll say that for you.'

'You won't shoot me,' I said, smiling.

'Why not?'

'I'm not insured for a million and a half.'

Her eyes widened. 'Does that mean that you think that I . . . I . . . *shot Chrysalis*?'

'It's possible.'

She stared. 'You're a goddam fool.'

'So are you, if I may say so. That gun goes off very easily.'

She looked down at it vaguely and before I could stop her she threw it away from her on to the paving stones. The jar as it hit the ground inevitably fired it. Flame streaked out of the barrel, and the bullet smashed through the whisky glass which stood on the ground beside her long chair, nine inches from her body.

It took her a second to realize what had happened, then she shuddered heavily and put her hands over her face. I walked across to fetch the gun, and put the safety on, and then perched on the bed facing her.

'Games,' she said in a shattered voice. 'What do I have but games? Bridge and golf. All games.'

'This too?' I put the Luger back in the under-arm niche and buttoned the strap.

'I just thought I'd make you sweat.'

'Why?'

'That's a bloody good question. A bloody good question. All games. Life is all bloody games.'

'And we're all poor bloody losers,' I agreed sardonically.

She put her hands down and looked at me. Her eyes were dry, but half her assurance had drained away.

'It was only a game. I didn't mean you any harm.'

She thought she was telling the truth, but I'd met too many of the tricks the unconscious mind gets up to. Perhaps because I'd saved her husband, or was looking for his horse, or merely represented some obscure form of male challenge, she'd had an undoubted urge to destroy me. And she was a very troubled lady in far more obvious ways than that.

'Give me your drink,' she said abruptly.

'I'll get you some more whisky,' I said.

'Yours will do,' she insisted.

I gave her the glass, but one sip was enough. Dry ginger ale. On the rocks.

'Do you cheat all along the line?'

'Whenever it's kinder, or safer, or gets better results.'

I walked away across the lawn and brought her back another glass. She took a moderate pull and put it down amid the ruins of the first one.

'Stay to dinner,' she said. She made it a casual suggestion rather than a warm invitation, and I answered her need, not her tone.

'All right.'

She nodded briefly and flattened herself face down, to roast her back. I lay with one arm over my eyes to shield them from the direct sun, and thought about all the things she hadn't asked, like how was Dave when I saw him and how bad was the broken thigh.

After a while she went back to floating.

'Come on in,' she called.

I shook my head.

'Don't be so prissy,' she said. 'I'm not a swooning virgin. If your legs are like that, the rest of you must be the same. Take that bloody shirt off and give yourself a break.'

It was indeed very hot, and the clear blue water looked good. I sighed, stood up, took the shirt off, and slid down into the pool. Its lukewarm antigravitational gentleness unlocked knots and tensions in my nerves and muscles that I hadn't even realized were there, and I swam and floated tranquilly for nearly an hour. When finally I hauled myself out over the edge she was smoothing on another coating of oil. Her whisky glass was empty.

'Is Dave in that state too?' she asked, eyeing me.

'Pretty much.'

She grimaced slightly and said nothing when I put my shirt back on.

The sun had begun to lose its height in the sky and shadows were fanning out from the trees. A golden sheen lay on the big cream colonial type house across the green lawn. The pool water stilled, and the quietness of the place crept subtly into all the senses.

'It's so beautiful here,' I said. A banal enough phrase for the promise of peace.

She looked round casually. 'I suppose it is. But we're moving, of course.'

'Moving?'

'Yes. To California.'

'Moving the stud? Horses, and everything?'

'That's right. Dave's just bought a farm down near Santa Barbara, and we're moving over there in the fall.'

'I would have thought you were settled here for life. Wasn't this Dave's father's place?'

'Oh no. We moved here about ten years ago. The old farm was on the other side of Lexington, out on the Versailles Road.'

'California is a long way,' I commented. But she didn't respond with a reason for the move, and after a pause I said, 'If it wouldn't be much trouble to you,

I'd like very much to see the horses and stables you have here.'

She narrowed her eyes. 'Business or pleasure?'

'Both,' I smiled.

She shrugged. 'Help yourself. But get me another drink first.'

A pool-side icebox, I reflected, would save a lot of walking: but maybe she still needed the illusion that she didn't drink in the afternoon. I fetched her a refill, changed into my clothes, and found her still face down in the bikini.

'Say I sent you,' she said.

Before I could move, however, Dave rang from England, and Eva brought a portable telephone out and plugged the long cord into a socket in the hut. Dave's wife made three or four unanxious inquiries about her husband's condition, and then said, 'Yes, he's here right now.' She held out the receiver to me. 'He wants to talk to you.'

'Gene?' His voice was as clear as if he'd been in Lexington, and much stronger than it had been the previous morning.

'Hi,' I said.

'Look fella, Sim and I want you back here for a conference. Can you get a plane tomorrow?'

'But the fare . . .' I protested mildly.

'To hell with the fare. You've got a return ticket.'

'All right.'

'You haven't found the horse yet?'

'No.'

'Do you think you will?'

'I don't know yet.'

He sighed. 'See you Thursday, then,' and the line went dead.

The stables lay some distance away on the far side of the house. I walked round there and was shortly talking to the stud groom, Chub Lodovski, a large good-natured man with slow speech, a bird head, and great ham-like hands. He showed me round the whole setup with unlimited patience and an obvious pride in his job. The state of the place was his testimonial. The mares and foals ate peacefully in neatly railed paddocks reached by impeccable narrow drives with sharply cut grass edges. The stallions lived in a short row of six large airy box-stalls in a spacious barn, with a wooden railed exercise paddock in front, flanked by two high-walled mating compounds.

Only five of these stalls were occupied. The vacancy was for Chrysalis.

'Is this where you kept Allyx?' I asked.

'That's right. Second stall from the end. He was only in it four days.'

'And where was the fire?'

He frowned. 'It started in some straw one night, just about here.' We were fairly central. 'It wasn't much. Mostly smoke.'

'And you turned the horses out into the exercise paddock in front here?'

'That's right. Just as a precaution. But one of those doggone animals got scared and broke a rail on the far side, and the whole bunch got out across that stretch of grass on to that dirt road over there. We never did find Allyx. There hasn't been sight nor sound of him since.'

We talked for a while about the search they'd made next morning, but, Lodovski said, the whole of Kentucky was plastered with horses, and no one thought much about it if they saw one loose, and although a reward had been offered, and the insurance people had swarmed around like bloodhounds, they'd never found him.

'And now Chrysalis,' I sighed sympathetically.

'Sure. And they say lightning never strikes the same place twice!'

He was moderately upset that the stud looked like losing another major attraction, but it wasn't his money that was involved, and besides that he was proud enough of the stallions remaining in residence. I asked him if he'd ever been to California.

'The farm's moving out there, did you know?' he said.

'Are you going, yourself?'

'Mebbe, mebbe not. Depends on the missus, and she can't make up her mind.' He grinned comfortably and accepted the note I gave him with dignity.

When I got back to the pool Dave's wife had got her dress on again and Eva was brushing the splinters of whisky glass into a dustpan, which she carried carefully away across the lawn.

'Well, what did you think of the place?'

'The horses all looked very well. The stallions especially.'

'So would you, if all you had to do was . . .' she began, and then stopped and shrugged. 'So would you.'

Apart from an occasional 'bloody' which crept in from habit, that was the last of her verbal squibs for the day. But my lack of scandalized reaction didn't have the same effect on her drinking, and she kept up a slow but steady intake right through dusk and dinner. Her mental brakes remained half on, half off, as before.

Over thick slices of rare beef she said, 'Are you married?'

'No.' I shook my head.

'Divorced?'

'No,' I said. 'I've never been married at all.'

'Are you queer?' she asked, as simply as if she'd said, 'Are you comfortable?'

I smiled slightly. 'No.'

'Then why aren't you married?'

'I haven't found anyone who will marry me.'

'Don't be ridiculous. You must have women lying down for you in droves.'

'It's not the same thing.'

She looked at me broodingly over the rim of her glass. 'So you live all alone?'

'That's right.'

'No parents?'

'They're both dead,' I said. 'And I've no brothers, no sisters, no uncles, aunts, or cousins.' I smiled. 'Anything else?'

'Stay the night.'

She said it abruptly, as if it came from a deeper level than her fairly harmless interrogation, and there was an element of surprise and alarm on her face afterwards.

'I'm sorry,' I said matter-of-factly, 'but I can't.'

She looked at me without expression for about ten seconds.

'I have a mother,' she said. 'And sisters, and brothers, and dozens of relations. And a husband, and a son, and all this.' She waved a hand around the millionaire bracket walls. 'I have everything.' Her eyes filled with tears, but she went on looking straight across the table, without blinking.

'I have . . . bloody . . . everything.'

CHAPTER SIX

There was an envelope from Walt in my room at the motel containing a short note and a list.

Gene,
This is all the drivers came up with. I think it's
safe to bet that they actually did see these
vehicles. The top three, they both remembered.
The others, only one of them remembered. No
horse vans, though.

Walt

The list read:
'Impala, lilac, two years old, California number plates. Passengers included a fat child who made faces out of the rear window. Both days.

Grey station wagon trailing a load of furniture. Both days.

Dark green Ford Mustang, Nevada plates. Young couple, no description. The horse van drivers remember this one because they were discussing whether the Mustang was a good car or not. Second day only.

White convertible: young woman with blond hair wound on rollers. Second day only.

Army green pick-up truck with white lettering on the doors. Second day only.

The pick-up, one of the drivers thinks, was probably on Inter-state 70, after Zanesville and before they turned off south. He doesn't remember clearly.'

I read the list through three times while I dressed. The load of furniture looked the most promising, but none of it exactly inspired.

Walt, driving to the airport in the morning, damped even the furniture.

'It was only one of those Snail Express trailers.'

'Like the U-Haul,' I said.

'That's right. "Carry your house on your back, but let us take the weight",' he said, quoting the Snail Express advertising slogan. 'The drivers said it wasn't big enough to put a horse in.'

There were furniture trailers of all sizes all over the country: people moving house hired one at their old home, loaded up, and drove off to the new, maybe six states away. There they unloaded and simply left the trailer in a local depot, from where the haulage firm hired it to the next removing client. The bright orange U-Haul trailers and the aluminium and blue ones of the Snail Express were as frequent on the roads as the Greyhound buses.

'How about the pick-up?' I asked.

'Much too small for a horse,' Walt said gloomily.

He came back with me to New York and rubbed his thumb continuously over the finger pads while I went through the file we had made on the case.

There was a batch of photographs of the missing horse, mostly taken from stud book advertisements, by the look of them. Not a very remarkable creature on paper, I thought.

Sam Hengelman had sent his two most careful drivers to fetch Chrysalis. He had had a call from Mrs Teller informing him of the date fixed for the horse to fly over, and also a cable from England when he was on his way. Hengelman had telephoned Kennedy Airport and been told the horses would be through the twenty-four hour immigration regulations at noon, Tuesday. He had sent the van as soon as he got the cable, on Sunday. There was, he agreed, a system like the U-Haul in operation among horse vans, to avoid the need for long empty journeys, but some folks liked personal service, and Mr Teller was one of them.

The Buttress Life Insurance covered transport. Sam Hengelman had not had to take out a policy for the trip, and neither stood to lose nor gain from the hi-jacking.

Both drivers had clean records going way back.

Both grooms had been in their present jobs for more than three years. One of them came from Midway Farm; the other from another farm which had a horse coming in on the same trip.

An interview with Mrs Eunice Teller had produced no helpful information.

I shut the folder with a smile, and gave it back to Walt.

'How about checking with Snail Express, on the off-chance?'

He looked sceptical. 'The drivers said the trailer wasn't high enough.'

'They're used to thinking in terms of ordinary horse vans. And they were looking down, from their cab. You could squeeze a racehorse into a box about seven feet by four, by six feet high, if you were ruthless enough. Find out how many trailers that size or larger Snail Express had out last Monday or Tuesday, which might conceivably have been on the turnpike.'

'All right,' he said expressionlessly. 'If you say so.'

With the time lag working in reverse it was 3 AM Thursday morning when I landed at Heathrow, and 12 before I walked into Dave Teller's room in a Reading hospital. Flaming June had come and gone: it was raining again.

If one discounted the ropes, pulleys, slings, and plaster suspending his leg in mid air, the patient looked healthy enough. He greeted me without fuss, the direct eyes steady and bright.

'Tiring trip?'

'So so.'

'You've eaten?' He waved vaguely at a collection of chocolates and grapes.

'I had breakfast over Ireland, at two o'clock.'

He laughed, eased himself on the pillows, and stretched out a hand for a cigarette.

'How's my wife?'

'Very well.'

He lit his cigarette and flicked shut the lighter.

'What was she doing, when you called?' His apprehension was pretty well concealed.

'Sunbathing. Swimming. There's a heatwave coast to coast.'

A couple of muscles relaxed in his forearm and he inhaled deeply. 'She gave you a drink . . . I hope?'

'Sure. And a swim. And I stayed to dinner.'

He looked at me directly for some time without speaking. Then he said merely, 'A good one?'

'Very, thank you. And I saw your horses. Chub Lodovski showed me round.'

He talked much more naturally about the horses: no problems there.

'I hear you're moving to California,' I said, after a while.

The tenseness instantly came back; the small give-away tightening of eye, neck, and respiratory muscles that I looked for every day in my job, and couldn't be blind to in my friends.

'Yes,' he said, tapping off ash. 'Eunice loves the ocean, and in Kentucky we're as far from it as can

104

be . . . and of course, the horse breeding business in California is every bit as profitable. We will do very well out there, I've no doubt.'

Eunice would take her problems right along with her, I thought: though with a bit of luck they would recede for a year or two. Perhaps Teller considered the upheaval worth it.

'What's the new place like?' I asked.

'It's good land, pretty well irrigated. And the stable and general layout are as good as Midway. Better even, in some respects. It's Davis L. Davis's old place.'

I looked blank, and he explained. 'Made his money out of roadside hamburger stands. Well, he died early this year, and last month they held a dispersal sale of his brood mares and stallions, to divide up his estate for inheritance. I put in a bid for the farm to his executors before I came over here this time, and they wrote me a week or so back to say they're accepting it. The contracts are in hand right now, but I don't foresee any difficulties. I'm sure glad to have got it settled at last.'

'At last?'

'Been looking for a farm in southern California for over a year now, but there were too many snags to most of them. Eunice and I took a trip over in March of this year, and we saw the Davis farm then, and liked it. So . . .' He waggled his fingers to finish the sentence.

The door opened and Keeble came in, mild

spectacles reflecting the pallid light from the window, eyes blinking rapidly, and the usual patch of bristle growing grey where he had short-sightedly missed with the razor. He said hellos all round and settled himself comfortably into the spare armchair.

'Well, how's it with the States?' he said: and I told them everything Walt had told me. They thought it over for a while in silence.

'So what do you think now?' Keeble said.

I glanced doubtfully at Teller, but he tapped ash off his cigarette and remarked simply, 'Sim says you were convinced I was pushed into the river on purpose. I guess what he's asking you is, have you changed your mind?'

'No, I haven't.'

Keeble and Teller looked at each other. Then Teller said, sighing, 'We've come up with one or two things which makes it almost certain you are right.'

Keeble nodded. 'I went to Dave's hotel in London to collect his luggage and pay his bill, and explained where he was if anyone wanted him. The young man at the reception desk asked me if the lady journalist from *Stud and Stable* had found Dave all right on Saturday. She had, he said, been most insistent, owing to a deadline on the magazine, and he had given her my address and telephone number, which Dave had left with him in case he was wanted hurriedly in connection with Chrysalis.'

'And that', I remarked, 'is how boy and girl knew where to find you.'

'Quite,' Keeble agreed. 'From the house to the river was no doubt a simple piece of following. Incidentally, I checked with *Stud and Stable*. They didn't want Dave, and their deadline is the first day of each month.'

'Nice,' I said.

Keeble took an envelope from his pocket and fished out some three by three inch black-and-white photographs. 'There are Peter's snaps,' he said. 'Take a look.'

I took them from him and looked. The ducks had come out splendidly; better than one of Lynnie, who had been moving. The picnic lunch was there, and the *Flying Linnet* in Marsh Lock, and one of Dave Teller standing on the bows, and a rather grim one of myself staring down into the water. There was one of the four men fallen in a heap in the punt at the hotel where we'd had our morning drinks, and another, taken with the photographer's back to the river, of Keeble, Joan, Dave, Lynnie, and myself sitting round the little table under the sun umbrella, with glasses in our hands.

Keeble waited without blinking. With this in mind I started through the pile again, and found what he had seen. I looked up at him. He nodded, and from an inside pocket produced a magnifying lens, which he threw over to me. With the help of that, the two figures were clear. A girl with long hair and white trousers, a young man with pale trousers and a check shirt, standing side by side in the background of the photograph of us all drinking at the pub.

'It's them,' I nodded.

'Yes,' Keeble agreed. 'They were there in the morning. So I'll grant you they could have followed us by car from Henley . . . you can see the river from several places along that road . . . and also that they saw Dave standing on the bows when we left Henley and when we left the pub. And possibly also when we arrived at the pub, and at Marsh Lock. They would know there was a good chance of him being there again when we came back through Harbour.'

I smiled. 'And the five feet which was missing from the punt's mooring rope had been used to tie it securely to the Danger post while they waited for us.'

'I agree,' Keeble said. 'We took that punt right out of the water after you'd gone on Monday, and we found that the cleat for the stern rope had been unscrewed from the stern, and screwed on again under the water line at the bow end.'

'So both mooring points were at one end,' Teller said. 'The safe rope was under water all the time, hidden by the punt itself and the girl's body and arms. And, of course, we weren't looking for anything like that at the time, so we'd never have seen it.'

Keeble finished it. 'Once they'd got the visible rope safely in Joan's hands, and we were all looking anxiously for you and Dave to surface, the girl had only to pull some sort of quick release knot, and the punt was free. So I'll agree, Gene, that that was an accident which could be staged, and was staged, and you were right and I was wrong. Which, I seem to remember vaguely, has happened once or twice before.'

He smiled at me with irony, and I reflected that there were few superior officers who would say that sort of thing so utterly ungrudgingly.

A nurse clattered in with Teller's lunch, which proved to be chicken salad and tinned mandarin oranges. The patient poured the oranges on to the salad and ate the combined course with resignation.

'The food is lousy,' he said mildly. 'I've forgotten what a good steak looks like.'

We watched him eat without envy, and I asked Keeble if he'd had any results with the handkerchief.

'Only negative ones. None of the Yogi Bear concessionists in this country imported it. They say, from the material and the sort of paint used for the bear, that it was probably made in Japan. And some of them had doubts it was done by the Hanna-Barbera artists. Not well enough drawn, they said.'

'I'll take it back to the States and try there,' I said. 'After all, boy and girl were almost certainly American.'

Teller raised his eyebrows with his mouth full.

'The boy shouted "Can you help us, sir," and that "sir" comes a great deal more commonly from Americans, than from the English. Also, the boatman said their accent was "same as on the telly" and there's as much American as English on our television.'

'The same argument might apply to public school-boys,' Keeble said casually. 'But they were Americans, I agree.'

'So all we need to know now, apart from who were they,' I said to Teller, 'is why they wanted you dead.'

No one had any constructive ideas on that point. Teller drank his coffee and a maid in a green overall came to take the tray.

'You're guarding against them having another go?' I said to Keeble, watching the maid's back disappear through the door.

Keeble followed my eyes. 'All precautions,' he nodded. 'The works. I got the Radnor-Halley Agency. Only the best for Dave!'

'They won't let me open any packages,' Teller complained. 'I think they take them outside, dunk them in a bucket, and wait for the ticking to start. And the only chocolates I have were bought by Sim personally. You'd never believe the half of what goes on in here.'

I laughed. 'It's when you get out of here you'll notice it.'

'He'll stay here till you've wrapped it up,' remarked Keeble; and he wasn't joking.

I stared. 'I'm in anti-infiltration, remember? Not the CID.'

'Oh sure. But the same motivation, I imagine. Just

let your hunter instincts loose . . . and tell us what you plan to do next.'

I stood up restlessly and went to the window, still raining. Two nurses ran from one building to another, clutching capes around them and skitting mud up the backs of their stockings. Useful people, nurses. Needed people. Constructive, compassionate, tough people . . .

'Well?' said Keeble, behind me.

I turned round and leaned against the wall. 'How's the exchequer?'

Teller answered, 'Look, Gene, I've enough to launch a minor space programme. And as I said before, if it weren't for you I wouldn't be here at all. So spend what you need to, and I'll pick up the chits.'

'Right . . . then I think it would be best to let the Radnor-Halley Agency deal with anything which crops up here . . . I suppose they did the handkerchief inquiry?'

Keeble nodded.

'And I'll go back to the States tomorrow. I can't believe the attempted murder isn't tied in with the horse theft, so the springboard for everything must be in America. Unless some Irish fanatic disapproves of you skimming off the cream of British bloodstock!'

'Is Chrysalis Irish, then?' Keeble asked seriously.

'Irish-bred dam,' I said. 'That's all. His sire was Purple Emperor, in the Read Stud at Newmarket.'

'How do you know?' Teller asked, surprised.

'I looked it up,' I said briefly. 'Also his markings.

111

And that is important.' I paused. 'Whoever took Allyx and Chrysalis knew a lot about horses. Allyx was one of six stallions loose in a paddock at night. Chrysalis was one of five horses in a horse box. Yet each time the right horse was singled out for removal. We have to believe it was the right horse, not just chance, because each time it was by far the most valuable one of the collection which disappeared. Well . . . Chrysalis is a dark bay with no distinguishing marks. No socks, no blaze, no star. One colour all over. And Allyx was exactly the same. There are literally thousands of horses like that.'

The two men didn't stir.

I went on, 'This means that if we ever do find Chrysalis, there will be an enormous problem of identification. English horses have no tattooed numbers, like American.'

'Christ,' Teller said.

'I wouldn't know him if he came up and ate sugar out of my hand. Would you?' He shook his head. I went on, 'The only people at all likely to be able to pick him out for us with any certainty are those who handled him in England. And that's where we hit a very big snag. The stud groom at Read's died of a heart attack two months ago and the new man couldn't be sure of knowing Chrysalis again. Read himself is too short sighted, apparently, to be of any help. This means we have to go back nearly five years, to the season when Chrysalis last raced. To his owner at that time, and his trainer. Though the only one I'd pin any faith on would be the lad who looked after him. And it's the lad, I think, who we'll need to take to the States, if we find a horse which might be Chrysalis.'

'We could easily find out who the lad is,' Keeble nodded, 'and shunt him over.'

'His name is Sam Kitchens, and he'll be at Ascot at this moment, as one of his horses is running in the four-thirty. It's Gold Cup day today.' I smiled faintly. 'I thought I might just drift along to the races when I leave here.'

'Just tell me,' Teller said in a small voice, 'how and when you found out all this?' He spread his fingers. 'I only ask.'

'I spent an hour this morning at the British Blood-stock Agency... I was practically camped on their doorstep at nine o'clock. And then I did some tele-phoning. That's all.'

'When do you sleep, fella?'

'Between meals. Very bad for the appetite.'

'He's mad,' Teller said to Keeble.

'You get used to it,' Keeble assured him. 'The first eight years are the worst.'

'And this is the guy you'd trust your daughter to?'

'Hm,' said Keeble. 'We haven't mentioned that.'

'What?' I said suspiciously.

'We'd ... er ... like you to take Lynnie back with you, to the States,' Teller said. 'She's going to visit with Eunice for a while.'

113

I glanced at Keeble and saw that he knew what I was inevitably thinking: that Eunice's special need for company was more compelling than the rest of Lynnie's finishing-school term.

'I'd be glad to,' I said to them both with formality. 'On a slow boat via New Zealand, if you like.'

'She's too young for you,' said Keeble, without anxiety.

'She is indeed.' I pushed myself away from the wall and stood upright. 'Where will I collect her?'

Keeble handed me an envelope. 'Air tickets for you both. She'll be at the Victoria Air Terminal at eight-thirty tomorrow morning. Is that all right?'

I took the tickets and nodded. 'Can I have the handkerchief?'

He obligingly produced it, in another envelope. I put that and the air tickets away, and picked up Peter's snaps. Holding the negatives up to the light I singled out the drinking group and put it in my wallet.

'I'll get it blown up tomorrow in New York,' I said. 'Then it'll only be a matter of sifting through two hundred million inhabitants.'

Drizzle was wilting the fluffy hats when I got to Ascot, but the turf looked greener for it, and the horses glossier. I spotted the trainer I wanted and walked across to where he was talking to a large woman in a creased pink dress under a dripping pink umbrella. He caught sight of me over her shoulder, and I watched the initial memory-jog pass through mind-search to recognition. He smiled warmly at his success.

'Gene Hawkins.'

The large woman turned round, saw she didn't know me, decided she didn't want to, and departed.

'Mr Arkwright.' We shook hands, and I thought how little age had changed him. Still the upright, brisk, grey-headed neighbour from my father's days in Yorkshire.

'Come and have a drink,' he said, 'and let's get out of this rain.' There were misty beads of water fuzzing his tall grey hat. 'Though it's much better than it was an hour ago, isn't it?'

'I've only just come.'

He led the way up the staircase into the balcony bar and ordered vodka and tonic. I asked if I could have the tonic without the vodka and he remarked that my father, an enthusiastic alcoholic, would have turned in his grave.

'What are you doing now then?' he said, sipping the clear fizzy mixture. 'Still in the Civil Service?'

'Yes,' I nodded. 'But I'm on leave at present.'

'It always seemed rum to me, you doing something so . . . so tame,' he said. 'Considering the sort of boy you were.' He shrugged. 'Never would have thought it. Your old father always thought you'd do something in racing, you know. You rode well enough, you knew your way around. Can't understand it.' He looked at me accusingly. 'Those two years in the Army did you no good.'

I smiled. 'It was while I was in the Army that they offered me this job.'

'Safe, I suppose,' he said, making allowances. 'Prospects, pension, and all that.'

'Mm,' I said non-committally. 'Actually, I really came here today to see you, to ask you about Chrysalis.'

'Have they found him, do you know?' he said.

'Not yet, no. The American who bought him is a friend of my boss, and they've asked me, as I know you, to see if you would do them a favour.'

'If I can,' he said promptly. 'If I can.'

'Their problem is', I explained, 'that if and when a loose horse is found, especially if he's some distance from where he was lost, how are they to be sure it is Chrysalis.'

He looked startled and then amused. 'That certainly is a problem. But Chrysalis hasn't been in my yard since ... let's see ... four years last October. I don't know whether I'd be certain of him, not absolutely certain, if I saw him, for instance, among twenty others rather like him. And you'd want it to be more positive than that.'

'Yes,' I agreed. 'Actually I rang your home this morning and your secretary said I'd find you here. And he also said Chrysalis's old lad would be here. Sam Kitchens. Would you mind if I had a word with him?'

'That's right, he came with Milkmaid for the four-thirty. No, I don't mind, you ask him what you like.'

'Mr Dave Teller, who bought Chrysalis, wonders whether you would let Sam Kitchens go over to the States for a few days, if and when the horse turns up, to identify him. Mr Teller will pay his fare and expenses.'

Arkwright laughed. 'Sam will like that. He's not a bad chap. Pretty reliable.'

'Then if he's needed, you'll get a cable saying which flight he's to go on, and so on. Will that be all right?'

He nodded. 'You tell the American I'll let him go.'

I thanked him. 'They'll be very grateful.' I bought him another vodka and tonic and we talked about horses.

Sam Kitchens walked his fair young Milkmaid around the parade ring and I risked ten bob on her, but she turned out to be a cow. I joined Arkwright while he ran his hand down the filly's legs and listened to the jockey explaining forcibly that it wasn't down there that the trouble lay, but up in her pea-sized brain.

Lads usually resent criticism of their charges, but from his expression Kitchens, a short stocky man of about thirty, held much the same view. I asked him, after introductions from Arkwright, whether he would know Chrysalis again with enough certainty to testify if necessary in a court of law.

'Sure,' he said without hesitation. 'I'd know the boy.

117

I had him three years. Sure, I'd know him. Maybe I couldn't pick him out of a herd, now, but I'd know him close to. The way his hide grows, and little nicks in his skin, I wouldn't have forgotten those.'

'That's fine,' I said, nodding. 'Was there . . . is there . . . anything special about him, which might help someone who'd never seen him before to recognize him?'

He thought it over for several minutes. 'It's four years. More, nearly five, see. The only thing I remember is, we had trouble with his off hind hoof. It was thin, used to crack at the same place every time. But the stud he went to might have cured it, as he wasn't racing any more. Or he might just have grown out of it, being older now.' He paused. 'Tell you something, he liked sardines. He's the only horse I know of who had a taste for sardines.'

I smiled. 'That's pretty odd. How did you find out?'

'Took my tea into his box once. Sardines on toast. I put it down for a minute on the window sill, and when I looked round he'd scoffed the lot. It tickled me, it did. I used to share a tinful with him sometimes, after that. He always liked them.'

I stayed for the last race and picked another loser. I would have made a lousy trainer, anyway.

CHAPTER SEVEN

I reached the Air Terminal at eight-fifteen, but Lynnie was there first.

'I couldn't sleep much,' she said. 'I've never been to America before.'

I'd been to America a dozen times. I hadn't slept much either.

Lynnie's clothes, a deep pink shiny PVC raincoat over the orange tan dress, were having an anti-soporific effect on everyone in sight. Resisting an urge to grope for dark glasses I felt an uncommon lift to the spirits, which lasted to mid Atlantic. There Lynnie went to sleep and a strong wave of non-enthusiasm for finding Chrysalis invaded my mind like one enormous yawn. I wouldn't mind, I thought idly, I really wouldn't mind lazing around that swimming pool with Eunice and Lynnie, doing nothing at all but drink in sunshine, peace, Scotch, and an uninterrupted view of two well-shaped females in bikinis. Peace most of all. Lie like a log, and not think, not feel. And sleep. Sleep for sixteen hours a day and mindlessly laze away the other

eight: a programme as near to death as dammit. A
very small step from there to eternity, to make the
peace permanent . . .

'What are you thinking about?' Lynnie said.

She had opened her eyes and was watching my face.

'Heaven,' I said.

She shook her head slightly. 'Hell, more like.' She
sat up briskly. 'How long before we land?'

'About an hour.'

'Will I like Mrs Teller?'

'Haven't you met her before?' I asked.

'Once, when I was little. I don't remember her.'

I smiled. 'She isn't easy to forget.'

'Exactly,' Lynnie said. 'There's something odd about
me going to stay with her. Of course I said I'd love
to, and who wouldn't go off on any trip to get away
from school, let alone a super one like this, but I
distinctly think that Daddy and Mr Teller have an
ulterior motive and I want to know what it is.'

'They want her to have company, to stop her
drinking too much alone.'

'Wow!' She looked surprised. 'You're not serious?'

'They didn't say so. I'm only guessing.'

'But I can't stop her drinking,' she protested.

'Don't try. She doesn't get drunk. And you'll like
her all right, as long as your ears don't fall off.'

She laughed. 'My mother wouldn't approve of her?'

'Quite likely not.'

'I expect that's why I've only met her once.' She

grinned at me mischievously without a shred of self-consciousness, Joan's influence waning visibly with every hundred miles.

It was late morning, local time, when we checked in at the Biltmore. From there Lynnie departed on foot for a private tour of New York, and I cabbed down town to Buttress Life. The heatwave was still in position, the air still saturated. Lethargy and haze hung over the city, and buildings shivered like mirages through the blue exhausts of the cars. Once over the Buttress building's threshold the temperate zone took over: I rode up to the seventh floor with the humidity in my clothes condensing into water, and sagged damply into Walt's spare chair in four seven.

'Good trip?' he said. 'You look . . .' he hesitated.

'Yeah,' I said. 'Pooped.'

He smiled. It was worth waiting for. There's a load to be read in a smile, and Walt's was a good one.

'How's it with the Snail Express?' I asked.

He picked a list off his desk. 'They were very co-operative. Only trouble is, they had about thirty-five trailers out on those dates which just might have been going west on the turnpike.' He handed me the paper sympathetically. 'It was a pretty long shot, of course.'

'Hm.' I looked at the list of names and addresses, and at my watch. 'I think we'd better check them.'

'I had a feeling you'd say that.' A touch of gloom.

I smiled at him. 'I'll start it, if you like. Do you know where we can get good enlargements of a

121

snapshot done quickly?' He nodded and mentioned a name, and I gave him the negative. 'The top left hand corner. A couple. Man and girl.' He nodded again. 'And there's this handkerchief.' I produced it. 'Would you mind making a tour of all the offices on this floor, and perhaps the fifth as well, and finding out what everyone associates with it?'

Walt took the small white square curiously.

'Yogi Bear,' he said. 'What's the point?'

'It belonged to a girl who may know more than she ought about Chrysalis. The girl on the negative.'

'Find her, find the horse?' He was half incredulous, a fraction excited.

'Maybe.'

'Right then,' he said at the door. 'See you.'

I studied the list. Snail Express had done their best. Most names had two addresses, the old and the new. All were followed by a place and a date, the depot where the trailer had been checked in after its trip. There were several telephone numbers for the eastern addresses, a few for the west.

Working stolidly down the list, with long pauses while new inhabitants went to find the new telephone numbers of the old, I said I was calling from Snail Express, wanting to know that the service had been satisfactory, or if the customers had any suggestions or complaints. I listened to more praise than criticism, and eventually checked off twenty-seven genuine hirings.

Walt came back while I was biting the end of one of his pencils and wondering what to do next. It was three o'clock. He'd added lunch to his itinerary but he carried a large white package, which he opened carefully. Six enlargements of the corner of Peter's negative. Various sizes, from postcard to nine by seven. The faces were clearest on the smallest print, too fuzzy on the largest.

'He says he'll run off as many as you want by this evening, if you let him know at once.'

'Ask him for six, then. Postcard size.'

'OK.' He picked up the receiver, pressed the buttons, and asked.

The boy and girl stood side by side, their heads turned slightly to the left, towards where we had sat under the sun umbrella. Their faces were calm, good-looking, and somewhat alike. The boy's hair was darker. They were of almost the same height. The checks of the boy's shirt stood out clearly, and one of its buttons was either undone or missing. The girl had a watch with an extra wide strap on her left wrist. She hadn't been wearing it while she hung on to the post.

'All-American kids,' Walt commented. 'So what?'

'So how did you get on with the handkerchief?'

Walt produced it. A little limper, a little grubbier than before.

'Fifteen Yogi Bears, ten don't-bother-me-nows, six lewd suggestions, and one Yellowstone Park.'

'One where?'

'Yellowstone Park?'

'Why Yellowstone Park?'

'That's where Yogi Bear lives. At least, it's called Jellystone in the cartoons, but it's Yellowstone really.'

'Real live bears still in Yellowstone?'

'Oh sure.'

'A natural beauty spot . . . holiday place, isn't it?' I remembered vaguely.

Walt nodded.

'With souvenirs?' I suggested.

'Great lot of help that would be to us.'

I agreed. It would only narrow the field down to one of the thousands who'd been to Yellowstone sometime, or one of the other thousands who knew someone who'd been to Yellowstone sometime. But I remembered a Jamaican would-be assistant to the Biological Warfare Defence Laboratory at Porton who'd been turned down because of a Russian-made bust of Castro in his bedroom. Souvenirs sometimes had their uses.

'The handkerchief probably came from Japan. Do you have a leg-man who can check who imported it, and where it was sold over here?'

'Leg-man?' Walt echoed dismally. 'That's me.' He put the handkerchief away in its envelope, chased up a few answers on the telephone, and heaved himself reluctantly to his feet. 'I may as well go see a man about a Yogi, then. How're the trailers?'

'Twenty-seven are OK. Of the other eight, five don't answer, and three have no telephone.'

I tried two of the non-answerers yet again. Still no reply. Walt looked through the shorter list I'd made of the unchecked.

'They sure went all over, didn't they?' He said, 'Nebraska, Kentucky, New Mexico, California, Wyoming, Colorado, Texas, and Montana. Just don't ask me to leg it around all those places!' He drifted out of the door and his solid footsteps diminuendoed down the passage.

I went on trying the numbers now and then. After two hours I had crossed Texas off the list, bitten the end right off Walt's pencil and started on it an inch farther down, decided I couldn't work many days in his rabbit hutch of an office, and wondered how Eunice was making out beside her pool.

The telephone buzzed.

'Are you staying at the Biltmore again?' Walt said.

'Yes.'

'Meet me in the bar there,' he suggested. 'I'm nearer there than to you.'

'Sure,' I said. 'I'm on my way.'

Lynnie wasn't back. I left a message at the desk for her and joined Walt. His pale blue suit looked as if it had just come out of a spin dryer and there was a damp translucent look to his skin. Repentant, I bought him a large Scotch on the rocks and waited until he had it where it would do most good. He sighed, rubbed

125

the back of one wrist across his eyes, fished a crumpled piece of paper out of his pocket, and spread it open on the bar.

'To start with,' he said disgustedly, 'it's not Yogi Bear.'

I waited in sympathetic silence and beckoned to the barman for a refill. On the paper a list of about eight souvenir manufacturers and distributors had been crossed out, a single line through each. The top lines were neat and straight, the last three a great wild slash across the paper. Walt had had a very bad day.

'The handkerchief came from Japan, like you said.' He took a swallow of his second drink and began to revive. 'Several of the firms phoned their west coast offices for me. No dice. It seems as if at least half of the souvenirs sold in the west are made in Japan, but all these Yogi Bear concessionists say that this isn't Yogi Bear at all, it's the wrong shaped head.'

He pulled out of the by now battered envelope a very bedraggled looking handkerchief and looked at it with loathing.

'If it was sold at or near Yellowstone Park, it could have come from any two-bit import business. As it's not Yogi Bear, no one will have had to pay commission to use the picture, and there isn't any way that I know of finding who brought it into the country and who sold it to where.'

After ten seconds I suggested diffidently, 'We could start from the other end.'

He glared at me incredulously. 'Are you plumb nuts? You can't mean what I think you mean.'

The rocks in my drink had melted to pebbles. I tasted the drowned whisky and put the glass back on the bar.

I said, 'One of the Snail Express trailers was checked in at Rock Springs, Wyoming. It's still there: they haven't had another customer for it yet. I've asked them to hold it until I've had a look at it.'

'Why that one? Why that one particularly?' Walt asked. Irritation only half repressed sharpened his voice.

'Because it's one of the three with no phone number. Because it's in the same state as Yellowstone. And because it gives me an itch.'

'Yellowstone is clear across Wyoming from Rock Springs,' he said. 'Must be four hundred miles.'

'Three hundred. I looked at the map.'

He drank and rubbed his thumb over his fingers much faster than usual. Tired lines had appeared round his eyes.

'I think it's a futile waste of time,' he said abruptly.

'I've time to waste.'

'And I haven't.'

He put the glass down with a thump, reached into an inner pocket and brought out another white package which he tossed down in front of me.

'These are your photographs.'

'Thanks.'

127

The look he gave me was a long way from the smile of that morning. I wondered whether I would have let him go looking for answers if I'd known he was short on stamina, and decided I probably would. He hadn't given up half way: only at the end.

Lynnie appeared in the bar doorway in her orange dress and the tired looking men there straightened their spines in a hurry. She wouldn't come in. I eased Walt with me across the heavy carpet and introduced him to her in the hall outside. He made only a few perfunctory remarks and left in a short time with a glowering face and solid back.

'Whatever's bitten him?' said Lynnie, looking after him.

'He's had a tiring day and he's going home to his wife.'

She looked at me quickly, half laughing. 'Do you always know what you're saying?'

'Frequently.'

She chuckled. 'Anyway, you look a lot tireder than he does.' We started to walk over to the desk to collect our keys.

'That's most encouraging.'

'What shall we do this evening? Or do you want to sleep?' She was unselfish enough to keep anxiety entirely out of her voice, but when I said we'd go wherever she wanted there was an extra bounce in her stride. She decided on a two hour taxi ride to everywhere in the city she'd ever heard of that she hadn't managed to see that afternoon, followed by dinner in a second-floor glass-walled restaurant, looking down and across the lights of Broadway and Times Square. At eleven-thirty, when we got back to the Biltmore, she was still wide awake.

'What a fabulous, fantastic day,' she said in the lift.

'Good.'

'I'll remember it as long as I live.'

I smiled at her enthusiasm. It was a thousand years since I'd been as happy as that, but sometimes I could still imagine how it felt. That evening it had been quite easy.

'You are far from drizz,' she said, contentedly grinning.

'You'd be no great drag to be stuck in a lift with yourself.'

But the lift stopped unimaginatively at the eighth floor as scheduled and we walked along to our rooms. Her door was opposite mine.

I kissed her cheek. 'Goodnight, little Lynnie.'

Her brown eyes smiled serenely back. 'Goodnight, Gene. Sleep well.'

'You too,' I said. 'Kentucky first stop in the morning.'

It took four more days to find the girl in the photograph, though maybe I could have done it in two if it hadn't been for Lynnie. Privately aware that it wasn't necessary for me to do the job myself I dredged up a cast iron-sounding reason for having to accompany her to Lexington, and we flew down via Washington, which involved another quick taxi tour instead of a lengthy wait at the airport. Lynnie didn't intend to miss a thing.

Eunice met us at Lexington airfield and drove us to Midway, and after a prawn and avocado lunch lent me her car to go on my errand. I greased Chrysalis's ex-groom into going with me with twenty dollars of his employer's money, and took him off to Sam Hengelman's. The horse van, Sam said out of the corner of his mouth as he watched an old movie on a cyan-heavy colour set, was still in care of the police department. If I wanted to look at it, go talk to them.

At the police department a state trooper listened to what I had to say, said 'Yeah,' several times, consulted higher authority, and sorted out some keys. Higher authority turned out to be a good-looking detective in his twenties, and we all four repaired to the parking lot behind the police building, where the horse van stood in one corner.

Chrysalis's lad pointed out the stall the stallion had inhabited, and the state trooper came up with a successful conclusion to the expedition: four long shining bay hairs.

'From his mane,' said the groom authoritatively.

The detective kept two for the State and sent off

the other two special delivery to Walt at Buttress Life, and the groom and I drove back to Midway.

Eunice and Lynnie were both in the pool, and the rest of the day and night came close enough to my daydream on the plane, except that the sixteen hours' sleep shrank to six, but even that was spectacular by recent standards.

When Lynnie said over large cups of breakfast coffee the next morning that she wished I wasn't going, I very nearly didn't. If I'd stayed, Buttress Life would have paid the insurance and a load of grief would never have happened. Yet if I could go back to that cross-roads moment again I know I would inevitably make the same decision. Once a hunter, always a hunter: the inner compulsion hadn't loosened its grip: the quality they'd hauled me out of the Army for was too basic in my nature, and being what I was, what I am, slopping out of the chase was impossible. Keeble had known, I admitted wryly, that he had only to get me hooked.

'I must go,' I said, 'if I'm to find the horse.'

'Damn the horse,' Lynnie said.

I laughed at her. 'You've learnt quickly.'

'I like Eunice,' she said defensively. 'She doesn't shock me.'

I gathered from that that she certainly did, but that Lynnie would never admit it.

'But you will come back here? Before you go home, I mean?'

'I expect so,' I said.

She fiddled with her coffee cup, looking down. 'It's only a week since I picked you up at your flat, last Sunday.'

'And you've aged a year.'

She looked up quickly, startled. 'Why did you say that?'

'It was what you were thinking.'

'I know,' she said, puzzled, 'but I don't know how you do.'

'Crystal set in the attic. Intermittent though, unfortunately.'

'Just as well, if you ask me.' There was a healthy mockery on her laughing face. 'How would you like to be tuned in permanently to Eunice?'

Eunice herself trailed through the doorway at that moment wearing an electric blue wrapper and a manageable hangover. With both still in place, after two cups of coffee and a cigarette, she trundled Lynnie and me to the airport.

'Goodbye, you son of a bitch,' she said to me, as I stood beside her window. 'I guess you can come back any time you want to.'

Lynnie glanced at her sharply, with sudden speculation: growing up in front of one's eyes. I smiled goodbye to them both and walked away into the airport. From there I bus-stopped a thousand miles to Denver, and chartered a twin-engined Piper from a local firm for the last two hundred to Rock Springs.

The pilot chewed his nails savagely beside me all the way as if he were a dedicated auto-cannibal, and I arrived feeling sick.

On the hot late Sunday afternoon the little desert town looked lifeless. Shimmering air rose endlessly over the dump of abandoned rusting motor cars, a Greyhound bus rolled past with passengers staring like fish through its green glass windows, and sprinklers on the richer front lawns kept the parching heat at bay. At the bus station I learnt that old man Hagstrom's boy was the agent for Snail Express, but when I found old man Hagstrom, fanning himself in a rocker on the front porch of his small frame house, he said that his boy was out calling.

Hagstrom himself seemed to be glad to have company and told me to go inside and bring two beers out of the icebox. The icebox was in the living room, just through the screen door. It was a shambles of a room with sagging broken-spring chairs, dirty worn out rag rugs, a scattered assortment of cups, glasses, and bottles, all unwashed, and a vast new television. I took the beer out on to the porch, sat on the top step, and drank from the bottle, like my host.

The old man rocked, scratched himself, drank, and said vaguely that his boy would be right along, I could bet on it. I looked up and down the hot empty street. There were other shapes rocking gently in the shade of the porches, half invisible because many had the insect screens round the outside rails. From behind them they watched the world go by: only thing was, the world rolled past in automobiles and didn't stop to talk.

Two beers later, while old man Hagstrom was telling me how he personally would have dealt with the Saigon situation in '67, his boy rolled up in a pock-marked Chrysler. His boy was literally a boy, not more than eighteen: old man Hagstrom's grandson. He rubbed his hands down his grease-marked T-shirt and jeans, and held one out to me with as easy going a welcome as his grandfather's. I explained what I wanted.

'Sure you can look at the trailer,' he said, amiably. 'Now?'

'If you don't mind.'

'You're welcome.'

He waved me into his baking car and whirled it casually round a few corners, drawing up with a jerk outside a rickety looking gate set in a head-high wall. Through the gate, in a dusty area, stood four Snail Express trailers, all different sizes.

'That one,' I said, pointing to the largest.

'Came in last Saturday. I think. I'll look it up.' He unlocked a small brick-built office on one side, and I followed him in. Hot enough in there to please Satan.

'That's right, Saturday,' he said, consulting the ledger. 'Came from New York State, renting charge paid in advance for one week. The week wasn't up until Monday.'

'Do you remember who brought it here?'

'Uh, let's see. Oh yes. An old guy. Can't remember much about him. He had white hair, I guess.'

'What sort of car did he have, to pull the trailer?'

'I helped him unhitch . . . a station wagon, I think. Grey, mebbe.'

'It wasn't these two?' I showed him the photograph.

'Nope.' He was definite. As far as he knew, he'd never seen them. Had I asked his grandfather? I had.

He said he'd swept out the trailer, but I could look inside if I wanted to.

'Why did you sweep it?' I asked.

'Usually do. It was pretty clean already, though.'

I looked anyway. There were no bay hairs. Nothing at all to suggest that Chrysalis had ever been squeezed into it. The only suggestive thing about it was the way it was built: the roof opened outwards right along the centre line, to make the loading of tall objects easier. It had been worrying me that Chrysalis would not have walked into a tiny dark trailer: but one open to the sky was a different matter.

Old man Hagstrom's boy obligingly dug out the Hertz agent, who rented me an air-conditioned black Chevrolet with only five thousand on the clock. Overnight I added three hundred and thirty-four more, and drove into Gardiner for breakfast.

The road there had led through Yellowstone Park itself where the dawn had crept in mistily between the pine trees, and glimpses of lakes had looked like flat puddles of quick-silver. I had seen an ugly great moose, but no bears. Yogi was asleep.

I spent all morning walking round the town. None of the shops were selling the handkerchief, or had ever stocked any like it. The photograph produced no reactions at all. After a toasted bacon, tomato, and lettuce sandwich at a lunch counter I left Gardiner and went fifty-four miles to West Yellowstone.

The afternoon's trudge produced exactly the same absence of results. Hot, tired, and frustrated, I sat in the Chevrolet and wondered what to do next. No trace of Chrysalis in the trailer, even though it seemed likely it was the one the drivers had seen. No matching handkerchiefs at Yellowstone Park. Walt had been right. The trip was one pointless waste of time.

I thought of the long forest drive back through the park, the canyon gradients at midway, and the final hundred miles of desert to Rock Springs, and decided to put it off until the next day. Sighing, I found the best-looking motel and booked the best room they had, stood under the shower until the day's aches had run down the drain with the dust, and stretched out for a couple of hours on the kingsized Slumberland.

The waitress who brought my steak at dinner was large, loosely upholstered, kind natured, and with an obvious conviction that a man alone liked a bit of gossip. I wanted her to go away and let me eat in peace, but custom was slack and I learnt more than I cared about her complicated home life. In the end, simply to stop the flow, I pulled out the crumpled handkerchief and asked if she knew where I could get a new one like it.

She thought 'the girls' might know, and went off to ask them. Relieved, I finished my steak. Then she came back and doubtfully put the white square down beside me on the tablecloth.

'They say you might get one in Jackson. They do have bears on ashtrays and things down there. Down in the Tetons. A hundred, hundred-fifty miles. It's a holiday town, Jackson.'

I'd driven straight through Jackson the night before on the way up from Rock Springs, and seen only a small western town fast asleep. When I went back on the Tuesday morning it was buzzing with holiday-makers and local inhabitants, dressed all alike in cowboy clothes. Dude ranch country, I learnt. The main street was lined with souvenir shops, and the first one I went into had a whole pile of small white handkerchiefs with bears on.

CHAPTER EIGHT

The girl in the punt opened the ranch house door, walked halfway to meet me from the car, and greeted me with professional instant welcome.

'Mr Hochner? How nice to have you with us.'

'I'm glad you could take me at such short notice, with the Fourth coming up next weekend.' I shook her hand, putting a slight touch of German accent into my voice because it was easier for me than American if I had to keep it up for any length of time. It didn't seem altogether wise to be English.

'We're seldom full this early in the season.' She smiled as far up her face as her cheek bones while her eyes skimmed my clothes, car, and luggage. Only a hotel keeper's check up: it hadn't occurred to her that she'd seen me before.

'I'll show you straight to your cabin, if you like? Then you can freshen up and come along here to the ranch house for dinner later on. There will be a bell, to let you know when.'

I parked the car, and carrying my two suitcases, the

old one and the new one from Jackson, followed her along a grassy woodland track towards one of several small log cabins scattered among the trees.

She was tall and strong, and older than she had seemed on the river: twenty-six or twenty-seven, I guessed. The fair hair no longer hung childishly loose, but was combed up into a round topknot, leaving her neck cool and uncluttered. She wore dark blue Levis instead of the white trousers, but the pink shirt on top looked identical. One of the storekeepers in Jackson, the fifth I tried, had known her immediately when I had artistically let the photograph drop face up in front of him as I took money for a local map out of my wallet.

'Yola Clive,' he said casually, picking it up. 'And Matt. Friends of yours?'

'I'd thought of looking them up,' I agreed, sorting out bills. 'How do I get there, do you know? I haven't been to their place before.'

He obligingly gave me clear directions for a fifteen-mile drive, finishing, 'and the High Zee Ranch is the only place along there, so you can't miss it. But if you're planning on staying, I'd give them a call and make a reservation. It's a mighty popular place they run.'

'I sure will,' I said: and I did. I also bought some Levis and shirts and a pair of riding boots, and the suitcase to put them in. In cowboy country guns passed without comment: I added a heavy black tooled leather belt with a silver buckle, and the clerk didn't show any surprise at my wanting to make sure that the small-of-the-back holster I sometimes used would slot on to it.

Jackson preserved its own wild western flavour to the extent of a small authentic stage coach waiting in front of the drug store: but the sleepy disillusioned horses between the shafts looked a poor prospect against galloping redskins. Broad raised boardwalks edged with hitching rails ran along in front of the stores in the short main street, though the mud they had been built to avoid had long been metalled over. Motels with signs saying 'air-conditioning and central heating' were called 'Covered Wagon' and 'Rustlers' Hideout'. Jackson was an uneasy mixture of evolution and make believe, and clearly a success.

I sat in the sun on a hitching rail most of the afternoon: did a bit of thinking, and made two calls to Walt at Buttress Life.

Yola Clive led me round a neat stack of sawn logs, up two steps, across a minimal porch and through a screen door and a wood door into the cabin.

'Bathroom through there,' she said, pointing. 'And you'll probably need to light the stove in the evenings. The snows only melted here two or three weeks ago, and the nights are cold.' She smiled briefly and indicated a small tubful of a crumbly mixture which stood beside the squat black stove. 'Light the logs with two or three handfuls of that.'

'What is it?' I asked.

'Pep,' she said. 'A mixture of diesel oil and sawdust.' Her eyes glanced professionally round the room, checking that everything was in order. 'There's an ice machine out back of the kitchen, if you want to make drinks. Most guests bring their own liquor . . . We don't sell it ourselves. I expect you'll want to go riding tomorrow. We usually fix that up over dinner.' The half smile came and went, and Yola walked quietly away along the track.

Sighing, I investigated my quarters. There had been a reasonable compromise between age-old materials and modern construction, resulting in a sturdy two-roomed cabin with a pitch roof and varnished tree trunk walls. Two single beds stood on the polished wood floor in the main room, covered with patchwork quilts. A curtain across a half-shelved recess acted as closet, and the two upright chairs and the table were all home built. So, too, I discovered, were the towel rail, stool, and shelf in the bathroom. But the backwoods stopped short of the plumbing: and the lighting was ranch generated electric.

I unpacked on to the shelves and hangers, and changed from town clothes into Levis and a blue-and-white check shirt. The complete vacationer, I thought sourly: and buckled the gun belt round my waist.

After that for an hour I sat on the porch and looked at the view, which was good enough for a chocolate box. The Teton range of the Rocky Mountains stretched north and south, with dark green pine forests washing up from the valley to meet spotless snow-capped peaks. Along the bottom ran a sparkling thread of blue and silver, a tributary to the upper reaches of the one thousand mile Snake River: and between the river and the woods on whose edge my cabin stood, a wide stretch of sage brush and scrub was dotted with yellow weed-like flowers.

The woods around the cabin stood on the lower slopes of another ridge of peaks which rose sharp and high behind the ranch, shutting it in, close and private. The stream ran right along, in and out, but the only road into the narrow valley stopped dead in the parking area of the High Zee.

A bell clanged loudly up at the ranch house. I went back into the cabin and put on a sloppy black sweater which hid the Luger and looked reasonable at nine thousand two hundred feet above sea level, though the still persisting heatwave was doing a good job in the mountains too. Walking slowly along the dusty grass track I wondered if Matt Clive would know me. I certainly had no clear memory of his face on the punt, though I now knew it well from the photograph. It was unlikely, since his full attention must have been concentrated on Dave Teller, that he had taken much notice of me; but he might possibly have a sharper impression than Yola, as I had been closer to him when I went in after Dave.

I needn't have wondered. He wasn't there.

Yola sat at one end of a long golden wood table flanked by chattering well-dug-in ranch guests. Family groups, mostly, and three married couples. No singles except me. A bright well-coiffured mother invited me to sit beside her, and her hearty husband opposite asked if I'd had a long drive. On the other side of me a small boy told his parents loudly that he didn't like stuffed pancakes, and every face round the table looked sunburned, vital, and overflowing with holiday spirits. I battened down a fierce urge to get up and go out, to get away from all that jollity. I didn't see how I was ever going to make the effort to look as if I were enjoying myself.

By the end of the meal it felt as if my smile were set in plaster, rigid and mechanical to the extent that my face ached with producing it. But the hearty man opposite, Quintus L. Wilkerson III, 'Call me Wilkie,' seemed pleased to have a practically non-speaking audience, and made the most of it. I endured a splash by splash account of his day's fishing. His wife Betty-Ann had ridden to the lake with him, and then gone on into the hills in a party containing her two children, Samantha and Mickey. I heard about that too, from all three of them. They asked me to ride with their party the next day, and I wrenched my tongue into saying I'd be glad to.

I lasted out the coffee. The Wilkersons promised

to see me at breakfast, and Yola asked if I were comfortable in the cabin.

'Thank you, yes.' Remembering the German accent. Smile.

'That's fine,' she said brightly, her eyes sliding past. 'Ask if there's anything you need.'

I walked stiffly out of the ranch house and along the dark track to the empty cabin; leaned wearily against one of the posts holding up the porch roof and looked at the row of peaks glimmering palely in shifting moonlight, with streaky cloud across the sky. My head ached with a feeling of compression, as if my brain wanted to expand and fill up with air.

How could I go on like this, I thought. Dinner had been about as much as I could manage. I didn't know what to do about it. No use praying: no faith. If I went to a doctor I'd get a bottle of tonic and a homily about pulling myself together. There was absolutely nothing to be done but endure it, and go on with that until it got better. If I could only convince myself that it would in the end get better, at least I would have something to cling to.

Somewhere in the valley a stallion shrieked.

Maybe it was Chrysalis. If he wasn't actually on the High Zee Ranch I thought the chances very high that he was somewhere near. Maybe Keeble did know what he was doing sending me to find him, because it was evident that I could still function normally on the work level: concentration acted like a switch which cut out the personal chaos. If I concentrated twenty-four hours a day, life would be simple.

One trouble with that. It was impossible.

The ranch held upwards of a hundred and twenty horses. About forty of them were penned in a big corral near the main ranch house, saddle horses for the ranch guests to ride.

Breakfast had been early, but the fitting of guests to horses took some time, even though everyone except me had been there two or three days and knew which animal they wanted. The head wrangler asked me if I could ride, and if so, how well.

'I haven't been on a horse for nine or ten years,' I said.

He gave me a dead quiet one with U-shaped hocks. The western saddle seemed like an armchair after the postage stamp I'd been teethed on: and there were no new-fangled things like buckles for raising and lowering stirrups. The head wrangler unlaced the thong holding the three-inch-wide leathers to the saddle, slid them down two or three holes, and laced them up again. Good soft leather, which could go all day and not rub the horse.

Over to one side of the ranch house, past its green watered lawn, there was a smallish sturdily railed paddock of not more than an acre. I'd spent all breakfast looking out of the window at the seven horses in it.

Three mares, two small foals, two stallions. Both the stallions were bays, but one had a white blaze and was no thoroughbred.

'What are those horses over there?' I asked the wrangler, pointing.

He paused a second while he worked out how to put it delicately to an ignorant dude, and foreigner into the bargain, and then said, 'We breed most of the horses, on this ranch.'

'Oh, I see,' I said. 'Do you have many stallions?'

'Three or four. Most of these', he glanced round the patiently waiting mounts, 'are geldings.'

'That's a nice looking bay,' I commented.

He followed my eyes over to the small paddock again. 'He's new,' he said. 'A half-bred Matt bought in Laramie two or three weeks back.' There was disapproval in his tone.

'You don't like him?' I said.

'Not enough bone for these hills,' he said briefly, finishing the second stirrup. 'Now, is that comfortable?'

'Fine,' I said. 'Thank you.'

He nodded with casual friendliness and went to see to someone else. The wranglers differed from the dudes only in the matters of age and dress. They were all boys or young men between eighteen and thirty, several of them college boys working their vacation. The dudes were either parents or children; scarcely one in the twenties. No one, Betty-Ann Wilkerson told me knowledgeably, called cowboys cowboys anywhere except in films. Cowhand was possible, but the right word was wrangler. There were no cattle on the High Zee. The wranglers herded the horses, and the horses were there for the dudes to ride.

In the matter of clothes the wranglers were less flamboyant, less well pressed, altogether dustier. They had been up since five-thirty and other people's holidays were their hard work.

'They turn the horses out on the hills every night,' Wilkie explained, 'and go up and herd them down in the morning.'

We set off from the ranch in two parties, about twelve guests and two wranglers in each. Down over a flat wooden bridge across the narrow river, and up into the main Teton range opposite. Wilkie rode in front of me and Betty-Ann behind as we wound upwards through the woods in single file; and neither of them tired of talking.

'They turn the horses out on the hills over here because there isn't enough pasture in the valley to feed them.' Wilkie turned half round in his saddle to make sure I could hear. 'They go miles away, most nights. The wranglers fix a bell on to some of them, like cowbells in Switzerland, so that they can find them in the morning. The ones they put bells on are the sort of natural leaders, the horses other horses like to be with.' He smiled heartily. 'It's sure difficult to see them sometimes, with the sun shining through the trees and making shadows.'

What he said was true because we passed a group of three in a hollow later on, and I didn't see them until one moved his head and clinked his bell.

'They only bring in the number they need,' Betty-Ann filled in. 'They just leave the rest out, and maybe bring some of them in tomorrow, if they come across them first.'

'So sometimes a horse could be out for a week at a time?' I suggested.

'I guess so,' Wilkie said vaguely. He didn't really know. 'Of course, if they want one particular horse, the wranglers will go right up the mountain to find him, I do know that.'

'Anyone who can ride well enough can go up with the wranglers in the morning,' Betty-Ann said. 'But they *canter* up and down here instead of walk.'

The path was steep and also rocky.

'These horses are born to it, honey,' said Wilkie kindly. 'Not like the riding school horses back home.'

At eleven thousand feet the path levelled out on to a small tree-shaded plateau overlooking a breathtaking pine-wooded valley with a brilliant blue lake in its depths. The cameras came out and clicked excitedly. The chattering voices exclaimed over an order of beauty that demanded silence. And eventually we rode down again.

Yola asked me at lunch if I had enjoyed my morning, and I said without difficulty that I had. The Wilkerson children were calling me Hans and asked me to swim in the stream with them in the afternoon. Wilkie clapped me heartily on the shoulder and told me I was a good guy, and Betty-Ann had irritatingly begun looking at me in a way which would change her husband's mind about that instantly, if he noticed.

I left the lunch table last and whisked away a large slice of bread in a paper napkin. Alone in my cabin I unpacked some specially acquired groceries, filled one pocket with sugar cubes, and on the bread scooped out a whole tin of sardines. With the bread still held in the napkin I walked down through the sage brush and along to the mares' and foals' paddock, reaching it on the far side from the ranch house.

There I offered sugar in one hand and sardines in the other. The mares came and sniffed, and all chose sugar. The foals chose sugar. The bay with the white blaze chose sugar. The dusty half-bred that Matt bought two or three weeks ago in Laramie came last, less curious than the rest.

He sniffed at the sardines and raised his head with his ears pricked, staring across at the high Tetons as if hearing some far off sound, smelling some distant scent. His nostrils quivered gently. I looked at the splendid lines of bone in the skull, the gracefully slanted eye, the perfect angle of head on neck. He had the crest of a thoroughbred stallion, and the hocks of a racehorse.

He bent his head down to the sardines and ate the lot.

*

Yola and Matt Clive lived in a cabin of their own, separate from the main ranch house, which contained only the dining room, kitchens, sitting room, and wet day games room for the guests.

Yola backed an olive-drab pick-up with small white lettering on its doors out of a shady carport beside her cabin, and drove away down the dusty road. I stared after her, half amazed, half smiling. Full marks to the horse van drivers, I thought. They'd seen both the Snail Express van and the pick-up. They must have seen them both several times, but even so, they'd remembered.

Guests were allowed to use the telephone, which was located in the Clives' cabin. I strolled over there, knocked on the door, and found the place empty. Not locked, though in this case there was a key. There were no locks on any of the guest cabin doors: one could only bolt them on the inside, with a simple wooden wedge slotted into the latch.

A quick tour of the Clives' cabin revealed two separate single bedrooms, living room, kitchen, bathroom, and office. I planted three hypersensitive listening devices as invisibly as possible, and unhurriedly left.

After that I climbed into the Chevrolet and drove myself back to Jackson, where the telephone was more private. My call to Buttress Life lasted a long time, and Walt's contribution to the second part of the conversation consisted of gasps and protests of 'You can't.'

'Listen, Walt,' I said in the end. 'We're not policemen. I imagine your company would settle for the property back and no questions asked? And my brief is to restore Chrysalis to Dave Teller. Just that. Nothing more. If we start things the way you want, we'll end up with a lot of smart lawyers and most probably a dead horse.'

There was a long pause. 'All right,' he said slowly. 'OK. You win.'

He wrote down a long list of instructions. 'This is Wednesday,' I said, thinking aloud. 'Sunday morning. That gives you three clear days. Should be enough.'

'Only just.'

'Never mind,' I said soothingly. 'You can do most of it sitting down.'

Walt wasn't amused. 'And you, what exactly will you be doing?' he asked sarcastically.

'On a dude ranch,' I said reasonably, 'one dudes.'

At the Post Office I mailed off to him by express delivery six hairs from the mane of the sardine horse, and motored back to the grim business of acting the holiday I'd feared from the start.

The three days seemed eternal. Riding took up the mornings and most afternoons and that was the best of it. Meals continued to be a desperate trial. The nights were long. I wished that Lynnie could have come with me, because in her company the depression seemed to retreat, but she was Eunice's crutch, not mine. And her father, trust me as he might, would have found it hard to believe I would only ask for her

151

daytime closeness. And maybe I couldn't have done it. So no props. No props at all.

Yola ran the ranch with a sort of super-efficiency which looked easy, juggling staff and guests into harmony without a single wrinkle of anxiety and without any show of aggression. The fair hair continued to be worn tidily on top. Her clothes were jeans and shirt and soft flat shoes. No boots: no masculinity. She radiated friendliness and confidence, and her smile never once reached her eyes.

She didn't go riding with her guests, and I never sat next to her at meals because most of the husbands and many of the wives conducted a dignified scramble for her favours, but on Thursday evening, when with several others I was drinking after-dinner coffee out in the open on the long porch, she dropped gracefully down into the empty chair beside me, and asked if I were enjoying my holidays, and was finding my cabin comfortable.

I answered with half-true platitudes, to which she half listened.

'You are young,' I said next, with great politeness, 'to own so beautiful a place.'

She replied to this small probe with frank ease. 'It belonged to my grandfather and then to my mother. She died a year or two back.'

'Has it always been a dude ranch? I mean, it seems a bit hilly for cattle . . .'

'Always a dude ranch,' she agreed. 'My grandfather

built it about forty years ago . . . How did you hear of us?'

I glanced at her unhurriedly, but she was merely curious, not suspicious.

'I asked in Jackson for somewhere good and fairly quiet, out in the mountains.'

'Who recommended us?'

'Just a man in the street.'

She nodded, satisfied.

'What do you do in the winter?' I asked.

There was a flicker in the eyes and a quick private smile on the mouth: whatever she did in the winter pleased her more than hotel keeping.

'We move down south. Snow completely blocks this valley from November through March. Most years it's May before we come back . . . We usually open the ranch the second week in June, but the canyons are often impassable then.'

'What do you do with the horses?'

'Oh, they go down to the plain, on a friend's ranch.'

Her voice was as strong and capable as the rest of her. I watched her eyes slide round towards the paddock with the mares and foals, and pause there calmly, and return to me. Expressionless.

I smiled her a force five version of an adults-only smile, and asked if she ever found it lonely, so far out in the wilds. To this mild but unmistakable come-on there was no reaction beyond a crisp shake of the head. I was the only man there not guarded by a watchful wife: Yola wasn't in the least bit interested.

I complimented her on the ranch food, and on the helpfulness of the wranglers. She said she was glad I was pleased. I yawned and apologized, and said it must be all the fresh air ... she'd heard it all dozens of times a year, said everything she'd said so often that she no longer had to think. No use on this occasion using any jolting technique to force out an unguarded phrase: jolting her was roughly the last thing I wanted to do.

After a while I stood up lazily and said I would turn in, and she gave me the usual meaningless half-way-up smile. She hadn't really seen me at all: wouldn't remember me in another month. Unless I inadvertently gave her cause.

The three bugs in her cabin worked on the audio-switch principle: any noise, and speech especially, which they picked up, automatically started the recording machine which occupied the back half of the ordinary looking transistor radio standing beside my bed. But there was little to overhear. Yola slept alone, and apart from one evening when she invited four of the guests in for a drink, the only conversations were telephone calls.

In my cabin each evening, warming by the squat black stove, I played back the day's 'take'. Nearly all the calls were to do with business: grocery orders, laundry, blacksmith's supplies, and future bookings.

But one call, on Friday evening, was worth all the trouble.

'Uncle Bark?' Yola's voice said, low and clear. One of the bugs was behind a picture of drooping roses on the wall over the telephone table.

'. . . honey.' The occasional word escaped from the receiver in return, but Yola must have been holding it close to her ear.

'Sure. Everything's fine here,' she said. 'Absolutely no kind of trouble.'

'. . . Matt? . . .'

'That's what I called about, Uncle Bark. Matt wrote me he's having to give up in Europe. He says he can't get near to you-know-who, they've got him holed up as tight as Fort Knox. So I guess we'll just have to keep everything under wraps for a while longer.'

'. . .'

'It sure is a nuisance, yeah. But as long as we get him to you before the snows come again . . .'

'. . .'

'How can we? You know it isn't built for that.'

'. . . stay . . .'

'We certainly can't send him down to Clint's with the others. We'd waste a whole year and he might break a leg or something.'

'. . . desert.'

'We don't want him at Pitts, it isn't built for it. But there's a good long time for Matt to arrange something.'

155

'. . . hadn't started.'

'Yeah, I'm sure you would. But it's too late now. How were we to know that something so goddam stupid would happen? Matt will probably be home some time tomorrow. I'll have him call you.'

She put down the receiver soon after that: and I wound back the tape and played the conversation over again. Two unsubstantial points emerged. If Dave Teller had been too obviously guarded, Matt would have realized that the punt episode was not considered to be an accident. And the something 'goddam stupid' which had somewhere or other upset the Clives' original plans might be that I'd been there to fish Dave out of the river, or might be something else quite different; something which had made the removal of Dave necessary in the first place. The horse had been stolen on June 15th, Tuesday, and Yola had asked the London hotel for Dave's weekend address on June 19th, Saturday. So what, if anything, had happened in the four days between? Something goddam stupid . . .

I told Yola after breakfast on Saturday morning that I had enjoyed my stay immensely and would be leaving the following day. She smiled the regulation smile without clearly focusing, and thanked me for letting her know.

'So if I could have my bill at breakfast tomorrow?' I suggested.

'Sure,' she said. 'But you can't stay over Monday for the Fourth?'

'I'm afraid not.'

She nodded, not caring one way or the other. 'I'll get it ready for you, then.'

The Wilkersons exclaimed over my going. 'You'll miss the barbecue,' Samantha said. 'And the float trip down the river.'

A local man took parties down the fast flowing Snake on black inflated rubber raft dinghies: one of the area's attractions, like the rodeo and the ski lift. The Wilkersons had asked me to join them. 'Maybe I'll come back next year,' I said. And maybe I wouldn't.

I looked after the children that afternoon while Betty-Ann went to the hairdresser and Wilkie drove to a distant lake for the fishing. They swam in the stream, where I refused to join them in case my head in the water jogged Yola's sleeping memory, and we fed sugar and handfuls of grass through the rails to the leggy foals in the little paddock. The rails were solid young tree trunks dove-tailed and nailed into even sturdier posts, and the gate was just as substantial. Its hinges were bolted through the gatepost, and a heavy padlock fastened it through two strong hasps. None of this strength was new.

Samantha and Mickey didn't think much of the sardine bay.

'Too spindly,' Mickey said. 'His legs would snap if he went up the mountain.' I looked across at the Teton range, the tops shining white in the hot sun. The sure-footed born-to-it ranch horses picked their way easily

157

up and down the steep rocky paths over there, through the woods growing with flat huckleberry leaves, across the screes left from landslips, and on to the bare stony patches above the snow line.

'Why don't you stay till Monday night?' said Mickey. 'If you go tomorrow, you'll miss the fireworks.'

CHAPTER NINE

At one o'clock, early Sunday morning, I stood on the porch of my cabin waiting for my eyes to dilate, and listening to the night.

A slight wind, riffling the trees. A car horn, very distant. The faint hum of the electric generator in its special house. No sound from Yola's cabin. None all evening. Matt hadn't yet come home.

With some misgivings I had left my riding boots in the cabin, and wore only thin rubber-soled plimsolls, with a pair of socks on top. I walked quietly through the sage brush on the long way round to the little paddock, the spicy fragrance rising into my nose as I disturbed the silver-grey leaves. The half moonlight was enough to see by without a torch and streaky clouds made shifting shadows across the ground: it couldn't have been better if I'd sent in an order.

The padlock's strength was illusory. It had a simple lever movement inside which took me less than five minutes to fiddle open. No one could have heard the click of success. Nor the tiny squeak of the gate opening. I slipped through and distributed sugar to the mares and foals. The bay with the white blaze greeted this with a trumpeting whinny; but no lights went on in Yola's cabin or the wranglers' bunkhouse.

The sardine horse flared his nostrils at me but ate the sugar and let me slip over his head the simple rope halter I had come armed with. I spent some time rubbing his nose and patting his neck, and when I walked towards the gate he came with me docilely enough. I opened the gate and led him through, and the mares and foals quietly followed, their unshod hooves making dull little clops on the loamy ground.

The gentle procession went slowly across towards the river, over the flat bridge with hollow thuds, and up into the darkness of the pine woods. The mares soon stopped to graze, and the foals with them, but the bay stallion with the blaze suddenly realized he was free again, and crashed past me at high speed, squealing and cantering up the path and making as much noise as a train-load of football supporters. Anxious, heart-quickened moments passed: but still no reaction from below.

The sardine bay tugged hard to follow. I soothed him and steadied him, and we presently walked on. He picked his way too cautiously over the stones and corners of rocks sticking up in the narrow path, but I couldn't hurry him without risk; my neck prickled at the thought of being slung into a Wyoming jail for horse stealing; but it was nothing to the fear I had that Mickey might be right about those spindly legs.

In places all the way up the width of the path dwindled to two feet, with a wall of rock on one side and a steep slope on the other. Riding along them by day one simply had to trust that one's horse wouldn't tumble over the edge, as nothing could then have stopped a rock-strewn descent of two or three hundred feet. At these points there wasn't room to walk side by side with a horse one was leading: I inched up the path ahead of him, and slowly, cautiously, he put his feet delicately down between the bigger stones, and scrunched after me.

Two or three times we passed small groups of horses from the ranch, the cow bell clanking gently round the neck of the leader and betraying their presence. Their dark shapes melted into the jumbled background of woods and rocks, and the moonlight picked out only an eye, a rump, a swishing tail. The wranglers found them each morning by tracking, as the bells were only audible for a furlong. I'd had a long talk with one of the boys about tracking, and he'd shown me how they did it. They were going to be able to follow my way up the mountain as clearly as if I'd given them directions, and to tell the time I went by the amount of dew which formed in the hoof prints. The boy had shown me hoof prints, told me how many horses had gone by and when, and all I had seen were some scattered dusty marks. They read the ground like a book. If I tried to obliterate the sardine horse's hoof prints, I obliterated also any chance of the Clives believing he had wandered off by accident. The fuzzy outline of plimsolls under socks was, I hoped, going to pass unnoticed: nothing less was worth the discomfort of wearing them on such jagged going.

It took two hours to reach twelve thousand feet and to come to the end of the tracks I'd learnt in the past four days. From there it was a case of trusting my own nose. The drifting streaks of cloud made black shadows like pits across the rocks and several times I stood still and felt ahead with one toe to make sure that the ground was in fact still there, and I was not stepping straight off a precipice. The moon itself, and the cold mountain air moving against my right cheek, kept me going in the right general direction, but the dotted-line trail I had studied on the map proved more optimistic than actual.

The horse's legs stood up to it remarkably well. Mine had already had enough. Mountaineering was not among Civil Service requirements.

The peak of the Grand Teton rose to thirteen thousand seven hundred feet. The summit loomed very close. Patches of snow, half melted, exposed black looking banks of scree. I came suddenly across a narrow trail winding past them like an eel: people had walked along there recently, scraping into the snow. I had, with some luck, come the right way. The cold bit down under my black jersey and through the thin shirt underneath, and I wished I had had the sense to bring gloves. But it couldn't be a great deal farther: through the short canyon pass, and out the other side. I looked at my watch. The climb had taken nearly three hours and I was late.

It was darker in the canyon, but also invisible from the valley below. I took the small torch out of my jeans pocket, and shone it in front of my feet. Because of that, the whole expedition came unstuck.

A man suddenly rounded a corner a short way ahead and stood foursquare in the centre of the trail. Startled even more than I was, the horse backed instantly away, tore the rope out of my hand, pulled me flat over as I tried to hang on, and skipped sharply away along a narrow ridge branching off to the left.

Sick and furious I got back on my feet and turned to go after him. The man took a tentative step down the trail and called out.

'Gene?'

It was Walt.

I bit my tongue literally to stop the rage in my mind from spilling over him. There wasn't time for it.

'I saw you coming. The light,' he explained. 'I thought I'd come along to meet you. You're later than you said.'

'Yes.' I shut my mouth. There was half a million pounds loose in a death trap. My responsibility, and my fault.

The moon pushed out a feeble twenty watts. I

couldn't see the horse. The path he had taken in panic was a ledge eighteen inches wide with sheer rock on the left and a fierce slope of scree on the right. A gradient so steep that it was as dangerous as a straight down drop: and in its black invisible depths there would be the usual big slabs with upjutting edges.

'Stay here,' I said to Walt. 'And keep quiet.'

He nodded without speaking, understanding that the situation was beyond apology. His instructions had been expressly to wait for me at one arranged spot.

The ledge was thirty feet long with a bend to the left. I walked along it slowly, not using the torch, my left hand trailing along the rock wall, the grey light just enough to show the crumbly uneven outer edge.

After thirty feet the ledge widened into a saucer-shaped bowl three quarters surrounded by towering rocks. The sloping floor of the bowl led directly into the sharper slope of the scree. On the floor of the bowl, patchy snow and rough black pebble.

The horse was standing there, sweating. Quivering in every rigid limb. There was no way out except back along the ledge.

I stroked his muzzle and gave him four lumps of sugar, speaking gently to him in a voice much calmer than my feelings. It took ten minutes for the excessive tension to leave his body, and another five before he would move. Then I turned him carefully round until he was facing the way he had come.

Horses react instantly to human fear. The only

chance I had of getting him safely back was to walk round there as if it were a broad concrete path across his own stable yard. If he smelt fear, he wouldn't come.

Where the ledge began, he baulked. I gave him more sugar and more sweet talk. Then I turned my back on him and with the halter rope leading over my shoulder, walked slowly away. There was the faintest of protesting backward tugs. Then he came.

Thirty feet had never seemed so interminable. But an animal's sixth sense kept him from putting a foot over the edge, and the slithering clop of his hooves on the broken ground came steadily after me all the way.

Walt, this time, made no sound at all. I came across him standing motionless several yards up the intended trail and he turned without speaking and went on ahead.

Less than half a mile farther the path descended and widened into a broad sweeping basin: and there, where Walt had been supposed to meet me, waited another man, stamping his feet to keep warm.

Sam Kitchens. Holding another horse.

With a powerful torch he inspected every inch of the one I'd brought, while I held his.

'Well?' I said.

He nodded. 'It's Chrysalis all right. See that tiny scar up there, under his shoulder? He cut himself on a metal gate post one day when he was a two-year-old and a bit full of himself. And these black dots, sort of freckles, along that patch of his belly. And the way his hide grows in a whirl just there inside his hock. He always had clean legs. There's a mark or two on them now that wasn't there when I had him. But apart from knowing him from his general shape, like, I'd certainly swear to those other things in any court you'd like to mention.'

'Was the cut from the gate post bad enough to be treated by a vet?'

He nodded. 'Five or six stitches.'

'Good,' I said. 'Then off you go with him. And take good care.'

Sam Kitchens grinned. 'Who'd have thought I'd have seen him again up the Rocky Mountains in the middle of the night? Never you mind, I'll take care all right.'

He turned Chrysalis expertly round, clicking his tongue affectionately, and began the mile-long walk down to the Teton camping ground, to where he and Walt and Sam Hengelman had come in a horse box.

Walt said, 'It's too late for you to go back. Come with us.'

I shook my head. 'I'll meet you in Idaho Falls as we arranged.'

Walt moved uncomfortably. 'It's not safe to go back.'

'I'll be fine. You just get the two Sams cracking. They've got to be well on their way before dawn. They've got that bill of sale?'

Walt nodded, looking at the big mountain pony beside me.

'He cost five hundred dollars. One bay horse, no markings, entire, aged seven or eight. As ordered. That's what the bill of sale says, and that's what we've got in the van, if anyone asks. Sam Kitchens chose it. Said it was as near as you would get, without actually paying thousands for a blood horse.'

'This one looks fine. See you, then, Walt.'

He stood in silence while I levered myself on to the new horse's bare back and gathered up the reins. I nodded to him, turned away, and started back up the trail to the canyon.

Late, I thought. Almost too late, now. The wranglers would be high up in the hills by six, rounding up the horses. Dudes rode as usual on Sunday mornings. It was already five, and the first greyness of dawn had crept in as the moon faded. If they saw me out so early, I was in trouble.

At a jog trot, his sturdy legs absolutely at home on the terrain, the new horse took me back up into the canyon, past the fearful little ridge that Chrysalis had taken, and out on to the Clive valley side of the Tetons. From there down I looked out for a bunch of High Zee horses, but I was well below the snow line before I heard any of the bells.

There was a little group in a tree-filled hollow. They moved away at my approach, but slowly, and when I was among them and stopped, they stopped also. I slid off the horse I was riding, threaded my fingers through the mane of one of the High Zee group, and transferred the bridle from one to the other. Then, leaving Dave Teller's five-hundred-dollar purchase free on the hill, I pointed my new mount's nose homewards, and gave him a kick.

He knew the way, and he consequently could go much faster. The Wilkersons had told me the wranglers cantered down those steep rocky inclines, but until I did it I hadn't imagined what a hair-raising business it would be. The horse put his feet where I would have said no man could balance, let alone a quadruped, and when I turned him off the regular path he hardly slackened his pace. We went headlong downwards through pines and alders and groves of silver-trunked dead trees, back to the thicker woods with patches of grass underfoot, and more undergrowth of huckleberry and sapling. There was one sticky incline of black bog where a mountain stream had spilled out sideways on to a slope of earth, but my pony staggered across it, tacking downwards, sinking in to his knees at every step. Farther on, he crossed the tumbling stream itself, picking his way through a mass of underwater rocks, and lower still he went straight down a bare pebbly slope where the normal path ran from side to side in easier zigzags. Whippy branches caught at us under the trees, but I laid my head flat beside his ears, and where he could go, I went too.

The gentle dude rides had been no preparation for

this reckless descent, and the one or two point-to-points I'd tried in my teens were distant memories and milksop stuff in comparison. But skills learnt in childhood stay for ever: balance still came instinctively. I didn't fall off.

We kept up the pace until there was less than a mile to go, then I veered the pony along to the right, up along the valley and away from the bridge to the ranch.

The wranglers would no doubt follow him up there to round him up, but I hadn't time to do the whole detour on foot. It was too light and too late to get back into the ranch across the bridge. I was going to have to cross the stream higher up and go down to my cabin through the woods on the far side.

I slid off the pony nearly half a mile upstream, and took off the bridle. The rough brown hide was streaked dark with sweat, and he didn't look at all like an animal who had spent a peaceful night grazing. I gave him a slap and he trotted away, wheeling round and upwards, back on to the hill. With luck the wranglers wouldn't find him until he'd cooled down, especially as it wouldn't be him they'd be looking for.

I could hear the panic going on down by the ranch house as soon as I stepped cautiously out of the woods and began the freezing cold traverse of the stream. The stones dug into my bare feet, and the water splashed my rolled-up trouser legs. But as I couldn't from where I was see any of the buildings, I trusted

169

that no one there could see me. The shouts came up clearly, and then the thud of several horses cantering across the bridge. By the time I was across the stream and sitting down to put on my shoes again, they were going up towards the woods, and I could see them. Six wranglers, moving fast. If they looked back, they could see my head and shoulders sticking up out of the stretch of sage brush.

A hundred yards of it between me and the safety of the trees on the ranch-house side of the valley. I lay down flat on the ground for a few exhausted minutes, looking up at the dawn-filled sky: a high clear pale blue taking over from grey. The tracks of the mares and foals and both the stallions led straight uphill. I gave the wranglers time to go some way after them, and then quietly got to my feet and slipped unhurriedly across the sage brush and down through the trees to my cabin.

It was ten past six. Broad daylight.

I pulled off my filthy sweaty clothes and ran a deep hot bath. Tiredness had gone down to the bone, and the water tingled like a friction rub on my skin. Relaxing, reviving, I stayed in it for half an hour.

The tape played back for me the heavy knocking on Yola's door and the head wrangler telling her that the mares and stallions were out.

'What do you mean, out?'

'The tracks lead down to the bridge. They're out on the hills.'

'What?' Yola's voice screeched as the full meaning hit her. 'They can't be.'

'They sure are.' The wrangler's voice was much calmer. He didn't know the size of the disaster: wasn't in the game. 'But I can't understand it. The padlock was fastened like you said it must be, when I checked around yesterday evening.'

'Get them back,' said Yola sharply. 'Get them back.' Her voice rose hysterically. 'That new stallion. Get him. Get him back.'

There were sounds after that of drawers being pulled roughly open, and a door slamming, and silence. Yola was out looking for Chrysalis. And, Chrysalis was on his way to Kentucky.

The ranch guests knew all about it, at breakfast.

'What a fuss,' Wilkie said. 'You'd think they'd lost the deeds to a goldmine.'

They had.

'I'm glad they found the dear little foals anyway,' Samantha said.

'They've found them?' I asked. The small paddock was still empty.

'They've put them in the barn,' agreed Mickey. 'With their mothers.'

'Someone left the gate unlocked,' Betty-Ann told me. 'Isn't it a shame? Yola's obviously in a fearful state.'

171

Yola had been in the dining room when I strolled in to breakfast, standing silent and rigid by the kitchen door, checking that all the guests were there, looking for signs of guilt.

Poise had deserted her. The hair was roughly tied with a ribbon at the nape of her neck and the lipstick was missing. There had been no professional reassuring smiles. A muscle twitched in the strong jaw and she hadn't been in control of the wildness in her eyes.

I ate a double order of bacon and buckwheat hotcakes with maple syrup, and drank three cups of coffee.

Betty-Ann opposite me lit a cigarette and said did I have to leave, couldn't I stay another few days. Wilkie gruffly said they shouldn't try to keep a feller. Wilkie had cottoned on, and was glad to see me go.

Strong footsteps came into the room from the door behind me. Betty-Ann looked over my head and her eyes widened.

'Why hello there,' she exclaimed warmly, transferring her attentions. 'How good to see you.'

Wilkie, I thought in amusement, should be used to it by now. But the Wilkersons' problems blinked out of my mind for ever when someone else called the new man by his name.

Matt.

Matt Clive spoke from behind my shoulder; a drawling bass voice under strict control.

'Listen folks. I guess you know we've had a little

trouble here this morning. Someone let out the mares and horses from their paddock over there. Now if it was any of you kids, we'd sure like to know about it.'

There was a short silence. The various children looked uncomfortable and their parents' eyebrows peaked into question marks.

'Or if anyone knows that the gate wasn't properly fastened yesterday at any time?'

More silence.

Matt Clive walked tentatively round the long table, into my line of sight. About Yola's age, Yola's height. Same jawline. Same strong body, only more so. I remembered the two bedrooms in their cabin: the ringless fingers of Yola's hand. Yola's brother, Matt. I drank my coffee and avoided meeting his eyes.

One or two of the guests laughingly mentioned rustlers, and someone suggested calling in the police. Matt said they were seriously thinking of it. One of the stallions was quite valuable. But only, of course, if it was absolutely certain that none of the guests had left the gate open by accident.

Sympathetic murmurs were all he got. He might indeed be brave enough, or desperate enough, to call in the police. But if he did, they wouldn't recover Chrysalis, who should by now be hundreds of miles away on a roundabout route, accompanied by a strictly legal bill of sale.

Matt eventually went away, trailing a thunderous aura and leaving the guests unsettled and embarrassed.

I asked the girl who waited at table if she could fetch my account for me, as I wanted to pay up before leaving, and after an interval she returned with it. I gave her cash, and waited while she wrote a receipt.

The Wilkerson family said their goodbyes, as they were hoping to go riding if any of the wranglers had come back from searching for the missing horse, and I walked unhurriedly back to my cabin to finish packing. Up the two steps, across the porch, through the two doors, and into the room.

Yola came out of the bathroom carrying a rifle. The way she handled it showed she knew how to use it. Matt stepped from behind the curtained closet, between me and the way out. No rifle for him. A shotgun.

I put on the puzzled act, German accent stronger.

'Excuse me. I do not understand.'

'It's the same man,' Matt said. 'Definitely.'

'Where's our horse?' said Yola furiously.

'I do not know,' I said truthfully, spreading my hands out in a heavy shrug. 'Why do you ask such a question?'

Both the guns were pointing steadfastly my way.

'Excuse me,' I said, 'I have my packing to finish. I have paid the bill. I am leaving this morning.'

'You're not going anywhere, friend,' Matt said grimly.

'Why not?'

'You get that horse back here, and then you can go. Not before.'

He was going to have a fine old time if he intended to keep a prisoner silent indefinitely on a ranch full of holiday guests.

'I can't get him back,' I said. 'I don't know where he is. Several friends of mine, however, do know where I am. They will be expecting me to be leaving here this morning.'

They stared at me in silent fury. Children in crime, I thought, for all their ingenuity. They had walked straight in with their guns without thinking clearly through. They were, however, lethal children, ruled by impulse more than reason.

I said, 'I am unlikely to go around saying "I stole a horse from the Clives." If you do nothing, and I now drive safely away, you may hear no more of it. That's the best I can offer. You will not, whatever you do, recover the horse.'

The only sensible course open to them was to let me go. But Yola's finger tightened on the trigger, and I reluctantly decided it was time for the Luger. Watching her, I saw a split second too late in the looking glass that Matt had taken a step behind me and was swinging his gun butt like a bludgeon.

He caught me solidly across the back of the skull and the patchwork quilt on the bed dazzled into kaleidoscopic fragments in my glazing eyes as I went down.

CHAPTER TEN

When I woke up it was pretty clear that I wasn't intended to be a hostage, but a corpse.

The cabin was full of smoke, and small flames rose in a long uneven swathe across the floor. I couldn't remember anything at first. Looked at the scene muzzily, half sitting up, my head dizzy and splitting with pain. The Clives, I thought. They'd emptied the whole tub of pep out into a straggling line, and set it alight. Sawdust and diesel oil burning slowly and billowing out unbreathable gases.

They'd laid me against the stove so that it would seem as if I'd fallen and hit my head on it. The empty pep tin rolled away from my foot as I tried to get up, and my hand brushed against a cigarette and a book of matches.

Most deaths in fires weren't caused by burns but by asphyxia. The cabin wouldn't burn down from fire on the floorboards: fire never burnt downwards, only up. The Clives were staging my exit for no better motive than revenge. And as an accident it was one of their poorer efforts.

Having staggered its way through those useless random thoughts, my brain cleared enough for me to decide it was high time to move if I was going to do anything about living. And I supposed I would have to.

I stumbled on to my feet, pulled the quilt off one of the beds, tottered into the bathroom with it and soaked it under the taps in the bath. Smoke was well down in my lungs, thick and choking. It's bloody stupid, I thought groggily, it's damn bloody stupid that boy-and-girl keep trying to shove me where I want to go, and I keep trying not to let them. Ridiculous. Ridiculous . . .

I found myself on my knees, half unconscious. The bath water still running. Pulled myself up a little, hauled out the dripping quilt, flung it over the worst of the fire. Silly, I thought. Much better to go out of the door. Tried that. Damn thing was stuck.

Window, then. Stuck.

Wrapped my hand in the curtain and pushed it through one of the panes of glass. Some air came in. The insect screen stopped more.

Down on my knees again. Terribly dizzy. A black hell in my head. Smelt the quilt burning, lifted it off one lot of fire, and on to the next. Damped it all out into a smelly black faintly smouldering path and felt old and weak from too much scrambling up and down mountains and deeply ill from the crash on the brain and too much smoke.

Opened the front of the fat black stove. Shapleigh, it said. Gradually the smoke began to clear away up its stackpipe while I lay in a poor state beside the cabin door and breathed the fresh air trickling in underneath.

Several eras later I stopped feeling like morgue material and the hammer in my head died to a brutal aching throb. I began to wonder how long it would be before Matt and Yola returned to make their horrified discovery of my death, and wearily decided it was time for action.

I stood up slowly and leaned against the door. They'd fastened it somehow from the outside, in spite of there being no lock: and it was simple enough to see when one's eyes weren't filled with smoke. The screen door opened outwards, the wooden door inwards. A small hook leading in through the latch was holding the two together. I pushed it up, and it slid away as the inner door opened.

My wallet lay on the table, not in my pocket. They'd been looking. Nothing for them to find, except their own photograph. They'd taken that. But they hadn't searched very far: the Luger was still in its holster at my back, under my outhanging shirt. I checked the magazine – still loaded – and put it back in place.

The only other thing I really wanted to take with me was my radio. I squashed down its extended an-

tenna aerial and shoved it into my old suitcase on top
of the things I'd packed before breakfast. Then, picking it up and fighting down the whirling chaos which
resulted, I opened the screen door. Behind me the
cabin lay in a singed shambles. Ahead, the comparatively short walk to the car seemed a marathon.

I might have made it in one if I hadn't felt any
worse: but at the end of the woodland track, when all
that was left to go was the open expanse of the car
park, a wave of clammy sweating faintness seethed
through me and I dropped the suitcase and leaned
against a tree, waiting weakly for it to pass.

Yola came out of the kitchen door and saw me. Her
mouth fell open, then she turned on her heel and
dived back into the ranch house. For the rifle. Or for
Matt. My hand closed on the pistol at my back, but I
was very loath to use it. Too many explanations to
authority would be involved, and I preferred to avoid
them at this stage.

'Hello,' said a cheerful voice behind me. 'We
thought you'd gone ages ago.'

I turned my wonky head and let my hand fall away
from the gun. Mickey and Samantha were coming
down the track from the branch which led to the
Wilkersons' cabin.

'And I thought,' I said, 'that you'd gone riding.'

'The wranglers haven't brought in enough horses,'
Mickey explained sadly.

'Are you sick or something?' asked his sister, coming to a halt and staring up into my face.

'A bit,' I admitted. 'I'd be awfully glad if you'd carry my suitcase for me, across to that black car.'

'Sure,' said Mickey importantly, and Samantha took my hand in motherly solicitude. With one child at each side I completed the trip.

It was the rifle Yola fetched. She stood with it stiffly in her hands and watched the children put the suit-case in the car and stand close to my window while I started the engine. An accidental drowning, an acci-dental smothering she could manage: but three public murders by shooting were outside her range. Just as well. If she'd lifted that rifle towards the children, I would have shot her.

'Bye,' they said, waving. Nice kids.

'Bye.'

I released the brakes and rolled away down the drive in a plume of dust, accelerating fast as soon as I hit the metalled road, and taking the main branch down to Jackson. If Yola thought of following in the pick-up, she didn't do it fast enough. Repeated inspec-tion in the mirror showed no Clives chasing on my tail. The only things constantly before my eyes were bright dancing spots.

Through Jackson I turned north and west on the winding road to Idaho Falls. Along there the Snake River and the Pallisades Reservoir, sparkling blue against the dark pines, were stunningly beautiful. But my several stops weren't for appreciation: the cold sweating waves of dizziness kept recurring, like twenty-two over seven. I drove slowly, close to the side, never overtaking, ready to pull up. If I hadn't wanted to put a hundred miles or so between me and the Clives, I wouldn't have started from Jackson. Most of the time I wished I hadn't.

Walt was pacing the motel lobby like a frenetic film producer when I finally showed up at five-thirty in the afternoon.

'You are four-and-a-half hours late,' he began accusingly. 'You said . . .'

'I know,' I interrupted. 'Book us some rooms. We're staying here.'

He opened his mouth and shut it tight.

'I'm sorry,' I said, softening it, 'but I feel ill.'

'What's the matter?'

'Concussion.'

Walt gave me a searching look, booked the rooms, and even went so far as to carry my suitcase. I lay straight down on the bed, and he sat in an easy chair in my room and rubbed his fingers.

'Do you need a doctor?' he said.

'I don't think so. It's not getting any worse.'

'Well . . . what happened?'

'I'll give you some free advice,' I said. 'Don't ever let Matt Clive come within bashing distance of your head.'

The dizziness wasn't so bad lying down.

'Do you want a drink?' he asked.

'No . . . Let's listen to a tape recording instead.' I told him how to open the back of the radio and to rewind the reels.

'Neat little job,' he commented. 'Where did you get it?'

'Had it specially made, two or three years ago.'

Walt grunted, and switched on. The head wrangler banged on Yola's door and told her that the mares and stallions were out. Walt's face lifted into a half grin.

The recorder played twenty seconds of silence after each take, and began again at the next sound. The next piece was very short.

'Yola?' A man's voice, very loud. 'Yola! Where the hell is everybody?' A door slammed. Silence.

'That's Matt Clive,' I told Walt. 'He came back before breakfast.'

The voices began again. Yola speaking, coming indoors. '. . . say the tracks go straight up the hill, but he turned back at the high patch of scree and came down again.'

That was a bit of luck.

'They'll just have to go on looking,' Matt said. 'Yola, for God's sake, we can't lose that horse.' His voice was strained and furious. 'I'll go over to the house and see if any of those kids had a hand in it.'

'I don't think so. Not a darned one of them looks nervous.'

'I'll try, anyway.' His footsteps receded.

Yola picked up the telephone and made a call.

'That you, Jim? Have you seen any horse vans coming through Pikelet since last night? . . .

'Well no, I just wondered if you'd seen one. Not this morning, early? . . .

'No, it was just a chance. Sure. Yeah. Thanks anyway.' She put down the receiver with a crash.

Walt raised his eyebrows. 'Pikelet?'

'Couple of shops and a filling station where the Clives' own road joins the main road to Jackson.'

'Just as well we didn't . . .' he began, and then changed it to, 'Is that why you insisted on the long way round?'

'Partly,' I agreed. 'I wanted it to look as if Chrysalis had gone off by himself. I wanted to avoid them realizing he'd been deliberately stolen. Keep them guessing a bit, give us time to get well clear.'

The tape began again. Matt came back running.

'Yola. That man. That damned man.'

'What man?' She was bewildered.

'The man that pulled Teller out of the river. How long has he been here?'

Yola said almost in a whisper, 'Here?'

Matt was shouting. 'Here. Having breakfast. Staying here, you stupid bitch.'

'I don't . . . I don't . . .'

'I saw him at Reading too,' Matt said. 'He called to see Teller in the hospital. They let him in past all the watchdogs. I saw him looking out of the window. How the hell did he get here? Why in God's name didn't you spot him, you stupid, stupid . . . He's the one that's taken the horse. And I'll damn well make him bring it back.'

'How?' Yola said, wailing.

'Excuse me,' said the voice of the girl who waited at table. 'Excuse me, Miss Clive. Mr Hochner wants his bill.'

'There on the desk,' Yola said.

'Which is Hochner?' Matt, urgent.

'The German in cabin three.'

'Where was he sitting at breakfast? What does he look like?'

'He had his back to the door from the hall,' the girl said. 'He's wearing a blue-and-white check shirt, and he's quite tall and has dark brown hair and a tired sort of face.'

'Give him the bill then,' Matt said, and waited until she had gone. 'Hochner!' The voice was almost incoherent with rage. 'How long has he been here?'

'Since . . . Tuesday.' Yola's voice was faint.

'Get your rifle,' Matt said. 'If he won't give us that horse back . . . I'll kill him.'

There were small moving about sounds, and the tape went quiet. The time they had spent in my cabin telescoped into twenty seconds of silence; and the recording began again.

'He was right, Matt,' Yola said. 'We should have let

him go.' Her voice had gone quiet with despair, but Matt's still rode on anger.

'He had his chance. He should have told us what he'd done with Chrysalis.'

After a pause Yola said, 'He wasn't going to do that. He said so. Whatever you do, he said, you won't recover the horse.'

'Shut up,' Matt said violently.

'Matt.' A wail in her voice. 'He was right. We won't recover the horse and his friends will come looking for him, like he said.'

'They'll only find an accident.'

'But they won't believe it.'

'They won't be able to prove any different,' Matt insisted.

After another pause Yola said almost without emotion, 'If he got the horse clean away ... if someone else has him now, and he's on his way back to Teller ... they'll know we had Chrysalis here. We'll be arrested for that.'

'Hochner wasn't going to say he'd stolen the horse from here.'

'But you wouldn't listen.' Yola suddenly flared into anger of her own. 'He was right all the time. We should have let him go. We'd have lost Chrysalis ... but this way we're in terrible trouble, they'll never believe he died by accident, we'll have the whole FBI here and we'll end up ... we'll end up in ...'

'Shut up,' Matt said. 'Shut up.'

'He might not be dead yet . . . can't we go and stop it?' Her voice was urgent, beseeching.

'And have him accuse us of attempted murder? Don't be such a fool. No one can prove it isn't an accident, can they? Can they?'

'I suppose not . . .'

'So you leave him, Yola. You just leave him. He had his chance. I gave him his chance . . . You just wait for some of the guests to see the smoke and come and tell you, like we said. Don't you try going up there. Just don't try it.'

'No . . .'

'And I'm going back on the mountain with the wranglers. Chrysalis went across the bridge. His tracks are there. Well . . . I'm going tracking. Mr Clever Hochner might be bluffing all along the line. He might have Chrysalis tied to some tree up there, and he might not have told anyone where he is, and no one will come asking.' He convinced himself that this view of things was reasonable, and in the end Yola halfway agreed.

'We'll have to tell Uncle Bark,' she said finally.

There was a blank pause while they considered this.

'He'll blow his top,' Matt said gloomily. 'After all that planning.'

'He'll have to know,' Yola said.

'I'll call him this evening, if we have to. But we might have found Chrysalis by then.'

'I sure hope so . . .'

186

Matt went away then on his search, and presently, after Yola had left to go back to the ranch house, there was continued silence on the tape.

Walt switched the recorder off and looked across at me with a complete absence of expression.

'What did they do?'

I told him.

'Would it have passed as an accident?'

'I expect so. Neat little picture: man lighting cigarette, throws match absentmindedly in tub of pep instead of waste basket, panics, spills the stuff, steps wildly back from flames, trips over stove and knocks himself out. Bingo.'

'Do you smoke, though?'

'Sometimes. They used my own pack from the bedside table. And my own matches. It was impulsive, unpremeditated. They just looked round and used what came to hand. They're quite good at it.'

'Lucky you woke up in time,' Walt said.

'I suppose so.' I shut my eyes and wondered how he would react if I asked him to go out for some codeine.

'I've worked with one or two people like you before,' he said. 'And I can't say I like it.'

'Thanks,' I said sardonically. No pills.

'With your kind,' he said, 'dying comes easy. It's living takes the guts.'

I opened my eyes. He was watching me steadily, his

sober face removing any possibility that he was intending to be funny.

'How are you on guts?' he asked.

'Fresh out.'

He sighed deeply. 'That figures.'

'Walt . . .' I began.

'It struck me first last night, on the mountain. You were sure anxious about Chrysalis, but you didn't give a goddam about falling off the top yourself. It made me freeze just to watch you leading him along that ledge . . . and you came back as calm as if it had been your own yard.'

He was apologizing, in his indirect way, for his startling appearance on the path.

'Walt,' I said, half smiling. 'Will you go get me something for a headache?'

CHAPTER ELEVEN

Eunice, Lynnie, Sam Kitchens, and stud groom Chub Lodovski leaned in a row on the rail of the stallions' paddock at Midway and watched Chrysalis eat Kentucky grass with opinions varying from Lodovski's enthusiasm to Eunice's resignation.

The half-a-million pounds' worth looked none the worse for his trip up the Tetons. Better than on the ranch, as Sam Kitchens had removed all the Wyoming dust from his coat on the journey back, and the bay hide shone with glittering good health in the sunshine. There wasn't, Lodovski assured me, the slightest chance of his going missing again.

Batteries of photographers and pressmen had come and gone: the stallion had been 'found' straying on the land of a friend of Dave Teller's about thirty miles from where he had disappeared. All the excitement was over.

I walked back to Dave's house with Eunice and Lynnie, and Eunice poured me a drink which was four-fifths whisky and one-fifth ice.

'Who put you through what meat grinder?' she said. 'You look like a honeymoon couple on the tenth night.'

Sam Hengelman had driven into Midway with Chrysalis at lunchtime (Tuesday). I had flown to New York with Walt the day before, and had just back-tracked to Lexington, in time to catch the tail end of Eunice interviewing the press. Several of that hard bitten fraternity had tottered out past me with pole-axed expressions and Lynnie had been halfway through a fit of giggles.

I made inroads into the hefty drink.

'I could do with a good long sleep,' I admitted. 'If you could give me a bed? Or there's the motel . . .'

'Stay here,' Eunice said abruptly. 'Of course you're staying here.'

I looked from her to Lynnie. I couldn't stay in the house with one alone: perfectly proper with both. Silly.

'Thanks, then. And I must call Dave, in England.'

Dave, still in hospital, sounded incredulous.

'I heard it on a news flash, not half an hour ago,' he said. 'Chrysalis just plain turned up.'

'He sure did,' I said dryly.

'Where had he been?'

'It's a long story,' I said, 'and wires have ears. But the expenses stand right now at somewhere near six thousand three hundred dollars. Is that enough for you, or do you want to go on for some answers?'

'To what questions, fella?' He sounded uncertain.

'To why Chrysalis was hi-jacked, and why you fell in the river. And another thing: do you want Allyx back?'

'For God's sake . . . do you know where he is?'

'No. But maybe I could find him. However, if I do, and we get as positive an identification as on Chrysalis, the insurance money on Allyx will have to be repaid to Buttress Life. That will be the equivalent of buying him all over again. He's three years older now, and you'll have lost three crops of foals. He may not be a good proposition for you or your syndicate any more. In which case you might prefer not to have him found. It's up to you.'

'Jeez,' he said.

'Will you think it over, and call back?' I suggested. 'Your wife and Lynnie are filling me up with food and drinks, and I guess I'll be staying here tonight. But if you want me to go on, will you clear it with Keeble? I'm due back at my desk at nine AM next Monday morning, and I might not make it.'

'Sure,' he said, somewhat weakly, and I handed the receiver to Eunice.

'How's it going, honey?' she said, and I took a good swallow, put my head back on the chair, and listened to her long-married-wifely conversation with my eyes shut.

'Don't ask me how he did it, Dave, I don't know. All I know is he rang from New York yesterday afternoon and asked me for the name of any close friend of ours who was influential and respected, preferably high up in horsebreeding circles, and whose word would be taken as gospel by the press. So, after a rake around I said I guessed Jeff Roots fitted the bill; and lo and behold Chrysalis turned up on Jeff's land this morning... Yeah, the horse is as good as new; wherever he's been they've treated him right... Look, Dave, surely enough's enough? I heard what Gene said about finding Allyx. Well, don't do it. We need Allyx like a dose of clap. And your boy here is no goddam Hercules, a puff of wind would knock him off, the way he's come back... Lynnie's fine, sure. We're taking a trip tomorrow out to California. I'll measure up the curtains for the new place, things like that, and Lynnie can have some days on the beach and maybe try some surfing with those de Vesey boys. So look, why don't we take Gene with us, huh?... Sure, I've made reservations at The Vacationer in Santa Barbara... they're bound to have another room...'

I listened to her plans with disappointment. If I wanted to laze anywhere, it was right where I was, on the Midway Farm. By the peaceful pool in the quiet green garden, sleeping, drinking, and looking at Lynnie.

Eunice put down the receiver, and we had dinner, and late in the evening Dave rang through again.

'Gene?' he said. 'Now listen, fella. Apart from curiosity, is there any good reason for finding those answers you talked about?'

'Forestalling repetition,' I said promptly.

'No more stolen stallions and no more attacks on me?'

'That's right.'

There was a pause.

'I'll buy the answers, then,' he said. 'If you can get them. And as for Allyx . . . if you think there's any chance of finding him alive and vigorous, then I guess I'm morally obliged to give you the go-ahead. I'd have to syndicate him all over again, of course. He'll be twelve now. That would give him only about six to eight more years of high potency . . . But his get from before his disappearance are winning all over Europe. Business-wise I'm not too happy about those three lost years. But blood-wise, it would be criminal not to try to get him back.'

'All right,' I said. 'I'll see what I can do.'

'What you spent on finding Chrysalis is less than his fee for covering a single mare. You've a free hand again for Allyx.'

'Right,' I said.

'Sim Keeble says you've got seven days' extension of leave. Something about it being due to you anyway, from a week you were entitled to at Christmas and didn't take.'

'I'd forgotten about that.'

'I guess I could fix it with him for more, if the extra week isn't enough.'

'If I haven't finished by then I'll have failed anyway, and might as well go home.'

'Oh.' He sounded disappointed. 'Very well, we'll leave it like that for the present.' He cleared his throat. 'Eunice didn't seem to think you looked too well.'

'The boy on the punt who knocked you out did the same thing for me.'

'Gene!' His voice was shocked.

'Yeah. Don't tell my boss I'm that incompetent. Though come to think of it, he knows.'

He laughed. 'When you find that boy again give him a one-two from both of us.'

'Sure,' I said. But I'd been taught my job by cerebral people who didn't reckon a screener would ever have to fight for his life, and by the time I proved them wrong I was too old to become expert at boxing or judo, even if I'd liked the idea, which I didn't. I had learnt instead to shoot straight, and the Luger had in the past three years extricated me unharmed from two sticky situations. But in a stand up hand-to-hand affair with that young bull Matt Clive I would be a five hundred to one loser, and 'giving him a one-two from both of us' in any physical sense was a very dim possibility indeed.

'Keep in touch, fella,' Dave said.

'Sure,' I answered again, meaning it as little: and we rang off.

Curled opposite in a tomato armchair, Eunice said gloomily, 'I gather we're stuck with that bloody Allyx.'

'Only if we find him.'

'Oh, you'll do that, blast you.' Her bitterness was so marked that Lynnie stared at her. Too young to understand, I thought, that it wasn't me particularly that Eunice wanted to hurt, but life in general.

They went upstairs shortly afterwards murmuring about California in the morning, and I switched off the light and sat in near darkness, finishing the fourth of Eunice's massive ideas on drink and working out the questions I would ask the next day. I could find Allyx on paper, if I were lucky: but he could hardly turn up loose after three years. Three weeks had been strictly the limit. The whole thing might have to be more orthodox, more public. And I wouldn't again, I decided mildly, put myself within accident reach of the murderous Clives.

After a while I deserted the last half of the drink and wandered upstairs to the spacious air-conditioned room Eunice had given me. With a tired hand I switched on the light inside the door, and yellow pools in frilly shades shone out on brown and gold and white furnishings.

One splash of jarring bright pink. Eunice herself, in a fluffy trimmed wrapper, was lying on my bed.

I walked slowly across the thick white carpet and sat beside her on the white spotted muslin coverlet.

'What do you want?' I said gently.

'What do you think?'

I shook my head.

'Does that mean no?' Her voice was abruptly matter of fact.

'I'm afraid it does,' I said.

'You said you weren't queer.'

'Well . . . I'm not.' I smiled at her. 'But I do have one unbreakable rule.'

'And that is?'

'Not to sleep with the wives . . . or daughters . . . of the men I work for.'

She sat bolt upright so that her face was close to mine. Her eyes had the usual contracted pupils of the quarter drunk.

'That includes Lynnie,' she said.

'Yes. It does.'

'Well, I'll be damned. You mean that night you spent in New York with her you didn't even try . . .'

'It wouldn't have been much good if I had,' I said, half laughing.

'Don't you believe it. She never takes her eyes off you, and when you were away she talked about nothing else.'

I stared at her in real surprise. 'You must be wrong.'

'I wasn't born yesterday,' she said gloomily. 'She has two photographs of you as well.'

'What photographs?' I was staggered.

'Some her brother took. That day on the river.'

'But she shouldn't . . .'

'Maybe she shouldn't,' Eunice said dryly. 'But she does.' She swung her legs carelessly around to sit on

196

the edge of the bed beside me and I saw that for someone bent on seduction she had come well wrapped up.

'You expected me to say no,' I said.

She made a face. 'I thought you might. But it was worth a try.'

'Eunice, you're nuts,' I said.

'I'm bored,' she said explosively, and with an undoubted depth of unbearable truth.

'That puts me into the golf and bridge category.'

She was still playing games.

'At least you're goddam human,' she said, her mouth cracking into a smile. 'More than you can say about most men.'

'What do you like best about moving to California?' I asked.

She stared. 'Your mind's like a bloody grasshopper. What has that to do with sex?'

'You tell me, and I'll tell you.'

'For God's sake . . .' But she made some effort at concentrating, and in the end came up with the answer I had been most expecting.

'Fixing up the rooms, I guess.'

'You did all these . . .' I waved my hand around, embracing the house.

'Yeah, I did. So what?'

'So why don't you start in business, doing it for other people?'

She half laughed, ridiculing the idea, and half clung

to it: and I knew she'd thought of it in the past, because I hadn't surprised her.

'I'm no bloody genius.'

'You have an eye for colour. More than that: for mood. This is the most comforting house I've ever been in.'

'Comforting?' she said, puzzled.

'Yeah. Laugh, clown, laugh. That sort of thing. You can fill other people even though you feel empty yourself.'

Tears welled up in her grey-green eyes, and she shut the lids. Her voice remained normal.

'How do you know?'

'I know.'

After a pause, she said, 'And I suppose what it has to do with sex is that interior decorating would be a suitable sublimation for a middle-aged woman whose physical attraction is fading faster than her appetite . . .' The bitterness came from long acquaintance with the jargon and its point of view.

'No,' I said mildly. 'The opposite.'

'Huh?' She opened her eyes. They were wet and shiny.

'Playing games is easier than working.'

'Spell it out,' she said. 'You talk in goddam riddles.'

'Sex . . . this sort of casual sex . . .' I patted the bed where she'd lain, 'can be a way of running away from real effort. A lover may be a sublimation of a deeper need. People who can't face the demands of one may opt for passing the time with the other.'

'For Christ's sake . . . I don't understand a bloody word.' She shut her eyes and lay flat back across the bed.

'Thousands of people never try anything serious because they're afraid of failing,' I said.

She swallowed, and after a pause said, 'And what if you do bloody fail? What then?'

I didn't answer her, and after a while she repeated the question insistently.

'Tell me what you do if you fail?'

'I haven't got that one licked myself, yet.'

'Oh.' She laughed weakly. 'Oh God. The blind leading the blind. Just like the whole bloody human race.'

'Yeah.' I sighed and stood up. 'We all stumble along in the dark, and that's a fact.'

'I don't know if you'll believe it, but I've been utterly bloody faithful to Dave . . . except for this . . .'

'I'm sure of it,' I said.

She got to her feet and stood swaying slightly.

'I guess I'm tight.'

'Better than loose,' I said smiling.

'For God's sake, spare me goddam puns at one o'clock in the morning. I suppose if you're looking for that so and so Allyx there's no chance of you coming to California?'

'I wish there were.'

'Goddam liar,' she said vaguely. 'Goodnight.'
She made straight for the door and didn't look back.

I drove them to the airport in the morning. Eunice
had lent me her car and the house for as long as I
needed them, and had passed off her overnight visit
with one sarcastic dig at breakfast.

'Better undersexed than sorry.'

'What?' said Lynnie.

'Eunice is offering a solution to the population
explosion,' I explained.

Lynnie giggled. Eunice showed me a double row of
teeth and told me to pass the cream.

When I'd seen them off I followed a local road
map and Eunice's inaccurate directions, and eventually
arrived at the Perry Stud Farm, home of Jefferson L.
Roots, chairman, among other things, of the Bloodhorse Breeders' Association. A houseboy in a spotless
white coat showed me through the house and on to
the patio: a house made of large cool concrete boxes,
with rough-cast white walls and bare golden wood
floors. The patio was shaded by a vine trained across
a trellis. There was a glass and metal table, and low
comfortable lounging chairs around it. From one of
these Jeff Roots extricated himself and held out a
welcoming hand.

He was a thick man with a paunch which had defied
health farms, and he worried about his weight. His

manner had the gentle, deprecating ease of the really tough American; the power was inside, discernible but purring, like the engine in a Rolls. He was dressed in a tropical-weight city suit, and while I was there an efficient girl secretary came to remind him that time and his connection to Miami would wait for no man.

'A drink?' he suggested. 'It's a hot day already. What would you like?'

'Lime juice?' I asked. 'Or lemon.'

I got lime, squeezed fresh on to crushed ice. My host drank sugar-free tonic water and made a face over it.

'Just the smell of french fries and I'm a size larger in shirts,' he complained.

'Why worry?' I said.

'Ever heard of hypertension?'

'Thin people can have it too.'

'Tell that to the birds ... or rather, tell it to my wife. She starves me.' He swirled his glass gloomily, ice and lemon rising perilously to the rim. 'So, anyway, Mr Hawkins, how can I help you today?'

He pushed a folded newspaper across the table and pointed at it with an appreciative smile.

'Chrysalis cocooned,' the headlines said. And underneath, in smaller letters, 'High price stallion loses liberty, corralled at Perry, reshipped to Midway. And are the mares there glad, or are they? Our tip is syndicators breathe again.' There was a picture of Chrysalis in his paddock, some mention of Dave's leg, and a few snide remarks about the police and the local horse folks who hadn't been able to spot a million dollars at ten paces.

'Where did you rustle him up from?' Roots asked. 'Sam Hengelman wouldn't say. Most unlike him.'

'Sam was an accessory to a conjuring trick. A little matter of substitution. We left a horse and took a horse . . . I guess he didn't want to talk himself into trouble.'

'And naturally you paid him.'

'Er, yes,' I agreed. 'So we did.'

'But I gather from your call that it's not about Chrysalis that you want to see me now?'

'No. It's about Allyx.'

'*Allyx*?'

'Yes, the other stallion which . . .'

'I know about all that,' he interrupted. 'They turned the whole state upside down looking for him and they found just as much trace as they did of Chrysalis.'

'Do you by any chance remember, ten years ago, another horse called Showman?'

'Showman? Showman? He got loose from a groom who was supposed to be exercising him, or something like that, and was killed in the Appalachians.'

'How certain was the identification?'

He put his tonic water down carefully on the table.

'Are you suggesting he's still alive?'

'I just wondered,' I said mildly. 'From what I've been told, they found a dead horse two years after Showman vanished. But although he was in a high state of decomposition, he'd only been dead about three months. So it easily might *not* have been Showman, just somewhat like him in colour and size.'

'And if it wasn't?'

'We might just possibly turn him up with Allyx.'

'Have you . . .' he cleared his throat. 'Have you any idea where they . . . er . . . might be . . . turned up?'

'I'm afraid not. Not yet.'

'They weren't . . . wherever you found Chrysalis?'

'No. That was only a shipping station, so to speak. Chrysalis was intended to go on somewhere else.'

'And at that somewhere else, one might find . . .?'

'There's a good chance, I think.'

'They might have been shipped abroad again. Down to Mexico or South America.'

'It's possible; but I'm inclined against it, on the whole.' Uncle Bark, whoever he was, lived somewhere in the States. Yola had not needed to call the overseas operator to get through to him, on the telephone. She hadn't even made it person to person.

'The whole thing seems so extraordinary,' Roots said, shaking his head. 'Some nut going around stealing stallions whose value at once drops to zero, because he can't admit he's got them. Do you think some fanatic somewhere is conducting experiments. Trying to produce a super-horse? Or how about a criminal syndicate all getting their mares covered by bluest blood stallions at donkey prices? . . . No, that wouldn't work, they'd never be able to sell the foals for stud, they wouldn't be able to cash in on the blood lines . . .'

'I think it's a good deal simpler than either of those,' I said, smiling. 'Much more down to earth.'

'Then what?'

I told him.

He chewed it over and I drank my lime juice.

'Anyway,' I said. 'I thought I'd try along those lines, and see if it leads anywhere.'

'It's fantastic,' Roots said. 'And I hope to God you're wrong.'

I laughed. 'Yes, I can see that.'

'It'll take you months to plough through all that work yourself . . . and I don't suppose you have too close a knowledge of the thoroughbred scene over here . . . so why don't I get you some help?'

'I'd be very grateful.'

There was an outside extension telephone close to his chair. He lifted the receiver and pressed buttons. I listened to him arranging with the publishers of a leading horse journal for me to have the run of their files and the temporary services of two long-memoried assistants.

'That's fixed, then,' he said, standing up. 'The office is on North Broadway, along in Lexington. I guess you'll let me know how you make out?'

'I certainly will.'

'Dave and Eunice . . . they're great guys.'

'They are.'

'Give her my best,' he said, looking at his watch.

'She's gone to California . . .'

'The new place?'

I nodded.

'Crazy idea of Dave's, moving to the coast. The centre of the bloodstock industry is right here in Lexington, and this is the place to be.'

I made the sort of non-critical, non-committal noise in my throat necessary on such occasions, and Jeff Roots thrust out a rounded hand.

'I have this stockholders' meeting in Miami,' he said, apologetically, and he walked with me through the house to where his secretary waited in a Cadillac parked beside Eunice's Toronado Oldsmobile.

At the newspaper offices, I found, anything Jeff Roots wanted done was done whole-heartedly and at the double. My two temporary assistants proved to be an elderly man who spent most of his time compiling an annual stallion register, and a maiden lady in her fifties whose horse face and crisp masculine voice were easy to take, as she had an unexpectedly sweet smile and a phenomenal memory.

When I explained what I was looking for they both stared at me in dumb-struck silence.

'Isn't it possible?' I asked.

Mr Harris and Miss Britt recovered themselves and said they guessed so.

'And while we're at it, we might make a list of

anyone whose name or nickname might be Bark. Or Bart, perhaps; though I think it's Bark.'

Miss Britt promptly reeled off six names, all Barkleys, living in and around Lexington.

'Maybe that's not such a good idea,' I sighed.

'No harm in it,' Miss Britt said briskly. 'We can make all the lists simultaneously.'

She and Mr Harris went into a huddle and from there to the reference room, and were shortly up to their elbows in papers and books. They told me to smoke and wait, which I did all day.

At five o'clock they came across with the results.

'This is the best we can do,' Miss Britt said doubtfully. 'There are well over three thousand stallions at stud in the States, you see. You asked us to sort out any whose fees had risen steadily over the past eight or nine years . . . there are two hundred and nine of them.' She put a closely typed list in front of me.

'Next, you wanted the names of any stallions who had been conspicuously more successful at stud than one would have expected from their own breeding. There are two hundred and eighty two of those.' She gave me a second sheet.

'Next, you wanted to know if any of this year's two-year-olds had proved conspicuously better at racing than one would normally have expected from their breeding. There are twenty-nine of those.' She added the third list.

'And lastly, the people who could be called Bark . . .

thirty-two of them. From the Bar K Ranch to Barry Kyle.'

'You've done wonders,' I said sincerely. 'I suppose it's too much to hope that any one farm is concerned on all four lists?'

'Most of the stallions on the first list are the same as those on the second. That stands to reason. But none of the sires of the exceptional two-year-olds are on either of the first two lists. And none of the two-year-olds were bred by any of the Barks.' Both of them looked downcast at such negative results after all their work.

'Never mind,' I said. 'We'll try another way tomorrow.'

Miss Britt snorted, which I interpreted as agreement. 'Rome wasn't built in a day,' she said, nodding. Mr Harris seemed to doubt that this particular Rome could be built at all with the materials available, but he turned up uncomplaining at nine the following morning, and they both dived in again, on new permutations.

By noon the first two lists had been reduced to twenty. We all adjourned for a sandwich. At two the searching began again. At three ten Miss Britt gasped sharply and her eyes went wide. She scribbled quickly on a fresh piece of paper, considered the result with her head on one side, and then looked across to me.

'Well . . .' she said. 'Well . . .' The words wouldn't come.

'You've found them,' I said.

She nodded, only half believing it.

'Cross-checking them all by where they raced, their years of purchase, their markings and their approximate ages, as you asked ... we came up with twelve possibles which appeared on the first two lists. And one of the sires of the two-year-olds fits your requirements and comes from the same farm as one of the first twelve. Er ... do you follow me?'

'On your heels,' I said, smiling.

Mr Harris and I both joined her and looked over her shoulder at what she had written.

'Moviemaker, aged fourteen years; present stud fee ten thousand dollars.

'Centigrade, aged twelve years; this year's stud fee fifteen hundred dollars, fee next year twenty-five hundred.

'Both standing at Orpheus Farm, Los Caillos.

'The property of Culham James Offen.'

Moviemaker and Centigrade: Showman and Allyx. As clear as a frosty sky.

Stallions were normally booked for thirty to forty mares each breeding season. Forty mares at ten thousand dollars a throw meant four hundred thousand dollars every year, give or take a live foal or two. Moviemaker had cost one hundred and fifty thousand dollars at public auction ten years ago, according to Miss Britt's researches. Since then Offen had been paid somewhere near two-and-a-half million dollars in stud fees.

Centigrade had been bought for a hundred thousand dollars at Keneland sales. At twenty-five hundred a time he would earn that hundred thousand next year alone. And nothing was more likely than that he too would rise to a much higher fee.

'Culham James Offen is so well regarded,' Miss Britt said in consternation. 'I simply can't believe it. He's accepted as one of the top rank breeders.'

'The only thing is, of course,' said Mr Harris, regretfully, 'that there's no connection with the name Bark.'

Miss Britt looked at me and her smile shone out sweet and triumphant.

'But there is, isn't there? Mr Harris, you're no musician. Haven't you ever heard of Orpheus in the Underworld . . . by Offenbach?'

CHAPTER TWELVE

Walt said 'For God's sake' four times and admitted Buttress Life might be willing to send him from coast to coast if Allyx were the pot of gold at the end of the rainbow.

'Los Caillos is a short distance north-east of Los Angeles,' I said. 'I thought of staying a bit farther north, on the coast.'

'If you like.'

'Come to The Vacationer, Grand Beach, Santa Barbara, then. I'll meet you there tomorrow.'

He repeated the address. 'Who's paying?' he said.

'Buttress Life and Dave Teller can fight it out between them. I'll put the motel on Teller's expenses. Can you wring the fare out of your office?'

'I guess so.' His sigh came wearily over the wire. 'My wife and kids aren't going to like it. I was fixing to take them on a picnic this Sunday.'

'Postpone it a week,' I suggested.

'It's been postponed twice already, on your account.'

'Oh.'

After a short pause, he said, 'Around six, tomorrow, local time. That do?'

'That would do very well.'

'See you,' he said briefly, and put down his receiver with a crash. I returned the Teller instrument more kindly to its cradle and surveyed the green and tomato room.

Nothing to do.

Mixed a drink with precision, and drank it. Wandered down to the pool, thought about a swim in the dusk, and couldn't be bothered to undress. Went back to the house, and ate a dinner cooked and served by Eva, who chattered so long in her pleasure at having someone to speak to in her own language that I heartily regretted I'd ever used it. Wished desperately she would stop and go away, and when at last she did, that was no good either.

Tried to read and turned six pages without taking in a word. Wandered restlessly again into the black velvet deep green garden, and sat in one of the chairs by the pool, looking at darkness inside and out. Unreasonable, I thought drearily, that I shouldn't have recovered normally from losing Caroline, that I didn't value the freedom other men envied, that I couldn't be content with all I had: cruel that depression was no respecter of status or achievement and struck so deep that no worldly success could alleviate it.

Great fame, universal honour, droves of personal friends had demonstrably failed to save a whole string of geniuses from its clutches, and every year it bagged its thousands from unimportant people like me who would never see their name in print or lights, and didn't necessarily want to. Probably depression was an illness as definite as jaundice, and one day they would inoculate babies against it. I supposed I could count myself lucky not to have had it in its acute form, where its grey-black octopus tentacles reached out and sucked into every corner of the spirit until quite quickly life became literally unbearable, and the high jump suddenly presented itself with blinding clarity as the only logical, the only possible relief.

I wouldn't come to that day, if I could help it. I would *not*.

The Vacationer was right down on the beach, with the sound of the bright blue Pacific creeping in a murmur under the transistors, the air-conditioning, the civilized chatter, the squalling of children, and the revving of cars. There were no ocean rooms left. Walt and I, next door to each other, overlooked the parking lot.

Eunice and Lynnie were out when I arrived and still out when Walt checked in at six, but they were back when I went down with him for a drink before dinner. I had left a note at the desk for Eunice, but I hadn't told Walt she would be there. He stopped dead in his tracks when he saw her sitting with Lynnie, and turned on me a narrow-eyed composite glance of dislike and anger. If I'd told him she was to be with us, he wouldn't have come: he knew that I knew it. He was entitled to his rage.

Eunice was, however, the wife of a very good client of his firm. He swallowed his feelings like a pill, and chased them down with a double bourbon in silence. Eunice and Lynnie were on frosted looking daiquiris and happy with it. They both looked marvellous, with honey-brown skin and a languorous and sun-filled way of moving. Eunice wore fluorescent green with bits of gold at anatomical points like ears, wrists, and feet. Lynnie had acquired a locally grown hot pink-orange tunic, and the few straps of her sandals seemed to be made of polished semi-precious stones. Even Walt, after a while, couldn't take his eyes away from them for long.

We had dinner outside, under a trellis lit by hundreds of tiny multi-coloured lights, on a shallow terrace which led directly out on to the sand. Eunice's language was for once as soft as the sea breeze, and consequently as a social evening it developed into a reasonable success.

Over the coffee I asked Eunice with a casualness which drew a piercing glance from Walt, 'Have you by any chance heard of a racehorse breeder called Culham James Offen?'

'Heard of him,' she said. 'Of course I have. Everyone has.'

'I haven't,' Walt said flatly. One couldn't expect complete capitulation. He was doing very well.

'I mean, everyone in the bloodstock world would have heard of him,' Eunice explained without obvious patience. 'He has that terrifically successful stallion Moviemaker. And Dave says one ought to think of sending mares to another one of his, Centigrade . . . The first crop of foals is winning two-year-old races this season all over the place. But quite apart from that,' she smiled broadly, 'I guess we'll be seeing a good deal of him from now on.'

'Er . . . why?' I asked diffidently.

'Our new place is right next to his.'

Walt's mouth fell open and I stopped stirring my coffee.

'What did you say?' I said, feeling my eyes go blank, as I knew they always did under shock.

'Our new place, where we're moving to, is right across the road from Offen. We can see his paddocks from our bedroom windows.' I gaped in fascination at Eunice while she outlined in such blissful ignorance the reason for the attempted murder of her husband. He himself had told me that the executors of the late Davis L. Davis had accepted his tender for the farm only recently, during the week before our momentous trip on the river. So the something 'goddam stupid' which had happened to Yola and Matt Clive's scheme was that they had discovered that of all the people on earth it was to be Dave Teller who was to be Offen's

214

new close neighbour. They had discovered it *after* they'd hi-jacked the horse, or they wouldn't have gone ahead with the plan.

'Why are you laughing?' Eunice asked, frowning. 'What's so funny?'

'It's not funny,' I agreed, straightening my face, 'Far from it. Do you know Culham James personally?'

'Not yet. Does it matter?' She still looked puzzled.

'It would be wiser not to make close friends with him in too much of a hurry.'

'Why not?'

'Might prove a prickly flower.' I had a mental vision of Dave looking out of his bedroom window day after day, looking over to the paddocks where Chrysalis and Allyx were let out to graze. He might never have recognized them. But also he might. Culham James simply couldn't take the risk. Yola and Matt had flown immediately to England to dispose of Dave a long way from the real scene of danger.

While Allyx remained at Orpheus Farm and Dave continued making active plans to move alongside, the explosive situation would still exist. Though Matt Clive might have given up temporarily, I fervently hoped that Radnor-Halley wouldn't let their vigilance slide a millimetre. A call to Keeble would be wise . . . even at California–London rates.

'I'm going for a walk on the shore,' said Lynnie, kicking off the pebbly sandals. 'Who's coming?'

I beat Walt to it by quicker reflexes, and collected

a grim look from him as I left him alone with Eunice. Lynnie remarked on it, grinning as we ambled silently away on the trickling sand.

'He's put off by the bloodies,' I explained. 'That's all.'

'She says it less often over here,' Lynnie commented. 'And she doesn't drink, except one or two before lunch, until after we've changed in the evening. Why is that, do you think?'

'She's escaped from the Lexington cage.'

'That heavenly house . . . a cage?'

'Uh huh.'

'The new one isn't half so beautiful,' she protested.

'It will be, when Eunice has finished. And then the walls will close in again.'

'Another cage, do you mean?' She sounded uncertain.

'Another cage,' I agreed.

'Life can't be just escaping from one cage and ending up in another,' she said explosively, repudiating violently so bleak a vision.

'Everyone lives inside bars,' I said. 'The trick is not to want to get out.'

'Stop it,' she said in distress. 'I don't want to hear that.'

'They used to keep linnets as pets,' I said. 'But there aren't any linnets in cages any more. Budgerigars instead. You'll be all right, little linnet.'

'I never know when you're being serious.'

'Always.'

'But half the time what you say is so . . . so crazy.'

'Life is serious, life is crazy. Anything crazy is serious, and everything serious is crazy . . . I'll race you along to that beach hut.'

She beat me to it in her bare feet, and leaned against the rough wooden wall laughing and getting her breath back while I tipped half-a-ton of sand out of my shoes. We walked on a little farther, and then sat down in the warm night and looked out across the shadowy peaceful ocean. No land between us and Japan, half a world away.

'Did you come out here to be with . . . us, or to find Allyx?' she said.

'Both.'

She shook her head. 'You brought Walt. That makes it to find Allyx.'

'Walt would have chosen to stay somewhere else,' I said, smiling. 'So California for Allyx, Santa Barbara for you. Satisfied?'

She murmured something unintelligible, and we sat in silence while she scuffed sand into a heap with her toes.

'Will you find him, do you think?' she asked in the end.

'Allyx? We might do.'

'When, roughly?'

'I don't know. Tomorrow, maybe.'

'And then . . . you'll go home?'

'I guess.'

'Back to an office . . .' She swept out an arm, embracing the wide sky. Back to an office, I thought coldly: and to the perpetual digging into people's privacy, to the occasional snaring of a bent applicant, to drizzle, to Putney, to the vacuum of the flat. To, in short, my normal life. The trick was not to want to slip through the bars.

'What are you going to do, now that you've left school?' I asked.

She sucked in a breath. 'After this, all the old things seem horribly dreary.'

'They'll soon give Dave a walking plaster . . .'

'I *know*,' she wailed. 'Don't think I don't know. I was supposed to be starting a secretarial course in September . . . I utterly don't want to, any more. Why can't everyone just live on the beach and be warm all the time . . .' She rocked with her arms laced round her bent up knees.

'Not enough beach.'

She giggled. 'You are just about the least romantic man alive. Comes of being a civil servant, I suppose. Like Daddy.'

In time we walked back along by the edge of the sea and paused when we came level with the motel. She put her hand on my arm and simply stood there waiting. I kissed her forehead, and then her nose, and finally her mouth. It was all very gentle, and utterly unnerving.

'This is no good,' I said, taking my hands from her shoulders. 'No good at all.'

'I've been kissed before,' she said anxiously. 'I really have.'

'That isn't what I meant,' I said, half laughing. 'You'd qualify for a diploma. No . . . it's just, little Lynnie, that we're a long way from home . . . and I never kiss brunettes more than once on a Friday.' I turned away towards the motel and jerked my head for her to follow. The best resolutions in the world would come a cropper faced with something like Lynnie, and immediate flight was the only course. It didn't seem to be popular with Lynnie herself, but I couldn't help that. I walked her briskly up the beach and made a joke about what Walt would be saying to Eunice, and we arrived in reasonable order to find that it was nothing: they were sitting across the table from each other in a miles-apart silence. Eunice gave us a long cool look and Walt one of disillusion, and Lynnie quite unnecessarily blushed, confirming their obvious suspicions. The harmless little walk hadn't been a good idea from any one of four points of view.

Walt and I drove quietly into Orpheus Farm the following morning. He did the talking: a thoroughly professional piece of work, insurance patter at the double. A survey for new fire regulations, he glibly explained, necessitated us seeing over the entire establishment.

We saw. Every stall in every barn, every hay loft, every straw bale, every inch. We saw Moviemaker. We saw Centigrade. We made a great many notes.

Culham James Offen himself escorted us round the coolest barn containing his four prize stallions. A great deal of self satisfaction sat on his shoulders like an impervious duck's-back mantle. I considered this with uneasy suspicion.

Uncle Bark was not only a man in his fifties with white hair, but he had a grey station wagon in a third of his large garage. I saw Walt giving it a sidelong glance. Undoubtedly it was Uncle Bark who had delivered the Snail Express trailer to old Hagstrom's boy at Rock Springs; and very likely Uncle Bark who had followed Sam Hengelman's van along the turnpike. Impossible to prove, though, at this distance.

The colour of his hair was premature. Very few wrinkles marked the smooth suntanned face, from which white eyebrows stood out like a bracket of snow, nearly meeting over the nose. His eyelashes were also white, but the albino non-pigmentation stopped short of the eyes: not pink, but a clear pale blue.

He carried his head stiffly on a thick muscular neck, and the large body beneath the airy white shirt looked solid more than soft. Not a man to ignore in any company. A physique which teemed naturally with success: and success had given him an arrogance of expression where a decent humility would have been more fitting.

The whole farm had the high gloss of money-no-object. Mathematically precise white-painted wood railings ringed the paddocks, and the approach to the Spanish-style house was landscaped with watered lawns and palms and an occasional bed full of spiky red flowers with sharp purplish leaves. We didn't penetrate the house: Walt's fire insurance only stretched to the stabling.

After we'd seen the stallions Offen handed us over to his stud groom, a fair, surprisingly young man he called Kiddo, who had a drawling western voice and an air of having been born without urgency. Every second word was 'uh', and his walk was thirty-two frames a second; slow motion.

'Been here long?' I asked him, as he pointed out the spotless foaling stalls.

'Five or six months,' he said, showing no resentment at a personal question; good natured, unsuspicious, no sign of nerves.

'You must be good, to get a job like this so young,' I congratulated him.

After a pause he said, 'I got a feeling for horses, see? Mares, they foal down nearly always at night. Comes from having to give birth in the dark out in the wild, you understand?'

'Why in the dark?' asked Walt, puzzled.

Another pause. Not for a deliberate choice of what or what not to say, I realized, but just a moment of waiting while the instinctive knowledge coalesced into words.

'They drop 'em by day, some hungry hyena comes along and kills the foal in the first half hour. Foals, now, they're readier to run at birth than most other critturs, but you've got to give 'em a half hour to dry off.'

'But they don't have to run, here,' Walt protested.

'Nature don't know that,' Kiddo pointed out reasonably. 'Another thing, mares mostly drop their foals pretty quick. Don't take some of them no time at all. And then, see, I always know when a mare's ready, and most often I go to the stall and make sure she's doing all right.'

'How do you know?' I asked, fascinated.

A much longer pause. Then he said, 'I don't know how I know, I got a feeling for it. I just wake up some nights and think, that Rose is about ready, and I go on out to her, and maybe there she is, not needing a bit of help, or maybe with the cord round the foal's neck, strangling it. I bin with horses, see, all my life.'

'Where were you before you came here?' I asked.

'Uh ... all over. Had a job in Lexington a while back, but they said I didn't keep good time turning up at work.' He grinned suddenly, a big mischievous lighting-up of the passive patient face. 'Then ... uh ... I was with a feller in Maryland ... he had a barn was falling down and honeysuckle breaking his fences and creeping into his windows, but he sure had some pretty

222

mares and one of them was the dam of the horse who won the Preakness a year back. Though I don't go to the races, myself.'

'Where after Maryland?' I asked.

'Uh . . . here. I seen this ad in the *Blood Horse*, and I wrote. It was a joke, mostly. I never expected to hear a word, knowing this was a big place and everything. But Mr Offen, it seems he didn't want no great business man, just someone with a feeling for the mares . . . and he's keeping me on, he says, though there was two before me he let go after they'd been here a month.'

It didn't seem to worry him. He had the God-will-provide nature which doesn't understand anxiety and never stores up winter nuts. Not that he had any need to. His 'feeling for mares' was in fact priceless: he would probably never cash in on it as he could but he'd never want for a job.

Kiddo watched us go in the same calm friendliness with which he'd shown us round. Walt and I agreed on the way back to Santa Barbara that he was only potentially an opponent. Loyalty might be given to Offen if he demanded it, but at present Kiddo had no idea what was going on.

'Unless,' Walt said thoughtfully, 'he's a brilliant actor.'

I shook my head. 'He wasn't acting. None of the signs.'

Walt looked at me curiously, taking his eyes too long off the road. 'Can you always tell?'

I smiled. 'That's one of those unanswerable questions. I've a feeling for it, like Kiddo with his mares. But if it lets me down sometimes, how am I to know?'

'You'd know soon enough when secrets started leaking to the other side,' Walt pointed out. 'Have you ever passed as clear anyone who turned out to be a spy?'

'Yes.'

'How often?'

'Once.'

'In your first year, I suppose,' Walt said with mild sarcasm.

'In my second year. He was the first serious spy I had to deal with, and I didn't spot him. The counter-espionage chaps turned him up six months later when he'd done a good deal of damage, and the press made the usual scathing remarks about the feebleness of our screening system.'

'Which you took to heart,' Walt said dryly.

'I guess so.'

He drove a mile and then said, 'And now you're so good at it that they beat you up. What do you think about things when that happens?'

'That there's a big fish coming down the pipeline and they want me out of the way.'

'So you look all the harder.' A statement, not a question.

'You might say so. Yes.'

'They'll kill you one of these days.'

I didn't answer. Walt flicked a glance sideways and sighed. 'I suppose you don't care.'

'There are a lot of others in the department.'

Walt drove into Santa Barbara without another word, where we joined Eunice and Lynnie in the terrace restaurant for lunch. They had, they said, bought that morning the big bright dangling earrings which swung with every turn of their heads. Lynnie's were scarlet, Eunice's acid green; otherwise identical. Still friends, I thought in some relief. Still in harmony. Whether Eunice would do a small chore for me was, however, another matter.

We had clam chowder with shrimp to follow, and Lynnie said with all this seafood she'd be growing fins. During coffee, when she stood up restlessly and said she was going down to the sea, it was Walt, after a pause, who said he would go with her. She looked at me questioningly, worriedly, and then turned and walked quickly off with him, talking a good deal too brightly.

'Don't you hurt that child,' Eunice said fiercely.

'I don't want to.'

'You're too bloody attractive.'

'Yeah. Charm the birds off the trees,' I agreed sardonically. 'Little wives spill their husbands' secrets into my bloody attractive ears.'

She looked shocked. Quite a change, I thought, from dishing it out.

'You mean you . . . *use* it?'

'Like a can opener. And as a catalyst. Who doesn't? Salesmen, politicians, actors, women, all using it like mad.'

'For God's sake . . .' Her voice was faint, but she was also laughing.

'But not on Lynnie,' I added wryly.

'You didn't need to, I guess. Dragging Dave out of the Thames was a lot more effective.'

I watched Lynnie's and Walt's backs as they reached the tide line.

'So that's why . . .?' I said, almost to myself.

'Hero worship,' Eunice said with barbs. 'Does it give you a kick?'

'Like a mule's in the stomach . . .'

She laughed. 'It's not that you're so madly hand-some in any obvious way.'

'No,' I agreed with truth, 'I'm not.'

She looked as if she were going to say more and then thought better of it. I jumped straight in while her mind was still half flirting, knowing, and despising the knowledge, that in that mood she was more likely to do what I asked.

'Has Lynnie still got those photographs of me?'

'Don't worry,' she said sarcastically. 'In a fire, she'd save them first.'

'I'd like Culham James Offen to see them.'

'You'd like *what*? What are you talking about?'

'About you and Lynnie driving over to pay a neighbourly call on Culham James this afternoon, and easily, dearest Eunice, you could tell him about me pulling Dave out of the Thames, and Lynnie could show him my photograph. Especially the one of me sitting by a table outside a pub. That group of all of us.'

She gaped and gasped, and then started thinking.

'You really can't be as pleased with yourself as all that ... so for God's sake, why?'

'An experiment.'

'That's no answer.'

'Earning my keep at The Vacationer.'

A look of disgust turned down her mouth.

'Finding that bloody horse?'

'I'm afraid so.'

'You don't mean ... surely you can't mean that Offen has anything to do with it?'

'I'd like to make sure he hasn't.'

'Oh, I see. Well, I guess that's not much to ask. Sure. I'll get Lynnie to come with me.'

'And tell him I'm looking for Allyx.'

She gave me a straight assessing stare, and said, 'How about Chrysalis?'

'Whatever you like. Say that Dave employed me to get him back.'

'I don't know why I'm doing it.'

'More interesting than golf?' I suggested.

'Is it a game?' She was sceptical.

'Well . . . like hunting bears,' I smiled.

'Oh, yes.' She nodded sardonically. 'A sport.'

CHAPTER THIRTEEN

I parked a hired car in some scrub off the road leading to Orpheus Farm, and smoked a rare cigarette. The fierce afternoon sun roasted through the metal roof and a water mirage hung in a streak over the dry road. A day for lizards to look for shade. They'd run out of air-conditioned heaps at the hire firms: I'd had to take one of those old fashioned jobs where you breathed fresh air by opening the window. The air in question was as fresh as last week's news and as hot as tomorrow's.

At five past four Eunice and Lynnie passed unseeingly across my bows, heading back to Santa Barbara. I finished the cigarette and stubbed it out carefully in the flaked chromium ashtray. I looked at my fingernails for ten minutes. No special inspiration. At half past four I started the car, pointed its nose towards Orpheus, and went to call on Uncle Bark.

This time I drove straight up to the house and rang the ornate bell. A houseboy came: all on the same scale as at Jeff Roots's. When he went to find Culham

James I followed quietly on his heels, so my host, even if he had meant to, had no chance to say he was out. The houseboy opened the door on to a square comfortable office–sitting room and Culham James was revealed sitting at his desk with a green telephone receiver to his ear.

He gave the houseboy and myself a murderous glare between us which changed to reasonable affability once he'd got control of it. 'I'll call you later,' he said to the telephone. 'A Mr Hawkins has this minute arrived . . . that's right . . . later then.' He put down the receiver and raised his eyebrows.

'Did you miss something this morning?' he asked.

'No . . . should we have done?'

He shook his head in mild annoyance. 'I am merely asking the purpose of this return visit.'

'My colleague and I wanted answers to one or two extra questions about the precautions you take against fire, especially as regards those two exceptionally valuable stallions . . . er . . . Moviemaker and Centigrade.'

Under his suntanned face, behind the white bracket of eyebrows, Culham James Offen was beginning to enjoy a huge joke. It fizzed like soda water in his pale blue eyes and bubbled in his throat. He was even having difficulty in preventing himself from sharing it: but after a struggle he had it nailed down under hatches, and calm with a touch of severity took over. We went solemnly through the farce of fire precautions, me leaning on his desk and checking off Walt's solid sounding inventions one by one. They mostly had to deal with the amount of supervision in the stallions' barn at night. Whether there were any regular patrols, any dogs loose on watch, any photoelectric apparatus for detecting opacity, such as heavy smoke?

Offen cleared his throat and answered no to the lot.

'We have the extremely expensive and reliable sprinkler system which you saw this morning,' he pointed out. 'It is thoroughly tested every three months, as I told you earlier.'

'Yes. Thank you, then. I guess that's all.' I shut my notebook. 'You've been most helpful, Mr Offen.'

'You're welcome,' he said. The joke rumbled in his voice, but was coloured now with unmistakable malice. High time to go, I thought: and went.

When I got back to The Vacationer some while later I found Eunice and Lynnie and Walt sitting in a glum row behind empty glasses. I flopped into a chair opposite them and said, 'Why the mass depression?'

'You're late,' Walt said.

'I told you not to wait dinner.' I caught a passing waiter on the wing and arranged refills all round.

'We were considering a search party,' Eunice said.

I looked at all three of them more carefully. 'You've been comparing notes,' I said resignedly.

'I think it's terrible of you ... *wicked*,' Lynnie burst out. 'To have made me go and deliberately ... *deliberately* ... put you in such frightful danger.'

'Lynnie stop it. I wasn't in any danger ... here I am, aren't I?'

'But Walt said ...'

'Walt needs his brains seen to.'

Walt glared and compressed his mouth into a rigid line. 'You didn't tell me you'd arranged for Offen to know you were the man who took Chrysalis. And you didn't tell me the Clives had tried to kill Mr Teller.'

'And you didn't tell *me*,' Eunice added, 'that the couple in the background of the photograph Lynnie showed Culham Offen had tried to kill you too.'

'Or you'd never have let Lynnie show it to him?'

'No,' she said slowly.

'Just as well I didn't.'

'And you deliberately misled me by saying you wanted to clear Offen. It wasn't true.'

'Er ... no. But I did want you to behave naturally with him. And anyway, why all the fuss?'

'We thought ...' Lynnie said in a subdued voice. 'We almost thought ... as you were gone so long ... that you ... that they ...'

'They didn't,' I pointed out obviously, smiling.

'But won't you please explain why?' Lynnie said. '*Why* did you want me to give you away like that?'

'Several reasons. One was to make Dave safer.'

'I don't see how,' Eunice objected.

'By letting Offen know, and through him the Clives, that we could prove the Clives were in England and beside the Thames on the day of Dave's accident.

Murder by accident is only a good idea as long as there's no apparent motive and the murderers have no apparent connection with the victim. We've shown them that we know their motive and their connection, and they must now be aware that if Dave were killed they would be the first suspects. This makes it less likely they will try again.'

'Crikey,' Lynnie said, 'Go on.'

'When Walt and I went to Orpheus Farm this morning saying we were making a survey for new fire precautions, Offen wasn't worried. He didn't know me from Adam then, of course. It was before you showed him my photograph. But he showed no anxiety at all about two strangers turning up on a pretext that he didn't even bother to check. None of the edginess one might have expected if he'd just had one stolen horse pinched back from him, and was in possession of two others standing in his barn. I didn't like it. It didn't feel right.'

'He hasn't got them,' Eunice said with relief. 'I was sure it couldn't possibly be right that Culham Offen would steal horses. I mean, he's *respected*.'

Walt and I exchanged a glance of barely perceptible amusement. To be respected was the best cover in the world for fraud. Fraud, in fact, could rarely exist without it.

'So,' I said, 'I thought it would be helpful if he knew for certain that I was especially interested in Moviemaker and Centigrade, and that I wasn't in fire

233

insurance, but was the man he had to thank for losing Chrysalis. When I went back, after you two had left, he still wasn't worried. On the contrary, he was enjoying the situation. It amused him enormously to think that I believed I was fooling him. I asked him a lot of questions about the security precautions surrounding Moviemaker and Centigrade, and he was still completely untroubled. So,' I paused, 'it's now quite clear that the two horses standing in his barn called Moviemaker and Centigrade are in actual fact exactly what he says: Moviemaker and Centigrade. He isn't worried about snoopers, he isn't worried about me making clumsy preparations to steal them. He must therefore be confident that any legal proceedings will prove the horses to be the ones he says they are. He'd ambush me if I tried to steal them, and have me in real deep trouble, which would be to him some small compensation for losing Chrysalis.'

Walt nodded briefly.

Eunice said obstinately. 'I think it only proves that you're barking up the wrong damn tree. He isn't worried simply because he isn't guilty of anything.'

'You liked him?'

'Yes,' she said. 'He was bloody sweet.'

Lynnie nodded. 'I thought so too.'

'What did he say when you showed him the photographs?'

'He just glanced at them at first,' Lynnie said. 'And then he took them over to the window. And then he asked me who had taken them, and where, and when. So I told him about the day on the river, and about you and Dave going under the weir . . .'

At the side of my vision Eunice gave me an I-told-you-so smile.

'. . . and he said one or two nice things about you,' Lynnie finished. 'So I told him you came over here to look for Chrysalis, and somehow or other you found him.'

'He asked where you found him,' Eunice nodded. 'But we didn't know. I said you were now trying to find Allyx, and it certainly didn't worry him. I'm sure you must be wrong.'

I smiled at her. She didn't want the horse found, and as an ally she was as reliable as thin ice on a sunny day. I didn't intend to tell her anything in future which I wasn't prepared to have passed on to Offen. Like most law abiding citizens she had not grasped that a criminal mind didn't show, that an endearing social manner could co-exist with fraud and murder. 'Such a *nice* man,' the neighbours say in bewilderment, when Mr Smith's garden is found to be clogged with throttled ladies. 'Always so pleasant.'

Eunice, propelled by a strong semi-conscious wish for him not to have Allyx, might tell Offen anything, simply because she couldn't visualize a 'sweet' man being deadly. She might also tell him anything propelled by the same impulse which had made her point a gun at me.

'Let's have dinner,' I suggested; and Eunice and Lynnie went away to freshen up.

Walt looked at me thoughtfully, then raised his eyebrows.

I nodded. 'I put a bug on the underside of his desk, two feet from the telephone. I was late back because I was listening. He called Yola and told her about my visit but there wasn't much else. I left the set hidden, and came back here.'

'Do you mean it, that those two horses really are Moviemaker and Centigrade?'

'Sure. He bought them, remember. Openly. At bloodstock sales. And obviously he's kept them. I suppose he never could be certain that some ex-owner would turn up for a visit. Those horses will have been tattooed inside their mouths with an identity number when they first began to race. They have to be, over here, don't they? It'll be quite easy to establish that they're the right two.'

'You don't think Mrs Teller's right . . . that he never had Showman and Allyx after all?'

'I'll play you his call to Yola some time. He had the foresight to whisk those horses away from Orpheus when we got Chrysalis. He was more or less waiting for something like our visit this morning. No flies on Culham James, I'm afraid. Er . . . Walt, did you give Eunice and Lynnie any details about our jaunt in the Tetons?'

He looked uncomfortable. 'I was annoyed with you.'

'What exactly did you tell them?'

'Not much. I was horrified at Lynnie having shown Offen that picture of the Clives, and when Mrs Teller said you'd planned it I said you must be mad, they'd tried to kill you once already.'

'And you told them how?'

He nodded, not meeting my eyes.

'Did you tell them about the bugs and the wireless set?'

'No.'

'It's important, Walt.'

He looked up. 'I didn't mention them.'

I relaxed. 'How about our mountain walk?'

'No details.'

'Place?'

'I'm pretty sure I mentioned the Tetons.'

Nothing there that would hurt.

'How much did you say about Showman and Allyx?'

'I told them that you'd worked out through the stud books that Offen must have them.'

'Did you say the words "Uncle Bark"?'

He shook his head. 'I'd forgotten about that.'

I sighed. 'Walt. Mrs Teller doesn't want Allyx found any more than she wanted Chrysalis. Let's not entrust the state of the nation to the Indians.'

He flushed a little and compressed his mouth. Eunice and Lynnie came back shortly after, and, though we all four had dinner together it proved a taciturn and not over-friendly affair.

Walt rode up to my room for a conference after the coffee.

'How do we find them?' he said, coming bluntly to the point and easing himself simultaneously into the only armchair.

'They've made us a gift of them, in one way,' I said thoughtfully. 'We can send a bunch of lawyers in to query Moviemaker and Centigrade's identity, and get it established beyond doubt that the two Offen showed us are in fact those two horses. He'll be keen for them to do it: and once he's done it, he'll be stuck with them. We will meanwhile do another little vanishing trick with the other two and start our own identification parade on our ground. Once they are established as Allyx and Showman, Offen cannot possibly claim them back.'

'Two objections,' Walt said. 'We don't know where Allyx and Showman are. And if we find them, why not get lawyers into the act right away? Why go to all the danger and trouble of taking them?'

'Same as Chrysalis,' I pointed out. 'The first sign of any real trouble, and they'd be shot. It's not illegal to kill a horse and whisk it smartly off to the dog food people. And vastly more difficult to identify a dead one. Impossible, I'd almost say, for the degree of certainty we need here.'

'Even if we take them, and establish their identity, and everything goes smoothly, Offen will still be raking in those colossal stud fees of half a million dollars a year, because we'd never be able to prove that for the past ten years Showman has been siring every foal that's down in the book as Moviemaker's . . .'

I smiled. 'We'll do something about that, once we've sorted out the rest.'

'Which brings us back to square one,' Walt said flatly. 'Where the hell do we start?'

I perched on the window sill and looked down sideways into the brightly lit car park. Coloured bulbs on the face of the motel raised rainbow shimmers on glossy hard tops and struck me as a deeply melancholy commentary on human achievement. Yet I wouldn't have wanted to live without cars or electricity . . . if I'd wanted to live. My room was only two floors up, with none above. Too near the ground. I'd known of a woman who'd jumped from five and bungled it. A gun was better . . .

'Well?' Walt said insistently.

'I'm sorry . . .?' I said vaguely, turning my head back to him.

'Where do we look?'

'Oh . . . yes.'

'On the ranch?'

'Very doubtful, don't you think? They must know that's the first place we'd think of.'

'There's a lot of land there,' he said. 'And a lot of horses to lose them in.'

I shook my head. 'They'd have to keep them in a paddock close to the house. All the rest of the ranch is well named Rocky Mountains, and they couldn't turn them loose for fear of them breaking a leg. We'd better check, though.' I stared unseeingly at the carpet. 'But I guess the horses are with Matt. Offen is at Orpheus Farm, and Yola is tied to the ranch seeing to about thirty guests, so where's Matt?'

'Where indeed,' Walt said gloomily.

'He and Yola don't spend their winters on the ranch because the valley is blocked by snow. She told me that they go south . . . On one of those telephone calls she told Offen they couldn't keep Chrysalis at a place called Pitts, because it wasn't suitable. But that was when they didn't know we were after them . . . when it wasn't an emergency.'

'So somewhere south of the Tetons we find this Pitts, and Matt and the horses will be waiting for us?'

'Yeah.' I smiled briefly. 'Sounds too easy.'

'Easy!' Walt said.

'They must leave a forwarding address for mail,' I pointed out. 'They live a conventional law-abiding life with a longstanding business to give them obvious legal means of support. There must be dozens of people in Jackson who know their winter address.'

'Our Buttress agent could get that, then. First thing in the morning.'

'Fine.'

Walt levered himself out of the armchair and hesitated.

'Come along to my room,' he said. 'I've got a bottle.'

I wasn't sure that I wanted to, but he smiled suddenly, wiping out all resentments, and one didn't kick that sort of olive branch in the teeth.

'Be glad to,' I said.

The smile went deeper and lasted along the passage to his room, which was almost identical to mine. The window looked out on the same cars from a slightly different angle, and he had two armchairs instead of one. There was a bottle of Old Grandad on a round tray with glasses and a water jug, and on his bedside table stood a leather-framed photograph. I picked it up idly while he went to fetch ice from the machine along the passage. Walt with his family. A good-looking woman, a plain girl in her early teens, a thin boy of about ten: all four of them smiling cheerfully into the lens. He came back as I was putting them down.

'I'm sorry about the picnic,' I said.

'Next week will do just as well,' he said. 'We've got the whole of the summer, I guess.'

We sat in the armchairs, drinking slowly. I didn't like bourbon much; but that wasn't the point. He talked casually about the split-level ranch-type house they'd moved into the year before, and how his

241

daughter got along just fine with the folks next door, and how they'd had trouble with the boy's health, he'd had rheumatic fever . . .

'How about your own future, with Buttress Life?' I asked.

'I've gotten about as high as I'll get,' he said with surprising honesty. 'There's only one more step up that I really want, and that's to chief investigator, claims division, and that'll come along next year when the present guy retires.'

He poured more drinks, rubbed his thumb slowly over the round fingertips, and said Amy and the kids were asking him for a pool in their back yard, and that Amy's mother was a problem since Amy's father died last fall, and that he hadn't caught a single ball game last season, he'd been that busy . . .

We sat for more than an hour without mentioning the horses once. He yawned finally and I uncurled myself from the soft chair, putting down the third time empty glass. He said goodnight sleepily with easy friendliness and, for the first time since I'd known him, without tension. Back in my own room, undressing, I wondered how long it would last. Until I made the next unpopular suggestion, I supposed. I didn't know whether to envy him his enclosing domesticity or to feel stifled by it. I did know that I liked him both as a man and as a working companion, moods and all.

*

The Buttress Life agent in Jackson came through with the Clives' winter address within twenty minutes of Walt calling him: 40159 Pittsville Boulevard, Las Vegas, Nevada.

I remembered Yola's smile at the thought of winter. Las Vegas explained it. Yola liked to gamble.

'What now?' Walt said.

'I'll go on out there and take a look.'

'Alone?' There was a certain amount of anxiety in his voice, which I interpreted as a desire not to be left in Santa Barbara with Eunice.

'We need you here,' I said placatingly. 'And don't tell her where I've gone.'

He gave me a sharp glance. 'I won't.'

We drove in the hired car out to Orpheus Farm, where I showed him where I'd hidden the radio tape recorder between three rocks, with its aerial sticking up through the branches of a scrubby bush. The nearest neatly railed paddock was only feet away; the house, about four hundred yards. We picked up the radio and parked a short distance down the road.

'Supposing he sees us?' Walt said, watching me wind back the reel.

'He'll only think we're watching the farm routine, to know when to pinch Moviemaker. The radio will pick up the bug in his office from at least a quarter mile, but it gets fainter after that. It has to work on the air-vibration system. Not such a good amplification as electricity. Do you ever use them?'

'Bugs?' He shook his head. 'Not often. Cameras with telescopic lenses are better. Catch the claimants walking around on their paralysed legs.' Satisfaction echoed in his voice. Like me, a rogue hunter to the bone.

Smiling to myself, I switched on. Cutting in and out, Culham James' various conversations filled three-quarters of an hour of tape time, but nothing he said was of any use to us. I rewound the reels again and we put the radio in among the rocks, Walt agreeing that he would come back after sunset and listen to the day's take.

He drove me then to the Los Angeles airport, where I hopped on a plane to Las Vegas, arriving mid afternoon. The desert hit like a gust from an oven when they opened the plane doors, and from a nearby building the usual lighted numbers proclaimed to the populace that in the shade, if they could find any, it would be 108.

The air-conditioning at the edge of town motel I booked into was turning itself inside out under the strain, and the Hertz man who presently took my money admitted that this was a little old heatwave, sure thing. Had to expect them, in July. The incon-spicuous Pontiac he hired me was this time, however, a cooled one. I drove around for a while to get my bearings, and then took a look at Pittsville Boulevard.

The high numbers ran two miles out of the town, expensive looking homes along a metalled road with

the desert crowding in at their rear. The Clives' house
was flanked by others on both sides: not near enough
to touch, but too near for the invisible stabling of
stallions. The place on Pitts wasn't suitable, as Yola
had said.

It was low and white, with a flat roof and a frame
of palms and orange trees. Blinds and insect screens
blanked out the windows, and the grass on each side
of the drive was a pale dry biscuit colour, not green
watered like its neighbours. I stopped the car in the
roadway opposite and looked it over. Not a leaf moved
under the bleaching sun. Ten minutes ticked away.
Nothing happened in the street. Inside the car, with
the engine stopped, the temperature rose like Christmas prices. I started up again, sucked in the first cold
blast from the air-conditioner, and slid on along the
way I was heading.

A mile past the Clives' house the metal surface
ended, and the road ran out across the desert as a
dusty streak of gravel. I turned the car and went back,
thinking. The comparative dead-endedness of Pittsville
Boulevard explained the almost total lack of traffic
past the Clives', and also meant that I couldn't drive
past there very often without becoming conspicuous
to the neighbours. Keeping a check on an apparently
empty house, however, wasn't going to get me much
farther.

About five houses along on the town side of the
Clives' there was another with water-starved brownish

grass. Taking a chance that these inhabitants too were away from home I rolled the Pontiac purposefully into the palm-edged driveway and stopped outside the front door. Ready with some of Walt's insurance patter, I leant on the bell and gave it a full twenty seconds. No one came. Everything was hot, quiet, and still.

Strolling, I walked down the drive and on to the road. Looking back one couldn't see the car for bushes. Satisfied, I made the trip along to the Clives', trying to look as if walking were a normal occupation in a Nevada heatwave: and by the time I got there it was quite clear why it wasn't. The sweat burnt dry on my skin before it had a chance to form into beads.

Reconnoitring the Clives' place took an hour. The house was shut up tight, obviously empty. The window screens were all securely fastened, and all the glass was covered on the inside with blinds, so that one couldn't see in. The doors were fastened with safe-deposit locks. The Clives had made casual breaking-in by vagrants nearly impossible.

With caution I eased round the acre of land behind the house. Palms and bushes screened a trefoil-shaped pool from being overlooked too openly by the neighbours, but from several places it was possible to see the pools of the flanking houses some sixty yards away. Beside one of them, reminding me of Eunice, a woman in two scraps of yellow cloth lay motionless on a long chair, inviting heatstroke and adding to a depth of suntan which would have got her reclassified in South Africa. I moved even more quietly after I'd seen her, but she didn't stir.

The rear boundary of the Clives' land was marked by large stones painted white, with desert scrub on the far side and low growing citrus bushes on the near. From their windows, brother and sister had a wide view of hills and wilderness; two miles down the road neon lights went twenty rounds with the midday sun, and the crash of fruit machines out-decibelled the traffic. I wondered idly how much of Uncle Bark's illicit proceeds found their way into Matt and Yola's pocket, and how much from there vanished into the greedy slot mouths in Vegas. The stud fees went around and around and only Buttress Life were the losers.

On the way back to the motel I stopped at every supermarket I came to, and bought two three-pound bags of flour from each.

From a hardware store I acquired a short ladder, white overalls, white peaked cotton cap, brushes, and a half-gallon can of bright yellow instant drying paint.

CHAPTER FOURTEEN

Walt listened to what I had to say in a silence which hummed down the telephone wires more eloquently than hysterics.

'You're crazy,' he said at last, sounding as if he seriously meant it.

'Can you think of anything else?'

After a long pause he said grudgingly, 'Nothing quicker.'

'Right, then. I'll fix everything this end and give you a call in the morning. And let's hope it works.'

'What if it doesn't?'

'Have to try something else.'

Walt grunted gloomily and hung up.

I spent an hour at the airport, and then went back to the motel. The evening oozed away. I played some roulette without enthusiasm and lost backing black against a sequence of fourteen reds; and I ate a good steak listening to a girl singer whose voice was secondary to her frontage. After that I lay on my bed for a while and smoked, and kept the blues from crowding in too close by thinking exclusively of the job in hand.

At two I dressed in a dark green cotton shirt and black jeans, went downstairs, stepped into the car, and drove along Pittsville Boulevard to 40159. The town itself was wide awake and rocking: the houses along Pitts were dark and silent. With dimmed lights I rolled quietly into the Clives' driveway and stacked the bags of flour close to the front door. Then, holding the car door but not shutting it, I eased the Pontiac back along the road and parked it in the driveway of the same empty house that I had used in the afternoon. Again, not wanting any neighbours to remember hearing a car door slam, I left it ajar, and walked back to the Clives'.

The night was warm and gentle with a deep navy blue sky and stars like fluorescent polka-dots. Two miles away the blazing lights of Vegas raised a bell-shaped orange glow, but among the palms and orange trees the shadows were thick and black and comfortably concealing.

The Clives' was only the latest of a great many houses I had broken into. My short cuts to truth were scandalous by all public and private standards, and Keeble rarely asked how I got my information: and as I would have had the press, the police, and public opinion all balefully against me if I'd ever been caught, A gag on eggs would have been clumsy in comparison.

Law-abiding citizens never knew I'd been their guest. For the Clives', however, I had alternative plans.

Wearing surgeons' rubber gloves, and with my shoes stuck through my belt to the left of the Luger, I worked on the lock on the back door, and after not too bad a time, considering its complexity, the two sets of tumblers fell sweetly over, and the house was mine.

Inside, the air was stale and still, and dust sheets draped the furniture, looking like pale boulders in the dim light of my torch. The rear door opened into a spacious hall which led straight through to the front. I walked across, unbolted and unfastened the front door, brought in the bags of flour, and left the door ajar, like the one I'd come in by: the value of always being prepared for instant flight had been drummed into me by an ex-burglar who had once neglected it.

I went into the bedrooms. Large separate single bedded rooms again for Yola and Matt, and a guest bedroom, with a bathroom to each. I pulled all the covers off the furniture and flung on to the floor everything they had left in the chests and closets. Over the resulting mess in each room I shook six pounds of self-raising flour.

In the kitchen I emptied on to the floor a packet of soap flakes, a packet of rice, some cereal and four pounds of brown sugar, which were all lying handy in the pantry. I unlocked the pantry window and unfastened its outer screen, leaving both open: and as an afterthought tumbled some canned fruit off the shelf beneath it, to show that the intruder had come in that way.

In the spacious living room I again removed all the covers, put every ornament and small loose object in a heap on the floor, and flung flour over them and around the whole place. A smaller cosier room, facing the road, contained a desk full of papers, two large bookshelves, and a well-filled sewing box. Together the jumbled contents made a splendid ankle-deep mess on the floor. Pounds of flour fell over everything like snow.

It was while I was tearing open the last bag, ready for a final scatter round the hall, that I heard the distant police siren. Frozen, I doubted for a second that it was for me: then considered that either a too watchful neighbour had seen my torch in chinks through the blinds, or else that the Clives' complicated locks weren't their only protection, and that they had a direct burglar alarm line to the police.

Without wasting much time I shut the front door and heard the lock engage. Emptied the last bag of flour over a plastic flower arrangement on a table in the hall. Flitted through the rear door and clicked it shut behind me. Thrust the torch into my pocket.

The siren wailed and stopped at the front of the house. Doors slammed, men shouted, boots ran. Someone with a megaphone urged me to come out with my hands on my head. The edges of the house were outlined by a spotlight shining on its front.

With bare seconds to spare before the first uniform appeared in silhouette around the corner I reached the nearest of the bushes flanking the trefoil pool and dived behind it. Being quiet enough was no problem, as the law were making an intimidating clatter all around the house, but staying invisible was more difficult. They brought another spotlight round to the rear and shone it full on the house. The shuttered windows stared blindly and unhelpfully back, reflecting the glare almost as far as my cover.

Lights appeared in neighbouring houses, and heads stuck like black knobs out of the windows. I eased gently away past a few more bushes and thought I was still a great deal too close to a spell in the zoo.

A shout from the side of the house indicated that they had found the open pantry window. Four troopers altogether, I judged. All armed to the teeth. I grimaced in the darkness and moved another few yards with less caution. I wasn't going to give them any forefinger exercise if I could help it, but the time was running out.

They were brave enough. One or more climbed in through the window and switched on the light. I more rapidly crossed the last stretch of garden, stepped over the white-painted stones, and headed straight out into the desert.

Five steps convinced me I needed to put my shoes on. Ten steps had me certain that the only vegetation was prickly pear, and close-ranked, at that. I should imagine I impaled myself on every one in the neighbourhood.

Back at the Clives' they had temporarily stopped oohing and ahing over the mess, and were searching the grounds. Lights moved round the next door houses as well. If they went five along and found the car, things would get very awkward indeed.

I had meant to be safely back in my motel long before I called the police early in the morning to say that I was a civic minded neighbour who had just seen a prowler coming out of the Clives' . . .

When they showed signs of shining the light out towards where I was stumbling along I lay down flat on the ground and listened to the thud of my heart. The spotlight beam flickered palely over the low scrubby bushes and outlined the flat spiky plates of the prickly pears, but in the shifting uneven shadows that they threw, I reckoned I must be just another clump. There was a good deal of shouted discussion about whether it was necessary to take a look-see in the desert, but to my relief no one came farther out than the boundary stones. Gradually, frustrated, the dazzle and commotion retreated and died away.

The lights inside the Clives' house went out. The police car drove off. The neighbours went back to bed. I got to my feet and brushed off the surplus of dry sandy earth. What with that and flour dust even the blindest cop would have little difficulty in buttoning me on to the crime.

With more care than on the outward trip I headed back towards the houses, but at an angle I hoped would bring me near the car. The sooner I beat it from that little neck of the woods, the better . . .

I stopped dead.

How might one catch a prowler? Just pretend to go away, and wait somewhere down the road, and when he thought everything was safe, he'd come carelessly along and fall into your waiting hands like a ripe plum.

I decided not to drive back towards Las Vegas from that quiet cul-de-sac. Just in case.

At the fifth house along, everything was quiet. I cat-footed through the grounds, around the house, and took a distant look at the car. Still there. No trooper beside it. I stood in the shadows for longer than was probably necessary, then took a deep breath and risked it. I completed the steps to the car and peered in through the window. Empty. Made a quick cautious tour of the row of spiky low-growing palms hiding it from the road.

Nothing. No irate shouts. All quiet. Car undiscovered. Sighing with relief, the vision of the malicious Clives dancing at my trial fading a little, I pulled wide the already open door and folded like an understuffed rag doll into the driving seat. For five minutes I did nothing more energetic than to breathe freely, and enjoy it.

There remained however the problem of telephoning to Walt: and I chewed it over thoughtfully while absent-mindedly pulling prickly pear needles out of my legs.

I was a fair hand at wire tapping, when I had the kit: but it was in Putney. No doubt there would be a telephone in the empty house alongside. But I wasn't sure that I wanted to risk this house too being directly connected to the police, if that was what had happened at the Clives'. On the other hand, I had been in the Clives' house twenty minutes before the police showed up. Yet they might be quicker, on a second call.

After half an hour I pulled on the rubber gloves, climbed out of the car, and picked the front door lock. It turned all right, but unfortunately the prudent householders had also used bolts. Always a toss up which door of the house people bolted. I walked round to the rear, and let myself in. There was a telephone on a table in the hall. I walked over to it, then turned, retraced my steps, left the door ajar, went round to the car, started up, and drove quietly away in the dead end direction, not stopping until I was off the metalled road on to the gravel, and round a couple of bends. I switched off the light and smoked a cigarette.

Another half hour passed. No lights went on along by the houses; no police sirens, no disturbances at all. I drove gently back, parked in the same spot as before, went round into the house, and called up Walt.

He wasn't amused at being woken at 5 AM.

'A slight change of timing,' I said apologetically. 'The police have already seen the mess.'

He drew in a sharp breath. 'They didn't catch you!'

'No.' No point in telling him how close it had been: he hadn't approved of my going in at all.

'I suppose you want me to come now, then?' he said, with resignation.

'Yes, please. As soon as you can. Leave the car keys at the inquiry desk at Los Angeles airport, and I'll pick them up. The helicopter pilot I've engaged at Las Vegas is Michael King. He's expecting you. Just ask for him. The helicopter radio will pick up the frequency of the bug I've got with me, so you won't need to bring my recorder. Was there anything on the tape today?'

'Yesterday,' Walt corrected. 'Not much. I went over after dinner last night and ran it through. Offen had a friend over. There was two hours of just ordinary yapping. I didn't get back here to bed until one.'

'When this is over you can sleep for a fortnight.'

'Yeah?' he said sarcastically. 'Tell it to the marines.'

He put down his receiver with less of a crash than usual. Smiling, I took out a five dollar bill and left it stuck half under the telephone. Then I let myself out, relocked the door behind me, and went back to the car.

Three hours uneventfully went by. Night changed to day. The air temperature began its morning climb. A few energetic birds sang: and I smoked another cigarette.

Soon after eight a patrol car went up the road, siren fortissimo. Pittsville Boulevard woke up. I eased out of the car, walked carefully down towards the road, and tucked myself invisibly between a palm and a bush, from where I had a clear view of everyone driving up towards the Clives'.

From along the road I could hear several excited voices, most of them children's: and a small boy and a girl came past close to me doing an Indianapolis on their tricycles.

Several cars drove down from the houses, all with men alone, going in to Las Vegas. One woman followed. Three women came the other way, all looking eager. At nine-thirty two men drove in from Vegas, one of them adjusting a large folding camera: the local press.

An hour later a quiet-engined helicopter drifted over and landed out of sight behind a fold of hill.

At ten-fifty the hawk came to the lure.

A sky blue convertible Ford, with the hood down. Matt, driving fast, hunched with anger. Youth, strength, and fury, knotted into one callous personality. Even in a speeding car the impression came across with the solidity of a shockwave. Standing on his brakes flamboyantly late, he screeched down from sixty to nil outside his own house, scattering children like pigeons.

Satisfied, I got stiffly to my feet and went back up the drive to the car. There I removed from the boot the white overalls, white cotton gloves and a cap, and put them on, along with a pair of sunglasses. With a screwdriver from the tool kit I opened the tin of paint and gave the oily yellow contents an encouraging stir; cleaned and replaced the screwdriver, and rested the paint lid gently back on the tin. Then, picking it up by its handle with my right hand, and carrying brushes and ladders with my left, I strolled out on to the road, and along to the Clives'.

Matt's Ford stood at the door at a crooked angle to the patrol car. A good many people were still standing around, staring and gossiping in the sun. I meandered slowly through them and took a closer look at the blue convertible, and then withdrew discreetly to the edge of the proceedings.

Taking the bug out of my pocket, I talked to Walt, hoping he could hear. He couldn't answer: it was strictly one way traffic on the midget transmitter.

'Do you read me, Walt? This is Gene. Our young friend came in his own car, not a hired one or a taxi. His name is on the registration. Pale blue new Ford convertible, at present with the top down. Grey upholstery. Nevada plates, number 3711–42. I'll do the paint if I possibly can, though he may deal with it, of course; and I'll put this bug in the car. When he starts up, you'll hear him. Good luck. And for God's sake don't lose him.'

Indirectly, vaguely, I again approached the car. No one took any notice. I was merely one of the time-passing onlookers, a workman who wasn't working. Several of the children and some of their mothers had seen the state of the well-floured rooms, and thought it a dreadful shame. I leaned my ladder against the rear wing of the blue convertible, put the brushes and paint pot down casually on the flat surface of the boot, and mopped not too imaginary sweat off my face and neck.

Some of the blinds in the Clives' house had been raised, so that in places one could see into the house. No one was looking out. I stretched a hand over the side of the car with the bug in my palm, and felt its sucker cling snugly under the glove shelf.

Still no faces at the windows.

I said to the nearest little boy, 'Someone told me the intruder got in through the pantry window, round that corner.'

'No kidding?' he said, his eyes wide.

'Sure thing.'

He told his mother. They went to look. Nearly everyone followed them, especially as someone nudged the press photographer, who said he would take a picture.

I took a last comprehensive look at the windows, turned to walk away, and with a quick backward flip of a gloved hand, tipped over the can of paint. The lid came off. The can rolled slowly across the flat top of the boot and clanked heavily to the ground. The result was a bright broad spreading pool of yellow on blue, and a proper lake on the gravel.

I was out on the road when the first child saw it and ran after me.

'Your paint's tipped over, mister.'

'Yeah, I know. Don't touch it. Don't let anyone touch it, huh? I'm just going to fetch the stuff to get it off.'

He nodded importantly and ran back, and I made it safely along to the hired car, and drove away in peace towards Las Vegas, taking off the useful cap and gloves as I went. Back at the motel I showered, changed, packed, and paid my account; drove to the airport and returned the car to the Hertz agent: kept a very wary eye open in case Matt Clive had decided to travel by air; ate a much needed sandwich, and caught the first plane out to Los Angeles.

When I collected the car keys at the inquiry desk, there was a note from Walt as well.

You're one great crazy guy. And don't think I don't realize what you risked. If you're reading this, I guess you've made it, and aren't behind bars. My pal in the CIA told me you could be relied on to do mad things, and boy, he was right. What do you use for nerves? Count me strictly out, next time.

Walt.

Surprised, and not ungrateful that he should have bothered, I slipped his letter into my pocket and drove into the city to look for a good place for tape

260

recorders. I managed in the end to hire for one week an elaborate recorder which would play at the ultra slow fifteen-sixteenths of an inch per second, the speed of my own, and with it sitting on the passenger seat beside me, pointed my nose towards Orpheus Farm, Los Caillos. Then I removed the full reel from the radio recorder and fixed it up with another: no one appeared to have disturbed it in its bush and boulder hiding place, and as far as I could tell, no one saw me come and go.

Lynnie and Eunice were just walking up from the beach when I got back to The Vacationer: but they both greeted me with ten degrees of frost and went straight on past, murmuring that they guessed they would see me at dinner.

Slightly puzzled, shrugging, I carried my bag and the recorder up to my room, rewound the tape I had collected, and started it to run through while I took off my city suit and turned the air-conditioning to high.

Yola rang up, in great agitation. The houseboy answered, and went to tell Offen, who was still in bed. By great good fortune the houseboy neglected to go back to replace the downstairs receiver when Offen lifted the bedroom extension, and the bug in consequence had picked up the whole conversation.

'I've had a call from the cops in Vegas . . .'

'Don't shout, Yola. I'm not deaf.'

She didn't listen. 'Some vandals have wrecked the

house at Pitts.' She really minded: there was grief as well as anger in her voice.

'How do you mean, wrecked?'

'They say everything in the house has been thrown on the floor, and flour and sugar and stuff have been tipped over everything. They want to know what's been stolen, they want me or better Matt to go down there and deal with it . . . and I can't, Uncle Bark, I simply can't. We've got thirty-two people in, and I can't possibly get away. Matt will have to go.'

'But Matt . . .'

'Sure,' she wailed. 'Do you think I don't *know*? But he'll have to. Those horses won't die if he leaves them for a few hours. It's much farther for me, I'd be away at least two days. It's *hopeless*. Everything's gone wrong since we took that damn Chrysalis.'

'And if you remember,' Culham James said tartly, 'that was your and Matt's idea. I always said it was too soon after the last one. You and Matt have been too greedy ever since you found out.'

'Relatives ought to share their good luck, not to keep it to themselves.'

'So you're always saying.'

Nothing like a little blackmail to cement a family together, I thought in amusement. Offen had been happy with his half million a year, it seemed: but Matt and Yola, stumbling on the honey pot, had been in a hurry for more. Impulsive, ingenious, greedy Clives; if they had only been content with a share from Showman and Allyx, Offen would never had been found out.

Yola glossed over the longstanding squabble and returned to the current disaster. 'I didn't get Matt's number. What is it?'

'I haven't got it here, it's in my book downstairs . . .'

'Well look, will you call him? Tell him to get right on over, the cops will be there waiting. Tell him to call me from there and tell me what gives . . . I can't bear it if those bastards have stolen my mink wrap . . . and there's all that money in the safe . . .'

'Better face up to it that it's gone,' Offen said, with the tiniest trace of malice.

'They might not have had time,' Yola said. 'The alarms go off when anyone goes in the den, and there isn't supposed to be time for anyone to find the safe and open it before the cops get there. We paid enough for it . . .'

It had been their bad luck that by the merest chance I had left the den until last.

Yola disconnected, and after the twenty second gap on the tape, Uncle Bark called up Matt from the downstairs telephone. Matt's comments were mostly inaudible though detectably explosive. He agreed to go to the house, but nothing Offen said gave any clue as to where Matt was at that moment. It appeared only that he was somewhere within a reasonable radius of Las Vegas, as he was going to be able to drive there, see to things at the house, and get back in time to feed the horses in the evening: which narrowed it down to somewhere in an area of roughly a hundred and fifty thousand square miles. A pocket handkerchief.

A brief telephone conversation of no interest followed and then, presumably in the afternoon, Offen had switched on his television set to watch a racing programme. As far as I could tell from spot checks, it had used up the whole of the rest of the four-hour playing time.

Sighing, I switched off, and went downstairs. Lynnie and Eunice, dressed in dazzling colours, were drinking daiquiris and watching the Pacific sunset. I got another cool welcome and monosyllabic replies to my inquiries about their day.

Finally Eunice said distantly, 'Did you have a good time in San Francisco?'

I blinked. 'Yes, thank you.'

They relapsed into a longer silence which was broken only by a waiter coming to tell me I was wanted on the telephone.

It was Walt.

'Where are you?' I said.

'Las Vegas airport.'

'How did it go?'

'You can relax,' he said comfortably. 'The horses are on a small farm in a valley in Arizona, out beyond Kingman. We landed there and I asked around some. Seems the couple who own the farm don't make much of a living, but last week they said a friend was giving them a trip to Miami, and a young fellow would be looking after the place while they were away.'

'That's great,' I said with emphasis.

'The paint made it easy. We heard him yelling blue murder when he saw it, but I guess it had dried on by then and he couldn't get it off, because it was way past midday, and I'd begun to worry that he'd gone already and we hadn't heard him or that they'd picked you up planting the bug . . . anyway, we took off when his engine started, and the yellow splash was easy to see from a height, just as you said. He went right through Las Vegas and out on to the Hoover Dam road and across into Arizona. I kept the binoculars on him and we never flew near enough for him to notice us, I'm certain of that. He went up a winding graded road into the hills south-east of Kingman, and that was it.'

'You've done marvels.'

'Oh, sure. It was simpler than we were prepared for, though. You could hear the bug pretty clearly through the helicopter's headsets as high as two thousand feet, and we could have followed him in the dark if we'd had to, especially as he had his radio on for most of the way. We could hear music and news broadcasts now and then.'

'Are you coming back tonight?'

'Yeah, there's a plane in a half hour from now. But it'll be better than midnight when I get in.'

'I'll be awake,' I said. 'And just by the way, Walt,

what did you tell Eunice and Lynnie I was doing in San Francisco?'

He cleared his throat. 'I said you had some unfinished business there.'

'What sort of business?'

'Uh . . . like . . . er . . . female.'

'Thanks,' I said sarcastically. 'You're a right pal.'

Something very like a laugh lingered in my ear as I disconnected.

CHAPTER FIFTEEN

Lynnie and Eunice talked brightly to each other over dinner and I sat making plans for the next day and didn't listen. Politely after coffee we parted for the night, and at eleven I drove out to Orpheus with a fresh reel for the receiver in the rocks, and brought back the one I had fitted earlier.

Walt came back into my room as I was running it through, and we both listened to Culham James Offen talking to Matt and then to Yola.

Yola was a better bet from our point of view, because her angry feminine voice scattered higher sound waves out of the receiver, and one could imagine Uncle Bark holding it inches away out of deference to his eardrums.

He was doing his best to soothe her. 'Matt says it could have been worse; some of these vandals have thrown molasses and preserves and even sewage around in people's houses . . .'

'He says the whole place is *covered* in flour . . . it'll take weeks to clear up.'

'It'll vacuum quite easily, won't it? It's not sticky and it doesn't stain.'

But she couldn't be consoled, even when he reminded her that the money was safe, and that her mink wrap hadn't been stolen.

'But Matt says', she wailed, 'that it was *white*.'

'Flour will shake out . . . and might even clean it.'

'You don't understand.'

'Sure I do, Yola,' he said patiently. 'You feel like it was you who was assaulted, not your house. You feel dirty and furious and you'd like to kick the bastards who did it. Sure, I know. We had thieves in here once, when your Aunt Ellen was alive. They stole all her rings, and she said it was like being raped.'

They talked about the break-in for a good while longer, and Walt raised an eyebrow and remarked that I seemed to have gotten reasonable revenge for that clap on the head.

We were both yawning by the time Offen was through for the evening. The last half hour consisted of him telling his houseboy his plans and requirements, and none of these betrayed any anxiety or uncertainty. Culham James was confident, and I was glad of it. Worried men patrol their defences.

Walt went off to bed, and although I hadn't slept at all the previous night I woke again after only three hours. The coloured lights on the outside of the motel threw prismatic reflections on the ceiling. I stared up at them, trying to make patterns and shapes, trying any silly ruse to stop my mind from nose-diving into the pit. The tug of the unfinished chase was very faint, and whether Allyx and Showman ever sired another foal seemed a matter of supreme unimportance. Fraud, theft, attempted murder . . . who cared?

I had left the Luger in its belt holster across the room on a chair. Neither the Clives nor Offen were likely to come creeping through the night to do me in, and my usual enemies were six thousand miles to the east. The only danger lay in myself, the deadliest enemy of the lot. The theory that going to bed with the gun out of reach would lessen its magnetic temptation was proving a dreary flop.

One more day, I thought in the end. Anyone could manage just one more day. If you said that firmly enough every night, one might even finish the course.

Dawn crept up on the coloured bulbs and washed them out. I took a shower and shaved, and admitted that I had seen healthier looking men than the one in my reflection.

Walt came along to my room when I was midway through orange juice and coffee at eight-thirty. 'What you need,' he said, eyeing this, 'is some good solid food.'

'I don't feel hungry.'

His eyes slid to my face and away. 'Come on down and eat with me.'

I shook my head. 'I'll wait for you.'

He wouldn't go alone. He ordered hot-cakes and eggs and coffee from room service, and we got straight down to business while he demolished them.

'It'll take two and a half days for Sam Hengelman to get to Kingman,' I said.

He nodded with his mouth full.

'He was starting early this morning,' I went on, 'I called him last night, after you'd been through from Las Vegas. He's driving the van himself, and he's coming alone. That means his journey time will be longer, but it seemed better that way from the secrecy point of view.'

'Did you tell him it was another snatch?' Walt said doubtfully.

I smiled. 'I engaged him to come and collect a horse belonging to Dave Teller. He asked if we were likely to be collecting this one in a lonely place at night, and I said yes, we probably would.'

'And he didn't back out?'

'He merely remarked that he had no great objection to an easy buck if I would assure him he couldn't go to jail for it.'

Walt wiped errant egg off his chin. 'And could he?'

'I couldn't tell him it was impossible. Odds of a thousand to one, I said. He said a thousand bucks against one chance of going to jail wasn't enough.'

Walt laughed. 'So how much is he coming for?'

'Fifteen hundred, plus the normal hiring fee, plus expenses.'

'Not bad for one week's work.' He paused, stirring sugar, then said tentatively, 'What do you get out of this yourself?'

'Me?' I said in surprise. 'I've no idea. Three weeks' heatwave instead of the English summer . . .'

'Didn't you negotiate a fee?'

'No.'

'How come?'

'It didn't occur to me.'

His face crinkled into a mixture of emotions with what appeared to be amazement and pity coming out on top.

'How about you?' I said.

'I'm not on vacation,' he pointed out. 'I get a pretty good salary, and also a cut of everything I save the company.'

'So Chrysalis has been worth the extra work?'

'At a million and a half, are you kidding?' Walt looked at me earnestly. 'Look, Gene, I'm going to give you one half of that cut . . .'

'No,' I said, interrupting. 'I don't want it.'

'You know darned well I wouldn't have found that horse, not in a million years. Nor got him back alive so quickly. And as for these other two . . .'

'You keep it for your kids,' I said. 'But thanks, anyway.'

He would have gone on insisting, but I wouldn't

listen, and after two attempts he gave it up. In the back of my mind, as I outlined what I suggested we should do next, there lingered a bitter suspicion that I hadn't accepted his gift because it would be a selfish waste if I didn't stick around to spend it. I had rejected any strings of conscience tying me to life. The death-seeking force was up to another of its tricks.

'A pincer movement, I think,' I said. 'Or rather, a simultaneous attack on two fronts.'

'Huh?'

'Keep Culham James Offen's attention riveted on the Moviemaker and Centigrade he has on his farm while we spirit away the others.'

'Er, quite,' Walt agreed.

'You can take Offen,' I said.

'And you take the horses?'

I nodded. Walt considered what might happen if we exchanged roles, and didn't argue.

'What are the chances of finding out which company Matt insures the Las Vegas house with?'

Walt thought about it. 'Our agent there might be able to. But why?'

'I . . . er . . . would rather take those horses when I know Matt is safely away.'

Walt smiled.

'So,' I went on, 'it shouldn't be too difficult to get him to go back to the house on Pitts. Say for instance his insurance company required him to make an inspection of his security arrangements and sign some document or other, before they would renew full cover? We know from the telephone calls to Offen that Matt and Yola have a safe in the den with a lot of money in it. Matt won't want to be uninsured for more than a minute, after having one break-in already.'

'We couldn't ask his company to do that . . .' Walt paused and looked at me with suspicion.

'Quite right,' I nodded. 'You can. You know all the jargon. As soon as we hear from Sam Hengelman that he has reached the Arizona border, you can start the spiel on Matt.'

'From here?'

'Yes. Ask him what time would be convenient for him, but try to manoeuvre him into coming late in the afternoon or early evening, say six or seven. Then it would be dark when he got home, and late, which should hamper him a bit when he finds the horses are gone . . . he might even stop off in Las Vegas for a couple of hours at the tables.'

Walt said thoughtfully, 'I reckon I'd better go to the house on Pittsville and meet him.'

'No,' I said abruptly.

He looked at me. 'You'd thought of it?'

'You are not going anywhere near Matt Clive.'

'And why not?'

'You want a split skull or something?'

'Like webbed feet.' The smiled hovered. 'All the same, what is Matt going to do when he arrives at his house and no insurance man turns up? What would

273

you do? Call the company, I guess. And then what? He discovers no one in the company knows anything about him having to come back to the house, and he starts thinking like crazy. And if I were him I'd call the local cops and get them whizzing out to the farm for a look-see. You didn't see the road there from Kingman. But I did. There are no turnings off it for the last ten miles to the farm. What if you met the cops head on, you and Sam Hengelman and two stolen horses?'

'He wouldn't risk calling in cops.'

'He might reckon that if he was losing everything anyway, he'd make sure you went down as well. And I mean down.'

Every instinct told me not to let Walt meet Matt Clive.

'Suppose he won't make a late appointment?' he said. 'When I grant most of the company would have gone home, and it would be more difficult to check. Suppose he insists on three in the afternoon, or even the next morning? Do you want to snatch those horses by day?'

'Not much. But it would take him at least two hours each way. Add an hour for waiting and checking. Even if he called the police, it wouldn't be for three hours after he left home. We'd have been gone with the horses for two of those.'

Walt obstinately shook his head. 'The limits are too narrow. A horse van won't be liable to do better than thirty miles an hour on the farm road, if that much. You have to go into Kingman, which is in the opposite direction from Kentucky, and then round and across Arizona . . . there aren't too many roads in that state, it's mostly desert. The police could find you too easily.'

'Down through Phoenix . . .'

'The road to Phoenix twists through mountains, with hairpin curves most of the way.'

'I don't want you walking into an empty house with Matt Clive.'

He looked at me without expression. 'But you would go. If he didn't know you, I mean.'

'That's different.'

'How?' he said, half insulted, half challenging.

I looked at him sideways. 'I bet I can run faster than you.'

His forehead relaxed. 'You're in pretty good shape, I'll give you that. All the same, I'm going to Las Vegas.'

He'd manoeuvred me into not being able to persuade him against it on the grounds of safety; and from all other points of view it was a good idea. Against my instinct I agreed in the end that he should go.

'I'll drift on out tomorrow and look at the farm beyond Kingman,' I said. 'I suppose you couldn't see whether there were any other horses there besides the two we're after?'

He looked startled. 'You mean there might be another identification problem?'

'Perhaps. Though I'd say it's certain our two have Moviemaker's and Centigrade's stud book numbers tattooed inside their mouths. They would have to, to satisfy visiting grooms, for instance, that their mares were being mated with the right stallion. But I've never seen then . . . Showman and Allyx. If there are other horses there, it'll simply mean going round peering into all their mouths until I find the right ones.'

Walt raised his eyes to heaven. 'You make everything sound so darned easy. Like it's only five miles to the top of Everest, and everyone can walk five miles, can't they?'

Smiling, I asked him for precise directions to the farm, and he told me.

'And now this end . . .' I said. 'How many strings can you pull with the Los Angeles fraud squad?'

'Not many,' he said. 'I don't know anyone out there.'

'But with Buttress Life behind you?'

He sighed. 'I suppose you want me to go and dip my toes in the water?'

'Jump right in,' I agreed. 'Talk your way to the top chap, and tell him Buttress Life suspect that Moviemaker and Centigrade are Showman and Allyx. Get everything nicely stirred up. Make Offen prove beyond any doubt that the two horses at Orpheus literally are Moviemaker and Centigrade.'

He nodded. 'OK. I'll start this morning. Have to go a little carefully, though, or Offen will come up so fast with a libel suit that we'll wonder what hit us.'

'You must be used to ducking.'

'Yeah.'

I gave him the page Miss Britt had written out for me in Lexington.

'Here are the figures. No one can question these, not even Offen. You might find them useful in getting the law moving.'

He tucked the paper into his pocket and nodded, and shortly after, with the habitual martyred sigh, levered himself out of his chair and ambled on his way.

I sat and thought for a while but got nowhere new. There was going to be little else for me to do but wait and watch for the next few days while Sam Hengelman rolled his way two thousand miles across the continent.

When I went down to lunch I found Eunice and Lynnie sitting in cool bright dresses under the dappled shade of the sea-facing terrace. Their hair was glossy and neat, their big earrings gently swinging, their legs smooth and tanned, the whites of their eyes a detergent white.

They didn't get the lingering scrutiny they deserved. With them, equally crisp, equally at ease, sat Culham James Offen, Uncle Bark.

All three seemed a scrap disconcerted when I folded myself gently on to the fourth chair round the low table on which stood their long frosted drinks.

Offen and I nodded to each other. There was still in his manner the superior, self-satisfied amusement he had treated me with at his house. Reassuring. Lynnie smiled, but with a quick sidelong glance at Eunice to make sure such treachery hadn't been noticed. Eunice had on an 'I-am-your-employer's-wife' face, which didn't wipe from my mind, nor hers, I imagine, the memory of the fluffy pink wrapper.

'We thought you'd gone to LA with Walt,' Lynnie said.

Eunice gave her a sharp glance which she didn't see. 'We ran into Mr Offen in the lobby here, wasn't that extraordinary?'

'Extraordinary,' I agreed.

Offen's white eyebrows went up and down in an embarrassment he couldn't entirely smother.

'It sure has been a pleasure,' he said, 'to get to know you folks better.' He spoke exclusively to Eunice, however.

She had warmed again to the charm he had switched on for her, and gave me the tag end of a scornful glance. How could I, she inferred, imagine this nice influential citizen could be a crook.

'How are Matt and Yola these days?' I said conversationally.

Offen visibly jumped, and a blight fell on the party. 'Such charming young people,' I said benignly, and watched Eunice remembering what had happened to Dave, and also perhaps what Walt had told her about their attack on me. 'Your nephew and niece, I believe?'

Offen's pale blue eyes were the least impressive

feature in his tanned face with its snow-white frame. I read in them a touch of wariness, and wondered whether in prodding Eunice to face reality I had disturbed his complacency too far.

'They would sure like to meet you again,' he said slowly, and the heavy ill-feeling behind the words curdled finally for Eunice his milk-of-human-kindness image.

'Are you expecting them within the next few days?' I asked, dropping in the merest touch of anxiety.

He said he wasn't, and his inner amusement abruptly returned. I had succeeded in convincing him I would be trying to remove his horses from Orpheus pretty soon now; and shortly afterwards he got purposefully to his feet, bent a beaming smile on Eunice, a smaller one on Lynnie and a smug one on me, and made an important exit through the motel.

After a long pause Eunice said flatly, 'I guess I was wrong about that guy being sweet.'

We ate an amicable lunch and spent the afternoon on the beach under a fringed umbrella, with the bright green-blue Pacific hissing gently on the sand. Out on the rollers the golden boys rode their surfboards, and flat by my side little Lynnie sighed to the bottom of her lungs with contentment.

'I wish this could go on for ever,' she said.

'So do I.'

Eunice, on the other side of Lynnie, propped herself

up on one elbow. 'I'm going to take a dip,' she said. 'Coming?'

'In a minute,' Lynnie said lazily, and Eunice went alone. We watched her tight well-shaped figure walk unwaveringly down to the water, and Lynnie said what I was thinking. 'She hardly drinks at all now.'

'You're good for her.'

'Oh sure.' She laughed gently, stretching like a cat. 'Isn't this heat just gorgeous?'

'Mm.'

'What are all those scars on you?'

'Lions and tigers and appendicitis.'

She snorted. 'Shall we go in and swim?'

'In a minute. What did you and Eunice and Offen say to each other before I arrived?'

'Oh . . .' She sounded bored. 'He wanted to know what you were doing. Eunice told him you and Walt were cooking something up but she didn't really know what. And . . . er . . . yes . . . he asked if Walt was really an insurance man, and Eunice said he was . . . and he asked other things about you, what your job was and so on, and why you were out here with us . . .'

'Did Eunice tell him I got her to show him that photograph on purpose? Did she tell him that I was certain that the horses he has at Orpheus Farm are Moviemaker and Centigrade?'

Lynnie shook her head.

'You're quite sure?'

'Yes, absolutely. Would it have been a nuisance if we had?'

'A fair way to being disastrous.'

'Don't worry then. He was only here about a quarter of an hour before you came down, and all Eunice said was that you were er . . . er . . . well her actual words were, some dim bloody little office worker on vacation.' Lynnie laughed. 'She said her husband had been grateful to you for saving his life and was paying your bill here, and that all you seemed to be interested in at present was a girl up in San Francisco.'

I looked down to where Eunice's head bobbed in the surf and wondered whether she'd given him perfect answers from design or bitchiness.

'What's she like?' Lynnie said.

'Who?'

'The girl in San Francisco.'

'You'd better ask Walt,' I said, turning my head to look at her. 'He invented her.'

She gasped and laughed in one. 'Oh good! I mean . . . er . . . then what were you really doing?'

'Ah, well,' I said. 'Now that's something I'd hate Eunice to have told Culham Offen.'

She lay looking back at me steadily for several seconds. So much more assurance, I thought idly, than on that day on the river, when she had still been a child.

'Is that why you've told us practically nothing? Don't you trust her?'

'She's never wanted the horses back.'

Lynnie blinked. 'But she wouldn't . . . she wouldn't have ruined on purpose what you're trying to do. After all, you're doing it for her husband.'

I smiled and she sat up abruptly and put her arms round her knees.

'You make me feel so . . . *naïve*.'

'You', I said, 'are adorable.'

'And now you're laughing at me.'

I wanted impulsively to say that I loved her, but I wasn't sure that it was true. Maybe all I wanted was an antedote to depression. She was certainly the best I'd found.

'I'm going away again in the morning,' I said.

'To San Francisco?'

'Somewhere like that.'

'How long for?'

'Two nights.'

'This is your last week,' she said, looking out to sea.

The thought leapt involuntarily, *if only it were* . . . I shook my head abruptly, as if one could empty the brain by force, and climbed slowly up on to my feet.

'There's today, anyway,' I said, smiling. 'Let's go and get wet.'

Walt came back at seven with dragging feet and a raging thirst.

'Those detectives from the DA's office will scalp me if they find out we're only using them,' he said gloomily, up in my room. 'Two of them have agreed to go out to Orpheus Farm tomorrow, and I'm meeting them on the LA road to show them the way. Day after tomorrow, some guy from the bloodstock registry office is going out. I got the DA's office to call him and fix it.'

'Couldn't be better.'

Walt recharged his batteries with Old Grandad and said, 'So what's new with you?'

'Offen came here on a fact-finding mission.'

'He did *what*?'

'Came looking for answers. Got some real beauties from Eunice which won't help him any, and went away believing we'd be back on his doorstep pretty soon.'

'I guess', Walt said, 'that he wanted to know if we'd called it off and gone home, and whether it was safe to bring those horses back again. It's days since he saw any sign of us. Must have been like sitting on an H-bomb with a tricky firing pin.' He swallowed appreciatively and rolled his tongue over his gums. 'He'll get all the action he wants, tomorrow.'

When he plodded tiredly off to shower before dinner, I telephoned Jeff Roots.

'How was Miami?' I said.

'Hot and horrible, and I gained four pounds.'

283

Commiserating, I thanked him for his help with the newspaper files and told him that owing to Miss Britt we had found the two stallions.

'I wish I didn't believe it. Are you certain?'

'Yes.'

His sigh was heartfelt. 'We'd better start proceedings . . .'

'I've . . . er . . . already started them. We may in a day or two have two horses on our hands which will need to be stabled somewhere eminently respectable while their identity is being investigated. Owing to the length of time they've been lost, it may take a couple of months to re-establish them. Where would you think it would be best to put them?'

After a pause, he said, 'I suppose you're asking me to have them here?'

'Not really,' I explained. 'Too much of a coincidence after Chrysalis, perhaps. I'd thought rather of a more official place . . . I don't know what you have.'

'I'll think of something.' He coughed slightly. 'There won't be anything illegal about their recovery?'

'No more than for Chrysalis.'

'That's no answer.'

'There shouldn't be any trouble with the police,' I said.

'I guess that'll have to do,' he sighed. 'When do I expect them?'

'If all goes well, they should reach Lexington on Sunday.'

'And if all doesn't go well?'
'You'll have no problem.'
He laughed. 'And you?'
'One more won't matter.'

CHAPTER SIXTEEN

For most of thirty hours I sat in the mountainous Arizona desert and looked down at Matt Clive leading a boring life.

Like his sister, he was capable, quick, efficient. He watered the stock and mended a fence, swept out the house and fed the hens; and spent a great deal of time in the largest barn on the place.

I had found myself a perch among the rocks on the east-facing side of the valley, half a mile off the dusty road to the farm. At nearly three thousand feet above sea level the heat was bearable, though the midday sun blazed down from nearly straight overhead, and eggs would have fried on the sidewalks if there had been any. Desert plants were designed to save themselves and no one else: at my back grew a large agave, its central stem rising six feet high with flat outspreading flowers turning from red to brilliant yellow. For leaves it had razor-sharp spikes springing outwards from the ground in one large clump. Stiff; angular; not a vestige of shade. The spindly buckhorn and the flat devil's fingers would have been pretty useless to a midget. I folded myself under the overhang of a jagged boulder and inched round with the meagre shade patch until the sun cried quits behind the hill.

Showman and Allyx had to be in the big barn: though I saw no sign of them, nor of any other horses, on the first afternoon.

By air to Las Vegas and hired car to Kingman had taken me all morning, and at the last fork on the way to the farm I'd had to decide whether to risk meeting Matt head on on the road or to walk ten miles instead. I'd risked it. Ten miles there was also ten miles back. The car had bumped protestingly off the road two miles short of his farm, and was now out of sight in a gulley.

Binoculars brought every detail of the meagre spread up clear and sharp. The small dilapidated house lay to the left, with the big barn on the right across a large dusty yard. Along most of a third side of the rough quadrangle stretched an uneven jumble of simple stone buildings, and behind those the rusting guts of two abandoned cars lay exposed to the sky.

Maintenance was at a minimum: no endemic prosperity here. The owners scratched for a living in a tiny valley among the Arizona hills, existing there only by courtesy of the quirk of rock formation which had brought underground water to the surface in a spring. The small river bed was easy to follow from where I sat: grass and trees circled its origin, sparse paddocks stretched away to sagging fences on each side of its upper reaches, a corn patch grew beside it near the farm buildings, and lower down it ran off into the desert in a dry wide shallow sandy trough. Heavy rain would turn it every time into a raging torrent, as destructive as it was vital. High behind the house, dominating the whole place, a huge onion-shaped water storage tank sat squatly on top of a spindly looking tower.

Mile after mile of plain dark poles stretched along the road to the farm, carrying an electric cable and a telephone wire, but civilization had fallen short of refuse collection. A sprawling dump at one side of the big barn seemed to consist of a brass bedstead, half a tractor, a bottomless tin bath, the bones of an old wagon, a tangled heap of unidentifiable rusting metal, and roughly fifty treadless tyres of varying sizes. Filling every crevice among this lot were bottles and empty food cans with labels peeling and jagged lids mutely open like mouths. Over the top the air shimmered with reflected heat.

Matt had already spent at least a week in this ugly oasis. Walt shouldn't find it too hard to persuade him to make an evening visit to Las Vegas.

I watched until long after dark. Lights went on and off in the house, and Matt moved about, visible through the insect screens because he didn't draw any curtains. If, indeed, there were any.

Cautiously at some time after one o'clock, when all

the lights on my side of the house had been out for more than two hours, I picked my way down to the farm. The night was still warm, but as the only light came from the stars it was black dark on the ground, and with agave clumps in mind I reckoned my torch held lesser risk.

I reached the farmyard. Nothing stirred. Quietly, slowly, I made the crossing to the barn. Matt in the house slept on.

No padlocks: not even bolts. There weren't any. The wide door of the barn stood open; and with this invitation, I went in. Inside, the barn was divided into six stalls along one side, with feed bins and saddlery storage racks along the other. Here and everywhere else dilapidation and decay were winning hands down: everything my torch flicked over looked in need of help.

Four of the stalls were empty, but in the two central ones, side by side, stood two horses. Gently, so as not to frighten them, I went over, talking soothingly in a murmur and shining the torch beam on the wall in front of their heads. Their eyes in the dim light rolled round inquiringly, but neither gave more than a single stamp of alarm.

The first one tried to back away when I shone the torch into his mouth: but an exceedingly strong looking head collar and a remarkably new chain kept him from going more than a few feet. I ran my hand down his neck and talked to him, and in the end got my inspection done. The tattooed mark, as often, was none too clear: but discernibly it was 752:07. The registration of Moviemaker.

The tattoo on the second horse was more recent and also clearer: the registration number of Centigrade.

Satisfied, I gave them each a friendly slap, and with great care left the barn. Matt still slept. I hesitated, thinking that enough was enough, but in the end went down to the end of the farmyard to take a quick look through the other buildings. In one only, a deep narrow garage, was there anything of interest: a car.

It was not Matt's pale blue convertible, but a tinny black saloon three or four years old. My flashlight picked out a piece of paper lying on the passenger seat, and I opened the door and took a look at it. A copy of a work sheet from a garage in Kingman. Customer's name: Clive. Work required: Remove yellow paint from Ford convertible. Further instructions: Complete as soon as possible.

I put the paper back on the seat and shone the light over the dashboard. A small metal plate screwed on to it bore the name of the garage in Kingman: Matt had rented this car while his own was being cleaned.

Outside, everything was still, and feeling like a shadow among shadows I went quietly out of the farmyard and along the dusty road towards Kingman. It seemed a lot farther than two miles to the flat stones I had left one on top of the other as a marker, and even after I had reached them it took me quite a while to find the hidden car and get it back on to the road.

It was well after three when I called Walt. He sounded resigned, but he'd known it would be some time in the night.

'Are they there?' he said.

'They are. They're quite unguarded, and there's only Matt on the place. How about things your end?'

'Oh.' Amusement crept in. 'Offen was full of offended dignity. Didn't know how anyone could suggest he was engaged in fraud; that sort of thing. It didn't impress the DA's squad at all, because they get that sort of bluster every time. Made them all the keener, if anything. They had quite a long session with him, all fairly polite but definitely needling. Artists, they are. From our point of view Offen said nothing significant except for one little gem. The DA's guys asked to see the stud groom. That's Kiddo, remember? The one who told us about the mares foaling at night?'

'I remember,' I said.

'Well, it seems it's a slow time around studs just now, and Kiddo went off on vacation the day after our first visit.'

'He didn't say anything about that when we were there.'

'He sure didn't. Offen says Kiddo will be back in three weeks. By then, I guess, he expects to have had Moviemaker and Centigrade identified as themselves, and then when the dust has settled he can bring

Showman and Allyx quietly back, and it'll be safe for Kiddo to return. I guess Offen didn't know which way he'd jump, and booted him off out of trouble.'

'I'm sure you're right,' I said. 'Anything interesting on the tape?'

'I've been listening to that damned machine until I'm bored to death with it,' he said wearily. 'Today's run was mostly the DA's men talking to Offen, so I heard all that twice over. He then called both Yola and Matt and told them about it, and he sounded pretty pleased with the way things were going. I'd say Matt was a mite annoyed at having to stay where he is: Offen was telling him not to be stupid, what was a week or two with so much at stake. Also Yola must be wanting Matt back, because Offen smoothed her down with the same spiel.' Walt paused and cleared his throat. 'What would you say is the relationship between Matt and Yola?'

Smiling into the receiver I said, 'Such thoughts, Walt, from you!'

'It's possible . . .' he said uncomfortably.

'It sure is. But there's nothing to indicate it except for their not being married.'

'Then you don't think . . .?'

'I'd say they're certainly centred on each other, but how far it goes I couldn't guess. The only time I've seen them together they've had their hands full of punts and guns.'

'Yeah . . . well, maybe crime is how it takes them.'

I agreed that it probably was, and asked him if he'd got Matt set up for the insurance meeting.

'I sure have,' he said with satisfaction. 'I called him this afternoon. It must have been soon after he'd been talking to Offen, I guess, because he seemed to be glad enough to be given a reason for going to Las Vegas. I suggested six PM which sounded all right, but he himself asked if I could make it later.'

'He'll probably want to feed the horses about then, when the day gets cooler,' I said. 'And those horses would come first.'

'Yeah. At three million for two, they sure would. It beats me why he doesn't guard them every minute.'

'Against what?' I said.

'You got a point,' he conceded. 'Only us. And we're obviously concentrating on the two at Orpheus. Right?'

'Right.'

'Anyway, Matt said could I make it later than six, and we agreed in the end on nine. That should mean he'll take that gander at the roulette tables on his way home, and maybe give us most of the night to get the horses clear.'

'Good,' I said. 'That's fine. But Walt . . .'

'Yes?'

'Take care.'

'Go teach your grandmother,' he said, and I smiled wryly and asked him if he'd heard from Sam Hengelman.

'Sure, he called this evening, like you asked. He'd reached Santa Rosa in New Mexico and he was going on to Albuquerque before stopping for the night. He said he'd be in Kingman by four or five tomorrow afternoon . . . today, I suppose, technically . . . and he'll meet you at the Mojave Motel. I told him the return trip wouldn't be starting before eight, so he's going to take a room there and catch a couple of hours' sleep.'

'Thanks, Walt, that's great,' I said.

'We're all set, then?' There was a hint of unease in his voice, and it raised prickles again in my early warning mechanism.

'You don't have to go to Las Vegas,' I said reasonably. 'We've time enough without it.'

'I'm going,' he said. 'And that's that.'

'Well . . . all right. I think we could do with a checkpoint, though, in case anything goes wrong. Let's say you wait in the lobby of the Angel Inn from eight to eight-thirty tomorrow evening. That's where I stayed. It's right on the edge of Las Vegas, but it's an easy trip to Pittsville Boulevard. I'll call you there sometime during that half hour; and if I don't, you stay put, and don't go out to Matt's house.'

'OK,' he said, and although he tried, there was distinct relief in his voice.

We disconnected, and I ate a sandwich and drank coffee at an all night lunch counter at the bus station before returning to my hired car and pointing its nose again towards the farm and the hills. The two flat stones came up again in the headlights, and re-stowing the car in its former hiding place, I finished the journey on foot.

Back in the shelter of the same jagged rock I tried for a time to sleep. There was still an hour or more before dawn, and the sun wouldn't be too hot for a while after that, but in spite of knowing that I'd get no rest at all during the following night, my brain stayed obstinately awake. I supposed an inability to sleep on open ground surrounded by cacti and within yelling distance of a man who'd kill me if he had a chance could hardly be classed as insomnia in the ordinary way: but I had no illusions. That was precisely what it was. The restless, racing thoughts, the electrical awareness, the feeling that everything in one's body was working full steam ahead and wouldn't slow down; I knew all the symptoms much too well. One could lie with eyes shut and relax every muscle until one couldn't tell where one's arms and legs were, and still sleep wouldn't come. Breathe deeply, count all the sheep of Canterbury, repeat once-learnt verses; nothing worked.

The sun came up and shone in my eyes. Inching out of its revealing spotlight I retreated round the side of the rock and looked down to the farm through the binoculars. No movement. At five-thirty Matt was still in bed.

I put down the glasses and thought about a cigarette. There were only four left in the packet. Sighing,

I reflected that I could easily have bought some in Kingman, if I'd given it a thought. It was going to be a long day. All I'd brought with me beside the binoculars was a bottle of water, a pair of sunglasses, and the Luger in my belt.

At seven-thirty Matt came out through the rickety screen door of the house, and stood in the yard stretching and looking around at the cloudless cobalt blue sky. Then he went across to the barn and poked his head briefly inside.

Satisfied that the gold was still in the bank, he fetched buckets of water and joined it for long enough to muck out the stalls and see to the feed. After a time he came out with a barrowful of droppings and wheeled it away to empty on the far side of the barn, out of my sight.

The hens got their grits, and the calves in a near compound their ration of water, and Matt retired for his breakfast. The morning wore on. The temperature rose. Nothing else happened.

At noon I stood up for a while behind the rock to stretch my legs and restore some feeling to the bits that were numb from sitting. I drank some water and smoked a cigarette, and put on the sunglasses to circumvent a hovering glare headache: and having exhausted my repertoire except for a few shots from the Luger, folded myself back into the wedge of slowly moving shade, and took another look at the farm.

Status quo entirely unchanged. Maybe Matt was

asleep, or telephoning, or watching television, or inventing systems for his trip to Las Vegas. He certainly was not doing much farming. Nor did he apparently propose to exercise the horses. They stayed in their stalls from dawn to dusk.

By two I knew intimately every spiny plant growing within a radius of ten feet of my rock, and found my eyes going far oftener to the broad sweep of desert on my left than to the dirty little farm below. The desert was clean in its way, and fierce, and starkly beautiful. All hills and endless sky. Parched sandy grey dust and scratchy cactus. Killing heat. A wild, uncompromising, lonely place.

When I first felt the urge just to get up and walk away into it I dragged my eyes dutifully back to the farm and smoked the second cigarette and thought firmly about Matt and the horses. That only worked for a while. The barren country pulled like a magnet.

I had only to walk out there, I thought, and keep on going until I was filled with its emptiness, and then sit down somewhere and put the barrel of the Luger against my head, and simply squeeze. So childishly easy; so appallingly tempting.

Walt, I thought desperately. I couldn't do it because of Walt and the unfinished business we were embarked on. The horses were there in front of me, and Walt and Sam Hengelman were on their way. It was impossible just to abandon them. I hit my hand against the rock and dragged my mind back to the farm and the night ahead. And when I'd gone through that piece by piece I concentrated one at a time on Yola and Offen, and Eunice and Dave Teller, and Keeble and Lynnie, trying to use them as pegs to keep me believing that what I did mattered to them. That anything I did mattered to anybody. That I cared whether anything I did mattered to anybody.

My hand had been bleeding. I hadn't even felt it. I looked dispassionately at the scraped skin, and loathed myself. I shut my eyes, and the desolation went so deep that for an unmeasurable age I felt dizzy with it, as if I were in some fearful pitch black limbo, with no help, no hope, and no escape. Spinning slowly down an endless shaft in solitary despair. Lost.

The spinning stopped, after a while. The internal darkness stayed.

I opened my eyes and looked down at the farm, only half seeing it, feeling myself trembling and knowing that there wasn't much farther to go.

Matt came out of the house, walked across the yard, took a look into the barn, and retraced his steps. I watched him in a disorientated haze: those horses in the barn, what did they matter? What did anything matter? Who cared a sixpenny damn about blood lines, it would all be the same in a hundred years.

Dave Teller cared.

Let him.

Dave Teller cared a ten thousand dollar damn what happened to them.

Crystal clear, like distilled water logic, it occurred to me that I could give us both what we wanted if I postponed my walk into the desert until later that night. I would pack the horses off with Hengelman, and instead of driving back to Kingman after him, I would set off on foot, and when it was nearly dawn, and everything looked grey and shadowy, and the step would be small ... then ...

Then.

I felt, immediately after making this firm decision, which seemed to me extremely sensible, a great invasion of peace. No more struggle, no more fuss. My body felt relaxed and full of well-being, and my mind was calm. I couldn't think why such an obvious solution hadn't occurred to me before. All the sweat and sleeplessness had dissolved into a cool, inner, steady light.

This stage lasted until I remembered that I had once been determined not to reach it.

After that, creeping in little by little, came the racking conviction that I had merely surrendered, and was not only despicable but probably insane.

I sat for a while with my head in my hands, fearfully expecting that with the false peace broken up and gone, back would come the shattering vertigo.

It didn't. There was only so great a tiredness that what I'd called tiredness before was like a pinhead on a continent. The dreary fight was on again; but at least I'd survived the bloodiest battle yet. Touched bottom and come back. I felt that after this I really could climb right out, if I went on trying.

A long way to go. But then, I'd have all the time I needed.

CHAPTER SEVENTEEN

I had cramp right down both legs. Matt came out of
the house and I woke up to find that the shade patch
had moved round while I hadn't. When he went into
the barn I started to shift the necessary two yards and
found my muscles in knots.

The shade wasn't much cooler, but much better
cover. I sat in it waiting for Matt to come out of the
barn and for my legs to unlock. What they needed
was for me to get to my feet and stamp about: but if
Matt caught sight of anyone moving so close to him
the whole project would lie in ruins.

He fetched water for the horses, for the calves, and
for the hens. I looked at my watch, and was horribly
startled to see it was nearly six. It couldn't be, I
thought; but it was. Four hours since I last checked.
Four hours. I shivered in the roasting air.

Matt brought the empty muck barrow around and
into the barn, and came out with it filled. For the
whole afternoon I'd fallen down on the surveillance,
but looking back I was fairly sure nothing had changed

at the farm. Certainly at this point things were as they had been: Matt had no helpers and no visitors, and when he left for Las Vegas the horses would be alone. For that piece of certainty I had been prepared to watch all day, and a poor job I'd made of it.

Matt shut the barn door and went into the house. Half an hour later he came out in a cream-coloured jacket and dark trousers, a transformation from his habitual jeans and a checked shirt. He opened the doors of the shed containing the car, went inside, started up, and drove out across the yard, round the bend on to the road, and away over the desert towards Kingman.

Satisfied, I finally got to my feet. The cramps had gone. I plodded tiredly off to the two-mile distant hidden car, and wished the night was over, not beginning. I hadn't enough energy to lick a stamp.

Matt's dust had settled when I followed him along the empty road, but when I got into Kingman he was still there. With shock I saw him standing outside a garage I was passing, and I drew into the kerb fifty yards on and looked back. The black saloon he had hired and his own blue Ford were both standing there in the forecourt. An overalled girl attendant was filling the Ford's tank from the pump, and Matt was looking in snatches at his watch and exhibiting impatience. Seven-twenty; and a hundred miles to Las Vegas. He would be a few minutes late for his appointment with Walt.

Slumping down in my seat I fixed the driving mirror so that I could watch him. He paid the girl for the petrol and hopped into his car over the top, without opening the door. Then he pulled out on to the road, turned in my direction, and went past me with his foot impressively on the accelerator. I gently followed for a while at a respectable distance, content to keep him only just in sight, and turned back to the town once he was conclusively topping the speed limit on Route 93 to Las Vegas.

Outside the unprosperous looking Mojave Motel Sam Hengelman's horse van took up a sixth of the parking space. Inside, they told me that he had arrived at four-thirty and was along in Room 6, sleeping. I left him to it, because we couldn't move anyway until I'd phoned Walt at eight, and went into the bus station for some coffee. It came in a plastic carton out of an automat, black but weak. I drank it without tasting and thought about some food, but I wasn't really hungry enough to bother, and I was too dirty and unshaven for anywhere good. Until after eight I sat on the bus station bench staring into space, and then used the bus station telephone to get through to Walt.

He came on the line with little delay.

'How's things?' he said.

'Matt left Kingman for Las Vegas at seven-thirty, so he will be a little late.'

'Left Kingman?' Walt sounded surprised.

I explained about Matt changing cars.

'I suppose his Ford wasn't quite ready when he got there. Anyway, he's coming in that, not the hired one.'

'Are you all right?' Walt said hesitantly.

'Of course.'

'You don't sound it.'

'Sam Hengelman's here,' I said, ignoring him. 'He's asleep along at the Mojave Motel. We'll start as soon as I get back there and wake him up.'

'It's all safe at the farm?' He seemed anxious.

'Deserted,' I assured him. 'Has been all yesterday, all last night, and all today. No one around but Matt. Stop worrying. You just see Matt and put on your act, and then head straight back to Santa Barbara. As soon as Sam's clear of the area I'll follow you. See you for breakfast about twelve hours from now.'

'Right,' he said. 'Well . . . keep your nose clean.'

'You too.'

'Sure thing. It's not me that's nuts.'

The line clicked clear before I found an answer, and it left me with a vague feeling that there was more I should have said, though I didn't know what.

I knocked on Sam's door at the motel, and he came sleepily stretching to switch on the light and let me in.

'With you in a minute,' he said, reaching for his shoes and looking round for his tie.

'Sam, you don't have to come.'

'Eh?'

'Go back to sleep. I'll go and fetch the horses. That way you won't be so involved.'

He sat on the edge of the bed looking down at the floor. 'I'm still driving them to Lexington?'

'Unless you want out. Leave the van, and fly home.'

'Nope.' He shook his head. 'A bargain's a bargain. And I may as well come all the way. That van's none too easy in reverse... don't know that you could handle it.'

I half smiled and didn't argue. I'd wanted him with me, but only willingly, and I'd got that. He knotted his tie and brushed his hair and then took a sidelong glance at my own appearance, which fell a ton short of his. He was a fleshy man of about fifty, bald, pale-skinned, and unexcitable. His nerves, I thought, were going to be at least equal to the evening's requirements.

'Let's go, then,' he said cheerfully. 'I paid in advance.'

I followed him across to the van and climbed up into the cab. Sam started the engine, told me he'd filled up with gas when he'd first reached Kingman, and rolled out south-east on the road to the farm. His broad face looked perfectly calm in the glow from the dashboard, and he handled his six-stall horsebox like a kiddicar. He went eight miles in silence, and then all he said was, 'I'd sure hate to live this far from town, with nowhere to get a beer.'

We passed the third of the three side roads and started on the last ten uninhabited miles to the farm. Three miles farther on Sam gave an alarmed exclamation and braked from his cautious thirty to a full stop. 'What is it?' I asked.

'That gauge.' He pointed, and I looked. The needle on the temperature gauge was quivering on red.

'Have to look see,' he grunted, and switched off the engine. My thoughts as he disappeared out of the cab were one enormous curse. Of all hopeless, dangerous places for his van to break down.

He came back and opened the door my side. I jumped down beside him and he took me round to show me the exhaust.

'Look,' he said unnecessarily. 'Water.'

Several drops slid out, glistening in the light of his torch.

'Gasket,' he said, putting into one word the enormity of the disaster, and what he thought of fate for trapping us in it.

'No water in the radiator,' I said.

'Right.'

'And if we go on, the engine will seize up.'

'Right again.'

'I suppose you don't carry any extra water in the van?'

'We sure do,' he said. 'Never travel without it.'

'Can't we pour some in the radiator . . .?'

'Yeah,' he said. 'We can. There's two gallons. We can pour in a quarter, and go three miles maybe before it's all leaked out, and then another quarter, another three miles. Four quarts, twelve miles. And that's it.'

Thirteen miles out from Kingman. We could just about get back. Seven to the farm. We could refill the radiator at the farm, but Sam couldn't set out on his two thousand mile journey with a stolen cargo in a van emptying like a dry dock.

'There's an extra gasket, of course,' he said.

'A spare one?'

'Sure. Always carry a full set of spares. Never know where you're going to need them. Universal joints, big ends, carburettors, I carry them all. Anyone with any sense does that.'

'Well,' I said in relief, 'how long will it take you to fit the spare?'

He laid the engine bare and considered it in the torch light.

'Cylinder head gasket. Say three hours.'

'*Three hours!*'

'Won't take much less,' he said. 'What do you want to do?'

I looked at my watch. Eight-fifty. Three hours made eleven-fifty; and if we then went on to the farm and picked up the horses we couldn't be back through Kingman until one-fifteen.

Matt would reach Pittsville Boulevard by nine-thirty, and finish his insurance business long before ten. If he drove straight home again he would be on the farm road at midnight. If Sam changed the gasket, so would we.

If Matt stopped to play the tables, he would be at

least an hour later. His clothes had suggested he would stop. But whether for one hour or six, there was no way of telling.

'Change the gasket,' I said abruptly. 'Then we'll see.'

Sam nodded philosophically. It was what he would have done in any case if the van had broken down anywhere else, and without more ado he sorted out what he wanted and started unscrewing.

'Can I help?' I said.

He shook his head and clipped his torch on to a convenient spar to give a steady working light. There seemed to be little haste in his manner, but also no hesitation and a good deal of expertise. The heap of unplugged parts grew steadily on a square of canvas at his feet.

I walked away a few steps and felt for the cigarettes. Two left. I'd still forgotten to buy more. The smoke didn't help much towards making the next decision: to go on, or to go back.

I'd already gambled on Matt staying to play. If it had been Yola, I would have felt surer that it would be for most of the night: but her brother might not have the fever, might only want a short break in his boring stint with the horses. How short? How long?

The decision I came to, if you could call it that, was to wait and see what time Sam restarted the engine.

The night, outside the bright pool by the van, was as dark as the one before. The stars glittered remotely, and the immensity of the American continent marked their indifference to the human race. Against such size, what did one man matter? A walk into the desert . . .

Carefully I pinched out the end of my cigarette and put the stub in my pocket. A good criminal, I thought wryly: I'd always been that. I had a job to do, and even when I'd finished it, I was going for no walks into the desert. I was going back to Santa Barbara, to have breakfast with Walt and Eunice and Lynnie. The prospect at that moment seemed totally unreal, so far were the Arizona hills from the lush coast, so far had I been into the wasteland inside me.

I went back to Sam and asked how it was going. He had the cylinder head off and was removing the cracked gasket.

'So, so,' he said calmly. 'I'm breaking the record.'

I did my best at a smile. He grunted, and said he could do with a cup of coffee, and I said so could I. We hadn't brought any.

He worked on. The air was still warmer than an English summer and he wiped sweat off his bald forehead with the back of a greasy hand. The light shone on his thick stubby fingers, and the click of his spanners echoed across the empty land. The hands on my watch went round in slow fractions. The gasket was wasting the night. And where was Matt?

After two hours Sam's spanner slipped on a nut and he cursed. In spite of his calm, the tension wasn't far from the surface. He stopped what he was doing, stretched upright, took three deep breaths and a look at the night sky, and waited for me to say something.

'You're doing fine,' I said.

He sniffed. 'What'll happen if they catch us here?'

'We won't get the horses.'

He grimaced at my non-answer and went back to his task. 'What have you been doing all day?'

'Nothing. Sitting still.'

'You look half dead,' he commented. 'Pass me those two washers, will you?'

I gave him the washers. 'How much longer?'

'Can't say.'

I stifled the urge to tell him to hurry. He was going as fast as he could. But time was ticking away, and the postponed decision had got to be made. Turning my back on the tugging desert I climbed up to sit in the cab. Eleven-twenty. Matt could be a bare quarter of an hour out from Kingman. Or glued to the green baize and the tricky numbers in Las Vegas.

Which?

For a long half hour I looked out of the back windows while no helpful telepathic messages flowed through them. A straightforward gamble, I thought. Just decide if the winnings were worth the risk.

An easier decision if I'd come alone: but if I'd come alone I couldn't have mended the gasket.

At eleven-forty Sam said gloomily that he was having to fix the water pump as well. It was sticking.

'How long?'

'Another twenty minutes.'

We stared at each other in dismay.

'Go on then,' I said in the end. There was nothing else to do.

I left the cab and walked restlessly a short way back along the road, fearing every second to see Matt's headlights and wondering how best to deal with him if we had to. I was all for stealing from him what wasn't his, but not for damaging his skin. He, however, would have no such inhibitions. There would certainly be blood. Not fair to make it Sam's.

At two minutes past midnight he called out that he had finished, and I walked quickly back to join him. He was pouring water into the radiator, and screwed on the cap as I came up.

'It should be OK now,' he said. His hands were covered in grease and his big body hung tiredly from the shoulders. 'Which way do we go?'

'On.'

He nodded with a wide slicing grin. 'I figured you'd say that. Well, I guess that's OK by me.'

He swung up into the cab and I climbed in beside him. The engine started sweetly at first try, and switching on his headlights, he released the brake and eased away along the road.

'If anyone catches us here from now on,' I said, 'duck.'

'Yeah?'

'Yeah.'

'Tell you something,' he said comfortably. 'I swing a mean left hook.'

'The chap we'd be taking on goes for the head. But with a club of some sort in his fist.'

'Nice guys you play with,' he said. 'I'll remember that.'

We covered the remaining distance at a good speed and in silence. The horsebox crept round the last corner and its headlights flickered over the farm ahead. I put my hand on Sam's arm, and he braked to a halt a short way from the yard.

'Switch off, would you? Lights too,' I said, and jumped quickly down from the cab to wait a few precious seconds until my eyes and ears got used to silence and dark.

No lights in the house. No sound anywhere except the ultra-faint ringing vibrations of limitless air. The calves and hens were asleep. The horses were quiet. I banged on the cab door and Sam switched his head-lights on again before climbing down to join me. The bright shafts lit up the back of the house and wouldn't shine straight into the horses' eyes when I led them from the barn. Over on the shadowy side of the yard the open doors of the shed where Matt had kept his car yawned in a deep black square. The jumbled rubbish dump just in front of us threw surrealistic shadows across the dusty ground, and its smell of decay brushed by our noses.

Sam swept it all with a practised glance. 'Not much of a place.' His voice was as low as a whisper.

'No . . . If you'll unclip the ramp, I'll go fetch the horses. One at a time, I think.'

'OK.' He was breathing faster and his big hands were clenched. Not used to it, after all.

I hurried down towards the barn. It wasn't far; about forty yards. Now that we were totally committed my mind raced with urgency to be done, to be away, to be safely through Kingman before Matt came back. He could have been on the road behind us, be rushing at this moment across the desert to the farm . . .

What happened next happened very fast, in one terrifying cataclysmic blur.

There was an urgent shout behind me.

'Gene!'

I turned, whirling. There were two sets of headlights where there should have been one.

Matt.

The voice again, yelling. 'Gene! Look out.' And a figure running down the yard towards me.

Then there was a roar behind me and I turned again and was met full in the eyes by the blinding glare of two more headlights, much closer. Much closer.

Moving.

I was dazzled and off balance and I'd never have got clear. The running figure threw himself at me in a rugger tackle with outstretched arms and knocked me over out of the way, and the roaring car crashed solidly into the flying body and left it crumpled and smashed and lying on top of my legs.

The car which had hit him turned in a wide sweep at the end of the yard and started back. The headlights lined themselves up like twin suns on their target and with a fraction of my mind I thought it ironic that now when I'd decided not to, I was going to die.

Half sitting, half kneeling, I jerked out the Luger and pumped all of its eight bullets towards the windscreen. I couldn't see to aim straight . . . my eyes were hurting from the glare . . . Not that bullets would do any good . . . the angle was wrong . . . they'd miss the driver . . . By the time I fired the last one the left headlight was six feet away. I uselessly set my teeth against the mangling, tearing, pulping collision . . . and in the last tenth of a second the straight line wavered . . . the smooth side of the front wing hit the back of my shoulder, the front wheel ran over a fold of my shirt, and the rear wheel gave me a clear inch.

Almost before I realized it had missed me, the car crashed head on into one of the buildings at my back with a jolting screech of wood and metal. The body-work crumpled and cracked. The stabbing lights went black. The engine stopped. Air hissed fiercely out of a punctured tyre.

Gasping, dreading what I would find, I leaned over the heavy figure lying on my legs. There were more running footsteps in the yard, and I looked up hopelessly, unable to do any more. I'd used all the bullets . . . none left.

'You're alive!' The voice came from the level of my ear, the man kneeling. Sam Hengelman. I looked at him in a daze.

'I thought . . .' I said, with no breath, '. . . this was you.'

He shook his head. 'No . . .'

He helped me raise and turn the man who'd saved me; and with sickness and unbearable regret I saw his face.

It was Walt.

We laid him on his back, in the dust.

'Look in the car,' I said.

Sam lumbered silently to his feet and went away. I heard his footsteps stop and then start back.

Walt opened his eyes, I leaned over him, lifting his hand, feeling with surging hope for his pulse.

'Gene?' his voice mumbled.

'Yes.'

'He didn't come.'

'Didn't . . .?'

'Came to help you . . .'

'Yes,' I said. 'Thanks, Walt . . .'

His eyes slid aimlessly away from my face.

'Christ,' he said distinctly. 'This is it. This is . . . really . . . it.'

'Walt . . .' His hand was warm in mine, but it didn't move.

'Sod it,' he said. 'I wanted . . . I wanted . . .'

His voice stopped. There was no pulse. No heart-beat. Nothing. Nothing at all.

I put gently down on the ground the warm hand with the rounded fingertips, and stretched out my own, and shut his eyes. It should have been me lying there, not Walt. I shook with sudden impotent fury that it wasn't me, that Walt had taken what I'd wanted, stolen my death . . . It would have mattered so little if it had been me. It wouldn't have mattered at all.

Walt . . . Walt . . .

Sam Hengelman said, 'Is he dead?'

I nodded without looking up.

'There's a young guy in the car,' he said. 'He's dead too.'

I got slowly, achingly, to my feet, and went to look. The car was a blue Ford convertible, and the young guy was Matt.

Without caring, automatically, I took in that the car had smashed the right-hand door of the garage shed and ploughed into the wall behind it. Most of the windscreen was scattered in splintered fragments all over the inside of the car, but in one corner, where some still clung to the frame, there was a finger-sized hole.

Matt was lying over the steering wheel, his arms dangling, his eyes open. The skull above the left eye-brow was pierced and crumpled inwards, and there was blood and hair on the chromium upright which had held the windscreen. I didn't touch him. After a while I went back to Walt.

'What do we do?' Sam Hengelman said.

'Give me a moment . . .'

He waited without speaking until eventually I looked up and down the yard. Two sets of headlights still blazed at the way in.

'That's Walt's car up there?'

'Yeah. He drove up with the devil on his tail and jumped out and ran down after you . . .'

I turned the other way and looked at the dark garage.

'The young guy must have been in there all the time, waiting for us,' Sam said. 'He came roaring out and drove straight at you. I couldn't have stopped him . . . too far away. Walt was halfway down the yard . . .'

I nodded. Matt had been there all the time. Not in Las Vegas. Not on the road. Lying in ambush, waiting.

He hadn't passed us on the road, and there was no other way to the farm. He must have gone back ahead of us. Turned round on the road to Las Vegas and driven back through Kingman while I was sitting in the bus station waiting to telephone to Walt.

But why? *Why* should he have gone back? He hadn't seen me following him, I'd been much too far behind, and in any case I'd left him once he was safely on the highway.

It didn't matter why. It only mattered that he had.

317

Sam Hengelman looked down at Walt and summed up the mess we were entangled in.

'Well . . . what the heck do we do now?'

I took a deep breath.

'Will you fetch that torch of yours?' I asked, and he nodded and brought it from his van. I went with it over to the Ford, and took a longer, closer look. There wasn't much to see that I hadn't seen before, except for a bottle of bourbon that had been smashed in the impact. The neck and jagged top half lay on the floor to Matt's right, along with several smaller pieces and an uneven damp patch.

I walked into the garage and looked at the Ford from the front. It wouldn't be driving anywhere any more.

The big torch lit up clearly the interior of the deep shadowy garage. Quite empty now, except for a scatter of cigarette stubs against the left-hand wall. Matt had been smoking and drinking while he waited. And he'd waited a very long time.

The bullet hole faced me in the windscreen and left me with the worst question unanswered.

I'd have to know.

I stood beside Matt and went over every inch of his body down to the waist. He'd taken off the cream-coloured jacket and was wearing the checked shirt he'd worked in. There were no holes in it: no punctures underneath. His head was heavy. I laid it gently on the steering wheel and stepped away.

None of the bullets had hit him. They'd only smashed the windscreen and blinded him, and he'd slewed a foot off course and run into the wall instead of me, and his head had gone forward hard against the slim metal post.

Slowly I returned to where Sam Hengelman stood beside Walt. He drooped with the utmost dejection and looked at me without hope.

'Did you unclip the ramp?' I asked abruptly.

He shook his head. 'Didn't have time.'

'Go and do it now. We're taking the horses.'

He was aghast. 'We can't!'

'We've got to. For Walt's sake, and your sake, and Dave Teller's sake. And mine. What do you propose? That we call the police and explain what we were all doing here?'

'We'll have to,' he said despairingly.

'No. Definitely not. Go and let down the ramp.'

He hesitated unbelievingly for a few seconds, and then went and did as I asked. The horses stood peacefully in the barn, apparently undisturbed by the racket, the shots, and the crash. I untied the nearest, Showman, and led him quietly up the yard and into the van.

Sam watched me in silence while I tied him into one of the stalls.

'We'll never get away with it.'

'Yes we will,' I said, 'as long as you take these horses safely back to Lexington and never tell anyone,

anyone at all, what happened here tonight. Blot it out of your mind. I'll let you know, when you get back, that you've nothing to worry about. And as long as you tell no one, you won't have.'

The broad fleshy face was set in lines of anxiety.

'You've collected two horses,' I said matter-of-factly. 'An everyday job, collecting two horses. Forget the rest.'

I returned to the barn, fetched Allyx, and loaded him up. Sam still hadn't moved.

'Look,' I said. 'I've ... arranged ... things before. There's a rule where I come from – you take a risk, you get into a mess, you get out.' He blinked. 'Walt threw himself in the way of that car,' I said. 'Matt didn't intend to kill *him* ... You didn't see a murder. Matt drove straight into the wall himself ... and that too was an accident. Only two automobile accidents. You must have seen dozens. Forget it.' He didn't answer, and I added brusquely, 'The water can's empty. You can fill it over there.'

With something like a shudder he picked up the container and went where I pointed. Sighing, I checked that he had brought three days' fodder for the stallions, which he had, and with his help on his return, shut the precious cargo up snugly for their long haul.

'You don't happen to have any gloves around?' I asked.

'Only an old cotton pair in the tool kit.'

He rooted about and finally produced them, two

filthy objects covered with oil and grease which would leave marks on everything they touched, as tale-bearing as fingerprints. I turned them inside out and found they were thick enough to be clean on the inside. Sam watched wordlessly while I put them on, clean side out.

'OK,' I said. 'Will you turn the van, ready to go?'

He did it cautiously as far away from Walt as he could, and when he'd finished I stepped with equal care into the car Walt had come in, touching it as little and as lightly as possible, and drove it down into the yard, stopping a little short of the screen door to the house. There I switched off the engine and lights, put on the brake, and walked back to talk to Sam where he sat in his cab.

'I've three jobs to do,' I said. 'I'll be back as quick as I can. Why don't you just shut your eyes for a couple of minutes and catch a nap?'

'You're kidding.'

I concocted a replica of a smile, and a fraction of the tension in his face unwound.

'I won't be long,' I said, and he nodded, swallowing.

With his torch I surveyed the yard. The Luger was an automatic pistol, which meant it threw out the cartridge after each shot. No one would find the spent bullets, but eight shiny metal shells scattered near Walt's body were something else. Seven of them winked in the light as I inched the torch carefully round, and I collected them into my pocket. The eighth remained obstinately invisible.

The ejection slot had been on the side of the gun away from Walt, but the cases sometimes shot out straight upwards instead of sideways, and I began to wonder if the eighth could possibly have travelled far enough over to be underneath him. I didn't want to disturb him: but I had to find the little brass thimble.

Then, when I'd decided I had no choice, I saw it. Bent and dusty, partly flattened, no longer shining. I picked it up from the spot where I had been half-lying in the path of Matt's car. He had run over it.

After that I attended to the ground itself. Tyre marks didn't show on the rough dusty surface, but the hoof prints did to some extent. I fetched a broom of twigs from the barn and swept them out.

The garage was next. I punched through into the car the remaining corner of the windscreen with its significant bullet hole, and I picked up every one of the cigarette stubs which told where and how long Matt had waited. They went into a trash can standing a few yards along from the house door.

Matt hadn't locked the house when he went out. I went in to look for one essential piece of information: the address of the place, and the name of its owner. The torchlight swept over the threadbare covers and elderly furniture, and in one drawer of a large dresser I found what the farmer used for an office. The jumble of bills and letters gave me what I wanted. Wilbur

Bellman, Far Valley Farm, Kingman. On the scratch pad beside the telephone, Matt had written a bonus. In heavy black ballpoint were the simple words: 'Insurance 9 PM.'

Before leaving I gave the big dilapidated living room a final circuit with the torch and the beam flickered over a photograph in a cardboard folder standing on a shelf. Something about the face in it struck me as familiar, and I swung the torch back for a second and closer look.

The patient passive face of Kiddo smiled out, as untroubled as it had been when he told Walt and me about Offen's mares. Loopy unformed writing straggled over the lower half of the picture. 'To Ma and Pa, from your loving son.'

If Offen had sent his stud groom to Miami to join his parents, Kiddo's loyalty to his employer was a certainty. I almost admired Offen's technique in furnishing himself in one throw with an obscure hideout for the horses and a non-talking employee.

After the house there remained only Walt. Nothing to do but to say goodbye.

I went down on my knees beside him in the dust, but the silent form was already subtly not Walt. Death showed. I took off one glove and touched his hand: still warm in the warm air, but without the firmness of life.

There was no point in saying to him what I felt. If

his spirit was still hovering somewhere around, he would know.

I left him lying there in the dark, and went back to Sam.

He took one slow look at my face and said in an appalled voice, 'You're not leaving him there?'

I nodded, and climbed up beside him.

'But you *can't* . . .'

I simply nodded again, and gestured to him to start up and drive away. He did it with a viciousness that must have rocked the stallions on their feet, and we went back to Kingman without speaking. His revulsion at what I had done reached me in almost tangible waves.

I didn't care. I felt only one grim engulfing ache for the man I'd left behind.

CHAPTER EIGHTEEN

Lynnie put her brown hand tentatively on mine and said, 'Gene . . . what's the matter?'

'Nothing,' I said.

'You look worse than you did when you came back with Chrysalis. Much worse.'

'The food doesn't agree with me.'

She snorted and took her hand away. We were sitting on the sea terrace, waiting for Eunice to come down for dinner, with the sun galloping the last lap to dusk and the daiquiris tinkling with civilized ice.

'Is Walt back yet?' Lynnie said.

'No.'

'He's a funny man, isn't he?' she said. 'All moods and glum looks, and then suddenly he smiles, and you realize how nice he is. I like him.'

After a pause I said, 'So do I.'

'How was San Francisco?' she asked.

'Foggy.'

'What's the matter?'

'Nothing.'

She sighed and shook her head.

Eunice arrived in a cloud of yellow chiffon and clanked her gold bracelet as she stretched for her drink. She was cheerful and glowing; almost too much to bear.

'Well, you son of a bitch, when did you crawl in?'

'This afternoon,' I said.

'So what's new?'

'I've given up trying to find the horses.'

Eunice sat up straight with a jerk. 'For crying out loud!'

'I'll be starting home soon. Tomorrow evening, I expect.'

'Oh no,' Lynnie said.

'Oh, yes, I'm afraid so. The holidays are over.'

'They don't look as if they've done you much good,' Eunice observed. 'So now how do you deal with it?'

'With what?'

'With flopping. With not making out.'

I said wryly, 'Look it smack in the eye and dare it to bite you.'

'It probably will,' said Eunice sardonically. 'It'll chew me to bloody bits.' She drank the second quarter of her drink and looked me thoughtfully over. 'Come to think of it, it seems to have done that to you already.'

'Maybe I'll take up golf.'

She laughed, more internally relaxed than I'd ever seen her. 'Games', she said, 'are a bore.'

When they went in to eat I couldn't face it, and drove off instead to fetch the tape recorder from the rocks at Orpheus Farm. The short journey seemed tiresomely long. It had been nearly four hundred and fifty miles back to Santa Barbara from Kingman, and neither bath, shave, nor two hours flat on the bed seemed to have had any effect.

Back in my room at The Vacationer I listened to the whole of the tape's four-hour playing time. The first conversations, two or three business calls, were from the previous morning, after Walt had put in a new reel. Then there was almost an hour and a half of an interview between Offen and a man from the Bloodstock Registry Office. They had already been out to see the horses, and Offen was piling proof on proof that the horses in his barn were veritably Moviemaker and Centigrade. A groom who had cared for Centigrade during his racing days was asked in to sign a statement he'd made that he recognized the horse and would if necessary swear to its identity in any inquiry.

The bloodstock man apologized constantly that anyone should have doubted Offen. Offen enjoyed the scene, the joke rumbling like an undertone. After they'd gone he laughed aloud. I hoped he'd enjoyed it. He wouldn't be laughing much for a long time to come.

Next on the tape was a piece of Offen giving his houseman instructions for replenishing the drink stocks, then an hour's television programme. And after that, Matt telephoned.

I couldn't hear his voice at all, only Offen's replies, but they were enough.

'Hello, Matt. . . .

'Slow down, I'm not taking this in. Where did you say you were? . . .

'What are you doing on the road to Las Vegas? . . .

'Well, I can see the house must be insured. . . .

'You found *what* under the glove shelf? . . .

'How do you know it's a homer? . . .

'All these minute transmitters are a mystery to me . . .

'Who could have put it there? . . .

'I don't follow you. What was that about yellow paint? . . .

'But the police said it was vandals . . .

'All right, Matt, don't shout. I'm doing my best. Now let's get this clear. You were fumbling for a pack of cigarettes and you dislodged this . . . thing. Bug, whatever you said. And you're worried now that Hawkins and Prensela put it in your car, and that they used that and the yellow paint to follow you, so that they know where you've been staying, or maybe. Is that right? . . .

'Matt, I think you're blowing this thing up too big . . .

'But did you actually *see* a plane following you? . . .

'Well, yes, sure, if you think you should go back, go

back. The horses are far more important than the
insurance on the house. But I think you're wrong.
Hawkins and Prensela have been concentrating on
Moviemaker and Centigrade here, they've stirred up
the DA's office from LA and the bloodstock registry,
and it's been a three ringed circus here for the last
couple of days. They wouldn't have been trying to find
any horses anywhere else, because they're sure they're
here in the barn . . .

'Well, I don't *know* who could have planted the
bug . . .

'Yeah. All right. Go on back, then . . .

'Call me in the morning . . .

'Goodnight, Matt.'

The receiver went down, and for a few seconds
there were the indistinct noises of Offen going over
the conversation again in his mind, punctuating it with
'umphs' and small doubtful grunts.

I switched the tape off temporarily and thought
bitterly about Matt finding the bug. I hadn't had a
chance to remove it: on my first night visit to the farm
the car in the garage had been the one he'd hired
while his own was being cleaned of paint. But neither
had I looked upon it as a very great hazard, because
the little capsules were light and clung tightly. It had
been long odds against him groping for cigarettes while
driving in the dark, and dislodging it. I hadn't taken
it into account.

Some time on his way back to the farm it must

have struck him that the insurance appointment might be phoney; that if we had tricked him into going to Las Vegas once already, we might be tricking him again. If we'd got him out of the way, it could only be to take the horses. So he'd wait; in the dark, ready to spring.

He must have begun to think, when he'd sat out the three hours it took to mend the gasket, that Uncle Bark was right and he was wrong: but all the same he'd gone on waiting. And, in the end, we had come.

I switched the tape on again for the rest. The whole night had been telescoped into the few seconds' silence, because when Offen made his next call it was clearly morning.

'Yola, is that you?'

A faint clacking reached the bug. Yola's higher pitched voice disturbed more air.

'Have you heard from Matt?'

'. . .'

'No, he said he'd call me this morning, and he hasn't. I can't get any answer from the farm.'

'. . .'

'Well, not really. He called me last night because he had some crazy idea Hawkins had traced the horses . . .'

A loud squawk from Yola.

'Something about a listening bug and yellow paint.'

Yola talked for some time and when Offen answered he sounded anxious.

'Yeah, I know he found the first one when we thought that was impossible ... do you really think Matt may be right?'

'...'

'Yola, that's right out. Why don't you go yourself?'

'...'

'Close the ranch then. Send them all home.'

'...'

'Look, if you're right, if Matt's right ... say when he went back last night the DA's men were sitting there waiting for him? Say they're sitting there right now, waiting for me to turn up and see why Matt doesn't answer his calls? No, Yola, I'm not walking into that farm and find I have to answer questions like what am I doing there, and what are those two horses in the barn, with Moviemaker and Centigrade's registrations tattooed inside their lips? I'm not going.'

'...'

'Matt may be off on some plan of his own.'

'...'

'No. I'll give him today. If I haven't heard from him by morning I'll ... well, I'll think of something.'

Yola's final remark was loud, and I heard it clearly. Full of anxiety, full of anguish.

'If anything's happened to Matt ...'

The end of the tape ran off the reel, and I switched off the recorder. For Yola, as for Walt's wife, life would never be the same again.

I went to bed and lay awake, feeling feverish from

331

lack of sleep. Relaxed every limb, but my mind would have none of it. It was filled too full, as it had been all day, of a picture of Walt still lying on his back in the farmyard. The sun had risen and blazed on him, and set again. He would have no shelter until tomorrow. I couldn't sleep until he had. I tried to, but I couldn't.

On my way back to Santa Barbara I'd stopped for coffee and a handful of change, and I'd telephoned to Paul M. Zeissen in the Buttress Life office on Thirty Third Street. It had been nearly 6 PM New York time. Zeissen was preparing to go home for the weekend. I was a little worried, I told him, about Walt. He had gone to do some life insurance business on a farm in Arizona, and I hadn't heard from him since. Zeissen and I talked it over for a few minutes in unurgent civilized tones, and arranged finally that if I hadn't heard from Walt by morning, Buttress Life would ring the Arizona State Police in Kingman, and ask them as a favour to go out to the farm, just to check.

In the morning I would ring Zeissen at his home. By noon, perhaps, the Kingman police would reach the farm. They would read the story: insurance salesman arrives for appointment, gets out of car. Matt Clive, hurrying back to meet him, swings into the yard, sees a dark figure too late, hits him, runs straight on into the wall because judgement suspended by horror at collision. Matt, with whisky inside him, and a bottle in the car. Inside the house the 9 PM insurance appoint-

ment written in Matt's hand. And nothing else. No
horses. No suggestion of visitors. No sign that it could
have been anything but a tragically unlucky accident.

Matt had been good at accidents.

So was I.

I lay on my stomach on the beach all morning while
Lynnie sat beside me and trickled sand through her
fingers. Eunice had gone to Santa Monica, down the
coast.

'Are you really going home this evening?' Lynnie
said.

'First hop, yes.'

'Would you mind . . . if I came with you?'

I stirred in surprise.

'I thought you wanted to stay here for ever.'

'Mm. But that was with you . . . and Eunice. Now
you're going . . . and Eunice hasn't been here much
this week, you know. I've spent ages all on my own,
and there isn't that much to do on a beach, when you
do it every day . . .'

'Where had Eunice been?'

'Santa Monica, like now. There's some place there
she spends all her time in, where they import vases
and bits of sculpture and expensive light fittings, and
things like that. She took me there the day before
yesterday . . . I must say it's pretty gorgeous. Marvellous fabrics, too.'

'She might feel hurt if you just pack up and leave her.'

'Well, no. I mentioned it to her before she went this morning, and honestly I think if anything she was relieved. She just said if I really wanted to go, OK, and she would probably be moving down to Santa Monica in a day or two anyway.'

'If you really want to, then. I'm catching the night flight to Washington . . . I've a visit to make in Lexington tomorrow morning. After that, back to New York, and home.'

'You don't mind if I tag along?' She sounded a scrap uncertain.

'Come to think of it,' I said, 'you can wake me at the stops.'

We had a sandwich for lunch which I couldn't eat, and at two the girl from the reception desk came to say I was wanted on the telephone. Paul M. Zeissen told me in a suitably hushed voice that the Arizona police had been most co-operative and had gone to Bellman's farm as asked, and had found Walt dead. I made shocked noises. Zeissen said would I pack Walt's things and send them back? I said I would.

'I suppose,' he suggested diffidently, 'that you and he had not completed your other business?'

'The horses?'

'One horse. Allyx,' he said reprovingly. 'Showman was insured with another company.'

'Oh . . . yes. Allyx should be in circulation, safe and

authenticated within a month or so. I expect the Bloodhorse Breeders' Association will be getting in touch with you. Walt worked very hard at this, and it was entirely owing to his efforts that Buttress Life will be recovering most of the million and a half it paid out.'

'Where did he find the horse?'

'I can't tell you. Does it matter?'

'No . . .' he said thoughtfully. 'Goods back, no questions asked . . . we work on that principle, the same as any other company.'

'Right then,' I said. 'And you'll of course pay his commission to his widow?'

'Uh . . . of course. And naturally Walt had insured his life with us . . . Mrs Prensela will be well provided for, I feel sure.'

Provided for. Money. But no Walt. No picnic.

I said goodbye to Zeissen and went slowly back to Lynnie. When I told her Walt was dead, she cried for him.

Upstairs, when I packed his clothes, I lingered a good while over the framed photograph of him with Amy and the kids, and in the end put it in my suitcase, not his. It could hardly be the only photograph his wife would have of him, and I didn't think she'd worry much if it didn't return with his baggage.

Eunice came back tired and abstracted from Santa Monica, and after absorbing the shock of Walt's death was unaffected when Lynnie told her over early dinner that she was going home with me.

'Much better to travel with a man to look after you, honey,' she agreed absent-mindedly: and then, giving me a more characteristic sharp glance, added, 'Don't let him get up to any tricks.'

Lynnie sighed. 'He wouldn't.'

'Huh,' she said, but without conviction, and then asked me, 'Will you be seeing Dave when you get back?'

I nodded. 'Very soon after.'

'Tell him then, will you, that I've found a darling little business in Santa Monica. They're looking for a partner with some capital, to open another branch, and if the accounts are right I'd like to do it. I'll write to him, of course, but you could explain ... I guess you could explain better than anyone.'

'I'll explain.'

She said she was too tired to come all the way back to Los Angeles to see us off, and we said goodbye to her in the lobby, where she kissed Lynnie and then me on the cheek with a quite surprising strength of feeling.

Lynnie said, as we drove away, 'I'll miss her. Isn't that extraordinary. I'll really miss her.'

'You'll come back.'

'It won't be the same ...'

I returned the hired car to the Hertz agent at the airport, we caught the plane to Washington, and I made up on parts of the way for the three nights without sleep. Lynnie said at Lexington that she could quite see why I needed someone to wake me at the stops.

We went in a taxi to Jeff Roots's house and his teenage daughters took Lynnie off for a swim in the pool while I sat with him under his vine-covered trellis and thought how cool and substantial he looked in his bright open-necked Sunday shirt.

'Sam Hengelman should reach Lexington some time this afternoon or early evening,' I said. 'He'll call you to know where to take the horses.'

'That's all fixed,' Roots nodded.

'Would you give him a message from me?'

'Sure.'

'Just tell him everything's OK: that I said so.'

'Sure. You are, aren't you, one hundred per cent certain that those two definitely are Showman and Allyx?'

'One hundred per cent. There isn't the slightest doubt.'

He sighed. 'I'll get the identification started. Though who is to know Showman after ten years? A bay with no markings ... and only a four-year-old when he came from England.' He paused, then said, 'Have you any suggestions as to how we can start prosecuting Offen for fraud and theft?'

I shook my head. 'I'm not a policeman. Not interested in punishment, only prevention.' I smiled briefly. 'I came to get the horses back. Nothing else. Well . . . they're back. I've done what I was engaged for, and that's as far as I go.'

He eyed me assessingly. 'Do you want Offen to go on collecting huge stud fees, then?'

'He won't,' I said. 'Not if someone starts a quick rumour immediately that both Moviemaker and Centigrade have been suffering from an obscure virus which will certainly have affected their virility. Owners of mares can be quietly advised to insist they don't pay any stud fees until the foals have shown their quality. After that . . . well, Offen does legally own Moviemaker and Centigrade, and he's entitled to the fees they earn on their own merits.'

'You're extraordinary,' he said. 'Don't you want to see Offen behind bars?'

'Not passionately,' I said. Offen had enjoyed his prestige almost more than his income. He would be losing both. And Yola . . . she was going to have to work hard, without Matt, and probably without the expensive house on Pitts. Bars seemed superfluous.

He shook his head, giving me up as a bad job. 'We'll have to prosecute, I'm sure of it. I'll have to get the lawyers to see about it.'

He called the houseman to bring our drinks, and merely sighed when I said I'd as soon share his sugar free tonic.

We sipped the well-iced innocuous stuff and he said again that Offen would have to be prosecuted, if only to provide a reason for Allyx and Showman having disappeared for so many years, and to account for tattoo marks inside their mouths.

'I can see you would think that,' I said. 'I also think you'll have a terrible job proving that any of the mares booked to Moviemaker and Centigrade were actually covered by Showman and Allyx. I didn't find Showman and Allyx on Offen's farm. I doubt if anyone would testify that they were ever there. Certainly Offen would deny it, and go on denying it to the bitter end. It's his only hope.' I paused. 'I did manage to get some tape recordings, but unfortunately, even if they could be used as evidence, they are inconclusive. Offen never mentioned Showman or Allyx by name.'

Roots stared gloomily into space.

'This makes it difficult,' he said. 'What you are in fact saying is that we know Offen switched the stallions, because of the tattoo marks, but no one will be able to prove it?'

I looked down to where Lynnie was jumping into the pool in a big splash contest with Roots's daughters. Her lighthearted laughter floated up, carefree and very young.

'I wouldn't try,' I said. 'Rightly or wrongly I decided to repossess the stolen goods by stealing them back. First, so that Offen would have no chance of destroying them. Second, so that there shouldn't be years of delay while lawyers argued the case, years of the stallions standing idle, with their value diminishing day by day and their blood lines wasting. Third, and most important, that there should be no chance of Offen getting them back once the dust had settled. Because if he had any sense he would swear, and provide witnesses to swear, that the horses in dispute were two unraced halfbred animals of no account, and he'd explain the tattoos on their lips by saying he'd used them to try out some new type of ink. What more likely, he would say, than that he should repeat the numbers of his two best horses? He could make it sound a lot more reasonable than that he should have stolen two world famous stallions and conducted a large scale fraud. He has great personal charm.'

Roots nodded. 'I've met him.'

'Showman and Allyx were being looked after by Offen's nephew,' I said. 'Offen can say he'd lent him two old nags to hack around on, and he can't imagine why anyone would want to steal them.'

'He could put up an excellent defence, I see that,' he admitted.

'His present stud groom is innocent,' I added. 'And would convince anyone of it. If you leave things as they are, Offen won't get Allyx and Showman back. If you prosecute him, he may.'

He looked shattered, staring into his glass but seeing with experienced eyes every side of the sticky problem.

'We could try blood tests,' he said at last.

'Blood tests?'

'For paternity,' he nodded. 'If there is any doubt about which horse has sired a certain foal, we take blood tests. If one disputed sire's blood is of a similar group to the foal's, and the other disputed sire's is different, we conclude that the foal was sired by the similar sire.'

'And like in humans,' I asked, 'you can tell which horse could *not* have sired which foal, but you couldn't say which, of a similar blood group, actually did?'

'That's right.'

We thought it over. Then he said cheerfully, 'If we can prove that none of the so-called Moviemaker foals could in fact have been sired by Moviemaker, but could all have been sired by Showman, we'll have Offen sewn up tight.'

'Couldn't he possibly have made sure, before he ever bought Moviemaker, that his and Showman's blood groups were similar? I mean, if he's a breeder, he'd know about blood tests.'

Roots's gloom returned. 'I suppose it's possible. And possible that Centigrade and Allyx are similar too.' He looked up suddenly and caught me smiling. 'It's all right for you to think it's funny,' he said, wryly matching my expression. 'You don't have to sort out the mess. What in God's name are we going to do about the Stud Book? Moviemaker's . . . that is, Showman's . . . get are already siring foals, in some cases. The mix up is in the second generation. How are we ever going to put it straight?'

'Even if,' I pointed out, trying hard to keep the humour out of my voice and face, 'even if you prove Moviemaker couldn't have sired the foals he's supposed to have done, you can't prove Showman *did*.'

He gave me a comically pained look. 'What other sire could have got such brilliant stock?' He shook his head. 'We'll pin it on Offen in the end, even if we have to wait until after Showman and Allyx have been re-syndicated and their first official crops have won as much stake money as all the others. Offen wouldn't be able to say then that they were two halfbred nags he'd given his nephew to hack around on. We'll get him in the end.'

'The racing scandal of the year,' I said smiling.

'Of the year? Are you kidding? Of the century.'

Lynnie and I flew from Kennedy that night on a Super VC 10, with dinner over Canada at midnight and breakfast over Ireland three hours later. I spent the interval looking at her while she slept beside me in her sloped-back chair. Her skin was close textured like a baby's, and her face was that of a child. The woman inside was still a bud, with a long way to grow.

Keeble met us at Heathrow, and as usual it was raining. Lynnie kissed him affectionately. He went so far as to shake my hand. There was a patch of stubble on his left cheek, and the eyes blinked quickly behind the mild glasses. Santa Barbara was six thousand miles away. We were home.

Keeble suggested a cup of coffee before we left the airport and asked his daughter how she'd enjoyed herself. She told him non-stop for twenty minutes, her suntan glowing in the grey summer morning and her brown eyes alight.

He looked finally from her to me, and his face subtly contracted.

'And what have you been doing?' he said.

Lynnie answered when I didn't. 'He's been with us on the beach a good deal of the time,' she said doubtfully.

Keeble stroked her arm. 'Did you find the horses?' he asked.

I nodded.

'All three?'

'With help.'

'I told Dave I'd drop you off at the hospital when we leave here,' he said. 'He's still strung up, but he hopes to be out next week.'

'I've a lot to tell him, and there's a lot he'll have to decide.' The worst being, I thought, whether to carry on with his move alongside Orpheus Farm, or to disappoint Eunice in her new found business. Nothing was ever simple. Nothing was easy.

'You don't look well,' Keeble said abruptly.

'I'll live,' I said, and his eyes flickered with a mixture

of surprise and speculation. I smiled lopsidedly and said it again, 'I'll live.'

We stood up to go. Instead of shaking hands Lynnie suddenly put her arms round my waist and her head on my chest.

'I don't want to say goodbye,' she said indistinctly. 'I want to see you again.'

'Well,' I said reasonably. 'You will.'

'I mean . . . often.'

I met Keeble's eyes over her head. He was watching her gravely, but without disquiet.

'She's too young,' I said to him, and he knew exactly what I meant. Not that I was too old for her, but that she was too young for me. Too young in experience, understanding, and wickedness.

'I'll get older,' she said. 'Will twenty-one do?'

Her father laughed, but she gripped my arm. 'Will it?'

'Yes,' I said recklessly, and found one second later that I really meant it.

'She'll change her mind,' Keeble said with casual certainty.

I said, 'Of course,' to him, but Lynnie looked up into my eyes and shook her head.

It was late afternoon when I got back to the flat. The tidy, dull, unwelcoming rooms hadn't changed a bit. When I looked at the kitchen I remembered Lynnie making burnt scrambled egg, and I felt a fierce disturbing wish that she would soon make some more.

I unpacked. The evening stretched greyly ahead.

I sat and stared vacantly at the bare walls.

If was a grinding word, I thought. If Sam Hengelman had taken longer to mend that gasket, Walt would have found us on the road and would have stopped us going to the farm. If Sam had mended it faster, we'd have reached the farm well before Walt, and Matt would have killed me, as he'd meant.

If I hadn't decided to recover the horses by stealing them, Walt would be alive. They might collectively be worth nearly five million dollars, but they weren't worth Walt's life.

I wished I'd never started.

The grey day turned to grey dusk. I got up and switched on the light, and fetched two objects to put on the low table beside my chair.

The Luger, and the photograph of Walt with his wife and kids.

The trouble with being given a gift you don't really want is that you feel so mean if you throw it away. Especially if it cost more than the giver could afford.

I won't throw away Walt's gift. Even if Lynnie changes her mind, I'll survive.

Tired beyond feeling, I went to bed at ten. I put the Luger under the pillow, and hung the photograph on the wall.

And slept.

SHATTERED

To
Her Majesty Queen Elizabeth, The Queen Mother
in celebration of her 100th birthday
With endless gratitude, love and every good wish,
from Dick Francis

My thanks also to
Stephen Zawistowski, glass-blower
Stephen Spiro, Professor of Respiratory Medicine
Tanya Williams, West Mercia Police

to Matthew Francis, my grandson, for the title

and to my son, Felix, for everything

CHAPTER ONE

Four of us drove together to Cheltenham races on the day that Martin Stukely died there from a fall in a steeple-chase.

It was 31 December, the eve of the year two thousand. A cold midwinter morning. The world approaching the threshold of the future.

Martin himself, taking his place behind the steering wheel of his BMW, set off before noon without premon-ition, collecting his three passengers from their Cotswold hills bases on his way to his afternoon's work. A jockey of renown, he had confidence and a steady heart.

By the time he reached my sprawling house on the hillside above the elongated tourist-attracting village of Broadway, the air in his spacious car swirled richly full of smoke from his favourite cigar, the Montecristo No 2, his substitute for eating. At thirty-four he was spending longer and longer in a sauna each day, but was all the same gradually losing the metabolic battle against weight.

Genes had given him a well-balanced frame in general,

and an Italian mother in particular had passed on a love of cooking, and vivacity.

He quarrelled incessantly with Bon-Bon, his rich, plump and talkative wife, and on the whole ignored his four small children, often frowning as he looked at them as if not sure exactly who they were. Nevertheless his skill and courage and rapport with horses took him as often as always into the winner's enclosure, and he drove to Cheltenham calmly discussing his mounts' chances that afternoon in two fast hurdle races and one longer 'chase. Three miles of jumping fences brought out the controlled recklessness that made him great.

He picked me up last on that fateful Friday morning, as I lived nearest to Cheltenham's racecourse.

Already on board, and by his side, sat Priam Jones, the trainer whose horses he regularly rode. Priam was expert at self-aggrandisement but not quite as good as he believed at knowing when a horse in his care had come to a performance peak. That day's steeplechaser, Tallahassee, was, according to my friend Martin on the telephone, as ready as he would ever be to carry off the day's gold trophy, but Priam Jones, smoothing his white late-middle-age thinning hair, told the horse's owner in a blasé voice that Tallahassee might still do better on softer ground.

Lounging back beside me on the rear seat, with the tip of one of Martin's cigars glowing symmetrically to ash, Tallahassee's owner, Lloyd Baxter, listened without noticeable pleasure, and I thought Priam Jones would have done better to keep his premature apologies in reserve.

It was unusual for Martin to be the one who drove Tallahassee's owner and trainer anywhere. Normally he took other jockeys, or me alone, but Priam Jones from arrogance had just wrecked his own car in a stupid rash of flat tyres, thanks to his having tried to ignore head-on a newly installed deterrent no-parking set of rising teeth. It was the council's fault, he insisted. He would sue.

Priam had taken it for granted, Martin had told me crossly, that he – Martin – would do the driving, and would take not only Priam himself but would also chauffeur the horse's owner, who was staying overnight with Priam for the Cheltenham meeting, having flown down from the north of England to the local Staverton airfield in a small rented air taxi.

I disliked Lloyd Baxter as thoroughly as he disliked me. Martin had warned me of the Priam tyre situation ('keep your sarcastic tongue behind your splendid teeth') and had begged me also to swamp the grumpy, dumpy millionaire owner with anaesthetizing charm in advance, in case Priam Jones's fears materialized and the horse drew a blank.

I saw Martin's face grinning at me in the driving mirror as he listened to me sympathize with the flat tyres. He more than paid any debt he owed me by ferrying me about when he could, as I'd lost my licence for a year through scorching at ninety-five miles an hour round the Oxford ring road (fourth ticket for speeding) to take him and his broken leg to see his point-of-death old retired gardener. The gardener's heart had then thumped away insecurely for six further weeks – one of life's little ironies. My loss of licence now had three months to run.

The friendship between Martin and myself, unlikely at first sight, had sprung fully grown in an instant four or more years ago, the result of a smile crinkling round his eyes, echo, I gathered, of my own.

We had met in the jury room of the local crown court, chosen for jury duty to hear a fairly simple case of domestic murder. The trial lasted two and a half days. Over mineral water afterwards, I'd learned about the tyranny of weight. Though my life had nothing to do with horses, or his with the heat and chemistry of my own days, we shared, perhaps, the awareness of the physical ability that we each needed for success in our trade.

In the jury room Martin had asked with merely polite curiosity, 'What do you do for a living?'

'I blow glass.'

'You do *what*?'

'I make things of glass. Vases, ornaments, goblets. That sort of thing.'

'Good grief.'

I smiled at his astonishment. 'People do, you know. People have made things of glass for thousands of years.'

'Yes, but . . .' he considered, 'you don't look like someone who makes ornaments. You look . . . well . . . tough.'

I was four years younger than he and three inches taller, and probably equal in muscles.

'I've made horses,' I said mildly. 'Herds of them.'

'The Crystal Stud Cup,' he said, identifying one of Flat racing's more elaborate prizes. 'Did you make that?'

'Not that one, no.'

'Well . . . Do you have a *name*? Like, say, Baccarat?'

I smiled lopsidedly. 'Not so glamorous. It's Logan, Gerard Logan.'

'Logan Glass.' He nodded, no longer surprised. 'You have a place on the High Street in Broadway, side by side with all those antique shops. I've seen it.'

I nodded. 'Sales and workshop.'

He hadn't seemed to take any special notice, but a week later he'd walked into my display gallery, spent an intense and silent hour there, asked if I'd personally made all the exhibits (mostly) and offered me a lift to the races. As time went by we had become comfortably accustomed to each other's traits and faults. Bon-Bon used me as a shield in battle and the children thought me a bore because I wouldn't let them near my furnace.

For half the races that day at Cheltenham things went as normal. Martin won the two-mile hurdle race by six lengths and Priam Jones complained that six lengths was too far. It would ruin the horse's position in the handicap.

Martin shrugged, gave an amused twist to his eyebrows and went into the changing room to put on Lloyd Baxter's colours of black and white chevrons, pink sleeves and cap. I watched the three men in the parade ring, owner, trainer and jockey, as they took stock of Tallahassee walking purposefully round in the hands of his stable lad. Tallahassee stood at odds of six to four with the bookmakers for the Coffee Forever Gold Trophy: clear favourite.

Lloyd Baxter (ignoring his trainer's misgivings) had put his money on, and so had I.

It was at the last fence of all that Tallahassee uncharacteristically tangled his feet. Easily ahead by seven lengths he lost his concentration, hit the roots of the unyielding birch and turned a somersault over his rider, landing his whole half-ton mass upside down with the saddle-tree and his withers crushing the rib cage of the man beneath.

The horse fell at the peak of his forward-to-win acceleration and crashed down at thirty or more miles an hour. Winded, he lay across the jockey for inert moments, then rocked back and forwards vigorously in his struggle to rise again to his feet.

The fall and its aftermath looked truly terrible from where I watched on the stands. The roar of welcome for a favourite racing home to a popular win was hushed to a gasp, to cries, to an endless anxious murmur. The actual winner passed the post without his due cheers, and a thousand pairs of binoculars focused on the unmoving black and white chevrons flat on the green December grass.

The racecourse doctor, though instantly attending him from his following car, couldn't prevent the fast gathering group of paramedics and media people from realizing that Martin Stukely, though still semi-conscious, was dying before their eyes. They glimpsed the blood sliding frothily out of the jockey's mouth, choking him as the sharp ends of broken ribs tore his lungs apart. They described it, cough by groan, in their news reports.

The doctor and paramedics loaded Martin, just alive, into the waiting ambulance and as they set off to the hospital they worked desperately with transfusions and oxygen, but quietly, before the journey ended, the jockey lost his race.

Priam, not normally a man of emotion, wept without shame as later he collected Martin's belongings, including his car keys, from the changing rooms. Sniffing, blowing his nose, and accompanied by Lloyd Baxter who looked annoyed rather than grief-stricken, Priam Jones offered to return me to my place of business in Broadway, though not to my home in the hills, as he intended to go in the opposite direction from there, to see Bon-Bon; to give her comfort.

I asked if he would take me on with him to see Bon-Bon. He refused. Bon-Bon wanted Priam alone, he said. She had said so, devastated, on the telephone.

Lloyd Baxter, Priam added, would now also be off-loaded at Broadway. Priam had got him the last available room in the hotel there, the Wychwood Dragon. It was all arranged.

Lloyd Baxter glowered at the world, at his trainer, at me, at fate. He should, he thought, have won the gold trophy. He had been robbed. Though his horse was unharmed, his feelings for his dead jockey seemed to be resentment, not regret.

As Priam, shoulders drooping, and Baxter, frowning heavily, set off ahead of us towards the car park, Martin's changing-room valet hurried after me, calling my name. I stopped, and turned towards him, and into my hands he thrust the lightweight racing saddle that, strapped firmly to Tallahassee's back, had helped to deal out damage and death.

The stirrups, with the leathers, were folded over the saddle plate, and were kept in place by the long girth wound round and round. The sight of the girth-wrapped piece of professional equipment, like my newly dead mother's Hasselblad camera, bleakly rammed into one's consciousness the gritty message that their owners would never come back. It was Martin's empty saddle that set me missing him painfully.

Eddie, the valet, was elderly, bald and, in Martin's estimation, hardworking and unable to do wrong. He turned to go back to the changing room but then stopped, fumbled in the deep front pocket of the apron of his trade and, producing a brown-paper-wrapped package, called after me to wait.

'Someone gave this to Martin to give to you,' he shouted, coming back and holding it out for me to take. 'Martin asked me to give it back to him when he was leaving to go home, so he could pass it on to you . . . but of course . . .' he swallowed, his voice breaking . . . 'he's gone.'

I asked. 'Who gave it to *him*?'

The valet didn't know. He was sure, though, that Martin himself had known, because he had been joking about it being worth a million, and Eddie was clear that the ultimate destination of the parcel had been Gerard Logan, Martin's friend.

I took the package and, thanking him, put it into my raincoat pocket, and we spent a mutual moment of sharp sadness for the gap we already felt in our lives. I supposed, as Eddie turned to hurry back to his chores in the changing room, and I continued into the car park, that I might have gone to the races for the last time, that without Martin's input the fun might have flown.

Priam's tears welled up again at the significance of the empty saddle, and Lloyd Baxter shook his head with disapproval. Priam recovered enough however to start Martin's car and drive it to Broadway where, as he'd intended, he off-loaded both me and Lloyd Baxter outside the Wychwood Dragon and then departed in speechless gloom towards Bon-Bon and her fatherless brood.

Lloyd Baxter paid me no attention but strode without pleasure into the hotel. During the journey from the racecourse he'd complained to Priam that his overnight bag was in Priam's house. He'd gone by hired car from Staverton airfield, intending to spend the evening at Priam's now-cancelled New Year's Eve party, celebrating a win in the Gold Coffee Cup before flying away the following morning to his thousand-acre estate in Northumberland. Priam's assertion that, after seeing Martin's family, he would himself ferry the bag to the hotel, left Tallahassee's owner unmollified. The whole afternoon had been a disaster, he grumbled, and in his voice one could hear undertones of an intention to change to a different trainer.

My own glass business lay a few yards away from the Wychwood Dragon on the opposite side of the road. If one looked across from outside the hotel, the gallery's windows seemed to glitter with ultra-bright light, which they did from breakfast to midnight every day of the year.

I walked across the road wishing that time could be reversed to yesterday: wishing that bright-eyed Martin would march through my door suggesting improbable glass sculptures that in fact, when I made them, won both commissions and kudos. He had become fascinated by the actual composition of glass and never seemed to tire of watching whenever I mixed the basic ingredients myself, instead of always buying it the easy way – off the shelf.

The ready-made stuff, which came in 200-kilo drums, looked like small opaque marbles, or large grey peas, half the size of the polished clear-glass toys. I used the simple option regularly, as it came pure and clean and melted without flaws.

When Martin first watched me load the tank of the furnace with a week's supply of the round grey pebbles, he repeated aloud the listed ingredients. 'Eighty per cent of the mix is white silica sand from the Dead Sea. Ten per cent is soda ash. Then add small specific amounts of antimony, barium, calcium and arsenic per fifty pounds of weight. If you want to colour the glass blue, use ground lapis lazuli or cobalt. If you want yellow, use cadmium, which changes with heat to orange and red and I don't believe it.'

'That's soda crystal glass,' I nodded, smiling. 'I use it all the time as it's safe in every way for eating or drinking from. Babies can lick it.'

He gazed at me in surprise. 'Isn't all glass safe to suck?'

'Well ... no. You have to be exceedingly careful making things with lead. Lead crystal. Lovely stuff. But lead is mega mega poisonous. Lead silicate, that is, that's used for glass. It's a rusty red powder and in its raw state you have to keep it strictly separate from everything else and be terribly meticulous about locking it up.'

'What about cut lead-crystal wine glasses?' he asked. 'I mean, Bon-Bon's mother gave us some.'

'Don't worry,' I told him with humour. 'If they haven't made you ill yet, they probably won't.'

'Thanks a bunch.'

I went in through my heavy gallery door of bevelled glass panes already feeling an emptiness where Martin had been. And it wasn't as if I had no other friends. I had a pack of beer and wine cronies for whom fizzy water and sauna sweats were on their anathema lists. Two of those, Hickory and Irish, worked for me as assistants and apprentices, although Hickory was approximately my own age and Irish a good deal older. The desire to work with glass quite often struck late in life, as with Irish, who was forty, but sometimes, as with me, the fascination arrived like talking, too early to remember.

I had an uncle, eminent in the glass-blowing trade, who was also a brilliant flameworker. He could heat solid glass rods in the flame of a gas burner until, among other things, he could twiddle them into a semblance of lace, and make angels and crinolines and steady flat round bases for almost anything needing precision in a science laboratory.

He was amused at first that an inquisitive kid should shadow him, but was then interested, and finally took it seriously. He taught me whenever I could dodge school, and he died about the time that my inventiveness grew to match his. I was sixteen. In his will he left me plans and instructions for the building of a basic workshop, and also, much more valuably, his priceless notebooks into which he'd detailed years of unique skill. I'd built a locked safe-like bookcase to keep them in, and ever since had added my own notes on method and materials needed when I designed anything special. It stood always at the far end of the workshop between the stock shelves and a bank of four tall grey lockers, where my assistants and I kept our personal stuff.

It was he, my Uncle Ron, who named his enterprise Logan Glass, and he who drilled into me an embryonic business sense and an awareness that anything made by one glass-blower could in general be copied by another, and that this drastically lowered the asking price. During his last few years he sought and succeeded in making pieces of uncopyable originality, working out of my sight and then challenging me to detect and repeat his methods. Whenever I couldn't, he generously showed me how; and he laughed when I grew in ability until I could beat him at his own game.

In the late afternoon of Martin's death both the gallery and showroom were crowded with people looking for ways of remembering the advent of the historic millennium day. I'd designed and made a whole multitude and variety of small good-looking calendar-bearing dishes in every colour combination that I knew from experience attracted most tourist dollars, and we had sold literally hundreds of them. I'd scratched my signature on the lot. Not yet, I thought, but by the year 2020, if I could achieve it, a signed Gerard Logan calendar dish of 31 December 1999 might be worth collecting.

The long gallery displayed the larger, unusual, one-off and more expensive pieces, each spot-lit and available: the showroom was lined by many shelves holding smaller, colourful, attractive and less expensive ornaments, which could reasonably be packed into a tourist suit-case.

One side wall of the showroom rose only to waist height, so that over it one could see into the workshop beyond, where the furnace burned day and night and the little grey pebbles melted into soda crystal at a raised heat of 2,400 degrees Fahrenheit.

Hickory or Irish, or their colleague Pamela Jane, took turns to work as my assistant in the workshop. One of the other two gave a running commentary of the proceedings to the customers and the third packed parcels and worked the till. Ideally the four of us took the jobs in turn, but experienced glass-blowers were scarce, and my three en-thusiastic assistants were still at the paperweight and penguin stage.

Christmas sales had been great but nothing like the New Year Two Thousand. As everything sold in my place was guaranteed hand-made (and mostly by me), the day I'd spent at the races had been my first respite away from the furnace for a month. I'd worked sometimes into the night, and always from eight onwards in the morning, with one of my three helpers assisting. The resulting exhaustion hadn't mattered. I was physically fit, and as Martin had said, who needed a sauna with 2,400 degrees in one's face?

Hickory, twirling colour into a glowing paperweight on the end of a slender five-foot-long steel rod called a punty iron, looked extremely relieved at my return from the races. Pamela Jane, smiling, earnest, thin and anxious,

14

lost her place in her commentary and repeated instead, 'He's here. He's here . . .' and Irish stopped packing a cobalt-blue dolphin in bright white wrapping paper and sighed, 'Thank God' very heavily. They relied on me too much, I thought.

I said, 'Hi, guys,' as usual and, walking round into the workshop and stripping off jacket, tie and shirt, gave the millennium-crazy shoppers a view of a designer-label white string singlet, my working clothes. Hickory finished his paperweight, spinning the punty iron down by his feet to cool the glass, being careful not to scorch his new bright trainers. I made, as a frivolity, a striped hollow blue, green and purple fish with fins, a geodetic-type of ornament that looked impressively difficult and had defeated me altogether at fourteen. Light shone through it in rainbows.

The customers, though, wanted proof of that day's origin. Staying open much later than usual, I made endless dated bowls, plates and vases to please them, while Pamela Jane explained that they couldn't be collected until the next morning, New Year's Day, as they had to cool slowly overnight. No one seemed deterred. Irish wrote their names and told them jokes. There were hours of good nature and celebration.

Priam Jones called in fleetingly at one point. When he had been at Martin and Bon-Bon's house, he'd found my raincoat lying on the back seat in the car. I was most grateful, and thanked him with New Year fervour. He nodded, even smiled. His tears had dried.

When he'd gone I went to hang up my raincoat in my locker. Something hard banged against my knee and I remembered the package given to me by Eddie, the valet. I put it on a stock shelf out of the way at the rear of the workshop and went back to satisfy the customers.

Shop closing time was elastic but I finally locked the door behind the last customer in time for Hickory, Irish and Pamela Jane to go to parties, and for me to realize I hadn't yet opened the parcel that Priam Jones had returned in my raincoat. The parcel that had come from Martin . . . he'd sat heavily on my shoulder all evening, a laughing lost spirit, urging me on.

Full of regrets I locked the furnace against vandals and checked the heat of the annealing ovens, which were full of the newly made objects slowly cooling. The furnace, that I'd built to my uncle's design, was constructed of fire-bricks and fuelled by propane gas under pressure from a fan. It burned day and night at never less than 1,800 degrees Fahrenheit, hot enough to melt most metals, let alone burn paper. We were often asked if a memento like a wedding ring could be enclosed in a glass paper-weight, but the answer was sorry, no. Liquid glass would melt gold – and human flesh – immediately. Molten glass, in fact, was pretty dangerous stuff.

I slowly tidied the workshop, counted and recounted and then enclosed the day's takings in their canvas bag ready to entrust to the night safe of the bank. Then I put on my discarded clothes and eventually took a closer look at my neglected parcel. The contents proved to be exactly what they felt like, an ordinary-looking videotape, a bit disappointing. The tape was wound fully back to the beginning, and the black casing bore no label of any sort. There was no protective sleeve. I stacked it casually beside the money, and the sight of it reminded me that my videotape player was at my home, that I'd sold my car, and that rising midnight on a thousand years' eve wasn't the best time to phone for a taxi.

Plans for my own midnight, with a neighbourhood dance next door to my house, had disintegrated on Cheltenham racecourse. Maybe the Wychwood Dragon, I thought, not caring much, still had a broom cupboard to rent. I would beg a sandwich and a rug and sleep across the dark night into the new century, and early in the morning I would make an obituary for a jockey.

Just as I was about to cross to the Wychwood Dragon someone tapped heavily on the glass-paned door, and I went to open it, intending to say it was far too late, the year two thousand lay fifteen minutes ahead in Broadway, even if it had been tomorrow for hours in Australia. I unlocked the door and, prompted by inexorable courtesy, faced politely an unexpected and unwanted visitor in Lloyd Baxter, telling him with a half-smothered yawn that I simply hadn't enough energy to discuss the disaster at Cheltenham or anything else to do with horses.

He advanced into the brightest area on the threshold and I saw he was carrying a bottle of Dom Pérignon and two of the Wychwood Dragon's best champagne glasses. The heavily disapproving expression, despite these pipes of peace, was still in place.

'Mr Logan,' he said formally, 'I know no one at all in this place except yourself, and don't say this isn't a time for rejoicing, as I agree with you in many ways . . . not only because Martin Stukely is dead but because the next century is likely to be even more bloody than the last and I see no reason to celebrate just a change of date, particularly as there's no doubt the date is incorrect to begin with.' He took a breath. 'I therefore decided to spend the evening in my room—' He stopped abruptly, and I would have finished the tale for him, but instead I merely jerked my head for him to come right in, and closed the heavy door behind him.

'I'll drink to Martin,' I said.

He looked relieved at my acquiescence, even though he thought little of me and was old enough to be my father. Loneliness, though, still propelling him, he set the glasses on the table beside the till, ceremoniously popped the expensive cork and unleashed the bubbles.

'Drink to whatever you like,' he said in depression. 'I suppose it was a bad idea, coming here.'

'No,' I said.

'I could hear the music, you see . . .'

Music in the distance had forced him out of his lonely room. Music powerfully attracted the gregarious human race. No one welcomed two thousand years in silence.

I looked at my watch. Only nine minutes to ring-the-bells time.

Regardless of cynical withdrawals from organized enjoyment, regardless even of thrusts of raw unprocessed grief, I found there was inescapable excitement after all in the sense of a new chance offered, a fresh beginning possible. One could forgive one's own faults.

New numbers themselves vibrated with promise.

Five minutes to ring-the-bells ... and fireworks. I drank Lloyd Baxter's champagne and still didn't like him.

Tallahassee's owner had changed, thanks to his transferred bag, into formal clothes, complete with black tie. His almost Edwardian type of grooming seemed to intensify rather than lighten his thunderous personality.

Even though I'd been introduced to him at least two years earlier, and had drunk his fizz on happier occasions, I'd never before bothered to read his face feature by feature. Rectifying that, I remembered that he'd earlier had thick strong dark hair, but as his age had advanced from fifty there were grey streaks that to my eyes had multiplied quite fast. His facial bone structure was thick and almost Cro-Magnon, with a powerful-looking brow and a similar no-nonsense jaw.

Perhaps in the past he had been lean and hungry, but as the twentieth century rolled away he had thickened round the neck and stomach and taken on the authoritative weight of chairman. If he looked more like an industrialist than a landowner, it was because he'd sold his majority share in a shipping line to buy his racehorses and his acres.

He disapproved, he'd told me severely, of young men like myself who could take days off work whenever they cared to. I knew he considered me a hanger-on who sponged off Martin, regardless of Martin's insisting it was more likely the other way round. It seemed that when Lloyd Baxter formed a set of opinions he was slow to re-arrange them.

Distantly, out in the cold night, bells in England pealed the passing of the all-important moment, celebrating the artificial date change and affirming that humankind could impose its own mathematics on the unresponsive planet. Lloyd Baxter raised his glass to drink to some private goal, and I, following his gesture, hoped merely that I would see in January 2001 in safety. I added in fact with banal courtesy, that I would drink to his health outside, if he'd forgive me my absence.

'Of course,' he said, his voice a mumble.

Pulling open the gallery door I walked out into the street still holding my golden drink, and found that dozens of people had felt impelled in the same way. A host, myself included, had been moved by an almost supernatural instinct to breathe free new air under the stars.

The man who sold antique books in the shop next to my gallery shook my hand vigorously, and with warm goodwill wished me a happy new year. I smiled and thanked him. Smiling was easy. The village, a fairly friendly place at any time, greeted the new year and the neighbours with uncomplicated affection. Feuds could wait.

Nearby, a large group of people had linked arms and were swaying across the road singing 'Auld Lang Syne' with half the words missing, and one or two cars crept along slowly, headlights full on, horns blaring, with enthusiastic youths yelling from open windows. Up and down the High Street local sophistication found its own level, but everywhere with a benign slant of mind.

Perhaps because of that, it was longer than I'd intended before I reluctantly decided I should return to my shop, my ready-for-the-bank takings and my unwelcome visitor, whose temper wouldn't have been improved by my absence.

Declining with regret a tot of single malt from the bookseller, I ambled along to Logan Glass feeling the first twitch of resignation for the lack of Martin. He had known always that his job might kill him, but he hadn't expected it. Falls were inevitable but they would happen 'some other time'. Injuries had been counted a nuisance that interfered with winning. He would 'hang up his boots', he'd told me lightheartedly, the minute he was afraid to put them on.

It was the *thought* of fear that bothered him, he'd once said.

I pushed open the heavy door preparing my apologies and found that an entirely different sort of action was essential.

Lloyd Baxter lay face down, unmoving and unconscious, on my showroom floor.

Dumping my empty glass rapidly on the table that held the till I knelt anxiously beside him and felt for a pulse in his neck. Even though his lips were bluish he hadn't somehow the look of someone dead, and there was to my great relief a slow perceptible thud-thud under my fingers. A stroke, perhaps? A heart attack? I knew very little medicine.

What an appallingly awkward night, I thought, sitting back on my heels, for anyone to need to call out the medics. I stood up and took a few paces to the table which held the till and all the business machines, including the telephone. I dialled the come-at-once number without much expectation, but even on such a New Year's Eve, it seemed, the emergency services would respond, and it wasn't until I'd put down the receiver on their promise of an instant stretcher that I noticed the absence beside the till of the ready-for-the-bank canvas bag. It had gone. I searched for it everywhere, but in my heart I knew where I'd left it.

I swore. I'd worked hard for every cent. I'd sweated. My arms still ached. I was depressed at that point as well as furious. I began to wonder if Lloyd Baxter had done his best; if he'd been knocked out trying to defend my property against a thief.

The black unidentified videotape had gone as well. The wave of outrage common to anyone robbed of even minor objects shook me into a deeper anger. The tape's loss was a severe aggravation, even if not on the same level as the money.

I telephoned the police without exciting them in the least. They were psyched up for bombs, not paltry theft. They said they would send someone in the morning.

Lloyd Baxter stirred, moaned and lay still again. I knelt beside him, removed his tie, unfastened his belt and in general rolled him slightly onto his side so that he wasn't in danger of choking. There were flecks of blood, though, around his mouth.

The chill of the deep night seeped into my own body, let alone Baxter's. The flames of the furnace roared captive behind the trapdoor which rose and fell to make the heat available, and finally, uncomfortably cold, I went and stood on the treadle that raised the trap, and let the heat flood into the workshop to reach the showroom beyond.

Normally, even in icy winter, the furnace in constant use gave warmth enough, supplemented by an electric convector heater in the gallery, but by the time help arrived for Baxter I had wrapped him in my jacket and everything else handy, and he was still growing cold to the touch.

The ultra-efficient men who arrived in the prompt ambulance took over expertly, examining their patient, searching and emptying his pockets, making a preliminary diagnosis and wrapping him in a red warming blanket ready for transport. Baxter partially awoke during this process but couldn't swim altogether to the surface of consciousness. His gaze flickered woozily once across my face before his eyes closed again into a heavier sleep.

The paramedics did some paperwork and had me provide them with Baxter's name, address, and as much as I knew (practically nothing) of his medical history. One of them was writing a list of all the things they had taken from him, starting with a Piaget gold watch and ending with the contents of a pocket of his trousers – a handkerchief, a bottle of pills, and a businesslike hotel-room key in the shape of a ball-and-chain deterrent to forgetfulness.

I didn't even have to suggest that I should return the key myself to the hotel, the paramedics suggested it themselves. I rattled it into my own trousers without delay, thinking vaguely of packing Lloyd Baxter's things into his much-travelled case and more positively of sleeping in his bed, since the paramedics were adamant that he would have to stay in hospital all night.

'What's wrong with him?' I asked. 'Has he had a heart attack? Or a stroke? Has he been . . . well, attacked and knocked out?'

I told them about the money and the tape.

They shook their heads. The most senior of them discounted my guesses. He said that to his experienced eyes Lloyd Baxter wasn't having a non-fatal heart attack (he would be awake, if so) nor a stroke, nor were there any lumpy bruises on his head. In his opinion, he announced authoritatively, Lloyd Baxter had had an epileptic fit.

'A *fit*?' I asked blankly. 'He's seemed perfectly well all day.'

The medics nodded knowledgeably. One of them picked up the pill bottle whose contents were listed as phenytoin and said he was certain that this was the preventative for epilepsy.

'Epilepsy,' the chief medic nodded, 'and who'll bet that he was overdue with a dose? We have all the other symptoms here. Alcohol.' He gestured to the depleted bottle of Dom. 'Late night without sleep. Stress . . . isn't he the one whose jockey was done for at the races today? Then there's the slow pulse and bluish lips, the blood flecks from where he's bitten his tongue . . . and did you notice that his trousers are wet? They urinate, you know.'

CHAPTER TWO

The resident Dragon of the Wychwood Dragon Hotel being its fierce lady manager, I could ooze in and out of the halls unseen (as it were) owing both to the collection of small coloured glass animals marching round her dressing table, and to her occasional invitations to bed. The glass animals weren't so much trophies as apologies, however, as she was fortunately resigned to accepting that a thirty-year difference in age was a fair enough reason for me to say no. Her habit of calling me 'Lover' in public was embarrassment enough, though, and I knew that most of Broadway believed she ate me with eggs for breakfast.

Anyway, no one questioned my takeover of Lloyd Baxter's room. In the morning I packed his belongings and, explaining all to the Dragon, arranged for the hotel to send them to the hospital. Then I walked down and across to the workshop, where Martin, though vivid in my mind, refused to fly as a statement in glass. Inspiration operated at its own good speed, and many a time I'd found that trying to force it didn't work.

The furnace roared in its firebox. I sat beside the stainless-steel table (called a marver) on which I should have been rolling eternity into basic balls of liquid glass, and thought only of Martin alive in the body, Martin laughing and winning races, and Martin's lost message on videotape. Where was that tape, what did it contain and who thought it worth stealing?

These profitless thoughts were interrupted by the door-bell ringing early at nine o'clock, when we'd said we'd open at ten.

On the doorstep stood no recognizable customer but a young woman in a vast sloppy sweater hanging round her knees, topped by a baseball cap over a shock of brassily dyed streaky hair. We stared at each other with interest, her brown eyes alive and curious, her jaw rhythmic with chewing gum.

I said politely, 'Good morning.'

'Yeah. Yeah.' She laughed. 'Happy New Century and all that rubbish. Are you Gerard Logan?'

Her accent was Estuary, Essex or Thames: take your pick.

'Logan.' I nodded. 'And you?'

'Detective Constable Dodd.'

I blinked. 'Plain clothes?'

'You may laugh,' she said, chewing away. 'You reported a theft at twelve thirty-two this a.m. Can I come in?'

'Be my guest.'

She stepped into the gallery spotlights and glowed.

From habit I dramatized her in glass in my mind, an abstract essence as a conduit of feeling and light, exactly the instinctive process I'd tried in vain to summon up for Martin.

Oblivious, Detective Constable Dodd produced a down-to-earth warrant card, identifying her in uniform and adding a first name, Catherine. I handed the warrant card back and answered her questions, but the police opinion was already firm. Too bad I'd left a bagful of money lying around, she said. What did I expect? And videotapes came by the dozen. No one would think twice about snapping one up.

'What was on it?' she asked, pencil poised over a notepad.

'I've no idea.' I explained how it had come to me originally in a brown-paper parcel.

'Pornography. Bound to be.' Her pronouncement was brisk, world-weary and convinced. 'Unidentified.' She shrugged. 'Would you know it from any other tape if you saw it again?'

'It hadn't any labels.'

I dug the wrapping out of the rubbish bin and gave her the wrinkled and torn paper. 'This came to me by hand,' I said. 'There's no postmark.'

She took the paper dubiously, enclosed it in a plastic bag, got me to sign across the join and tucked it away somewhere under the extra-loose sweater.

My answers to her questions about the stolen money caused her eyebrows to rise over the amount, but she obviously thought I'd never again see the canvas bag or the mini bonanza inside. I still had cheques and credit card slips, of course, but most of my tourist customers paid in cash.

I told her then about Lloyd Baxter and his epileptic fit. 'Maybe he saw the thief,' I said.

She frowned. 'Maybe he *was* the thief. Could he have faked the fit?'

'The paramedics didn't seem to think so.'

She sighed. 'How long were you out in the street?'

'Bells. "Auld Lang Syne", fireworks, happy new thousand years . . .'

'Getting on for half an hour?' She consulted her notebook. 'You phoned the ambulance service at twelve twenty-seven.'

She wandered through the showroom looking at the small colourful vases, the clowns, sailing boats, fishes and horses. She picked up a haloed angel and disapproved of the price sticker under the feet. Her swathe of hair fell forward, framing her intent face, and I again clearly saw the bright analytical intelligence inside the sloppy hippie-type disguise. She was through and through a police officer, not primarily a come-hither female.

Replacing the angel with decision on the shelf, she folded her notebook, stored it out of sight and with body language announced that the investigation, despite its lack of results, was over. It was the go-to-work version of Constable Dodd that prepared to step into the street.

'Why?' I asked.

'Why what?' She concentrated on her change of character.

'Why the too big sweater and the baseball cap?'

She flashed me an aware, amused glance and turned back to the world outside. 'You happened to have been robbed on my allotted beat. My assignment in Broadway is to spot the gang stealing cars on bank holidays in this area. Thanks for your time.'

She grinned with cheerfulness and shuffled off down the hill, pausing to talk to a homeless-looking layabout sitting in a shop doorway, huddling against the chill of morning.

A pity the hippie and the hobo hadn't been car-thief spotting at midnight, I thought vaguely, and telephoned the hospital to enquire about Baxter.

Awake and grumbling, I gathered. I left a message of goodwill.

Bon-Bon next.

She wailed miserably into my ear. 'But, darling Gerard, *of course* I didn't tell Priam not to bring you with him. How could you believe it? You are the *first* person Martin would want to come here. Please, please come as soon as you can, the children are crying and everything's dreadful.' She drew a shaky breath, the tears distorting her voice. 'We were going to a midnight party . . . and the baby-sitter came and said she wanted her full money anyway, even if Martin was dead, can you believe it? And Priam talked about the inconvenience of finding

30

another jockey halfway through the season. He's an old fool and he kept patting me . . .'

'He was seriously upset,' I assured her. 'A matter of tears.'

'*Priam?*'

I frowned at the memory, but the tears had looked real.

'How long did he stay with you?' I asked.

'Stay? He didn't stay long. Ten to fifteen minutes, maybe. My mother descended on us while he was here and, you've met her, you know what she's like. Priam was mostly in Martin's den, I think. He kept saying he had to be back for evening stables, he couldn't sit still.' Bon-Bon's despair overflowed. 'Can't you *come*? Please, please come. I can't deal with my mother by myself.'

'As soon as I've done one job, and found some transport. Say . . . about noon.'

'Oh yes, I forgot your bloody car. Where are you? Did you get home?'

'I'm in my workshop.'

'I'll come and fetch you . . .'

'No. First, fill your mama with gin and let the children loose on her, then shut yourself in Martin's den and watch the tapes of him winning his three Grand Nationals but don't drive anywhere while you're so upset. I'll find transport, but at the worst we could persuade your remarkable parent to lend me Worthington and the Rolls.'

Bon-Bon's mother's versatile chauffeur raised his eye-

31

brows to heaven frequently at Marigold's odd requirements, but had been known to drive a roofless Land
Rover at breakneck speed at night across stubble fields,
headlights blazing in the dark, while his employer stood
balancing behind him with a double-barrelled shotgun
loosing off at mesmerized rabbits over his head. Martin
said he'd been afraid to watch, but Worthington and
Marigold had achieved a bag of forty and freed her land
of a voracious pest.

Worthington, bald and fifty, was more an adventure
than a last resort.

On New Year's Day 2000 in England the world in general
came to a stop. Saturday's running of one of the best
steeplechasing afternoon programmes of the whole midwinter season was stuck in a silly halt because the people
who worked the Tote betting machines wanted to stay at
home. There was no racing – and no football – to
entertain the non-workers on or off the television.

Logan Glass astounded the other residents of Broadway by opening its doors to the day-before's customers,
who arrived to collect their overnight-cooled souvenirs.
To my own astonishment two of my assistants turned up,
even though bleary-eyed, saying they couldn't leave me
to pack the whole delivery job alone, so it was with speed
and good humour that my new century began. I looked
back later at the peace of that brief morning with a feeling

of unreality that life could ever have been so safe and simple.

Pamela Jane, twittery, anxious, stick-thin and wanly pretty, insisted on driving me to Bon-Bon's place herself, leaving me in the driveway and departing with a wave, hurrying back to the shop as she'd left Irish alone there.

Martin and Bon-Bon had agreed at least on their house, an eighteenth-century gem that Marigold had helped them buy. I admired it every time I went there.

A small van stood on the gravel, dark-blue with a commercial name painted on it in yellow: '*Thompson Electronics*'. I suppose it was because I'd been working myself that I didn't immediately remember that that day was a national holiday; definitely a moratorium for television-repair vans.

Chaos was too weak a word to describe what I found inside Martin's house. For a start, the front door was visibly ajar and, when I touched it, it swung wide. It was normally the kitchen door the family left hospitably unlocked, both for friends and visiting tradesmen.

Beginning to feel slight unease, I stepped through the heavily carved front doorway and shouted, but there was no response, and a pace or two later I learned why I had misgivings.

Bon-Bon's mother Marigold, frothy grey hair and floaty purple dress in disarray as usual, lay unconscious on the stairs. Worthington, her eccentric chauffeur, sprawled like a drugged medieval guard dog at her feet.

The four children, out of sight, were uncannily quiet, and the door to Martin's room, his den, was closed on silence.

I opened this door immediately and found Bon-Bon there, lying full-length on the wood-block floor. Again, as with Lloyd Baxter, I knelt to feel for a pulse in the neck, but this time with sharp anxiety; and I felt the living ga-bump ga-bump with a deeper relief. Concentrating on Bon-Bon I saw too late in peripheral sight a movement behind my right shoulder ... a dark figure speeding from where he'd been hiding behind the door.

I jerked halfway to standing but wasn't quick enough on my feet. There was a short second in which I glimpsed a small metal gas cylinder – more or less like a quarter-sized fire extinguisher. But this cylinder wasn't red. It was orange. It hit my head. Martin's den turned grey, dark grey, and black. A deep well of nothing.

I returned slowly to a gallery of watchers. To a row of eyes dizzily in front of my own. I couldn't think where I was or what was happening. It had to be bad, though, because the children's eyes looked huge with fright.

I was lying on my back. Into the blank spaces of memory slowly crept the picture of an orange gas cylinder in the hands of a figure in a black head-mask with holes cut out for eyes.

As a return to awareness grew clearer I focused on Bon-Bon's face and tried to stand up. Bon-Bon, seeing this minor revival, said with great relief, 'Thank God you're all right. We've all been gassed and we've all been sick since we woke up. Totter to the loo next door, there's a chum. Don't be sick in here.'

I had a headache, not nausea. My head had collided with the outside of a metal gas cylinder, not with the contents. I felt too lethargic to explain the difference.

Worthington, notwithstanding the muscular physique he painstakingly developed by regular visits to a punch-bag gym, looked pale and shaky and far from well. He held each of the two youngest children by the hand, though, giving them what comfort and confidence he could. In their eyes he could do everything, and they were nearly right.

Bon-Bon had once mentioned that Worthington's top value to her mother was his understanding of book-makers' methods, because, as Marigold herself disliked walking along between the rows of men shouting the odds, Worthington got her the best prices. A versatile and compulsive good guy, Worthington, though he didn't always look it.

Only Marigold herself was now missing from the sick parade. I asked about her, and the eldest of the children, a boy called Daniel, said she was drunk. She was snoring on the stairs, the elder girl said. So pragmatic, 2000-year children.

While I peeled myself slowly off the wood blocks,

Bon-Bon, with annoyance, remarked that her doctor had announced he no longer made house calls, even for those recovering from bereavement. He said all would be well with rest and fluid. 'Water,' he'd said.

'Gin,' corrected one of the children dryly.

I thought it scandalous that Bon-Bon's doctor should have refused to tend her and had a go at him myself. Capitulating with apologetic grace he promised he would 'look in', New Year's Day holiday notwithstanding. He hadn't understood Mrs Stukely, he excused himself. He didn't realize she'd been attacked. She'd been partly incoherent. Had we informed the police?

It did seem obvious that robbery had been the purpose of the mass anaesthesia. Three television sets with integral tape players were missing. Bon-Bon had been angry enough to count things.

Also gone was a separate video player on which she'd been watching Martin, together with dozens of tapes. Two lap-top computers, with printers and racks of filing disks were missing too, but Worthington prophesied that the police would offer little hope of recovering these things, as Martin had apparently not recorded any identifying numbers anywhere.

Bon-Bon began crying quietly from the strain of it all and it was Worthington, recovering and worth his weight in videotapes, who talked to the overburdened local nick. My Constable Catherine Dodd, he found, was attached to a different branch. Detectives, however, would arrive on the Stukely doorstep soon.

Not surprisingly, the '*Thompson Electronics*' van had gone.

Marigold went on snoring on the stairs.

Worthington made calming sandwiches of banana and honey for the children.

Feeling queasy, I sat in Martin's black leather chair in his den, while Bon-Bon, on an opposite sofa, dried her complicated grief on tissues and finally gave no complete answer to my repeated question, which was, 'What was on the tape that Martin meant to give me after the races, and where did it come from? That's to say, who gave it to Martin himself at Cheltenham?'

Bon-Bon studied me with wet eyes and blew her nose. 'I know Martin wanted to tell you something yesterday, but he had those other men in the car, and I know he wanted to talk to you without Priam listening so he planned to take you home last, after the others, even though you live nearest to the racecourse.'

Even in distress she looked porcelain pretty, the plumpness an asset in a curvy black wool suit cut to please a living husband rather than a mourning neighbourhood.

'He trusted you,' she said finally.

'Mm.' I'd have been surprised if he hadn't.

'No, you don't understand.' Bon-Bon hesitated and went on slowly. 'He knew a secret. He wouldn't tell me what it was. He said I would fret. But he wanted to tell *someone*. We did discuss *that*, and I agreed it should be you. *You* should be his back-up. Just in case. Oh dear . . .

He had what he wanted you to know put onto a plain old-fashioned recording tape, not onto a CD or a computer disk, and he did that, I think, because whoever was giving him information preferred it that way. I'm not sure. And also it was easier to play, he said. Better on video than computer because, darling Gerard, you know I never get things right when it comes to computers. The children laugh at me. I can play a videotape easily. Martin wanted me to be able to do that if he died, but of course . . . of *course* . . . he didn't think he'd die, not really.'

I asked, 'Could you yourself make a home movie on a videotape?'

She nodded. 'Martin gave me a video camera for Christmas. It makes your own home films but I've hardly had time to learn how to use it.'

'And he didn't say *anything* about what was on that tape he meant for me?'

'He was awfully careful not to.'

I shook my head in frustration. The tape stolen from the glass showroom was surely the one with the secret on it. The one passed to Martin, then to Eddie the valet, and then to me. Yet if the Broadway thieves, or thief, had viewed it – and they'd had all night to do so – why were they needing to rob Martin's house ten hours later?

Did the tape taken from the showroom actually contain Martin's secret?

Perhaps not.

Was the second robbery carried out by a *different* thief, who didn't know about the first one?

I had no answers, only guesses.

Marigold at that point tottered into the den as if coming to pieces in all directions. I had been used to Marigold for the four years since Martin had straight-facedly presented me to his buxom mother-in-law, a magnified version of his pretty wife. Marigold could be endlessly witty or tiresomely belligerent according to the gin level, but this time the effect of gas on alcohol seemed to have resulted in pity-me pathos, a state that aroused genuine sympathy, not serve-you-right.

In Bon-Bon's house it was the police that turned up first, and Bon-Bon's children who described down to the laces on his shoes the clothes worn by their attacker. He had stared with wide eyes through his black head-mask while he'd pointed the orange cylinder at them and squirted a nearly invisible but fierce mist, sweeping from face to face and knocking them out before they'd realized what was happening. Asked about it, Daniel, the eldest child, described the black-masked man having something white tied over his face underneath. An elementary gas mask, I surmised. Something to prevent the robber from inhaling his own gas.

Worthington had been attacked most strongly and had fallen unconscious first, and Bon-Bon – in the den – last. The gas had perhaps been exhausted by the time I arrived; a direct bang on the head had sufficed.

Worthington had been right in guessing the police would offer no hope of Bon-Bon ever again seeing the missing goods. She felt less pain than I would have expected over the loss of tapes showing Martin winning the Grand National because, as she explained, she could get duplicates.

Scarcely had the police notebooks been folded away than Bon-Bon's doctor hurried in without apology, giving the impression he was making an exception, out of the goodness of his heart.

It was the colour orange that slowed him into frowns and more thorough care. He and the police all listened to Daniel, brought out paper, and took notes. The doctor told the departing detectives to look for villains with access to the anaesthetic gas cyclopropane, which came in orange cylinders, and wasn't much used because of being highly flammable and explosive.

Slowly, after decently thorough peerings into eyes and throats and careful stethoscope chest checks, each of the family was judged fit to go on living. Sweet Bon-Bon, when her house was finally free of official attention, sat sprawling on the office sofa telling me she was utterly exhausted and needed help. Specifically she needed *my* help and Martin would have asked for it.

So I stayed and looked after things, and because of that I saved myself at least another sore head, as thieves broke into my house on the hill that night and stole everything that could remotely be called a videotape.

On the Monday, after an early morning session in the workshop making new little items for stock, I went to

Cheltenham races again (by taxi) to talk to Martin's valet, Eddie Payne.

Ed or Eddie (he answered to both) was ready to help, he said, but he couldn't. He'd spent all weekend thinking it over and he said, his gaze darting over my shoulder and back again to my face, he couldn't – however hard he tried – remember any more than he'd told me on Friday. I thought back to the moment of empathy between us, when we had each realized what we'd lost. That moment of genuine emptiness had gone.

The difference between Friday and Monday was a fierce-eyed woman of approaching forty, now standing a pace or two behind me, a woman Ed referred to as his daughter. He slid a second glance at her expressionlessly and like a ventriloquist not moving his lips, said to me almost too quietly for me to hear, '*She* knows the man who gave Martin the tape.'

The woman said sharply, 'What did you say, Dad? Do speak up.'

'I said we'd miss Martin badly,' Eddie said, 'and I'm due back in the changing room. Tell Gerard – Mr Logan – what he wants to know, why don't you?'

He walked away with a worried shuffle, apologetically saying to me as he went, 'Her name's Rose. She's a good girl really.'

Rose, the good girl, gave me such a bitter flash of hate that I wondered what I'd ever done to annoy her, as I hadn't known of her existence until moments earlier. She was angularly bony and had mid-brown hair with frizzy sticking-out curls. Her skin was dry and freckled, and although her clothes looked too big for the thin body inside, there was about her an extraordinary air of magnetism.

'Er . . . Rose—' I started.

'Mrs Robins,' she interrupted abruptly.

I cleared my throat and tried again.

'Mrs Robins, then, could I buy you some coffee, or a drink in the bar?'

She said, 'No, you could *not*.' She bit the words off with emphasis. She said, 'You'd do better to mind your own business.'

'Mrs Robins, did you see who gave a brown-paper parcel to Martin Stukely at Cheltenham races last Friday?'

Such a simple question. She primped her lips together tightly, swivelled on her heel, and walked away with an air of not intending to come back.

After a short pause, I followed her. Looking down from time to time at my racecard as any prospective punter would, I trickled along in her wake as she made for the ranks of bookmakers' pitches in front of the open-to-the-public Tattersalls stands. She stopped at a board announcing *Arthur Robins, Prestwick, Established 1894*, and talked to an Elvis Presley lookalike with heavy black side-whiskers who was standing on a box, leaning down to take money from the public and dictating his transactions to a clerk, who was punching the bets into a computer.

Rose Robins, established long after 1894, had a fair

amount to say. The Elvis lookalike frowned, listening, and I retreated: I might have strength and reasonable agility but Rose's contact made my muscle-power look the stuff of kindergartens. Whichever Robins filled the shoes of Arthur nowadays, if he were the Elvis lookalike, he weighed in with grandfather-gorilla shoulders.

Patiently I climbed the stands and waited while the *Arthur Robins, Est. 1894* bookmakers – three of them – took bets on the final two races of the afternoon, and then I watched their chief, the Elvis lookalike, pack up the board and take charge of the money bag and walk towards the exit with Rose and his two helpers beside him. I watched them go out of sight. As far as I could tell, they all left the racecourse. As a group, they equalled an armoured tank.

From experience with Martin, I knew that jockeys' valets finished their work after most of the crowds had gone home. A valet was a man who helped the jockeys change rapidly between races. He also looked after and cleaned their gear, saddles, breeches, boots and so on, so it was all ready for next time they raced. Martin had told me that a single valet would look after a whole bunch of jockeys, and the valets would work as a team to cover all the race meetings. While Eddie packed up his hampers of saddles, kit and clothes for laundering, I waited with hope for him to reappear out of the changing room at the end of his day.

When he came out and saw me, he was at first alarmed, and then resigned.

'I suppose,' he said, 'Rose wouldn't tell you.'

'No,' I agreed. 'So would you ask her something, for Martin's sake?'

'Well . . .' he hesitated. 'It depends.'

I said, 'Ask her if the tape Martin gave you was the one she thought it was.'

He took a few seconds to work it out.

'Do you mean,' he asked doubtfully, 'that my Rose thinks Martin had the wrong tape?'

'I think,' I confessed, 'that if Martin's tape ever surfaces after all the muddle and thieving, it'll be a matter of luck.'

He protested self-righteously that he'd given me Martin's tape in good faith. I insisted that I believed him. No more was said about Rose.

Eddie knew, as did the whole racing world after that day's newspapers, that Martin's funeral was planned for Thursday, providing no jinx upset Wednesday's inquest. Eddie, eyes down, mumbled a few words about seeing me there, he supposed, and in discomfort hurried away to the inner realms of the changing rooms, from where the public with awkward questions were banned.

Rose Robins and her enmity added complexity to an already tangled situation.

I caught a bus from the racecourse which wound its way from village to village and, in the end, to Broadway. In spite of my having spent all the time tossing around in my mind the unexpected involvement of Eddie's scratchy daughter I came to a no more satisfactory or original conclusion than that someone had given some tape or other to Martin who had given it to Eddie who had given it to me who had carelessly lost it to a thief.

Still drifting in outer space was whatever confidential data Martin had meant to entrust to me. In some respects that didn't matter, and never would, just as long as the hidden nugget of information didn't heat up or collide with an inconvenient truth. Additionally, as I had no road map to the ingredients of the nugget, I had no way either of foreseeing or preventing trouble.

Unrealistically, I simply hoped that Martin's secret would remain forever hidden in uncharted orbit, and all of us could return to normal.

It was after five-thirty by the time I reached the doors of Logan Glass, and again my assistants were there, two of them making paperweights with enthusiasm and the third keeping shop. Bon-Bon had telephoned, they told me, saying she was begging me to go on organizing her household in return for transport; at least until after the funeral, and, much to the amusement of my assistants, the transport she sent that afternoon wasn't her own runabout, but was Marigold's Rolls.

Whenever we were alone together, I sat beside Worthington as he drove. He had offered me the comfort and prestige of the rear seat usually taken by his employer, but I felt wrong there. Moreover, on the showing of the last few days, if I sat at the back he tended both to call me 'sir' and to favour respectful silence instead of pithy and irreverent observation. When I sat in the front, Marigold was 'Marigold': when in the back, 'Mrs Knight'. When I sat beside her chauffeur, he showed his inner self.

In addition to being bald, fifty and kind to children, Worthington disliked the police force as a matter of principle, referred to marriage as bondage and believed in the usefulness of being able to out-kick any other muscle-man in sight. It wasn't so much as a chauffeur that I now valued Worthington at my elbow, but as a prospective bodyguard. The Elvis lookalike had radiated latent menace at an intensity that I hadn't met before and didn't like; and for detonator there was fierce thorny Rose, and it was with her in mind that I casually asked Worthington if he'd ever placed a bet at the races with *Arthur Robins, Est. 1894*.

'For a start,' he said with sarcasm, fastening his seat belt as if keeping to the law were routine, 'the Robins family don't exist. That bunch of swindlers known as Arthur Robins are mostly Veritys and Webbers, with a couple of Browns thrown in. There hasn't been a bona-fide Arthur Robins *ever*. It's just a pretty name.'

Eyebrows raised in surprise I asked, 'How do you know all that?'

'My old man ran a book,' he said. 'Fasten your seat-belt, Gerard. The cops in this town would put eagles out of business. Like I said, my old man was a bookmaker, he taught me the trade. You've got to be real sharp at figures, though, to make a profit, and I never got quick enough. But Arthur Robins, that's the front name for some whizzers of speed merchants. Don't bet with them, that's my advice.'

I said, 'Do you know that Eddie Payne, Martin's valet, has a daughter called Rose who says her last name is Robins and who's on cuddling terms with an Elvis Presley lookalike taking bets for Arthur Robins?'

Worthington, who had been about to start the car outside Logan Glass to drive us to Bon-Bon, sat back in his seat, letting his hands fall laxly on his thighs.

'No,' he said thoughtfully, 'I didn't know that.' He thought for a while, his forehead troubled. 'That Elvis fellow,' he said finally, 'that's Norman Osprey. You don't want to mix with *him*.'

'And Rose?'

Worthington shook his head. 'I don't know her. I'll ask around.' He roused himself and started the purring car.

By Thursday, the day of Martin's funeral, the police as predicted hadn't found one identifiable videotape in a country awash with them.

On the day before the funeral a young woman on a motor bike – huge helmet, black leather jacket, matching trousers, heavy boots – steered into one of the five parking spaces at the front of Logan Glass. Outside in the January chill she pulled off the helmet and shook free a cap of fair fine hair before walking without swagger into the gallery and showroom as if she knew the way well.

I was putting the pre-annealing final touches to a vase, with Pamela Jane telling a group of American tourists how it was done, but there was something attention-claiming about the motor cyclist, and as soon as I thought of her in terms of glass, I knew her infallibly.

'Catherine Dodd,' I said.

'Most people don't recognize me.' She was amused, not piqued.

With interest I watched the tourists pack somewhat closer together as if to elbow out the stranger in threatening clothes.

Pamela Jane finished her spiel and one of the American men said the vases were too expensive, even if they were hand-made and handsome. He collected nods and all-round agreement, and there was relief in the speed with which the tourists settled instead on simple dolphins and little dishes. While Hickory wrapped the parcels and wrote out bills I asked the motor cyclist if there were any news of my lost tape.

She watched me handle the vase in heat-proof fibre and put it to cool in the annealing oven.

'I'm afraid,' said Detective Constable Dodd in plain – well, plainer – clothes, 'your tape is gone for good.'

I told her it held a secret.

'What secret?'

'That's the point, I don't know. Martin Stukely told his wife he was giving me a secret on tape for safekeeping – that's a bit of a laugh – in case he was killed in a car crash, or something like that.'

'Like a steeplechase?'

'He didn't expect it.'

Catherine Dodd's detective mind trod the two paths I'd reluctantly followed myself since Normal Osprey and his Elvis sideburns had appeared on my horizon. First, *someone* knew Martin's secret, and second, *someone*, and maybe not the same someone, could infer, one way or another, that that secret was known to me. Someone might suppose I'd watched that tape during the evening of Martin's death, and for safety had wiped it off.

I hadn't had a tape player on the Logan Glass premises, but the Dragon over the road made one available generously to the paying guests, and she distributed brochures by the hundred advertising this.

'If I'd had a tape player handy,' I said, 'I probably *would* have run that tape through early in the evening, and if I thought it awful I *might* have wiped it off.'

'That's not what your friend Martin wanted.'

After a brief silence I said, 'If he'd been sure of what he wanted he wouldn't have fiddled about with tapes, he would just have *told* me this precious secret.' I stopped abruptly. 'There are too many ifs. How about you coming out for a drink?'

'Can't. Sorry. I'm on duty.' She gave me a brilliant smile. 'I'll call in another day. And oh! There's just one loose end.' She produced the ever-essential notebook from inside her jacket. 'What are your assistants' names?'

'Pamela Jane Evans and John Irish and John Hickory.

We leave off John for the men and use their last names, as it's easier.'

'Which is the elder?'

'Irish. He's about ten years older than both Hickory and Pamela Jane.'

'And how long have they all worked for you?'

'Pamela Jane about a year, Irish and Hickory two to three months longer. They're all good guys, believe me.'

'I do believe you. This is just for the records. This is actually . . . er . . . what I dropped in for.'

I looked at her directly. She all but blushed.

'I'd better go now,' she said.

With regret I walked with her as far as the door, where she paused to say goodbye as she didn't want to be seen with me too familiarly out in the street. She left, in fact, in the bunch of winter tourists, all of them overshadowed by the loud voice of a big man who judged the whole afternoon a waste of time and complained about it all the way back to the group's warm tour bus. His broad back obscured my view of the departure of Detective Constable Dodd, and I surprised myself by minding about that quite a lot.

On Bon-Bon's telephone, the night before Martin's funeral, I learned from the Dragon herself that Lloyd Baxter had deemed it correct to fly down for 'his jockey's last ride' (as he put it) but hadn't wanted to stay with Priam Jones, whom he was on the point of ditching as his trainer. The Dragon chuckled and went on mischievously, 'You didn't have to go all that way to stay with Bon-Bon Stukely, if you didn't fancy sleeping in your burgled house, lover boy. You could have stayed here with me.'

'News gets around,' I said dryly.

'You're always news in this town, lover, didn't you know?'

In truth I did know it, but I didn't feel it.

On that evening before Martin's funeral Priam Jones telephoned, meaning to talk to Bon-Bon but reaching me instead. I had been fielding commiserations for her whenever I was around. Marigold, Worthington and even the children had grown expert at thanks and tact. I thought how Martin would have grinned at the all-round grade A improvement in his family's social skills.

Priam blustered on a bit, but was, I gathered, offering himself as an usher in the matter of seating. Remembering his spontaneous tears I put him on the list and asked him if, before he'd picked me up from my home on Friday morning, Martin had by any chance mentioned that he was expecting delivery of a tape at the races.

'You asked me that the day after he died,' Priam said impatiently. 'The answer is still yes. He said we wouldn't leave the racecourse until he'd collected some package or other to give to you. And I did give it to you, don't you remember? I brought it back to Broadway after you'd left it in your raincoat in the car ... Well, I'll see you tomorrow, Gerard. Give my regards to Bon-Bon.'

Also, on the evening before Martin's funeral, Eddie

Payne went to his local Catholic church and in the confessional recited his past and present sins, asking for pardon and absolution. He told me this with self-righteousness when I intercepted his condolences to Bon-Bon. He'd tried and tried to get someone else to do his racecourse work, he said, but such was life, he hadn't succeeded, and he was going to have to miss the funeral, and it grieved him sorely as he'd been Martin's racecourse valet for six or seven years. Eddie, to my disparaging ear, had plucked up half a bottle of Dutch courage before stretching out his hand to the phone, and wouldn't remain long in a state of grace owing to his distance from the fact that he could more easily have got stand-ins to free him to go to that particular funeral than if it was for his own grandmother.

On the same evening, before Martin's funeral (though I didn't learn of it until later), Ed Payne's daughter, Rose, described to a small group of fascinated and ruthless knaves how to force Gerard Logan to tell them the secret he'd been given at Cheltenham races.

CHAPTER THREE

On the first Thursday of January, the sixth day of the next thousand years, I, with Priam Jones and four senior jump jockeys carried Martin into church in his coffin and later delivered him to his grave.

The sun shone on frosty trees. Bon-Bon looked ethereal, Marigold stayed fairly sober, Worthington took off his chauffeur's cap, baring his bald pate in respect, the four children knocked with their knuckles on the coffin as if they could wake their father inside, Lloyd Baxter read a short but decent eulogy and all the racing world, from the Stewards of the Jockey Club to the men who replaced the divots, everyone crowded into the pews in church and packed the wintry churchyard grass outside, standing on the moss-grown ancient slabs of stone. Martin had been respected, and respects were paid.

The new burial ground lay on a hillside a mile away by hearse and heavy limousines. Among banks of flowers Bon-Bon cried as the man who'd quarrelled with her daily sank into the quiet embracing earth and I, who'd stage-managed the second farewell party in a month (my mother the other), prosaically checked that the caterers had brought enough hot toddy and that the choristers were paid, along with other mundane greasings of the expensive wheels of death.

After the hundreds who had turned up for Martin had drunk and eaten and had kissed Bon-Bon and left, I sought her out to say my own goodbye. She was standing with Lloyd Baxter, asking about his health. '*Do* take the pills,' she was saying, and he with embarrassment promised he would. He nodded to me coldly as if he had never brought Dom Pérignon to me for company.

I congratulated Baxter on his eulogy. He received the praise as his due, and stiffly invited me to dine with him in the Wychwood Dragon.

'Don't go,' Bon-Bon exclaimed to me, alarmed. 'Stay here one more night. You and Worthington have tamed the children. Let's have this one more night of peace.'

Thinking of Martin, I excused myself to Baxter and stayed to help Bon-Bon, and after midnight, when only I was awake, I sat in Martin's squashy chair in his den and thought intently of him. Thought of his life and of what he'd achieved, and thought eventually about that last day at Cheltenham, and about the videotape and whatever he'd had recorded on it.

I had no minutest idea what he could have known that needed such complex safe-keeping. I did see that, much as I thought Bon-Bon a darling and as sweet as her name, she wasn't the most reticent person on earth. To Bon-Bon a secret would be safe until her next nice chat with her best friend. Many of her and Martin's shouting matches had been the result of Bon-Bon repeating publicly what she'd been privately told or overheard about some horse or other's prospects.

I slouched in Martin's chair, deep in regret. One had so few close friends in life. None to spare. His personality filled the room to the extent that it seemed that if I turned I would see him standing by his bookcase, looking up some race's result in the form book. The feeling of his presence was so intense that I actually swivelled his chair round to see, but of course there were only books, row on row, and no Martin.

It was time, I supposed, to make sure the outside doors were locked and to sleep away the last hours in Martin's house. I'd lent him a couple of books a few weeks earlier on ancient glass-making techniques, and as they were lying on the long table by the sofa, it seemed a good time to pick them up to take home without bothering Bon-Bon too much. One of the things I would most miss was, I thought nostalgically, Martin's constant interest in historic difficult-to-make goblets and bowls.

In the morning, saying goodbye, I mentioned I was taking the books. 'Fine, fine,' Bon-Bon said vaguely. 'I wish you weren't going.'

She was lending me Worthington to drive me in her white runabout to Broadway. 'If you weren't getting your butt out of that house pronto,' Worthington said bluntly as we drove away, 'Bon-Bon would catch you like a Venus fly-trap.'

'She's unhappy,' I protested.

'Sticky, attractive, and once caught, you can't escape.' Worthington grinned. 'Don't say I haven't warned you.'

'And Marigold?' I teased him. 'How's the Marigold fly-trap?'

'I can leave her any day I want,' he protested, and drove for miles smiling, as if he believed it.

Stopping to unload me at my gallery door in Broadway he said more seriously, 'I got a low-life investigator to ask about that woman, Rose.' He paused. 'He didn't get much further than you did. Eddie Payne thinks she saw who gave that damned tape to Martin, but I wouldn't rely on it. Eddie's afraid of his own daughter, if you ask me.'

I agreed with him on that, and we left it there. My three assistants welcomed me back to a regular work-day, and I taught Hickory – as I'd taught Pamela Jane before Christmas – how to collect a third gather of glass, so hot that it was red and semi-liquid, and fell in a heavy tear-drop shape that drooped towards the floor (and one's feet) if one didn't marver it fast enough on the steel table. He knew how to press its lengthened tip into long heaps of dust-like colours before returning the revolving head into the heat of the furnace to keep the now heavy chunk of glass at working temperature. I showed him how to gather glass neatly on the end of a blowing iron, before lifting it into the air ready to blow, and how to keep the resulting slightly ballooned shape constant while he continued to develop his ideas towards a final goal.

Hickory watched the continuous process with anxious

eyes and said that, like Pamela Jane when she'd tried it, he couldn't go the whole way.

'Of course not. Practise handling three gathers. You can do two now easily.'

A gather was the amount of molten glass that could be brought out of the tank at one time on the tip of the steel punty rod. A gather could be of any size, according to the skill and strength of the glass-blower. Glass in bulk, very heavy, demanded muscle.

Owing to the space limitation of tourist suitcases, few pieces of 'Logan Glass' sold in the shop were of more than three gathers. Pamela Jane, to her sorrow, had never quite mastered the swing upwards and blow technique. Irish, in spite of enthusiasm, would never be a top-rated glass-blower. Of Hickory, though, I had hopes. He had ease of movement and, most importantly, a lack of fear.

Glass-blowers were commonly arrogant people, chiefly because the skill was so difficult to learn. Hickory already showed signs of arrogance but if he became a notable expert he would have to be forgiven. As for myself, my uncle (as arrogant as they came) had insisted that I learn humility first, second and third, and had refused to let me near his furnace until I'd shed every sign of what he called 'cockiness'.

'Cockiness' had broken out regularly after his death, humbling me when I recognized it. It had taken perhaps ten years before I had it licked, but vigilance would be necessary for life.

Irish had grown accustomed to brewing the large jugs

of tea to replace the sweat lost to the furnace. I sat on a box and drank thirstily and all day watched my apprentice improve considerably, even though, with exhausted rests, there was generally a lot of swearing and a whole heap of shattered glass.

There were few customers to interrupt the lesson and by five o'clock on this bleakly cold January afternoon I sent my three helpers home and with gloom did some long overdue paperwork. The cash stolen on New Year's Eve left a depressing hole in what was otherwise a cheerful season. It wasn't difficult, after a while, to lay aside the minus figures and pick up the books I'd lent to Martin.

My favourite of all historic goblets was a glowing red cup, six and a half inches high, constructed around the year 300 and something AD (a fair time ago, when one looked back from 2000). It was made of lumps of glass, held fast in an intricate gold cage (a technique from before blowing was invented), and would appear green in different lights. Flicking through the early pages in one of the books I came across the goblet's picture with my usual pleasure and a few pages later smiled over the brilliant gold and blue glass Cretan Sunrise necklace that I'd once spent days copying. Sleepily, by accident, I let the book begin to slide off my knees towards the smooth brick floor and, by luck, caught it without damage to its glossy construction.

Relieved at the catch, and berating myself for such clumsiness in not holding on more tightly to a valued treasure, I didn't notice at first a thin buff envelope that lay at my feet. With a reaction accelerating from puzzlement to active curiosity I laid the old book down carefully and picked up the new-looking envelope, which I supposed had been held within the pages and had fallen out when I made my grab.

The envelope from inside my book was addressed by computer printer not to me but to Martin Stukely Esq., Jockey.

I had no qualms at all in taking out the single-page letter inside, and reading it.

Dear Martin.
　　You are right, it is the best way. I will take the tape, as you want, to Cheltenham races on New Year's Eve.
　　This knowledge is dynamite.
　　Take care of it.
　　Victor Waltman Verity.

The letter too was typed on a computer, though the name given as signature had been printed in a different font. There was no address or telephone number on the letter itself, but faintly across the stamp on the envelope there was a round postmark. After long concentration with a magnifying glass, the point of origin seemed to me only 'xet' round the top and 'evo' round the bottom. The date alone was easily readable, though looking anaemic as to ink.

The letter had been sent on 17.XII.99.

17 December. Less than a month ago.

xet

evo

There weren't after all many places in Great Britain with an x in their name, and I could think of nowhere else that fitted the available letters other than Exeter, Devon.

When I reached Directory Enquiries I learned that there was indeed a Victor Verity in Exeter. A disembodied voice said, 'The number you require is . . .'. I wrote it down, but when I called Victor Verity I spoke not to him, but to his widow. Her dear Victor had passed away during the previous summer. Wrong Verity.

I tried Enquiries again.

'Very sorry,' said a prim voice, not sounding it. 'There is no other Victor or V. Verity in the Exeter telephone area which covers most of Devon.'

'How about an ex-directory number?'

'Sorry, I can't give you that information.'

Victor Waltman Verity was either ex-directory or had posted his letter far from home.

Cursing him lightly I glanced with reluctance at the money job half done on my computer . . . and there, of course, lay the answer. Computers. Internet.

The Internet, among other miracles, might put an address to a name anywhere. That's to say, it would if I could remember the open sesame code. I entered my Internet access number and typed in my password, and sat hopefully, flicking mentally through possibilities as the machine burped and whined until a connection was made.

After a while a web-site address drifted into my mind, but it was without certainty that I tried it: www.192.com.

192.com was right.

I started a search for Verity in Devon and, as if eager to be of service, the Internet, having surveyed every fact obtainable in the public domain (such as the electoral registers) came up with a total of twenty-two Devon-based Veritys, but none of them any longer was Victor.

Dead end.

I tried Verity in Cornwall: sixteen but still no Victor.

Try Somerset, I thought. Not a Victor Verity in sight.

Before reaching to switch off, I skimmed down the list and at the end of it noticed that at number 19 Lorna Terrace, Taunton, Somerset, there lived a *Mr Waltman* Verity. Good enough to try, I thought.

Armed with the address I tried Directory Enquiries again, but ran up against the same polite barrier of virtual non-existence. Ex-directory. Sorry. Too bad.

Although Saturday was a busier day in the showroom, my thoughts returned continuously to Taunton and Victor Waltman Verity.

Taunton . . . Having nothing much else urgently filling my Sunday, I caught a westbound train next morning, and in Taunton asked directions to Lorna Terrace.

Whatever I expected Victor Waltman Verity to look like, it was nothing near the living thing. Victor Waltman Verity must have been all of fifteen.

The door of number 19 was opened by a thin woman dressed in trousers, sweater and bedroom slippers, with a cigarette in one hand and big pink curlers in her hair. Thirty something, perhaps forty, I thought. Easy going, with a resigned attitude to strangers on her doorstep.

'Er . . . Mrs Verity?' I asked.

'Yeah. What is it?' She sucked smoke, unconcerned.

'Mrs Victor Waltman Verity?'

She laughed. 'I'm Mrs Waltman Verity, Victor's my son.' She shouted over her shoulder towards the inner depths of the narrow terraced house. 'Vic, someone to see you,' and while we waited for Victor Waltman Verity to answer the call, Mrs Verity looked me over thoroughly from hair to trainers and went on enjoying a private giggle.

Victor Waltman Verity appeared quietly from along the narrow hallway and regarded me with curiosity mixed, I thought, with the possibility of alarm. He himself was as tall as his mother, as tall as Martin. He had dark hair, pale-grey eyes and an air of knowing himself to be as intelligent as any adult. His voice, when he spoke, was at the cracked stage between boy and man, and his face had begun to grow from the soft lines of childhood into adult planes.

'What've you been up to, young Vic?' his mother asked, and to me she said, 'It's bloody cold out there. Want to come in?'

'Er,' I said. I was suffering more from the unexpected than the cold, but she waited for no answer and walked back past the boy until she was out of sight. I pulled the envelope sent to Martin out of a pocket and immediately set the alarm racing above the curiosity in young Victor.

'You weren't supposed to find me,' he exclaimed, 'and, in any case, you're dead.'

'I'm not Martin Stukely,' I said.

'Oh.' His face went blank. 'No, of course, you aren't.' Puzzlement set in. 'I mean, what do you want?'

'First of all,' I said plainly, 'I'd like to accept your mother's invitation.'

'Huh?'

'To be warm.'

'Oh! I get you. The kitchen is warmest.'

'Lead on, then.'

He shrugged and stretched to close the door behind me, and then led the way down beside the staircase to the heart of all such terrace houses, the space where life was lived. There was a central table covered with a patterned plastic cloth, four attendant unmatched upright chairs and a sideboard deep in clutter. A television set stood aslant on a draining-board otherwise stacked with unwashed dishes, and checked vinyl tiles covered the floor.

In spite of the disorganization, there was bright new paint and nothing disturbingly sordid. I had an overall impression of yellow.

Mrs Verity sat in one of the chairs, rocking on its back legs and gulping smoke as if she lived on it.

She said pleasantly enough, 'We get all sorts of people here, what with Vic and his wretched Internet. We'll get

a full-sized genie one of these days, I shouldn't wonder.'
She gestured vaguely to one of the chairs, and I sat on it.

'I was a friend of Martin Stukely,' I explained, and I
asked Vic what was on the videotape that he had sent or
given to Martin at Cheltenham.

'Yes, well, there wasn't a tape,' he said briefly. 'I
didn't go to Cheltenham.'

I pulled his letter to Martin out of the envelope and
gave it to him to read.

He shrugged again and handed it back when he'd reached the end.

'It was just a game. I made up the tape.' He was nervous, all the same.

'What knowledge was it that was dynamite?'

'Look, none.' He grew impatient. 'I told you. I made
it up.'

'Why did you send it to Martin Stukely?'

I was careful not to let the questions sound too
aggressive, but in some way that I didn't understand, they
raised all his defences and coloured his cheeks red.

His mother said to me, 'What's all this about a tape?
Do you mean a *video* tape? Vic hasn't got any videotapes.
We're going to get a new video machine any day now,
then it will be different.'

I explained apologetically. 'Someone did give to Martin a videotape at Cheltenham races. Martin gave it to Ed
Payne, his valet, to keep safe, and Ed gave it to me, but
it was stolen before I could see what was on it. Then all

the videotapes in Martin's house and all the videotapes in my own house were stolen too.'

'I hope you're not suggesting that *Vic* stole anything, because I can promise you he wouldn't.' Mrs Verity had grasped one suggestion wrongly and hadn't listened clearly to the rest, so she too advanced to the edge of anger, and I did my best to retreat and placate, but her natural good humour had been dented, and her welcome had evaporated. She stubbed out a cigarette instead of lighting another from it, and stood up as a decisive signal that it was time I left.

I said amiably to young Victor, 'Call me,' and although he shook his head I wrote my mobile number on the margin of a Sunday newspaper.

Then I stepped out of number 19 Lorna Terrace and walked unhurriedly along the street pondering two odd unanswered questions.

First, how did Victor happen to come to Martin's attention?

Second, why had neither mother nor son asked my name?

Lorna Terrace curved sharply to the left, taking number 19 out of sight behind me.

I paused there, wondering whether or not to go back. I was conscious of not having done very well. I'd set off expecting to unearth the mysteries of the videotape, if not with ease, then actually without extreme trouble. Instead, I seemed to have screwed up even what I'd thought I'd understood.

Irresolutely I wasted time and missed the train I'd thought of catching. I might be OK at glass, but not excellent at Sherlock Holmes. Dim Dr Watson, that was me. It grew dark and took me a long time to reach Broadway, luckily finding a willing neighbour on the train to give me a lift from the station.

Without Martin, I reflected with depression, I was either going to spend a fortune on cabs or thumb a thousand lifts. There were still eighty-one days before I could apply to get my licence-to-speed out of the freezer.

I thanked my generous companion with a wave as he drove away and, fishing out a small bunch of keys I plodded towards the gallery door. Sunday evening. No one about. Brilliant lights shining from Logan Glass.

I hadn't learned yet to beware of shadows. Figures in black materialized from the deep entrance to the antique bookshop next door and from the dark line of the rubbish bins put out ready for collection on Monday morning.

I suppose there were four of them leaping about in the dark; an impression, not an accurate count. Four was profligate, anyway. Three, two, maybe only one could have done the job. I guessed they'd been waiting there for a long time and it hadn't improved their temper.

I hadn't expected another physical attack. The memory of the orange cylinder of cyclopropane had faded. The cylinder, I soon found, had delivered a less painful message than the one on my doorstep. This one consisted of multiple bashes and bangs and of being slammed two or three times against the lumpy bit of Cotswold stone wall that joined the bookshop to my own place.

Disorientated by the attack itself I heard demands as if from a distance that I should disclose information that I knew I didn't have. I tried to tell them. They didn't listen.

All that was annoying enough, but it was their additional aim that lit my own inner protection furnace and put power into half-forgotten techniques of kick-boxing left over from my teens.

It seemed that a straightforward pulping was only half their purpose, as a sharp excited voice specifically instructed over and over again, 'Break his wrists. Go on. *Break his wrists . . .*' And later, out of the dark, the same voice exulting, 'That got him.'

No, it bloody didn't. Pain screeched up my arm. My thoughts were blasphemy. Strong, whole and flexible wrists were as essential to a glass-blower as to a gymnast on the Olympic high rings.

Two of the black-clad agile figures waved baseball bats. One with heavily developed shoulders was recognizably Norman Osprey. Looking back later from a huddled sort of collapse on the pavement, I saw that only one of those two had the bright idea of holding my fingers tightly together in a bunch against the wall before getting his colleague to aim just below them with the bat.

I had too much to lose and I hadn't been aware of how desperately one could fight when it was the real thing.

My wrists didn't get broken but my watch stopped, in pieces from a direct hit. There were lumps and bruised areas all over everywhere. A few cuts. Torn skin. Enough. But my fingers worked, and that was all that mattered.

Maybe the fracas would have ended with my taking a fresh hole in the ground beside Martin, but Broadway wasn't a ghost town in a western desert; it was somewhere that people walked their dogs on a Sunday evening, and it was a dog-walker who yelled at my attackers, and with three toothy Dobermanns barking and pulling at their leashes, got the shadowy figures to change their minds smartly and vanish as fast as they'd come.

'Gerard *Logan*!' The tall dog-walker, astounded, bending to look at me, knew me by sight, as I did him. 'Are you all right?'

No, I wasn't. I said, 'Yes,' as one does.

He stretched down to help me to my feet, when all I really wanted to do was lie on a soft mattress.

'Shall I call the police?' he asked, though he wasn't a police lover; far from it.

'Tom . . . Thanks. But no police.'

'What was it all about?' He sounded relieved. 'Are you in trouble? That looked to me like pay-back business.'

'Muggers.'

Tom Pigeon, who knew a thing or two about the rocky sides of life, gave me a half-smile, half-disillusioned look, and shortened the leashes of his hungry life-preservers.

More bark than bite, he'd assured me once. I wasn't certain I believed it.

He himself looked as if he had no need to bark. Although not heavily built and without a wrestler's neck, he had unmistakable physical power, and, at about my own age, a close-cut dark pointed beard that added years of menace.

Tom Pigeon told me there was blood in my hair and said if I would give him my keys he would open the door for me.

'I dropped them,' I said and leaned gingerly against the lumpy bit of wall. The dizzy world revolved. I couldn't remember ever before feeling so pulverized or so sick, not even when I'd fallen bottom of the scrum in a viciously unfriendly school rugby match and had my shoulder blade broken.

Tom Pigeon persevered until he kicked against my keys and found them by their clinking. He unlocked and opened the gallery door and with his arm round my waist got me as far as the threshold. His dogs stayed watchfully by his legs.

'I better not bring the canines in amongst your glass, had I?' he said. 'You'll be all right now, OK?'

I nodded. He more or less propped me against the door frame and made sure I could stand up before he let go.

Tom Pigeon was known locally as 'The Backlash', chiefly on account of being as quick with his wits as his fists. He'd survived, unharmed, eighteen months inside for aggravated breaking and entering and had emerged as a toughened hotshot, to be spoken of with awe. Whatever his dusty reputation, he had definitely rescued me, and I felt in an extraordinary way honoured by the extent of his aid.

He waited until I could visibly control things and stared shrewdly into my eyes. It wasn't exactly friendship that I saw in his, but it was . . . in a way . . . recognition.

'Get a pit-bull,' he said.

I stepped into my bright lights and locked the door against the violence outside. Pity I couldn't as easily blot out the woes of battery. Pity I felt so stupid. So furious. So wobbly, so dangerously mystified.

In the back reaches of the workshop there was running water for rinsing one's face, and a relaxing chair for recovery of all kinds of balance. I sat and ached a lot, and then phoned the taxi firm, who apologized that this Saturday and Sunday had already overstretched their fleet, but they would put me on their priority list from now on . . . yeah . . . yeah . . . never mind . . . I could have done with a double cyclopropane, shaken, with ice. I thought of Worthington, tried for him on the phone, got Bon-Bon instead.

'Gerard, darling. I'm so *lonely*.' She sounded indeed in sorrowing mode, as her elder son would have put it. 'Can't you come over to cheer me up? Worthington will come to fetch you, and I'll drive you home myself. I promise.'

I said with regret that I didn't want to give her flu (which I hadn't got) and simply went on doing very little through a highly unsatisfactory evening. Worthington's fly-trap vision itched. I loved Bon-Bon as a friend, but not as wife.

At about ten-thirty I fell asleep in the soft chair and half an hour later was awakened again by the doorbell.

Disorientated as I woke, I felt stiff, miserable and totally unwilling to move.

The doorbell rang insistently. I went on feeling shivery and unwilling, but in the end I wavered upright and creaked out of the workshop to see who wanted what at such an hour. Even then, after the dire lessons I'd been given, I hadn't enough sense to carry with me a weapon of defence.

As it happened, my late-evening visitor looked pretty harmless. In addition, she was welcome. More than that, I thought that with a kiss or two and a hug she might prove therapeutic.

Detective Constable Catherine Dodd took her finger off the doorbell when she saw me, and smiled with relief when I let her in.

'We had reports from two separate Broadway residents,' she said first. 'They apparently saw you being attacked outside here. But we had no complaint from yourself, even though you were hardly walking, it seemed

. . . so anyway, I said I would check on you on my way home.'

She again wore motor-cycle leathers, and had parked her bike at the kerb. With deft speed, as before, she lifted off her helmet and shook her head to loosen her fair hair.

'One of the reports,' she added, 'said that your attacker had been Tom Pigeon, with his dogs. That man's a damned pest.'

'No, no! It was he who got rid of the pests. Really depressing pests.'

'Could you identify them?'

I made a non-committal gesture and meandered vaguely through the showroom to the workshop, pointing to the chair for her to sit down.

She looked at the chair and at the sweat I could feel on my forehead, and sat on the bench normally the domain of Irish, Hickory and Pamela Jane. Gratefully I sank into the soft armchair and half answered her who? and why? queries, not knowing whether they had a police basis or were ordinary curiosity.

She said, 'Gerard, I've seen other people in your state.'

'Poor them.'

'Don't laugh, it's hardly funny.'

'Not tragic, either.'

'Why haven't you asked my colleagues for more help?'

Well, I thought, why not?

'Because,' I said lightly, 'I don't know who or why,

and every time I think I've learned something, I find I haven't. Your colleagues don't like uncertainty.'

She thought that over with more weight than it deserved.

'Tell *me*, then,' she said.

'Someone wants something I haven't got. I don't know what it is. I don't know who wants it. How am I doing?'

'That makes nonsense.'

I winced and turned it into a smile. 'It makes nonsense, quite right.' And in addition, I thought to myself with acid humour, I have the Dragon and Bon-Bon on my watch-it list, and policewoman Dodd on my wanted-but-can-I-catch-her list, and Tom Pigeon and Worthington on my save-my-skin list, Rose Payne/Robins on my black-mask possible list and young Victor Waltman on my can't-or-won't-tell list.

As for Lloyd Baxter and his epilepsy, Eddie Payne keeping and delivering videotapes, Norman Osprey running a book with the massive shoulders of 1894, and dear scatty Marigold, often afloat before breakfast and regularly before lunch, all of them could have tapes on their mind and know every twist in the ball of string.

Constable Dodd frowned, faint lines crossing her smooth clear skin, and as it seemed to be question time I said abruptly, 'Are you married?'

After a few seconds, looking down at her ringless hands, she replied 'Why do you ask?'

'You have the air of it.'

'He's dead.'

She sat for a while without moving, and then asked, 'And you?' in calm return.

'Not yet,' I said.

Silence could sometimes shout. She listened to what I would probably ask quite soon, and seemed relaxed and content.

The workshop was warmed as always by the furnace, even though the roaring fire was held in control for nights and Sundays by a large screen of heat-resistant material.

Looking at Catherine Dodd's face above the dark close-fitting leather, I most clearly now saw her in terms of glass: saw her in fact so vividly that the urge and desire to work at once couldn't be stifled. I stood and unclipped the fireproof screen and put it to one side, and fixed instead the smaller flap which opened to allow access to the tankful of molten glass.

I pressed extra time into the light switch, overriding the midnight cut-off, and with boringly painful movements took off my jacket and shirt, leaving only normal working gear of bare arms and singlet.

'What are you doing?' She sounded alarmed but had no need to be.

'A portrait,' I said. 'Sit still.' I turned up the heat in the furnace and sorted out the punty blowing irons I would need, and fetched a workable amount of glass manganese powder which would give me black in colour eventually.

'But your bruises . . .' she protested. 'Those marks. They're terrible.'

'I can't feel them.'

I felt nothing indeed except the rare sort of excitement that came with revelation. I'd burned myself often enough on liquid glass and not felt it. That Sunday night the concept of one detective darkly achieving insight into the sins of others, and then the possibility that good could rise above sin and fly, these drifting thoughts set up in me in effect a mental anaesthesia, so that I could bleed and suffer on one level and feel it only later after the flame of imagination had done its stuff. Sometimes in the disengagement from this sort of thing, the vision had shrunk to disappointment and ash, and when that happened I would leave the no-good piece on the marver table and not handle it carefully into an annealing oven. After a while, its unresolved internal strains would cause it to self-destruct, to come to pieces dramatically with a cracking noise; to splinter, to fragment . . . to shatter.

It could be for onlookers an unnerving experience, to see an apparently solid object disintegrate for no visible reason. For me, the splitting apart symbolized merely the fading and insufficiency of the original thought. On that particular Sunday I had no doubts or hesitation, and I gathered glass in muscle-straining amounts that even on ordinary days would have taxed my ability.

That night I made Catherine Dodd in three pieces that later I would join together. I made not a literal lifelike sculpture of her head, but an abstract of her daily occupation. I made it basically as a soaring upward spread of wings, black and shining at the base, rising through a black, white and clear centre to a high rising pinion with streaks of gold shining to the top.

The gold fascinated my subject.

'Is it *real* gold?'

'Iron pyrites. But real gold would melt the same way . . . only I used all I had a week ago.'

I gently held the fragile top wing in layers of heat-proof fibre and laid it carefully in one of the six annealing ovens, and only then, with all three sections safely cooling, could I hardly bear the strains in my own limbs and felt too like cracking apart myself.

Catherine stood up and took a while to speak. Eventually she cleared her throat and asked what I would do with the finished flight of wings and I, coming down to earth from invention, tried prosaically (as on other such occasions) just to say that I would probably make a pedestal for it in the gallery and light it with a spotlight or two to emphasize its shape.

We both stood looking at each other as if not knowing what else to say. I leaned forward and kissed her cheek, which with mutual small movements became mouth to mouth, with passion in there somewhere, acknowledged but not yet overflowing.

Arms round motor-cycle leathers had practical draw-backs. My own physical aches put winces where they weren't wanted, and with rueful humour she disengaged herself and said, 'Maybe another time.'

'Delete the maybe,' I said.

CHAPTER FOUR

All three of my assistants could let themselves in through
the gallery with a personal key, and it was Pamela Jane
alone whom I saw first with a slit of eyesight when I
returned unwillingly to consciousness at about eight
o'clock on Monday morning. I'd spent the first hour after
Catherine had gone considering the comfort of a Wychwood Dragon bed (without the Dragon herself) but in the
end from lack of energy had simply flopped back into the
big chair in the workshop and closed my eyes on a
shuddering and protesting nervous system.

Catherine herself, real and abstract, had kept me warm
and mobile through the darkest hours of night, but she'd
left long before dawn, and afterwards sleep, which practically never knitted up any ravelled sleave of care, had
made things slightly worse.

Pamela Jane said, horrified, 'Honestly, you look as if
you've been hit by a steamroller. Have you been here all
night?'

The answer must have been obvious. I was unshaven,
for a start, and any movement set up quite awful and

77

stiffened reactions. One could almost hear the joints creak. Never again, I promised myself.

I hadn't considered how I was going to explain things to my little team. When I spoke to Pamela Jane, even my voice felt rough.

'Can you . . .' I paused, cleared my throat and tried again. 'Pam . . . mug of tea?'

She put her coat in her locker and scurried helpfully around, making the tea and unbolting the side door which we were obliged to have ready to use as a fire escape if necessary. By the advent of Irish I was ignoring the worst, and Hickory, arriving last, found me lifting the three wing sections of the night's work out of the ovens and carefully fitting them together before fusing them into place. All three of my helpers wished they'd seen the separate pieces made. One day, I agreed with them, I would make duplicates to show them.

They couldn't help but notice that I found too much movement a bad idea, but I could have done without Hickory's cheerful assumption it was the aftermath of booze.

The first customer came. Life more or less returned to normal. Irish began building a plinth in the gallery to hold the wings. If I concentrated on blowing glass I could forget four black jersey-wool masks with eyeholes.

Later in the morning Marigold's Rolls drew up outside and occupied two of the parking spaces, with Worthington at the wheel looking formal in his badge-of-office cap.

Marigold herself, he reported through his wound-down

window, had gone shopping with Bon-Bon in Bon-Bon's car. Both ladies had given him the day off and the use of the Rolls, and he appreciated their generosity, he said solemnly, as he was going to take me to the races.

I looked back at him in indecision.

'I'm not going,' I said. 'And where am I not going?'

'Leicester. Jump racing. Eddie Payne will be there. Rose will be there. Norman Osprey will be there with his book. I thought you wanted to find out who gave the videotape to Martin? Do you want to know what was on it, or who stole it, and do you want to know who gassed me with the kids and the ladies, or do you want to stay here quietly and make nice little pink vases to sell to the tourists?'

I didn't answer at once and he said judiciously, making allowances, 'Mind you, I don't suppose you want another beating like you got last night, so stay here if you like and I'll mooch around by myself.'

'Who told you about last night?'

He took off his cap and wiped his bald crown with a white handkerchief.

'A little bird told me. A not so little bird.'

'Not . . . a pigeon?'

'Quick, aren't you.' He grinned. 'Yeah, a Pigeon. It seems he thinks quite a bit of you. He phoned me specially at Bon-Bon's. He says to put it around that in future any hands laid on you are laid on him.'

I felt both grateful and surprised. I asked, 'How well do you know him?'

He answered obliquely. 'You know that gardener of

79

Martin's that was dying? That you lost your licence for, speeding to get him there in time?'

'Well, yes, I remember.'

'That gardener was Tom Pigeon's dad.'

'Ah. He didn't die, though. Not then, anyway.'

'It didn't matter. Are you coming to Leicester?'

'I guess so.'

I went back into the workshop, put on my outdoor clothes and told Irish, Hickory and Pamela Jane to keep on making paperweights while I went to the sports. They had all known Martin alive, as my friend, and all of them in brief snatches, and in turn, had been to his sending off. They wished me luck with many winners at the races.

I sat beside Worthington for the journey. We stopped to buy me a cheap watch, and to pick up a daily racing newspaper for the runners and riders. In a section titled 'News Today' on the front page I read, among a dozen little snippets, that the Leicester Stewards would be hosts that day to Lloyd Baxter (owner of star jumper Tallahassee) to honour the memory of jockey Martin Stukely.

Well, well.

After a while I told Worthington in detail about my visit to Lorna Terrace, Taunton. He frowned over the more obvious inconsistencies put forward by mother and son, but seemed struck to consternation when I said, 'Didn't you tell me that the bookmaking firm of Arthur Robins, established 1894, was now owned and run by people named Webber, Brown . . . and Verity?'

The consternation lasted ten seconds. 'And the mother

and son in Taunton were Verity!' A pause. 'It must be a coincidence,' he said.

'I don't believe in coincidences like that.'

Worthington slid a silent glance my way as he navigated a roundabout, and after a while said, 'Gerard, if you have any clear idea of what's going on . . . what is it? For instance, who were those attackers in black masks last night, and what did they want?'

I said, 'I'd think it was one of them who squirted you with cyclopropane and laid me out with the empty cylinder, and I don't know who that was. I'm sure, though, that one of the black-masks was the fragrant Rose.'

'I'm not staying she wasn't, but why?'

'Who else in the world would scream at Norman Osprey – or anyone else, but I'm pretty sure it was him – to break my wrists? Rose's voice is unmistakable. And there is the way she moves . . . and as for purpose . . . partly to put me out of business, wouldn't you say? And partly to make me give her what I haven't got. And also to stop me from doing what we're aiming to do today.'

Worthington said impulsively, 'Let's go home, then.'

'You just stay beside me, and we'll be fine.'

Worthington took me seriously and body-guarded like a professional. We confirmed one of the black-mask merchants for certain simply from his stunned reaction to my being there and on my feet when anyone with any sense would have been knocking back aspirins on a sofa with an ice-pack. Martin himself had showed me how jump jockeys walked around sometimes with broken ribs and arms and other injuries. Only broken legs, he'd said, postponed actual riding for a couple of months. Bruises, to him, were every-day normal, and he dealt with pain by putting it out of his mind and thinking about something else. 'Ignore it,' he'd said. I copied him at Leicester as best I could.

When he saw me, Norman Osprey had stopped dead in the middle of setting up his stand, his heavy shoulders bunching; and Rose herself made the mistake of striding up to him in a carefree bounce at that moment, only to follow his disbelieving gaze and lose a good deal of her self-satisfaction. What she said explosively was 'Bloody hell.'

If one imagined Norman Osprey's shoulders in a black jersey, he was recognizably the figure who'd smashed my watch with his baseball bat, while aiming at my wrist. I'd jerked at the vital moment and I'd kicked his shin very hard indeed. The sharp voice urging him to try again had, without doubt, been Rose's.

I said to them jointly, 'Tom Pigeon sends his regards.'

Neither of them looked overjoyed. Worthington murmured something to me urgently about it not being advisable to poke a wasps' nest with a stick. He also put distance between himself and Arthur Robins 1894 and, with unobvious speed, I followed.

'They don't know exactly what they're looking for,' I pointed out, slowing down. 'If they knew, they would have asked for it by name last night.'

'They might have done that anyway, if Tom Pigeon

hadn't been walking his dogs.' Worthington steered us still further away from Norman Osprey, looking back all the same to make certain we weren't being followed.

My impression of the events of barely fifteen hours earlier was that damage, as well as information, had been the purpose. But if Tom Pigeon hadn't arrived, and if it had been to save the multiple wrist bones that Martin had said never properly mended, and if I *could* have answered their questions, then would I . . .?

Sore as I already felt all over, I couldn't imagine any piece of knowledge that Martin might have had that he thought was worth my virtual destruction, and I didn't like the probability that they – the black-masks – wrongly believed that I did know what they wanted, and that I was being merely stubborn in not telling them.

Mordantly I admitted to myself that if I'd known for certain what they wanted and if Tom Pigeon hadn't arrived with his dogs, I wouldn't at that moment be strolling round any racecourse, but would quite likely have told them *anything* to stop them, and have been considering suicide from shame. And I was *not* going to confess that to anyone at all.

Only to Martin's hovering presence could I even admit it. Bugger you, pal, I thought. What the sod have you let me in for?

Lloyd Baxter lunched at Leicester with the Stewards. His self-regarding nature found this admirable invitation to be merely his due. He told me so, condescendingly, when our paths crossed between parade ring and stands.

To Lloyd Baxter the meeting was unexpected, but I'd spotted him early and waited through the Stewards' roast beef, cheese and coffee, talking to Worthington outside, and stiffening uncomfortably in the cold wind.

Cold weather emphasized the Paleolithic-like weight of Baxter's facial structure and upper body, and even after only one week (though a stressful one) his hair seemed definitely to have greyed a further notch.

He wasn't pleased to see me. I was sure he regretted the whole Broadway evening, but he concentrated hard on being civil, and it was churlish of me, I dare say, to suspect that it was because I knew of his epilepsy. Nowhere in print or chat had his condition been disclosed, but if he was afraid I would not only broadcast but snigger, he had made a judgement of my own character which hardly flattered.

Worthington melted temporarily from my side and I walked with Lloyd Baxter while he oozed compliments about the Stewards' lunch and discussed the worth of many trainers, excluding poor old Priam Jones.

I said mildly, 'It wasn't his fault that Tallahassee fell at Cheltenham.'

I got an acid reply. 'It was Martin's fault. He unbalanced him going into the fence. He was too confident.'

Martin had told me that *it* – whatever *it* might be – was, with a disgruntled owner, normally the jockey's fault. 'Pilot error.' He'd shrugged philosophically. 'And then you get the other sort of owner, the cream to ride for, the ones who understand that horses aren't infallible, who say, "That's racing," when something shattering happens, and who comfort the jockey who's just lost them the win of a lifetime. And believe me,' Martin had said, 'Lloyd Baxter isn't one of those. If I lose for him, it is, in his opinion, my fault.'

'But,' I said without heat to Lloyd Baxter during his trainer-spotting at Leicester, 'if a horse falls, it surely isn't the trainer's fault? It wasn't Priam Jones's fault that Tallahassee fell and lost the Coffee Cup.'

'He should have schooled him better.'

'Well,' I reasoned, 'that horse had proved he could jump. He'd already won several races.'

'I want a different trainer.' Lloyd Baxter spoke with obstinacy: a matter of instinct, I saw.

Along with lunch, the Stewards had given Tallahassee's owner an entry ticket to their guests' viewing box. Lloyd Baxter was already apologizing for shedding me at the entrance when one of the Stewards, following us, changed our course.

'Aren't you the glass man?' he boomed genially. 'My wife's your greatest fan. We have lumps of your stuff all over our house. That splendid horse you did for her, you came to rig its spotlights, didn't you?'

I remembered the horse and the house with enough detail to be invited into the Stewards' guests viewing balcony, not entirely to Lloyd Baxter's delight.

'This young man's a genius, according to my wife,'

the Steward said to Baxter, ushering us in. The genius merely wished he felt less weak.

Lloyd Baxter's poor opinion of the Steward's wife's judgement was written plain on his heavy features, but perhaps it did eventually influence him because, after the cheering for the next winner had faded, he surprised me very much by resting his hand lightly on my arm to indicate that I should stay and hear what he felt like telling me. He hesitated further, though, so I gave him every chance.

'I've often wondered,' I said mildly, 'if you saw who came into my showroom on New Year's Eve. I mean, I know you were ill ... but before that ... when I'd gone out into the street, did anyone come?'

After a long pause, he faintly nodded. 'Someone came into that long gallery you have there. I remember he asked for you and I said you were out in the street. But I couldn't see him properly as my eyes ... my sight develops zigzags sometimes . . .' He stopped, but I continued for him.

'You surely have pills.'

'Of course I do!' He was irritated. 'But I'd forgotten to take them because of the terrible day it had been, and I hate those very small air taxis to begin with, and I do want a different trainer.' His voice died away, but his troubles had been laid out clearly enough for a chimpanzee to understand.

I asked if, in spite of the zigzag aura, he could describe my unknown visitor.

'No,' he said. 'I told him you were in the street and the next time I was properly awake I was in hospital.' He paused while I regretted the cut-short sequence, and then with diffidence he said slowly, 'I am aware that I should thank you for your reticence. You could still cause me much embarrassment.'

'There's no point in it,' I said.

He spent a while studying my face as in the past I'd learned his. The result surprised me. 'Are you ill?' he said.

'No. Tired. Didn't sleep well.'

'The man who came,' he said abruptly, making no other comment, 'was thin and had a white beard and was over fifty.'

The description sounded highly improbable as a thief, and he must have seen my doubt because he added to convince me, 'When I saw him, I immediately thought of Priam Jones, who's been saying for years he's going to grow a beard. I tell him he'd look weedy.'

I nearly laughed: the picture was true.

Baxter said the white-bearded man reminded him chiefly of a university professor. A lecturer.

I asked, 'Did he speak? Was he a normal customer? Did he mention glass?'

Lloyd Baxter couldn't remember. 'If he spoke at all, I heard him only as a jumble. Quite often things seem wrong to me. They're a sort of warning. Often I can control them a little, or at least prepare ... but on that evening it was happening too fast.'

He was being extraordinarily frank, I thought. I wouldn't have expected so much trust.

'That man with the whisker job,' I said, 'he must have seen the beginning at least of your . . . er . . . seizure. So why didn't he help you? Do you think he simply didn't know what to do, so ran away from trouble, as people tend to, or was it he who made off with the loot . . . er . . . that money, in the canvas bag?'

'And the videotape,' Baxter said.

There was an abrupt breath-drawing silence. Then I asked, 'What videotape?'

Lloyd Baxter frowned. 'He asked for it.'

'So you gave it to him?'

'No. Yes. No. I don't know.'

It became clear that, in fact, Lloyd Baxter's memory of that evening in Broadway was a scrambled egg of order into chaos. It wasn't certain that any university lecturer in any white beard existed outside fiction.

While we occupied for another ten uninterrupted minutes the most private place on a racecourse – the Stewards' guests' viewing balcony in between races – I managed to persuade Lloyd Baxter to sit quietly and exchange detailed memories of the last few minutes of 1999, but try as he might, he still clung to the image of the scrawny man in the white beard who probably – or maybe it was some other man at some other time – asked for a videotape . . . perhaps.

He was trying his best. His manner to me had taken a

ninety-degree angle of change, so that he'd become more of an ally than a crosspatch.

One of the things he would never have said in the past was his reassessment of my and Martin's friendship. 'I see I was wrong about you,' he admitted, heavily frowning. 'Martin relied on you for strength, and I took it for granted that it was the other way round.'

'We learned from each other.'

After a pause he said, 'That fellow in the white beard, he was real, you know. He did want a videotape. If I knew more than that, I would tell you.'

I finally believed him. It was just unlucky that Baxter's fit had struck at the wrong random moment; unlucky from White-Beard's point of view that Baxter had been there at all; but it did now seem certain that during the time I was out in the street seeing the year 2000 arrive safely, a white-bearded thin middle-aged professor-type individual had come into my showroom and had said something about a videotape, and had left before I returned, taking the tape and, incidentally, the money with him.

I hadn't seen any white-bearded figure out in the street. It had been a week too late for the ho ho ho joker from the North Pole. Lloyd Baxter said he couldn't tell whether or not the beard was real or left over from Father Christmas.

When we parted we shook hands for the first time ever. I left him with the Stewards and fell into step with Worthington, who I found shivering outside and obviously hungry. Accordingly we smelled out some food which he galloped through with endless appetite.

'Why don't you eat?' he demanded, chomping.

'Habit,' I said. A habit caught from a scales-conscious jockey. Martin seemed to have influenced my life more than I'd realized.

I told Worthington while he saw off two full plates of steak and kidney pie (his and mine) that we were now looking for a thin man, in late middle age, white beard, who looked like a college lecturer.

Worthington gazed at me earnestly while loading his fork with pastry. 'That,' he pointed out, 'doesn't sound at all like someone who would steal a bagful of money.'

'I'm surprised at you, Worthington,' I teased him. 'I thought you, of all people, would know that beards aren't automatic badges of honesty! So how does this sit with you? Suppose Mr White-Beard gives a tape to Martin, which Martin gives to Eddie Payne, who hands it on to me. Then, when Martin died, Mr White-Beard decided to take his videotape back again, so he found out where the tape would be . . . that's to say, he turned up in Broadway. He found the tape and took it back, and on impulse he also whisked up the bag of money that I'd stupidly left lying around, and in consequence he cannot tell anyone that he has his tape back.'

'Because he would be confessing he'd stolen the cash?'

'Dead right.'

My bodyguard sighed and scraped his plate clean. 'So what next?' he said. 'What happened next?'

'I can only guess.'

'Go on, then. Guess. Because it wasn't some old guy that gassed us with that cyclopropane. Young Daniel described the trainers that the gas-man wore, and nobody but a teenager, I don't think, would be seen dead in them.'

I found I disagreed. Eccentric white-beards might wear anything. They might also make erotic tapes. They might also tell someone the tape was worth a fortune, and that it was in Gerard Logan's hands. A few little lies. Diversionary tactics. Beat up Logan, make him ready to cough up the tape or, failing that, whatever information had been on it.

What had Martin been going to give me for safe-keeping?

Did I any longer really want to know?

If I didn't know, I couldn't tell. But if they believed I knew and I wouldn't tell ... dammit, I thought, we've almost been through that already, and I couldn't expect Tom Pigeon and Dobermanns to rescue me every time.

Not knowing the secret on the tape was perhaps worse than knowing it. So somehow or other, I decided, it wasn't enough to discover who took it, it was essential after all to find out what they expected as well as what they'd actually got.

Once Worthington's hunger had retreated temporarily

and we had lost our money on a horse Martin should have ridden, we walked back to where the serried ranks of bookmakers were shouting their offers for the getting-out stakes, the last race.

With Worthington's well-known muscle as guarantee of immunity from onslaught, we arrived in the living-and-breathing space of the 1894 Arthur Robins' operation 2000. Norman Osprey's raucous voice soared unselfconsciously above his neighbours' until he realized we were listening, at which point a sudden silence gave everyone else a chance.

Close enough to see the scissor marks on the Elvis sideburns, I said, 'Tell Rose—'

'Tell her yourself,' he interrupted forcefully. 'She's just behind you.'

I turned without haste, leaving Worthington at my back. Rose glared, rigid with a hatred I didn't at that point understand. As before, the dryness of her skin echoed the lack of generosity in her nature, but earlier, at our first and last racecourse encounter, neither of us held the subsequent memory of fists, stone walls, baseball bats, a smashed watch and a whole bunch more of assaults-to-the-person, all orchestrated and encouraged as Sunday evening entertainment for the troops.

Being as close to her as a couple of yards gave my outraged skin goose pimples, but she seemed to think a black mask and leotard had made her invisible.

I asked again the question she had already refused to answer.

'Who gave a videotape to Martin Stukely at Cheltenham races?'

She answered this time that she didn't know.

I said, 'Do you mean you didn't see anyone give Martin a parcel, or that you saw the transfer but didn't know the person's name?'

'Dead clever, aren't you,' Rose said sarcastically. 'Take your pick.'

Rose, I thought, wasn't going to be trapped by words. At a guess she had both seen the transfer and knew the transferor, but even Torquemada would have had trouble with her, and I hadn't any thumbscrews handy in Logan Glass.

I said without much hope of being believed, 'I don't know where to look for the tape you want. I don't know who took it and I don't know why. But I haven't got it.'

Rose curled her lip.

As we walked away Worthington sighed deeply with frustration.

'You'd think Norman Osprey would be the "heavy" in that outfit. He has the voice and the build for it. Everyone thinks of him as the power behind Arthur Robins. But did you see him looking at Rose? She can make any blunder she likes, but I'm told she's still the brains. She's the boss. She calls the tune. My low-life investigator gave me a bell. He finds her very impressive, I'm afraid to say.'

I nodded.

Worthington, a practised world-traveller, said, 'She hates you. Have you noticed?'

I told him I had indeed noticed. 'But I don't know why.'

'You'd want a psychiatrist to explain it properly, but I'll tell you for zilch what I've learned. You're a man, you're strong, you look OK, you're successful at your job and you're not afraid of her. And I could go on, but that's for starters. Then she has you roughed up, doesn't she, and here you are looking as good as new, even if you aren't feeling it, and sticking two fingers up in her face, more or less and, believe me, I'd've chucked a rival down the stairs for less if they as much as yawned in my presence.'

I listened to Worthington's wisdom, but I said, 'I haven't done her any harm.'

'You threaten her. You're too much for her. You'll win the tennis match. So maybe she'll have you killed first. She won't kill you herself. And don't ignore what I'm telling you. There are people who really have killed for hate. People who've wanted to win.'

Not to mention murders because of racism or religious prejudice, I thought, but it was still hard to imagine it applying to oneself – until one had felt the watch smash, of course.

I expected that Rose would have told Eddie Payne, her father, that I was at the races, but she hadn't. Worthington and I lay in wait for him after the last race and easily ambushed him in a pincer movement when he came out of the changing room on his way to his car.

He wasn't happy. He looked from one to the other of us like a cornered horse, and it was as if to a fractious animal that I soothingly said, 'Hi, Ed. How's things?'

'I don't know anything I haven't told you,' he protested.

I thought if I cast him a few artificial flies, I might startle and hook an unexpected fish; a trout, so to speak, sheltering in the reeds.

So I said, 'Is Rose married to Norman Osprey?'

His face lightened to nearly a laugh. 'Rose is still Rose Payne but she calls herself Robins and sometimes *Mrs* Robins when it suits her, but she doesn't like men, my Rose. Pity, really, but there it is.'

'But she likes to rule them?'

'She's always made boys do what she wants.'

'Were you with her yesterday evening?' I asked him the question casually, but he knew instantly what I meant.

'I didn't lay a finger on you,' he said quickly. 'It wasn't me.' He looked from me to Worthington and back again, this time with puzzlement. 'Look,' he said wheedlingly, as if begging for forgiveness, 'they didn't give you a chance. I told Rose it wasn't fair . . .' He wavered to a stop.

With interest I asked, 'Do you mean that you yourself wore a black mask in Broadway yesterday evening?' and almost with incredulity saw in his face an expression of shame that he had.

'Rose said we would just frighten you.' He stared at me with unhappy eyes. 'I tried to stop her, honest. I never thought you'd be here today. So it can't have been as bad as it looked ... but I know it was *awful*. I went to confession first to ask forgiveness ...'

'So there was you and Rose,' I said it matter of factly, though stunned beneath. 'And Norman Osprey, and who else? One of Norman Osprey's bookmaking clerks, was it?'

'No. Not them.'

Horror suddenly closed his mouth. He had already admitted far too much from his daughter's point of view, and if the other so far unidentified black-mask shape were one of the other two clerks working with Norman Osprey as Arthur Robins Est. 1894, Eddie was no longer going to admit it easily.

I tried another fly.

'Do you know anyone who could lay their hands on anaesthetics?'

A blank.

Try again.

'Or anyone with a white beard, known to Martin?'

He hesitated over that, but in the end shook his head.

I said, 'Do you yourself know anyone with a white beard who looks like a university lecturer?'

'No.' His reply was positive, his manner shifty.

'Was the brown-paper parcel you gave me at Cheltenham the self-same one that Martin gave you earlier in the day?'

'Yes,' he nodded this time with no need for thought. 'It was the same one. Rose was furious. She said I should have stuck onto it when Martin died, and I shouldn't have mentioned it. We should have kept it ourselves and then there wouldn't have been all this fuss.'

'Did Rose know what was in it?'

'Only Martin knew for sure. I did more or less ask him what was in it but he just laughed and said the future of the world, but it was a joke, of course.'

Martin's joke sounded to me too real to be funny.

Ed hadn't finished. 'A couple of weeks before Christmas,' he said, still amused, 'Martin said that what he was giving Bon-Bon – a few of the jockeys were talking about presents for their wives and girlfriends while they were changing to go home ... it wasn't a big deal – anyway, what he was giving Bon-Bon was a gold and glass antique necklace, but he was laughing and he said he would have to get you to make him a much cheaper and modern copy. He said you had a videotape to tell you how. But next minute he changed his mind because Bon-Bon wanted new fur-lined boots, and anyway he was mostly talking about the King George Chase at Kempton on Boxing Day and how much weight he'd have to take off by not eating turkey. I mean, he was always worried about his weight, like most of them are.'

'He talked to you a lot,' I commented. 'More than most.'

Ed didn't think so. He liked to chat with the boys, he said. He could tell us a thing or two about them. He winked on it, as if all jockeys were real sexual rogues, and with this confidence his manner more or less returned to the calm and efficient valet I'd met through Martin.

Worthington, driving us home, summed up the day's haul of information. 'I'd say Martin and the white-bearded guy were serious about this tape.'

'Yes,' I agreed.

'And somehow or other, through her father, Rose may have imagined that that tape showed how to make an antique necklace.'

I said doubtfully, 'It must be more than that.'

'Well . . . perhaps it actually says where the necklace can be found.'

'A treasure hunt?' I shook my head. 'There's only one valuable antique gold and glass necklace that I know of, and I do know a fair amount about antique glass, and it's in a museum. It's priceless. It was probably designed in Crete, or anyway somewhere round the Aegean Sea sometime about 3,500 years ago. It's called the Cretan Sunrise. I did make a copy of it, though, and I once lent it to Martin. I also made a videotape to explain the methods I used. I lent that to Martin too and he still has it – or rather, heaven knows where it is now.'

'What if there's another one?' Worthington asked.

'Are you talking about *two tapes* now? Or two neck-laces?'

'Why not two tapes?' Worthington reasoned, as if it had suddenly become likely. 'Rose could have muddled them up.'

I thought it just as likely that it was Worthington and I who'd muddled everything up, but we arrived safely at Bon-Bon's house richer with at least two solid new facts: first, that Rose, Norman Osprey and Eddie Payne had spent their Sunday evening in Broadway; and, second, that an elderly, thin, white-bearded, university-lecturer-type man had walked into my shop as the new century came in with bells, and had not stayed to help Lloyd Baxter with his epileptic fit.

As we scrunched to a halt on Bon-Bon's gravel, Marigold came with wide-stretched arms out of the front door to greet us.

'Bon-Bon doesn't need me any more,' she announced dramatically. 'Get out the maps, Worthington. We're going skiing.'

'Er . . . when?' her chauffeur asked, unsurprised.

'Tomorrow morning, of course. Fill up the petrol tanks. We'll call at Paris on the way. I need new clothes.'

Worthington looked more resigned than I felt. He murmured to me that Marigold bought new clothes most days of the week and prophesied that the skiing trip would last less than ten days overall. She would tire of it quickly, and come home.

Bon-Bon was taking the news of her mother's departure with well-hidden relief, and asked me with hope whether 'the upsetting videotape business' was now concluded. She wanted calm in her life, but I had no idea if she would get it. I didn't tell her of Rose's existence or the distinct lack of calm she represented.

I asked Bon-Bon about White-Beard. She said she'd never seen or heard of him. When I explained who he was, she telephoned to Priam Jones who, though with his self-esteem badly hurt by Lloyd Baxter's ditching of him, regretted he couldn't help.

Bon-Bon tried several more trainers, but thin, elderly, white-bearded owners of racehorses seemed not to exist. After she'd tired of it she persuaded her mother to let Worthington continue our journey, to take me where I wanted. I kissed her gratefully and chose to go straight home to my hillside house and flop.

Worthington liked skiing, he said as we drove away. He liked Paris. He liked Marigold. He regularly admired her more bizarre clothes. Sorry, he said, about leaving me with the lioness, Rose. Good luck, he said cheerfully.

'I could throttle you,' I said.

While Worthington happily chuckled at the wheel, I switched on my mobile phone again to call Irish at his home to find out how the day had finally gone in the shop, but before I could dial the number the message-service called, and the disembodied voice of young Victor W. V. said briefly in my ear, 'Send your e-mail address to me at vic@freenet.com.'

Holy hell, I thought, Victor had things to say. Flopping could wait. The only computer I owned that handled e-mail was in Broadway. Worthington with resignation changed direction, at length stopping by my main glass door and insisting he came in with me, to check the place for black masks and other pests.

The place was empty. No Rose in wait. Worthington returned with me to the Rolls, shook my hand, told me to look after myself and left lightheartedly, again prophesying his swift return well within two weeks.

Almost at once I missed the muscle man, missed him as a safety umbrella and as a source of a realistic view of life. Paris and skiing attracted powerfully. I sighed over my inescapable bruises, roused my sleeping computer into action, connected it to the Internet, and sent an e-mail message to Victor, with my address.

I expected I'd have to wait a good long time to hear from Victor, but almost immediately – which meant he had been sitting at his computer, waiting – the screen of my lap-top demanded 'Who are you?'

I typed and sent, 'Martin Stukely's friend.'

He asked, 'Name?' and I told him, 'Gerard Logan.'

His reply was, 'What do you want?'

'How did you know Martin Stukely?'

'I've known him for ages, saw him often at the races with my grandad.'

I wrote, 'Why did you send that letter to Martin? How had you heard of any tape? Please tell me the truth.'

'I heard my aunt telling my mother.'

'How did your aunt know?'

'My aunt knows everything.'

I began to lose faith in his common sense, and I remembered his saying he was playing a game.

'What is your aunt's name?' I expected nothing much: certainly not the breath-taker that came back.

'My aunt's name is Rose. She keeps changing her last name. She's my mother's sister.' There was barely an interval before his next remark. 'I'd better log off now. She's just come!'

'Wait.' Stunned by the revelation I rapidly typed, 'Do you know of a thin old man with a white beard?'

A long time after I'd settled for no answer three words appeared.

'Doctor Force. Goodbye.'

CHAPTER FIVE

To my considerable delight Catherine Dodd again stood her motor bike by my kerb and pulled off her helmet before walking across the pavement to the door I held open for her. It seemed natural to us both to kiss hello, and for her to stand in front of the soaring flight of wings that I had barely finished lighting.

'It's tremendous.' She meant it. 'It's too good for Broadway.'

'Flattery will get you an awfully long way,' I assured her, and took her into the workshop, where it was warmest.

The sheet printed of my e-mail conversation with Victor lay folded on the marver table and I passed it to her to read. 'What do you think?' I asked.

'I think you need better pain killers.'

'No. Think about Victor.'

She sat this time in the armchair on my promise that on the next day I would walk down the hill looking in second-hand and antique furniture shops to buy another one.

'If,' I amended the promise, 'if you will come and sit in it.'

She nodded as if it were an 'of course' decision and read Victor's e-mail. When she'd finished she laid the sheet on her black leather-clad knees and asked her own questions.

'OK,' she said. 'First of all, remind me, who is Victor?'

'The fifteen-year-old grandson of Ed Payne, Martin Stukely's racecourse valet. Ed gave me the videotape that was stolen from here, that you came to see about. Victor sent this letter to Martin.' I gave her the letter to read, which raised her eyebrows in doubt.

'Victor said he was playing games,' I acknowledged.

'You can't believe a word he says!' Catherine agreed.

'Well, yes, you can, actually. He's made a game of actual bits of fact. Or anyway, he's done what everyone does at some point – he's heard one thing and thought it meant another.'

'The wrong end of the stick?' Catherine suggested. 'How about the right end?'

'Well ... the stick as I see it, then.' I stopped for a minute or two to make coffee which, in spite of her being off duty, she said she preferred to wine. No milk, no sugar, cool rather than hot.

'Have to begin with a "suppose",' I said.

'Suppose away.'

'Start with a white-bearded man who looks like a university lecturer and who might be called Dr Force.

Suppose that this Dr Force has somehow got to know Martin. Dr Force has some information he wants to put into safekeeping so he takes it to Cheltenham races and gives it to Martin.'

'Crazy,' Catherine sighed. 'Why didn't he put it in a bank?'

'We'll have to ask him.'

'And you are crazy, too. How do we find him?'

'It's you,' I pointed out, smiling, 'who is the police officer.'

'Well, I'll try.' She smiled back. 'And what then?'

'Then Dr Force went to the races as planned. He gave his tape to Martin. After Martin crashed, our Dr Force must have gone through a lot of doubt and worry, and I'd guess he stood around near the changing room wondering what to do. Then he saw Ed Payne give the tape in its brown-paper parcel to me, and he knew it was the right tape as he'd packed it himself.'

'You should join the police,' Catherine teased. 'So, OK, Dr Force finds out who you are and takes himself here to Broadway, and when you leave your door unlocked for a spell in the new-age air, he nips in and takes back his own tape.'

'Right.'

'And steals your cash on impulse.'

'Right. But up to that point he hasn't realized that there is someone else in the depths of the shop, and that's Lloyd Baxter, who proceeds to have an epileptic fit.'

'Upsetting for Dr White-Beard Force.' She spoke dryly.

I nodded. 'He did a bunk.'

Catherine said thoughtfully, 'One of our detective constables interviewed Lloyd Baxter in hospital. Mr Baxter said he didn't see anyone at all come into the showroom.'

'Lloyd Baxter didn't care about getting the tape back, nor the money either. He did care very much about keeping his illness as private as possible.'

Catherine showed irritation. 'However can we solve cases if people don't give us the facts?'

'You must be used to it.'

She said that being used to something wrong didn't make it right. The starchy disapproval common to her profession had surfaced briefly. Never forget, I told myself, that the inner crime fighter is always there, always on duty, and always part of her. She shook herself free of the moment and made a visible gear-change back to a lighter approach.

'OK,' she nodded, 'so Dr Force has his tape back. Fine. So who squirted anaesthetic at the Stukelys and took their TVs, and who ransacked your own house, and beat you up last night? And I don't really understand how this boy Victor got involved.'

'I can't answer everything, but think Rose.'

'Pink?'

'Rose. She is Ed Payne's daughter, and Victor's aunt. She's sharp featured, sharp tongued, and I think is on the edge of criminal. She jumps a bit to conclusions, and she's all the more dangerous for that.'

'For instance?'

'For instance . . . I'd guess it was she who stole all the videotapes in Bon-Bon's house and mine because they could possibly have been mixed up with the one I brought from the racecourse.'

'But heavens!' Catherine exclaimed. 'Tapes do so easily get mixed up.'

'Rose probably thought so, too. I would think it likely that Rose chatters to her sister – Victor's mother – quite a lot and I think it's fairly certain that Victor did overhear her when she said she knew of a tape worth a fortune.'

If only Martin had explained what he was doing! There was too much guesswork, and definitely too much Rose.

Sighing, Catherine gave me back Victor's print-out and stood up, saying with apparent reluctance, 'I have to go. I was so glad to find you here, but I've promised to be with my parents tonight. I was wondering, though, if you by any chance want to go to your house now, then – um – you don't need a licence to ride pillion.'

She necessarily shed the police half of herself. I clasped her close round her waist, having more or less strapped on her spare helmet, which was too small and inclined to wobble. We set off insecurely, but the bike had guts enough to take both of us up the hills without stuttering, and she was laughing when she stopped by the weedy entrance to my drive.

I thanked her for the ride. She roared off still laughing.

107

I was conscious of wishing that Worthington, or failing him, Tom Pigeon and his Dobermanns, were by my side, but there were no thorny briar Roses lying in wait this time. When I unlocked a side door and let myself in, it seemed that the house gave back in peace the years the Logan family had prospered there, father, mother and two sons, each in a different way. I was the only one left, and with its ten rooms still filled with sharp memories, I'd made no move to find a smaller or more suitable lair. One day, perhaps. Meanwhile the house felt like home in all senses: home to me, the home of all who'd lived there.

I walked deliberately through all the rooms thinking of Catherine, wondering both if she would like the place, and whether the house would accept her in return. Once in the past the house had delivered a definite thumbs down, and once I'd been given an ultimatum to smother the pale plain walls with brightly patterned paper as a condition of marriage, but to the horror of her family I'd backed out of the whole deal and, as a result, I now used the house as arbiter and had disentangled myself from a later young woman who'd begun to refer to her and me as 'an item' and to reply to questions as 'we'. *We* think.

No, we don't think.

I knew that several people considered me heartless. Also promiscuous, also fickle. Catherine would be advised not to get herself involved with that fellow whose reputation was as brittle as his glass. I knew quite well what the gossips said, but it wasn't going to be to please any gossip that the house and I one day would settle on a mate for life.

The burglars who'd taken all my videotapes hadn't made a lot of mess. There had been television sets with video recorders in three rooms: in the kitchen, and in each of the sitting rooms in which for nearly ten years my mother and I had lived our semi-separate lives.

As I hadn't yet done anything about the rooms since her death, it seemed as if she would soon come out of her bedroom, chiding me for having left my dirty clothes on the floor.

There wasn't a single tape left anywhere that I could find. My parent had had a radically different taste from me in films and recorded TV programmes, but it no longer mattered. Out of my own room I'd lost a rather precious bunch of glass-blowing instruction tapes that I might be able to replace if I could find copies. I'd been commissioned to make some of them myself for university courses. Those courses were basic and mostly dealt with how to make scientific equipment for laboratories. I couldn't imagine those teaching tapes being the special target of any thief.

In the kitchen there had been game shows, tennis, American football and cooking. All gone. The police had suggested I list them all. What a hope!

There wasn't much left to tidy, except for patches of dust and a couple of dead spiders here and there where once the televisions had stood.

With the Rose-induced bruises growing gradually less sore, I slept safely behind bolted doors, and in the morning walked (as usual while sans car) downhill to Logan Glass, getting there before Irish, Hickory and Pamela Jane. Relief was the emotion I chiefly felt about the soaring wings; relief that somehow someone hadn't managed to smash them overnight.

Irish's pedestal and my lighting system had combined to make accidental breakage very difficult, but one couldn't easily guard against hurricane or axe.

I made a fleet of little ornamental sailing ships all morning and bought a comfortable armchair at lunchtime which minimized every remaining wince. Followed by a brown-overalled chair pusher (with chair), I returned to Logan Glass and rearranged the furniture. My assistants grinned knowingly.

I straightened out the worst of Hickory's growing hubris by giving him a sailing boat as an exercise, which resulted in a heap of sad lumps of stunted mast and a mainsail that no breeze would ever fill.

Hickory's good looks and general air of virility would always secure him jobs he couldn't do. In less than the first week of his attractive company I'd learned more of his limitations than his skills, but every customer liked him and he was a great salesman.

'It's all right for *you*,' he now complained, looking from the little boat I'd made in demonstration to the heap of coloured rubble he'd painstakingly achieved, 'you know what a sailing boat *looks* like. When I make them they come out flat.'

Half the battle in all I did, as I tried to explain to him without any 'cockiness' creeping in, was the draughtsman's inner eye that saw an object in three-dimensional terms. I could draw and paint all right, but it was the three-dimensional imagination that I'd been blessed with from birth that made little sailboats a doddle.

As Hickory's third try bit the dust amid commiserating murmurs from the rest of us, the telephone interrupted the would-be star glass-blower's spurious explanation of how drops of water had unfairly fallen on his work at the crucial moment and splintered it, which was definitely not his fault . . .

I didn't listen. The voice on the line was Catherine's.

'I've been a police officer all morning,' she said. 'Did you really get another chair?'

'It's here waiting for you.'

'Great. And I've collected some news for you. I'll be along when I go off duty, at six o'clock.'

To fill in time I e-mailed Victor, expecting to have to wait for a reply as he should have been in school but, as before, he was ready.

He typed. 'Things have changed.'

'Tell me.'

There was a long gap of several minutes.

'Are you still there?' he asked.

'Yes.'

DICK FRANCIS

'My dad's in jail.'

E-mail messages cross the ether without inflection. Victor's typed words gave no clues to his feelings.

I sent back, 'Where? What for? How long? I'm very sorry.'

Victor's reply had nothing to do with the questions.

'I hate her.'

I asked flatly, 'Who?'

A pause, then, 'Auntie Rose, of course.'

I itched for faster answers but got only a feeling that if I pressed too hard I would lose him altogether.

Without the tearing emotion I could imagine him trying to deal with, he wrote, 'He's been there ten weeks. They sent me to stay with my Uncle Mac in Scotland when the trial was on, so I wouldn't know. They told me my dad had gone on an Antarctic expedition as a chef. He is a chef, you see. He got sent down for a year, but he'll be out before that. Will you go on talking to me?'

'Yes,' I sent back. 'Of course.'

A long pause again, then: 'Rose sneaked on Dad.' I waited, and more came. 'He hit Mum. He broke her nose and some ribs.' After an even longer pause, he sent, 'E-mail me tomorrow,' and I replied fast, while he might still be on line, 'Tell me about Dr Force.'

Either he'd disconnected his phone line or didn't want to reply, because Dr Force was a non-starter. Victor's silence lasted all day.

I went back to the teaching session. Hickory finally fashioned a boat that might have floated had it been full-

112

size and made of fibreglass with a canvas sail. He allowed himself a smirk of satisfaction which none of us grudged him. Glass-blowing was a difficult discipline even for those like Hickory, who apparently had everything on their side – youth, agility, imagination. Hickory put the little boat carefully in the annealing oven, knowing I would give him the finished ornament to keep in the morning.

By six I'd managed to send them all home, and by six plus twenty-three Detective Constable Dodd was approving the new armchair and reading Victor Waltman Verity's troubles.

'Poor boy,' she said.

I said ruefully, 'As he hates his Aunt Rose for grassing on his Pa, he might not tell me anything else himself. Sneaking appears to be a mortal sin in his book.'

'Mm.' She read the printed pages again, then cheerfully said, 'Well, whether or not you have Victor's help, your Dr Force is definitely on the map.' It pleased her to have found him. 'I chased him through a few academic *Who's Who*s with no results. He's not a university lecturer, or not primarily, anyway. He is, believe it or not, a medical doctor. Licensed, and all that.' She handed me an envelope with a grin. 'One of my colleagues spends his time chasing struck-off practitioners. He looked for him, and in the end he did find him.'

'Is he struck off?' It would make sense, I thought, but Catherine shook her head.

'No, not only is he not struck off, he was working in

some research lab or other until recently. He took a lot of finding, because of that. It's all in this envelope.'

'And is he fiftyish with a white beard?'

She laughed. 'His date of birth will be in the envelope. A white beard's expecting too much.'

Both of us at that point found that there were more absorbing facets to life than chasing obscure medics.

I suggested food from the take-away; she offered another pillion ride up the hill: we saw to both. I'd left central heating on for comfort, and Catherine wandered all over the house, smiling.

'I've been warned that you'll dump me,' she said casually.

'Not in a hurry.'

I still held the envelope of Dr Force details, and I opened it then with hope, but it told me very few useful facts. His name was Adam Force, age fifty-six, and his qualifications came by the dozen.

I said blankly, 'Is that all?'

She nodded. 'That's all folks when it comes to facts. As to hearsay – well – according to a bunch of rumours he's a brilliant researcher who has published star-spangled work since his teens. No one could tell my colleague about a white beard. He didn't speak to anyone who'd actually met the subject.'

I asked, 'Does Dr Force have an address?'

'Not in these notes,' she answered. 'In the *Who's Who* we used, it gives only the information provided by the people themselves. Those reference books leave people out if they don't want to be in.'

'Utterly civilized.'

'No, very annoying.'

She didn't sound very annoyed, however, as she knew all about the Internet. The next morning, we decided, we would catch him on the Web.

We ate the take-away food, or a little of it, owing to a change of appetite, and I switched up the heating a little in my bedroom without any need for explanation.

She'd shed somewhere in her life whatever she had ever suffered in the way of overpowering shyness. The Catherine who came into my bed came with confidence along with modesty, an intoxicating combination as far as I was concerned. We both knew enough, anyway, to give to each other as much pleasure as we received, or at least enough to feel slumberous and fulfilled in consequence.

The speed of development of strong feeling for one another didn't seem to me to be shocking but natural, and if I thought about the future it unequivocally included Catherine Dodd. 'If you wanted to cover the pale plain walls with brightly patterned paper, go ahead,' I said.

She laughed. 'I like the peace of pale walls. Why should I want to change them?'

I said merely, 'I'm glad you don't,' and offered her thirst quenchers. Like Martin, it seemed she preferred fizzy water to alcohol, though in her case the cause wasn't weight but the combination of a police badge and a motor bike. She went soberly home before dawn, steady on two wheels. I watched her red rear light fade into what was left of the night and quite fiercely wanted her to stay with me instead.

I walked restlessly downhill through the slow January dawn, reaching the workshop well before the others. The Internet, though, when I'd accessed it, proved less obliging about Adam Force than the address of Waltman Verity in Taunton. There had been a whole clutch of Veritys. Adam Force wasn't anywhere in sight.

Hickory arrived at that point, early and eager to take his precious sailboat out of the Lehr annealing oven. He unbolted the oven door and lifted out his still warm treasure. Although he would get the transparent colours clearer with practice, it wasn't a bad effort and I told him so. He wasn't pleased, however. He wanted unqualified praise. I caught on his face a fleeting expression of contempt for my lack of proper appreciation of his ability. There would be trouble ahead if he tackled really difficult stuff, I thought: but, as I'd done once in the past with someone of equal talent, I would give him good references when he looked for a different teacher as, quite soon now, he would.

I would miss him most in the selling department for results and in the humour department for good company.

Irish, more humble about his skills, and Pamela Jane, twittery and positively self-deprecating, came sweeping in together in the cold morning and gave the sailboat the extravagant admiration Hickory thought it deserved. Harmony united the three of them as usual, but I hadn't much faith in its lasting much longer.

Watched and helped by all three of them I spent that day replacing the minaret-shaped scent bottles we'd sold at Christmas, working fast at eight pieces an hour, using blue, turquoise, pink, green, white and purple in turn and packing the finished articles in rows in the ovens to cool. Speed was a commercial asset as essential as a three-dimensional eye, and winter in the Cotswold hills was the time to stock up for the summer tourists. I consequently worked flat out from morning to six in the evening, progressing from sailboats via scent bottles to fishes, horses, bowls and vases.

At six in the evening when my semi-exhausted crew announced all six ovens to be packed, I sent them off home, tidied the workshop and put everything ready for the morrow. In the evening Catherine Dodd, straight off duty, rode her bike to Broadway, collected a pillion passenger and took him to his home. Every night possible that week Detective Constable Dodd slept in my arms in my bed but left before the general world awoke and, during that time, no one managed to stick an address on Adam Force.

Glass-blowing aside, by Friday afternoon, three days after Worthington and Marigold had joyfully left for Paris, the weekend held no enticements as Catherine had departed on Friday morning to a promised school-friends' reunion.

On the same Friday, aching, I dare say, from the

117

absence of their daily quarrel, Bon-Bon filled her need of Martin by driving his BMW, bursting at the seams with noisy children, to pick me up at close of day in Broadway.

'Actually,' Bon-Bon confessed as we detoured to my hill house for mundane clean shirts and socks, 'Worthington didn't like you being out here alone.'

'*Worthington* didn't?'

'No. He phoned from somewhere south of Paris and specially told me a whole gang of people jumped on you in Broadway last Sunday evening when there were dog-walkers about, and this place of yours out here is asking for trouble, he said. He also said Martin would have taken you home.'

'Worthington exaggerated,' I protested, but after we'd all unloaded at Bon-Bon's house, I used the evening there to invent a game for the children to compete in, a game called 'Hunt the orange cylinder and the shoelaces.'

Bon-Bon protested. 'But they told everything they know to the police! They won't find anything useful.'

'And after that game,' I said, gently ignoring her, 'we'll play "Hunt the letters sent to Daddy by somebody called Force", and there are prizes for every treasure found, of course.'

They played until bedtime with enthusiasm on account of the regular hand-outs of gold coin treasure (money), and when they'd noisily departed upstairs I laid out their final offerings all over Martin's desk in the den.

I had watched the children search uninhibitedly in places I might have left untouched so that their haul was in some ways spectacular. Perhaps most perplexing was the original of the letter Victor had sent a copy of to Martin.

Dear Martin, it said, and continued word for word as far as the signature, which didn't say Victor Waltman Verity in computer-print, but was scrawled in real live handwriting – Adam Force.

'The kids found that letter in a secret drawer in Martin's desk,' Bon-Bon said. 'I didn't even know there was a secret drawer, but the children did.'

'Um.' I pondered. 'Did any of these other things come out of the drawer?'

She said she would go and ask, and presently returned with Daniel, her eleven-year-old eldest, who opened a semi-hidden drawer in the desk for us with an easy twiddle, and asked if it were worth another hand-out. He hadn't emptied the drawer, he explained, as he'd found the letter straight away, the letter that was the point of the whole game, the letter sent to Daddy by someone called Force.

Of course, no one had found any trace of an orange cylinder or of recognizable laces for trainers.

I gladly handed over another instalment of treasure, as the hidden drawer proved to stretch across the whole width of the desk under the top surface, and to be about four inches deep. Daniel patiently showed me how it opened and closed. Observant and quick-witted, he offered other discoveries with glee, especially when I gave him a coin for every good hiding place with nothing in it. He found four. He jingled the coins.

Bon-Bon, searching the desk drawer, found with blushing astonishment a small bunch of love letters from her that Martin had saved. She took them over to the black leather sofa and wept big slow tears, while I told her that her son knew the so-called secret drawer wasn't a secret at all but was a built-in feature of the modern desk.

'It's designed to hold a lap-top computer,' I told Bon-Bon. 'Martin just didn't keep a lap-top in it, as he used that table-top one over there, the one with the full keyboard and the screen.'

'How do you know?'

'Daniel says so.'

Bon-Bon said through her tears, 'How disappointing it all is,' and picked up a tissue for mopping.

I however found the lap-top drawer seething with interest, if not with secrets as, apart from Adam Force's letter to Martin, there was a photocopy of Martin's letter to Force, a not much longer affair than the brief reply.

It ran:

Dear Adam Force,

I have now had time to consider the matter of your formulae and methods. Please will you go ahead and record these onto the videotape as you suggested and take it to Cheltenham races on New Year's Eve. Give it to me there, whenever you see me, except, obviously, not when I'm on my way out to race.

Yours ever,

Martin Stukely

I stared not just at the letter, but at its implications.

Daniel looked over my shoulder, and asked what formulae were. 'Are they secrets?' he said.

'Sometimes.'

When Bon-Bon had read the last loving letter and had dried her tears I asked her how well Martin had known Dr Adam Force.

With eyes darkened from crying she said she didn't know. She regretted desperately all the hours the two of them had spent in pointless arguing. 'We never discussed anything without quarrelling. You know what we were like. But I *loved* him ... and he loved *me*, I know he did.'

They had quarrelled and loved, both intensely, throughout the four years I'd known them. It was too late to wish that Martin had confided more in her, even in spite of her chattering tongue, but together for once they had decided that it should be I and not Bon-Bon who held Martin's secret for safekeeping.

What secret? *What secret*, dear God.

Alone in the den since Bon-Bon and Daniel had gone upstairs to the other children, I sorted through everything in the drawer, putting the many loose letters in heaps according to subject. There were several used old cheque books with sums written on the stubs but quite often not dates or payees. Martin must have driven his accountant crazy. He seemed simply to have thrust tax papers, receipts, payments and earnings haphazardly into his out-of-sight drawer.

Semi-miracles occasionally happen, though, and on one stub, dated November 1999 (no actual day) I came across the plain name Force (No Dr, no Adam). On the line below there was the single word BELLOWS, and in the box for the amount of money being transferred out of the account there were three noughts, ooo, with no whole numbers and no decimal points.

Searches through three other sets of stubs brought to light a number of similar unfinished records: Martin deserved secrets, curse him, when he wrote so many himself.

The name Force appeared again on a memo pad, when a Martin handwritten scrawl said, 'Force, Bristol, Wednesday, if P doesn't declare Legup at Newton Abbot.'

Legup at Newton Abbot . . . Say Legup was a horse and Newton Abbot the racecourse where he was entered? I stood up from Martin's desk and started on the form books in his bookcase, but although Legup had run in about eight races in the autumn and spring over four or five years, and seldom, as it happened, on Wednesdays, there wasn't any mention of days he'd been entered but stayed at home.

I went back to the drawer.

A loose-leaf notebook, the most methodically kept of all his untidy paperwork, appeared as a gold-mine of order compared with all the rest. It listed, with dates, amounts given by Martin to Eddie Payne, his racecourse valet, since the previous June. It included even the day he died, when he'd left a record of his intentions.

As there was, to my understanding, a pretty rigid scale of pay from jockeys to valets, the notebook at first sight looked less important than half the neglected rest, but on the first page Martin had doodled the names of Ed Payne, Rose Payne, Gina Verity and Victor. In a box in a corner, behind straight heavy bars, he'd written Waltman. There were small sketches of Ed in his apron, Gina in her curlers, Victor with his computer and Rose . . . Rose had a halo of spikes.

Martin had known this family, I reflected, for almost as long as Ed had been his valet. When Martin had received the letter from Victor Waltman Verity, he would have known it was a fifteen-year-old's game. Looking back, I could see I hadn't asked the right questions, because I'd been starting from the wrong assumptions.

With a sigh I put down the notebook and read through the letters, most of which were from the owners of horses that Martin's skill had urged first past the post. All of the letters spoke of the esteem given to an honest jockey and none of them had the slightest relevance to secrets on videotapes.

A 1999 diary came next, though I found it not in the drawer but on top of the desk, put there by one of the children. It was a detailed jockey's diary, with all race meetings listed. Martin had circled everywhere he'd ridden, with the names of his mounts. He had filled in Tallahassee on the last day of the century, the last day of his life.

I lolled in Martin's chair, both mourning him and

wishing like hell that he could come back alive just for five minutes.

My mobile phone, lying on the desk, gave out its brisk summons and, hoping it was Catherine, I switched it on.

It wasn't Catherine.

Victor's cracked voice spoke hurriedly.

'Can you come to Taunton on Sunday? Please say you will catch the same train as before. I'm running out of money for this phone. Please say yes.'

I listened to the urgency, to the virtual panic.

I said, 'Yes, OK,' and the line went dead.

I would have gone blithely unwarned to Taunton on that Sunday if it hadn't been for Worthington shouting in alarm over crackling lines from a mountain top.

'Haven't you learned the first thing about not walking into an ambush?'

'Not Victor,' I protested. 'He wouldn't lure me into a trap.'

'Oh yeah? And does the sacrificial lamb understand he's for the chop?'

Lamb chop or not, I caught the train.

CHAPTER SIX

Tom Pigeon, who lived within walking distance away
with his three energetic Dobermanns, strolled to the
gallery door of Logan Glass late on Saturday morning
and invited me out for a beer in a local pub. Any bar, but
not the Dragon's across the road, he said.

With the dogs quietly tied to a bench outside, Tom
Pigeon drank deep of a pint in a crowded dark inn and
told me that Worthington thought that I had more nerve
than sense when it came to the Verity–Paynes.

'Mm. Something about a wasps' nest,' I agreed.
'When, exactly, did he talk to you?'

Tom Pigeon looked at me over the rim of his glass as
he swallowed the dregs. 'He said you were no slouch in
the brain box. He told me this morning.' He smiled. 'He
phoned from Gstaad. Only the best for his lady employer,
of course.'

He ordered a second pint while I still dawdled with
my first. His slightly piratical dark little pointed beard
and his obvious physical strength turned heads our way. I

might be of his age and height, but no one sidled away at my approach, or found me an instinctive threat.

'It was only a week ago tomorrow,' he said, 'that they hammered you until you could hardly stand.'

I thanked him for my deliverance.

He said, 'Worthington wants you to stay away from any more trouble of that sort. Especially, he said, while he's in Switzerland.'

I listened, though, to the Tom Pigeon view of that course of inaction. He sounded as bored with the safe road to old age as Worthington himself had been the day he had goaded me to go to Leicester races.

'Worthington's coming across like a father,' Tom said.

'A bodyguard,' I commented wryly, 'and I miss him.'

Tom Pigeon said casually but with unmistakable sincerity, 'Take me on board instead.'

I reflected briefly that Tom's offer wasn't what Worthington had intended to spark off, and wondered what my dear Constable Dodd would think of my allying myself to an ex-jail occupant with a nickname like Backlash. I said regardless, 'Yes, if you'll do what I ask . . .'

'Maybe.'

I laughed and suggested how he might spend his Sunday. His eyes widened and came to vivid approving life. 'Just as long as it's legal,' he bargained. 'I'm not going back in the slammer.'

'It's legal,' I assured him, and when I caught the train the following morning I had a new rear defender in the guards' van, accompanied by three of the most dangerous-looking black dogs that ever licked one's fingers.

There was only one possible train combination to travel on which would achieve the same time of arrival at Lorna Terrace as I'd managed the previous Sunday. It would be the time that Victor meant. Tom had wanted to rethink the plan and go by car. He would drive, he said. I shook my head and changed his mind.

Suppose, I'd suggested, this is not the ambush that Worthington feared, but just the frantic need of a worried boy. Give him a chance, I'd said.

We would compromise, though, about the awkward return journey. We would hire a car with driver to follow us from Taunton station, to shadow us faithfully, to pick us up when we wanted and finally drive us to Broadway and home.

'Expensive,' Tom Pigeon complained.

'I'm paying,' I said.

Victor himself was waiting on the Taunton platform when the train wheels ran smoothly into the station. I'd travelled near the front of the train so as to be able to spot and to pass any little unwelcoming committee where I had plenty of space to assess them, but the boy seemed to be alone. Also, I thought, anxious. Also cold in the January wind. Beyond that, an enigma.

Tom's dogs, travelling at the rear of the train, slithered down onto the platform and caused a sharp local division between dog-lovers and those with anti-fang reservations.

I reckoned, or anyway hoped, that Victor himself

wouldn't know Tom or his dogs by sight, even though Rose and the rest of her family probably would, after the rout of the black-masks in Broadway.

I needed no black-mask to meet Victor but, learning from the plain-clothes police, I wore a baseball cap at the currently with-it angle above a navy-blue tracksuit topped with a paler-blue sleeveless padded jacket. Normal enough for many, but different from my usual grey trousers and white shirt.

Bon-Bon's children having sniggered behind their hands, and Tom having swept his gaze over me blankly as if I had been a stranger, I walked confidently and silently in my trainers to Victor's back and said quietly in his ear, 'Hello.'

He whirled round and took in my changed appearance with surprise, but chief of his emotions seemed to be straightforward relief that I was there at all.

'I was afraid you wouldn't come,' he said. 'Not when I heard them saying how they'd smashed you up proper. I don't know what to do. I want you to tell me what to do. They tell me lies.' He was shaking slightly, more with nervousness, I guessed, than with cold.

'First of all, we get off this windy platform,' I said, 'then you tell me where your mother thinks you are.'

Down in front of the station the driver I'd engaged was polishing a dark-blue estate car large enough for the occasion. Tom Pigeon came out of the station with his dogs, made contact with the driver and loaded the Dobermanns into the big rear space designed for them.

Victor, not yet realizing that the car and dogs had anything to do with him, answered my question and a dozen others. 'Mum thinks I'm at home. She's gone to see my dad in jail. It's visiting day. I listened to her and my Auntie Rose planning what they would say to me, and they made up some story about Mum going to see a woman with a disgusting illness that I wouldn't like. Every time she goes to see Dad they make up another reason why I stay at home. Then, when I listened some more, I heard them say they're going to try again, after Mum sees Dad, to make you tell them where the tape is you had from Grandad Payne. They say it's worth millions. My Auntie Rose says it's all nonsense for you to say you don't know. Please, please tell her where it is, or what's on it, because I can't bear her *making* people tell her things. I'd heard them twice up in our attic screaming and groaning and she just laughs and says they have toothache.'

I turned away from Victor so that he shouldn't see the absolute horror that flooded my mind and assuredly appeared on my face. Just the idea of Rose using teeth for torture melted at once any theoretical resistance I might have thought to be within my own capacity.

Teeth.

Teeth and wrists and hell knew what else . . .

The need intensified to a critical level to find out what secrets I was supposed to know, and then to decide what to do with the knowledge. Victor, I thought, might be able to dig from the semi-conscious depths of his memory the scraps I still needed if I were to glue together a credible whole. I had pieces. Not enough.

I asked with an inward shudder, 'Where is your Auntie Rose today? Did she visit your dad too?'

He shook his head. 'I don't know where she is. She doesn't usually go to the jail because Dad's not talking to her since she shopped him.' He paused, and then said passionately, 'I wish I belonged to an ordinary family. I wrote to Martin once and asked if I could stay with him for a while but he said they didn't have room. I begged him . . .' His voice cracked. 'What can I do?'

It seemed clear that Victor's need for someone to advise him stretched very far back. It wasn't odd that he was now close to breakdown.

'Come for a ride?' I suggested with friendliness, and held open for him the door behind the estate-car driver. 'I'll get you back home before you're missed, and before that we can talk about what you need.'

He hesitated only briefly. He had, after all, brought me there to help him, and it appeared he was reaching out to someone he trusted even though his family considered that person to be an enemy. Victor couldn't invent or act at this level of desperation.

If this were an ambush, then Victor was the lamb who didn't know it.

I asked him if he knew where I could find Adam Force. The question caused a much longer hesitation and then a shake of the head. He knew, I thought, but perhaps telling me came into the category of squealing.

Tom Pigeon sat beside the driver, making him nervous simply by being himself. Victor and I sat in the rear passenger seats with the dogs behind, separated from us by a netting divider. The driver, taciturn from first to last, set off as soon as we were all aboard and headed at first through winding Somerset country roads and finally out to the wide expanses of Exmoor. Even in the summer, I imagined, it would be a bare and daunting place, grim with sunny dreams unfulfilled and long skylines blurring into drizzly mist. On that Sunday in January the cloudless air was bright, cold and crisp and on the move. The driver pulled off the road onto an area consolidated for tourist parking, and with a few spare words pointed to a just perceptible path ahead, telling me it led onto trackless moorland if I went far enough.

He would wait for us, he said, and we could take our time. He had brought a packed picnic lunch for all of us, as I had arranged.

Tom Pigeon's dogs disembarked and bounded free ecstatically, sniffing with unimaginable joy round heather roots in rich dark red earth. Tom himself stepped out of the car and stretched his arms and chest wide, filling his lungs with deep breaths of clean air.

Victor's face, transformed by the exchange of terrace-house-Taunton for wide open sky, looked almost carefree, almost happy.

Tom and his black familiars set off fast along the track and were soon swallowed into the rolling scenery. Victor and I followed him but eventually more slowly, with

Victor pouring out his devastating home life and difficulties, as I guessed he'd never done before.

'Mum's all right,' he said. 'So's Dad really, except
when he comes home from the pub. Then if Mum or I
get too near him he belts us one.' He swallowed. 'No,
I didn't mean to say that. But last time he broke her ribs
and her nose and her face was black all down one side,
and when Auntie Rose saw it she went to the cops, and it
was funny, really, because other times I'd seen *her* hit
my dad. She's got fists like a boxer when she gets going.
She can deal it out until the poor buggers beg her to stop,
and that's when she laughs at them, and often when she's
clouted them once or twice more, she'll step back a bit
and smile . . . And then sometimes she'll *kiss* them.' He
glanced at me anxiously, sideways, to see what I made of
his Aunt Rose's behaviour.

I thought that possibly I'd got off fairly lightly at the
hands of the black-masks, thanks to Rose having met her
equal in ferocity, my friend with his dogs ahead now on
the moor.

I asked Victor, 'Has Rose ever attacked you, personally?'

He was astonished. 'No, of course not. She's my aunt.'

I'd give him perhaps another two years, I thought,
before his aunt looked on him as a grown man, not a
child.

We walked another length of track while I thought
how little I understood of the psychology of women like
Rose. Men who enjoyed being beaten by women weren't

the sort that attracted Rose. For her to be fulfilled they had to hate it.

The track had narrowed until I was walking in front of Victor, which made talking difficult, but then suddenly the ground widened into a broader flat area from which one could see distant views in most directions. Tom Pigeon stood out below us, his Dobermanns zigzagging around him with unfettered joy.

After watching them for several moments I gave life to an ear-splitting whistle, a skill taught me by my father and brother who had both been able to accomplish the near-impossible of summoning taxis in London in the rain.

Tom stopped fast, turned towards me from lower down the rolling hills, waved acknowledgement, and began to return to where I stood. His dogs aimed towards me without a single degree of deviation.

'Wow,' Victor said, impressed. 'How do you do that?'

'Curl your tongue.' I showed him how, and I asked him again to tell me more about Dr Force. I needed to talk to him, I said.

'Who?'

'You know damn well who. Dr Adam Force. The man who wrote the letter you copied and sent to Martin.'

Victor, silenced, took a while to get going again.

In the end he said, 'Martin knew it was a game.'

'Yes, I'm sure he did,' I agreed. 'He knew you well, he knew Adam Force, and Adam Force knows you.' I watched Tom Pigeon trudge towards us up the hill. 'You may know their secret, that one that was on the tape everyone's talking about.'

'No,' Victor said, 'I don't.'

'Don't lie,' I told him. 'You don't like liars.'

He said indignantly, 'I'm not lying. Martin knew what was on the tape, and so did Dr Force, of course. When I sent that letter to Martin I was just pretending to be Dr Force. I often pretend to be other people, or sometimes animals. It's only a game. Sometimes I talk to people who don't really exist.'

Harvey the rabbit, I thought: and I'd been engine drivers and jockeys in my time. Victor would grow out of it soon, but not soon enough for now in January 2000.

I asked him how he had obtained a copy of Dr Force's letter, which he had sent to Martin with his own name attached in place of Force's.

He didn't reply but just shrugged his shoulders.

I asked him yet again if he knew where I could find his Dr Force, but he said dubiously that Martin had for sure written it down somewhere.

Probably he had. Victor knew where, but he still wasn't telling that either. There had to be some way of persuading him. Some way of bringing him to the point of wanting to tell.

Tom Pigeon and his three bouncing companions reached us at the flattened viewing area, all clearly enjoying the day.

'That's some whistle,' Tom commented admiringly, so I did it again at maximum loudness, which stunned the dogs into pointing their muzzles in my direction, their noses twitching, their eyes alert. Tom patted them, and their stumpy tails wagged excessively.

Walking back towards the car Victor did his breathy best at a whistle that would equally affect the dogs, but they were unimpressed. Water in dishes and handfuls of dog biscuits, brought from home by their owner, suited them better as a prelude to lying down for a doze.

Tom himself, the driver, Victor and I ate sandwiches inside the car, out of the wind, and afterwards sleep came easily to the other three. I left the car and walked back slowly along the track sorting out and simplifying Victor's muddling game of pretence and reducing the Verity–Payne videotape roundabout to probabilities. Still, the absolutely first thing to do next, I concluded, was to find Adam Force, and the path to him still lay with Victor.

What I needed was to get Victor to trust me so instinctively that his deepest secret thoughts would pop out of him without caution. Also I needed to get him to that state fast, and I didn't know if that sort of total brainwash were possible, let alone ethical.

When there was movement around the car I returned to tell the yawning passengers that, according to my new cheap watch, it was time to leave if we were to get back to Lorna Terrace in advance of the time that Victor was expecting his mum.

Tom walked off to find comfort behind bushes, and jerked his head for me to go with him.

Contingency planning was in his mind. The day had gone too smoothly. Had I considered a few 'what ifs'?

We considered them together and returned to the car, where the taciturn driver had taken a liking for Victor and was deep in esoteric chat about computers.

The contentment of the day high on the moor slowly sank and evaporated as the estate car inevitably drew nearer to Lorna Terrace. Victor's nervous tremor reasserted itself and he watched me anxiously for signs of thrusting him back into his unsatisfactory life. He knew pretty well that at fifteen he would be at the mercy of the courts, and that the courts' mercy would undoubtedly be to consign him to the care of his mother. Gina, his mother, even a Gina chain-smoking in large pink curlers, would quite likely be seen as the badly-done-by parent of a thank'ess child. Gina Verity, unlike her sister Rose who co⋯n't help radiating a faint air of menace, would be seen by any court in the way that I had seen her at first, as a relaxed, tolerant and fond mother doing her best in difficult circumstances.

The driver stopped the car where Tom Pigeon asked him, which was round the bend that kept him out of sight of number 19. Victor and I disembarked at that point, and I sympathized very much with the misery and hopelessness reappearing in the droop of his shoulders. I went with him to the front door of number 19 which, as in many terraced houses, opened from a concrete path across a small square front garden of dusty grass. Victor produced a key from a pocket and let us in, leading me as before down the passage to the bright little kitchen where life was lived, and where I had promised to stay as company until his mother came back, even though she might not like it.

The door from the kitchen brought Victor to a standstill of puzzlement and unease.

He said, 'I'm sure I bolted the door before I went out.' He shrugged. 'Anyway, I know I bolted that gate from the backyard into the lane. Mum gets furious if I forget it.'

He opened the unbolted kitchen door and stepped out into a small high-walled square of backyard. Across the weeds and dead-looking grass, a tall brown-painted door was set into the high brick wall, and it was this door that freshly upset Victor by again not having its bolts, top and bottom, firmly slid into place.

'Bolt them now,' I said urgently, but Victor stood still in front of me in puzzlement and dismay, and although understanding flashed like lightning through my mind, I couldn't get round him fast enough. The door from the lane opened the moment I stepped towards it across the grass from the kitchen.

Rose had come into the backyard from the lane. Gina and the quasi-gorilla Norman Osprey marched out triumphantly from the house behind us. Both Rose and Osprey were armed with a cut-off section of garden hose. Rose's piece had a tap on it.

Victor at my side stood like a rock, not wanting to

believe what he was seeing. When he spoke, the words addressed to his mother were a scramble of 'You've come back early.'

Rose prowled like a hunting lioness between me and the door to the lane, swinging the heavy brass tap on the supple green hose, and almost licking her lips.

Gina, for once without curlers and pretty as a result, tried to justify the prospect ahead by whining to Victor that his caged father had told her to eff off, he wasn't in the mood for her silly chatter. In her anger she told Victor for the first time that his father was 'inside', and deserved it.

'He can be a mean brute, your dad,' Gina said. 'And when we'd gone all that way! So Rose drove me home again, and that bitch next door told me you'd sneaked off craftily to the station. She followed as she was going that way anyhow, and you met that fellow, that one over there, that Rose says is stealing a million from us. How *can* you, young Vic? So Rose says this time she'll make him tell us what we want to know, but it's no thanks to you, Rose says.'

I heard only some of it. I watched Victor's face, and saw with relief his strong alienation from Gina's smug voice. The more she said, the more he didn't like it. Teenage rebellion visibly grew.

The present and future scene here hadn't been exactly one of the 'what ifs' that Tom and I had imagined in the bushes, but now what if . . . if I could think it out fast enough . . . if I could use Victor's horrified reaction to his mother's outpouring ... if I could put up with a bit of Rose's persuasion ... then perhaps – on top of the carefree day on the moor – perhaps Victor would indeed feel like telling me what I was sure he knew. Perhaps the sight of his Aunt Rose's cruelty in action would impel him to offer a gift in atonement ... to offer me the one thing he knew I wanted. Maybe the prize was worth a bit of discomfort. So get on with it, I told myself. If you're going to do it, do it fast.

Last Sunday, I thought, the black-masks had jumped me unawares. It was different this Sunday. I could invite the assault head on and I did, at a run towards the door to the lane, straight towards Rose and her swinging tap.

She was fast and ruthless and managed to connect twice before I caught her right arm and bent it up behind her, her face close to mine, her dry skin and freckles in sharp focus, hate and sudden pain drawing her lips back from her teeth. Gina, yelling blasphemy, tore at my ear to free her sister.

I caught a glimpse of Victor's horror an instant before Norman Osprey lashed out at me from behind with his own length of hose. Rose wrenched herself out of my grip, pushed Gina out of her way and had another swing at me with her tap. I managed a circular kick-box which temporarily put the gorilla Norman face down on the grass, and in return got another fearful clout from Rose along the jaw that ripped open the skin.

Enough, I thought. Far and away too much. Blood trickled everywhere. I used my only real weapon, the piercing whistle for help, that Tom and I in the bushes had agreed meant 'come at once'.

What if I whistle and he doesn't come . . .?

I whistled again, louder, longer, calling not for a taxi in the rain in London, but quite likely for life without deformity and certainly for self-respect. I couldn't have told Rose from direct knowledge where to find that videotape, but if I'd needed to badly enough I would have invented something. Whether or not she would have believed me was another matter and one I hoped not to find out.

I fortunately also didn't find out what conclusion Rose intended for her Sunday afternoon sports. There was a vast crashing and tinkling noise and Tom's voice roaring at his dogs, and then three snarling Dobermann Pinschers poured like a torrent out of the house's wide open kitchen door into the confined space of the backyard.

Tom carried an iron bar he'd borrowed from local town railings. Norman Osprey backed away from him, his hose soft and useless in opposition, his Sunday pleasure no longer one long laugh.

Rose, the quarry of the dogs, turned tail and ignominiously left the scene through the gate into the lane, sliding through a small opening and pulling it shut behind her.

Trusting that the dogs knew me well enough to keep their fangs to themselves I walked among them and slid the bolts across on the wall-to-lane door, blocking Rose's immediate way back.

Gina screeched at Tom only once and without much

conviction, Tom's fierce physical closeness reducing her protests to nil. She was silent even when she discovered Tom's mode of entry had been to smash open her front door. She didn't try to stop her son when he ran past her along the passage from backyard to front, and called to me in the few steps before I reached the road.

Tom and the Dobermanns were already out on the pavement on their way back to the car.

I stopped at once when Victor called me, and waited until he came up. Either he would tell me or he wouldn't. Either the hose and tap had been worth it, or they hadn't. Pay-off time.

'Gerard . . .' He was out of breath, not from running but from what he'd seen in the yard. 'I can't bear all this. If you want to know . . . Dr Force lives in Lynton,' he said. 'Valley of the Rocks Road.'

'Thanks,' I said.

Victor unhappily watched me use tissues scrounged from his mother's kitchen to blot the oozing blood on my face. I said, 'There's always e-mail, don't forget.'

'How can you even speak to me?'

I grinned at him. 'I still have all my teeth.'

'Look out for Rose,' he warned me anxiously. 'She never gives up.'

'Try to arrange to live with your grandfather,' I suggested. 'It would be safer than here.'

Some of his misery abated. I touched his shoulder in parting and walked along Lorna Terrace to where Tom Pigeon waited.

Tom looked at my battered face and commented, 'You were a hell of a long time whistling.'

'Mm.' I smiled. 'Silly of me.'

'You delayed it on purpose!' he exclaimed in revelation. 'You let that harpy hit you.'

'You get what you pay for, on the whole,' I said.

Most bruises faded within a week, Martin had said; also, this time, I got a doctor on the Monday to stick together the worst of the cuts with small adhesive strips.

'I suppose you walked into another black-masked door,' guessed Constable Dodd, horrified. 'Rose may not frighten you but, from what I've heard, she'd terrify me.'

'Rose didn't bother about a mask,' I said, putting together a spicy rice supper on Monday evening in the kitchen of my house on the hill. 'Do you like garlic?'

'Not much. What are you planning to do about Rose Payne? You should go to the Taunton police and make a complaint against her for assault. That wound might even constitute GBH.'

Grievous Bodily Harm, I thought. Not half as grievous as she had intended.

'What would I tell them – a thin woman beat me up so a friend of mind with a criminal record smashed down her front door and set his dogs on her?'

She was not amused but simply repeated, 'So what are you going to do about her?'

I didn't answer directly. I said instead, 'Tomorrow I'm

going to Lynton in Devon and I'd rather she didn't know.'
I frowned over a green pepper. 'It's a wise man as knows
his enemies,' I asserted, 'and I do know our Rose.'

'In the biblical sense?'

'God forbid!'

'But Rose Payne is only one person,' Catherine said,
drinking fizzy water routinely. 'There were four black-
masks, you said.'

I nodded. 'Norman Osprey, bookmaker, he was Number
Two, and Ed Payne, who was Martin Stukely's racecourse
valet and is Rose's father, he was Number Three and he's
sorry for it, and all those three know I recognized them.
One other seemed familiar to me at the time but I can't
have been right. He was a clutcher setting me up for the
others and I think of him as Number Four. He was behind
me most of the time.'

Catherine listened in silence and seemed to be waiting.

Skidding now and then across a half-formed recollec-
tion went the so far unidentified figure that I called simply
Black-mask Four, and I remembered him most for the
inhumanity he took to his task. It had been Norman
Osprey who'd smashed my watch, but it had been Black-
mask Four who'd bunched my fingers for him. For all
Norman Osprey's awesome strength, in retrospect it was
Black-mask Four who'd scared me most, and who now,
nine days later, intruded fearsomely in my dreams, nightmares in which Black-mask Four intended to throw me
into the 1,800 degrees Fahrenheit of the liquid glass in
the tank in the furnace.

That night, while Constable Dodd slept peacefully in my arms, it was she whom Black-mask Four threw to a burning death.

I awoke sweating and cursing Rose Payne with words I'd rarely used before, and I felt more reluctant than ever to leave Catherine to the risks of her plain-clothes operation.

'Come back safe yourself this time,' she said worriedly, zooming off in the dawn, and I, with every intention of carrying out her instructions, walked down to my blameless furnace and did the day's work before my three helpers arrived.

The day before they had joked about my recurring Monday bruises, which Irish had sworn were the result of pub brawls. I hadn't disillusioned them, and on the Tuesday cheerfully left them practising dishes for the day while I walked out of the village for a mile to catch a bus.

Neither Rose nor Gina, nor anyone else I knew, came into sight, and I felt, when I disembarked outside a busy newsagents in the next town and climbed into another pre-arranged car with driver, that there could be no one on my tail. Tom Pigeon, who had designed 'the simple exit for glass-blowers', had begged me at least to take one of his dogs with me, if I wouldn't take *him*. Hadn't I been bashed enough? he asked. Hadn't I needed him to rescue me twice? Wasn't I now being insane to insist on travelling alone?

Yes, quite likely, I agreed. So give me advice.

Thanks to him, then, I went to Lynton on the north Devon coast unmolested, and in the electoral register found the full address of Dr Adam Force, in the Valley of the Rocks Road.

The chief disappointment to this successful piece of research was that there was no one in the house.

I knocked and rang and waited and tried again, but the tall grey old building had a dead air altogether and an empty-sounding reverberation when I tried the back door. The neighbours weren't helpful. One was out, and one was deeply deaf. A passing housewife said she thought Dr Force worked in Bristol during the week and only came to Lynton for the weekends. Not so, contradicted a shuffling old man angrily waving a walking stick, on Tuesdays Dr Force could be found up Hollerday Hill, at the nursing home.

The old man's anger, explained the housewife, was a form of madness. Dr Force went up to Hollerday Phoenix House every Tuesday, insisted the walking stick.

My driver – 'call me Jim' – long-sufferingly reversed and returned into the town's centre when the double bull's-eye more or less left us both laughing. Dr Force worked in Bristol half the time *and* opened up his Valley of the Rocks dreary house on Sundays and Mondays, *and* went up to Hollerday Phoenix House on Tuesdays. A small girl with plaited blonde hair pointed out the road to Hollerday Phoenix House, then told us not to go there because of the ghosts.

Ghosts?

145

The Phoenix House was haunted, didn't we know?

The town hall scoffed at the idea of ghosts, afraid of deterring holiday visitors in spring and summer.

That useful person 'A Spokesman' explained that the mansion, built by Sir George Newnes on Hollerday Hill, had been totally arsonized in 1913 by persons still unknown and later blown up as part of an army exercise. The Phoenix House recently built close to the grown-over ruins was a private nursing home. There were positively no ghosts. Dr Force had patients in the nursing home whom he visited on Tuesdays.

My driver, who believed in the supernatural, cravenly balked at driving up to the Hollerday Phoenix House, but swore he would wait for me to walk there and back, which I believed, as I hadn't yet paid him.

I thanked 'A Spokesman' for his help. And could he describe Dr Force, so I would know him if I saw him?

'Oh yes,' 'A Spokesman' said, 'you'd know him easily. He has very blue eyes, and a short white beard, and he'll be wearing orange socks.'

I blinked.

'He can't see red or green,' 'A Spokesman' said. 'He's colour blind.'

CHAPTER SEVEN

I took the quiet old back way through the woods, climbing the overgrown, gently sloping carriage road that thoughtful Sir George Newnes had had blasted through rock to save his horses having to haul a coach up a heart-straining incline to his house.

On that January Tuesday I walked alone through the trees. Traffic motored sparsely along a modern road on the other side of the hill, raising not even a distant hum on its way to the new complex that had risen on the memory of the old.

There were no birds where I walked; no song. It was dark even in daylight, the close-growing evergreens crowding overhead. My feet trod noiselessly on fallen fir needles and in places there were still bare upright slabs of raw grey blasted rock. Atmospherically, the hundred-year-old path raised goosebumps. There were ruins of a tennis court where long ago people had laughed and played in another world. Eerie, I thought, was the word for it, but I saw no ghosts.

I came down to Hollerday Phoenix House from above,

as 'A Spokesman' had foretold, and saw that much of the roof was covered with large metal-framed panes of glass, which opened and closed like roofs of greenhouses. The glass, of course, interested me – it was thick float glass tinted to filter out ultra violet A and B rays of sunlight – and I thought of the departed days of sanatoria, where people with tuberculosis most unromantically coughed their lives away in the vain hope that airy sunshine would cure them.

Hollerday Phoenix House spread wide in one central block with two long wings. I walked round to the impressive front door and found that the building I entered at the conclusion of the spooky path was definitely of the twenty-first century, and in no way the haunt of apparitions.

The entrance hall looked like a hotel, but I saw no further into the nursing home's depths because of the two white-coated people leaning on the reception desk. One was female and the other grew a coat-coloured beard, and did indeed wear orange socks.

They glanced briefly my way as I arrived, then straightened with resigned professional interest when I presented with cuts and bruises that actually, until they peered at me, I had forgotten.

'Dr Force?' I tried, and White-Beard satisfactorily answered, 'Yes?'

His fifty-six years sat elegantly on his shoulders, and his well-brushed hair, along with the beard, gave him the sort of shape to his head that actors got paid for. Patients would trust him, I thought. I might have been pleased myself to have him on my case. His manner held authority in enough quantity to show me I was going to have difficulty jolting him the way I wanted.

Almost at once I saw, too, that the difficulty was not a matter of jolting him but of following the ins and outs of his mind. All through the time I was with him I felt him swing now and then from apparently genuine and friendly responses to evasion and stifled ill will. He was quick and he was clever, and although most of the time I felt a warm liking for him, occasionally there was a quick flash of antipathy. Powerfully attractive overall, the charm of Adam Force, it seemed to me, could flow in and out like a tide.

'Sir,' I said, giving seniority its due, 'I'm here on account of Martin Stukely.'

He put on a sorry-to-tell-you expression, and told me that Martin Stukely was dead. At the same time there was a rigidity of shock on his facial muscles: it wasn't a name he'd expected to hear up Hollerday Hill in Lynton. I said I knew Martin Stukely was dead.

He asked with suspicion, 'Are you a journalist?'

'No,' I said. 'A glass-blower.' I added my name, 'Gerard Logan.'

His whole body stiffened. He swallowed and absorbed the surprise and eventually asked pleasantly, 'What do you want?'

I said equally without threat, 'I'd quite like back the videotape you took from the Logan Glass showroom in Broadway on New Year's Eve.'

'You would, would you?' He smiled. He was ready for the question. He had no intention of complying, and was recovering his poise. 'I don't know what you are talking about.'

Dr Force made a slow survey from head to foot of my deliberately conservative suit and tie and I felt as positive as if he had said it aloud that he was wondering if I had enough clout to cause him trouble. Apparently he realistically gave himself an honest but unwelcome answer, as he suggested not that I buzz off straight away, but that we discuss the situation in the open air.

By open air, it transpired he meant the path I'd just ascended. He led that way and sneaked a sideways glance to measure my discomfort level, which was nil. I smiled and mentioned that I hadn't noticed any ghosts on the prowl on my way up.

Should he be aware of small damages to my face and so on, I said, it was as a result of Rose Payne being convinced that I either had his tape in my possession, or that I knew what was on it. 'She believes that if she's unpleasant enough, I'll give her the tape or the knowledge, neither of which I have.' I paused and said, 'What do you suggest?'

He said promptly, 'Give this person anything. All tapes are alike.'

'She thinks your tape is worth a million.'

Adam Force fell silent.

'Is it?' I asked.

Under his breath Force said what sounded like the truth, 'I don't know.'

'Martin Stukely,' I murmured without hostility, 'wrote a cheque for you with a lot of noughts on.'

Force, very upset, said sharply, 'He promised never to say – '

'He didn't say.'

'But – '

'He died,' I said. 'He left cheque stubs.'

I could almost feel him wondering '*What else* did Martin leave?' and I let him speculate. In the end, in genuine-looking worry, he said, 'How did you find me?'

'Didn't you think I would?'

He very briefly shook his head and faintly smiled. 'It didn't occur to me that you would bother to look. Most people would leave it to the police.'

He would have been easy to like all the time, I thought, if one could forget Lloyd Baxter's epileptic fit, and a missing bank bag full of money.

'Rose Payne,' I said distinctly again – and somewhere in Adam Force this time her name touched a sensitive reaction – 'Rose,' I repeated, 'is convinced I know where your videotape is and, as I said before, she is certain I know what's on it. Unless you find a way of rather literally getting her off my back I may find her attentions too much to tolerate and I'll tell her what she's anxious to know.'

He asked, as if he hadn't any real understanding of what I'd said, 'Are you implying that I know this person, Rose? And are you also implying that I am in some way responsible for your . . . er . . . injuries?'

I said cheerfully, 'Right both times.'

'That's nonsense.' His face was full of calculation as if he weren't sure how to deal with an awkward situation, but wouldn't rule out using his own name, Force.

On the brink of telling him why I reckoned I could answer my own questions I seemed to hear both Worthington and Tom Pigeon shrieking at me to be careful about sticks and wasps' nests. The silence of the dark fir wood shook with their urgent warnings. I glanced at the benevolent doctor's thoughtful face and changed my own expression to regret.

Shaking my head, I agreed with him that what I'd said was of course nonsense. 'All the same,' I added, after quizzically checking with my two absent bodyguards, 'you did take the tape from my shop, so please can you at least tell me where it is now?'

He relaxed inwardly a good deal at my change of tone. Worthington and Tom Pigeon went back to sleep. Dr Force consulted his own inner safeguards and answered the question unsatisfactorily.

'Just suppose you are right and I have the tape. As Martin could no longer keep the information safe, there was no longer any need for it. Perhaps, therefore, I ran it through to record a sports programme from first to last. That tape might now show horse racing and nothing else.'

He had written to Martin that the knowledge on the tape was dynamite. If he'd wiped the dynamite out with racing, boasting he'd poured millions down the drain (or past the recording head) he still surely had whatever he needed for a clone.

No one would casually wipe out a fortune if not sure he could bring it back. Nobody would do it *on purpose*, that was.

So I asked him, 'Did you obliterate it on purpose, or by mistake?'

He laughed inside the beard. He said, 'I don't make mistakes.'

The frisson I felt wasn't a winter shudder from a daunting fir wood but a much more prosaic recognition of a familiar and thoroughly human failing: for all his pleasant manner, the doctor thought he was God.

He stopped by a fallen fir trunk and briefly rested one foot on it, saying he would go back from there as he had patients to see. 'I find business is usually completed by this point,' he went on and his voice was dismissive, 'I'm sure you'll find your own way down to the gate.'

'There are just a couple of things,' I said. My voice sounded flat, the acoustics dead between the trees.

He took his foot off the log and started to go back up the hill. To his obvious irritation I went with him.

'I said,' he commented with a stab at finality, 'that we'd completed our conversation, Mr Logan.'

'Well . . .' I hesitated, but Worthington and Tom

Pigeon were quiet and there wasn't even a squeak from the dogs, 'how did you get to know Martin Stukely?'

He said calmly, 'That's none of your business.'

'You knew each other but you weren't close friends.'

'Didn't you hear me?' he protested. 'This is not your concern.'

He quickened his step a little, as if to escape.

I said, 'Martin gave you a large chunk of money in return for the knowledge that you referred to as dynamite.'

'No, you're wrong.' He walked faster, but I kept up easily with him stride for stride. 'You completely do not understand,' he said, 'and I want you to leave.'

I said I feared I had no intention of leaving any time soon, now that I saw beside me the likely answer to multiple riddles.

'Did you know,' I asked him, 'that Lloyd Baxter, the man you abandoned to his epileptic fit in my showroom, is the owner of Tallahassee, the horse that killed Martin Stukely?'

He walked faster up the slope. I stayed close, accelerating.

'Did you know,' I asked conversationally, 'that in spite of the onset of an epileptic seizure, Lloyd Baxter was able to describe you down to the socks?'

'Stop it.'

'And of course you know Norman Osprey and Rose and Gina are as violent as they come . . .'

'No.' His voice was loud, and he coughed.

'And as for my money that you whipped with that tape . . .'

Adam Force quite suddenly stopped walking altogether, and in the stillness I could clearly hear his breath wheezing in his chest.

It alarmed me. Instead of pretty well bullying him, I asked him anxiously if he were all right.

'No, thanks to you.' The wheezing continued until he pulled from a pocket in his white coat the sort of inhaler I'd often seen used for asthma. He took two long puffs, breathing deeply while staring at me with complete dislike.

I was tempted to say 'Sorry', but in spite of his charming ways and pleasant looks he'd been the cause of my being chucked to both the black-masks in Broadway and to a piece of hosepipe in a Taunton backyard, and if that were all, I'd count myself lucky. So I let him wheeze and puff his way up the rest of the incline. I went with him to make sure he didn't collapse on the way, and inside the reception area I checked him into a comfortable chair and went to find someone to pass him on to, for safe keeping.

I heard his wheezy voice behind me demanding my return, but by then I'd hurried halfway down one of the wings of the building and seen no human being at all, whether nurse, patient, doctor, cleaner, flower-arranger or woman pushing a trolley of books. It wasn't that there weren't any beds in the rooms that lined the wing. In all the rooms there were beds, tray tables, armchairs and bathrooms off, but no people. Each room had glass French doors opening to a well-swept area of paving stones. Parts of the glass roof above were as wide open as they would go.

I stopped briefly at a room marked 'Pharmacy' which had an open skylight and a locked door of openwork grating to the passage. There was a host of visibly named pharmacy items inside, but still no people.

There had to be someone *somewhere*, I thought, and through the only closed door, at the end of the wing, I found a comparative bee-hive coming and going.

Twenty or more elderly men and women in thick white towelling bathrobes appeared to be contentedly taking part in comprehensive medical assessments, each test being brightly presented in play-school lettering, like 'Your blood pressure measured here' and 'Where does your cholesterol stand today?' A very old lady walked fast on 'a jolly treadmill', and on the wall of a separate hard-sided booth was the notice 'X-rays here. Please keep out unless asked to step in.'

Results were carefully written onto clipboards and then filed into computers at a central desk. An air of optimism prevailed.

My entrance brought to my side a nurse who'd been drawing curtains round a cubicle simply called Urology. Squeaking across a polished floor on rubber soles she smilingly told me I was late, and said only 'Oh dear' when I mentioned that the good Dr Force might be gasping his last.

'He often does have attacks when he has visitors,' the motherly nurse confided. 'When you've gone I expect he'll lie down and have a sleep.'

The good Dr Force was planning nothing of the sort. Registering annoyance like a steaming boiler, he wheezed to my side and pointed to a door coyly labelled 'Here it is', then 'Way out, too.' I explained, as if harmlessly, that I'd only come to find help for his asthma and he replied crossly that he didn't need it. He walked towards me with a syringe in a metal dish, advancing until I could see it almost full of liquid. He picked up the highly threatening syringe and then jabbed it towards me and the exit; and this time I thanked him for his attention and left.

The door out of the medical examination hall led past lavish changing rooms to a generous lobby, and from there to a forecourt outside.

Unexpectedly I found the Rover waiting there, Jim my driver nervously pacing up and down beside it. He held the door open for me while explaining that his concern for my welfare had overcome his natural instincts. I thanked him with true feeling.

Dr Force followed me out and waited until I was in the car and went indoors only after I'd given him a cheerfully innocent farewell wave, which he did not return.

'Is that the guy you came to see?' asked Jim.

'Yes.'

'Not very friendly, is he?'

I couldn't identify exactly what was wrong with that

place, and was little further enlightened when a large coach turned smoothly through the entrance gate and came to a gentle halt. The name, *Avon Paradise Tours*, read black and white on lilac along the coach's sides, with smaller letters underneath giving an address in Clifton, Bristol.

Jim drove rapidly downhill until we had returned to, in his eyes, the unsupernatural safety of the town centre. He did agree, though, subject to no further mention of things that go bump in the night, to drive round Lynton simply to enjoy it as a visitor.

Truth to tell, I was dissatisfied with myself on many counts and I wanted time to think before we left. I badly missed having my own car and the freedom it allowed, but there it was. I had indeed broken the speed limit often and got away with it before I'd been caught on the way to the dying gardener, and I could see that if policewoman Catherine Dodd had a permanent toe in my future, I would have to ration my foot on the accelerator.

Meanwhile, I persuaded Jim to stop in a side road. From there, town-hall map in hand, I found my way to North Walk, a path round the seaward side of a grassy cliff, cold in the January wind and more or less deserted.

There were benches at intervals. I sat for a while on one and froze, and thought about the Adam Force who was colour blind, asthmatic, volatile and changeable in nature, and who visited an obscure nursing home only to do good. A minor practitioner, it seemed, though with a string of qualifications and a reputation for sparkling research. A man wasting his skills. A man who took a visitor outside to talk on a noticeably cold day and gave himself an asthmatic attack.

I trudged slowly round, soaking up the spectacular views of the North Walk, wishing for summer. I thought of inconsequential things like coincidence and endurance and videotapes that were worth a million and could save the world. I also thought of the jewel I had made of glass and gold that not only looked truly old, but couldn't be distinguished from a 3,500-year-old original. A necklace worth a million ... but only one had that value, the genuine antiquity in a museum. The copy I had made once and could make again would be literally and only worth its weight in 18 carat gold, plus the cost of its coloured glass components, and as much again, perhaps, for the knowledge and ability it took to make it.

Like many an artist of any sort, it was to my own self alone that I could admit to the level I'd reached in my trade. It was also thanks to my Uncle Ron's embargo on arrogance that I let the things I made achieve birth without trumpets.

That the existence of the videotape explaining how to make the necklace was common knowledge among jockeys in the changing rooms didn't trouble me. I'd made it myself. It had my voice and hands on it, describing and demonstrating step by step what to do. I'd recorded it the way my Uncle Ron had taught me in my teens. The actual gold necklace I'd made was in my bank where I normally kept the tape as well. I'd better check on that,

I supposed. I'd lent the instruction tape to Martin, of course, and didn't care if he'd shown it to anyone else, although I dearly wished he had returned it before it disappeared, along with all the others from his den.

I made a fairly brisk return to the end of the Walk to find Jim striding up and down again and trying to warm his fingers. I thought perhaps he might not want to double the experience on the following day, but to my surprise, he agreed. 'Tom Pigeon'll set his dogs on me if I don't,' he said. 'He phoned me just now in the car to check on you.'

I swallowed a laugh. I prized those bodyguards, not resented them.

Jim apologized for not being in the same class as Worthington and Tom at kick-boxing.

'I can bash heads against walls,' he said.

I smiled and said that would do fine.

'I didn't know anything about you when I picked you up,' Jim confessed. 'I thought you were some useless sort of git. Then Tom tells me this and that on the phone and where Tom says he'll put his fists, you can count on mine.'

'Well, thanks,' I said weakly.

'So where do we go tomorrow?'

I said, 'How does Bristol grab you? A hospital area, best of all?'

He smiled broadly, transforming his face in one second from dour to delighted. He knew his way round Bristol. Up Horfield Road we would find a hospital, or on

Commercial Road down by the river. No problem at all. He'd driven an ambulance there one year, he said.

Jim said to count him out when it came to fists or feet, but no one could catch him in a car. We shook hands on it, and I acquired bodyguard number three, one who could slide round corners faster than Formula One.

Jim took me home and, apparently on Tom Pigeon's urging, came indoors with me and checked all ten rooms for uninvited occupants.

'You need a smaller pad,' he judged, finishing the inspection of the window locks. 'Or . . .' he looked sideways, 'a swarm of children.'

Catherine arrived at that moment on her motor bike. The driver gave her a leer, and I had to explain . . . a swarm of children. Constable Dodd seemed not to think it a bad idea.

Much amused, the driver left. Catherine fussed over my fresher crop of trouble and said she'd been bored by the class reunion from registration to wrap.

I said, 'Next time ditch the boredom and come home.'

The words slid out as if on their own. I hadn't intended to say 'home'. I'd been going simply to offer the house as a refuge. I explained. She nodded. It was later, holding her in bed, that I thought of Sigmund Freud and his telltale slip.

*

Bristol was wet with drizzle.

My driver – 'Call me Jim' – was short and stout and pronounced himself shocked that I preferred quiet in the car to perpetual radio.

Quite reasonably he asked where were we going exactly in the city. To find a phone book, I replied, and in the *Yellow Pages* singled out Avon Paradise Tours without trouble. They advertised that they operated adventures throughout Cornwall, Devon and Somerset and all points to London.

Jim, with his ambulance memory, more useful than any paper map, drove us unerringly to their lilac head-quarters and with a flamboyant gesture drew the busy bus depot to my attention like a rabbit from an abracadabra top hat.

Once they understood what I was asking, the women in the Avon Paradise Tours office were moderately help-ful but reluctant to say too much in case they broke house rules.

I did understand, didn't I?

I did.

They then opened the harmless floodgates and told me all.

On Tuesdays, members of a Bristol area Health Clubs Association went on a scenic coach tour to the Hollerday Phoenix House nursing home in Lynton for medical check-ups and advice on healthy living. Dr Force, who ran the clinic because he lived in Lynton, was paid jointly by the health clubs and Avon Paradise Tours for his one day's work per week. After extra consultation together, the office staff admitted they'd been told Dr Force had been *let* go (given the sack, did I understand?) by the research lab he used to work for.

Which research lab? They didn't know. They shook their heads in general, but one of them said she'd heard he'd been working on illnesses of the lungs.

Another phone book – listing all things medical – borrowed from the Avon Paradise ladies, had me trying all the remotely possible establishments, asking them via Paradise Tours phone if they knew a Dr Force. Dr Force? Unknown, unknown, unknown. The forever unknown Dr Force had me looking out of the window at the distant sheen of the River Avon at high tide and wondering what to try next.

Illnesses of the lungs.

Cheque stubs. A lot of zeros. The payee . . . Bellows. In Martin's handwriting, it had meant nothing to Bon-Bon and nothing to me.

There wasn't any listing for Bellows in the Bristol area phone book, nor had Directory Enquiries ever heard of it.

Martin, though, had written BELLOWS boldly in unmistakable capital letters.

Lungs were bellows, of course.

My mind drifted. Rain spattered on the window. The ladies began to fidget, implying I'd overstayed my time.

BELLOWS.

Well . . . maybe, why not?

Abruptly I asked if I might borrow their office telephone again and with their by now rather grudging permission I spelled out BELLOWS in phone dial numbers, which resulted in 235 5697. I punched them in carefully. There was nothing to lose.

After a long wait through maybe a dozen rings I was about to give up, when a brisk female voice hurriedly spoke, 'Yes? Who is that?'

'Could I speak to Dr Force, please,' I said.

A long silence ensued. I was about to disconnect and call it a waste of time when another voice, deep and male, enquired if I were the person asking for Dr Force.

'Yes,' I said. 'Is he there?'

'Very sorry. No. He left several weeks ago. Can I have your name?'

I wasn't sure how to answer. I was beginning to learn caution. I said I would phone back very soon, and clicked off. To the Paradise ladies' curiosity, I offered only profound thanks and left promptly, taking Jim in tow.

'Where to?' he asked.

'A pub for lunch.'

Jim's face lightened like a cloudless dawn. 'You're the sort of customer I can drive for all day.'

In the event he drank one half-pint of lemonade shandy, which was my idea of a good hired driver.

The pub had a pay phone. When we were on the point of leaving I dialled BELLOWS again and found the male voice answering me at once.

He said, 'I've been talking to Avon Paradise Tours.'

I said, smiling, 'I thought you might. You probably have this pub's public phone booth's number in front of your eyes at the moment. To save time, why don't we meet? You suggest somewhere and I'll turn up.'

I repeated to Jim the place suggested, and got a nod of recognition. 'Thirty minutes,' Jim said, and twenty-two minutes later he stopped the car in a no-waiting zone near the gate of a wintry public park. Against the united teaching of Worthington, Tom Pigeon and Jim not to go anywhere unknown without one of them close, I got out of the car, waved Jim to drive on, and walked into the park on my own.

The drizzly rain slowly stopped.

The instructions for the meeting had been 'Turn left, proceed to statue', and along the path, by a prancing copper horse, I met a tall, civilized, sensible-looking man who established to his own satisfaction that I was the person he expected.

CHAPTER EIGHT

He spoke as if to himself. 'He's six feet tall, maybe an inch or two more. Brown hair. Dark eyes. Twenty-eight to thirty-four years, I'd say. Personable except for recent injury to right side of jaw which has been medically attended to and is healing.'

He was talking into a small microphone held in the palm of his hand. I let him see that I understood that he was describing me in case I attacked him in any fashion. The notion that I might do that would have made me laugh on any other day.

'He arrived in a grey Rover.' He repeated Jim's registration number and then described my clothes.

When he stopped I said, 'He's a glass-blower named Gerard Logan and can be found at Logan Glass, Broadway, Worcestershire. And who are you?'

He was the voice on the telephone. He laughed at my dry tone and stuffed the microphone away in a pocket. He gave himself a name, George Lawson-Young, and a title, Professor of Respiratory Medicine.

'And 235 5697?' I asked. 'Does it have an address?'

Even with modern technology he didn't know how I'd found him.

'Old-fashioned perseverance and guesswork,' I said. 'I'll tell you later in return for the gen on Adam Force.'

I liked the professor immediately, feeling none of the reservations that had troubled me with Force. Professor Lawson-Young had no ill will that I could see, but on the contrary let his initial wariness slip away. My first impression of good humour and solid sense progressively strengthened, so that when he asked what my interest was in Adam Force I told him straightforwardly about Martin's promise to keep safe Dr Force's tape.

'Martin wanted me to keep it for him instead,' I said, 'and when he died the tape came into my hands. Force followed me to Broadway and took his tape back again, and I don't know where it is.'

Out on the road, Jim in the grey Rover drove slowly by, his pale face through the window on watch on my behalf.

'I came with a bodyguard,' I said, waving reassurance to the road.

Professor Lawson-Young, amused, confessed he had only to yell down his microphone for assistance to arrive at once. He seemed as glad as I was that he would not have to use it. His tight muscles loosened. My own Worthington-Pigeon-driven alertness went to sleep.

The professor said, 'How did you cut your face so deeply?'

I hesitated. What I'd done in the backyard of 19 Lorna

Terrace sounded too foolish altogether. Because I didn't reply Lawson-Young asked again with sharper interest, pressing for the facts like any dedicated news man. I said undramatically that I'd been in a fight and come off worst.

He asked next what I'd been fighting about, and with whom, his voice full of the authority that he no doubt needed in his work.

Evading the whole truth I gave him at least a part of it. 'I wanted to find Dr Force, and in the course of doing that I collided with a water tap. Clumsy, I'm afraid.'

He looked at me intently with his head on one side. 'You're lying to me, I'm sorry to say.'

'Why do you think so?'

'It's unusual to fight a water tap.'

I gave him a half-strength grin. 'OK then, I got hit with one that was still on a hose-pipe. It's unimportant. I learned how to find Adam Force, and I talked to him yesterday in Lynton.'

'Where in Lynton? In that new nursing home?'

'Phoenix House.' I nodded. 'Dr Force's clinic looks designed for children.'

'Not for children. For mentally handicapped patients. He does good work there with the elderly, I'm told.'

'They seemed pretty happy, it's true.'

'So what's your take-away opinion?'

I gave it without much hesitation. 'Force is utterly charming when he wants to be, and he's also a bit of a crook.'

'Only a bit?' The professor sighed. 'Adam Force was in charge here of a project aimed at abolishing snoring by using fine optical fibres and microlasers . . .' He briefly stopped. 'I don't want to bore you . . .'

My own interest however had awoken sharply as in the past I'd designed and made glass equipment for that sort of enquiry. When I explained my involvement, the professor was in his turn astonished. He enlarged into detail the work that Force had been busy with and had stolen.

'We'd been experimenting with shining a microlaser down a fine optical fibre placed in the soft tissues of the throat. The microlaser gently warms the tissues, which stiffens them, and that stops a person from snoring. What Adam Force stole was our results of the trials to find the optimum laser light wavelength needed to penetrate the tissues and heat them to the precise temperature necessary . . . Do you follow?'

'More or less.'

He nodded. 'A reliable way of abolishing snoring would be invaluable for severe sufferers. Adam Force stole such data and sold it to a firm of marketers whose business it is to advertise and inform prospective buyers of goods available. Force sold our latest but incomplete data to people we had dealt with occasionally before and who had no reason to suspect anything was wrong. Adam produced the right paperwork. It was weeks before the theft was discovered and really no one could believe it when we went to the marketers and they told us they had already bought the material and paid Adam Force for what we were now trying to sell them.'

'So you sacked him,' I commented.

'Well, we should have. He must have thought we might, but he was crucial to our research programme.' The professor however looked regretful, not enraged.

I said, 'Let me guess, basically you let him off. You didn't prosecute him because you all liked him so much.'

Lawson-Young ruefully nodded. 'Adam apologized more or less on his knees and agreed to pay the money back in instalments, if we didn't take him to court.'

'And did he?'

In depression the professor said, 'He paid on the dot for two months, and then we found he was trying to sell some even more secret information ... and I mean *priceless* information in world terms—' He stopped abruptly, apparently silenced by the enormity of Adam Force's disloyalty.

Eventually he went on, 'He repaid us for our generosity by stealing the most recent, the most dynamite-laden data in our whole laboratory, and we are certain that he is offering this work to the highest bid he can raise around the world. This is the information recorded on the tape Force took back from you, and it is this tape we have been praying you would find.'

I said with incredulity, 'But you didn't know that I existed.'

'We did know you existed, our investigators have been

very diligent. But we weren't sure you hadn't been in-
doctrinated by Adam, like your friend Stukely.'

'*Martin?*'

'Oh yes. Force can be utterly charming and persuasive,
as you know. We think it likely he also swindled Stukely
of a fairly large sum of money, saying it was to be
applied to our research.'

'But,' I protested, 'Martin wasn't a fool.'

'It is quite likely that Stukely had no idea that the
contents of the tape had been stolen. Believe me, you
don't need to be a fool to be taken in by a con man.
I wouldn't consider myself a fool, but he took *me* in. I
treated him as a friend.'

I said, 'Where did Martin meet Dr Force? I don't
suppose you know.'

'I actually do. They met at a fund-raising dinner for
cancer research. Adam Force was there raising money on
behalf of the charity, and Stukely was there as a guest of
a man for whom he raced, who was also a patron of the
charity. I too as it happens am a patron, and I also saw
Martin Stukely briefly on that evening.'

I vaguely remembered Martin mentioning the dinner
but hadn't paid much attention. It was typical of Martin,
though, to make friends in unexpected places. I had myself, after all, met him in a jury room.

After a while Lawson-Young said, 'We searched
absolutely everywhere for proof that Adam had in his
possession material that belonged to the laboratory. We

know ... we're ninety per cent certain ... that he recorded every relevant detail onto the videotape which he entrusted to the care of Martin Stukely.'

There was nothing, I heard with relief, about trying to make me reveal its whereabouts through the use of black-mask methods or threats of unmerciful dentistry. I was aware, though, that the former tension in the professor's muscles had returned, and I wondered if he thought I was fooling him, as Adam Force had done.

I said simply, 'Force has the tape. Ask him. But yesterday he told me he'd recorded a sports programme on top of your formulae and conclusions, and all that remained on the tape now was horse racing.'

'Oh God.'

I said, 'I don't know that I believe him.'

After a few moments the professor said, 'How often can you tell if someone's lying?'

'It depends who they are and what they're lying about.'

'Mm,' he said.

I glanced back in my mind to a long line of half-truths, my own included.

'Discard the lies,' George Lawson-Young said, smiling, 'and what you're left with is probably the truth.'

After a while he repeated, 'We've searched absolutely *everywhere* for proof that Adam had in his possession material that belongs to the laboratory. We believe that he recorded every relevant detail onto the videotape because one of our researchers thought he saw him doing it, but as he works in an altogether different field he believed Adam when he said he was making routine notes. Adam himself entrusted a tape into the care of Martin Stukely at Cheltenham races. When Stukely died, we learned from asking around that his changing-room valet had passed the tape on to Stukely's friend, as previously planned.' He paused. 'So as you are the friend, will you tell us where best to look for the missing tape? Better still, bring it to us yourself . . . as we believe you can.'

I said baldly, 'I can't. I think Force has it.'

Lawson-Young shivered suddenly in the cold damp wind, and my own thoughts had begun to congeal. I proposed that we found somewhere warmer if we had more to say and the professor, after cogitation and consultation with his microphone, offered me a visit to his laboratory, if I should care to go.

Not only would I like to go, I felt honoured to be asked, a reaction clearly visible on my face from the professor's own return expression. His trust, however, didn't reach as far as stepping into my car, so he went in one which arrived smoothly from nowhere, and I followed with Jim.

The professor's research laboratory occupied the ground floor of a fairly grand nineteenth-century town house with a pillared entrance porch. Antiquity stopped right there on the doorstep: everything behind the front door belonged to the future.

George Lawson-Young, very much the professor on his own turf, introduced me to his team of young research doctors whose chief if not only interest in my existence lay in my having long ago invented a way of making perfect glass joins between tiny tubes of differing diameters so that liquid or gases would move at a desired speed from one tube to the next.

They hadn't much else of my work there, but the words 'Logan Glass' etched on mini pipettes and a few specialized test tubes got me accepted as a sort of practitioner rather than simply a sightseer. Anyway, my ability to identify things like vacutaires, cell separators, tissue culture chambers and distillation flasks meant that when I asked what exactly had been stolen the second time by Adam Force, I got told.

'Actually, we now think there was a third thing,' a young woman in a white coat murmured sorrowfully. 'It seems likely that he also took out of here the formula of our new asthma drug aimed at preventing permanent scar tissue occurring on the airways of chronic asthmatics. Only recently did we realize what had happened, as, at the time, of course, we believed his assurances that he was borrowing some finished work from last year.'

The nods all round were indulgent. In spite of all, there were friendly faces for Adam Force. It was the professor himself, whose eyes had opened, who told me finally what I'd been in need of knowing all along.

'The videotape made and stolen by Adam Force showed the formation of a particular tissue culture and its ingredients. The tissue culture was of cancer cells of the commoner sorts of cancer like that of the lung and the breast. They were concerned with the development of genetic mutations that render the cancer cell lines more sensitive to common drugs. All common cancers may be curable once the mutated gene is implanted into people who already have the cancer. The tape probably also shows photographs of the chromatography of the different components of the cancer cell genetic constituents. It is very complicated. At first sight it looks like rubbish, except to the educated eye. It is, unfortunately, quite likely anyone might override the "don't record on top of this" tab.'

He lost me halfway through the technical details, but I at least understood that the tape that could save the world contained the cure for a host of cancers.

I asked the professor, 'Is this for real?'

'It's a significant step forward,' he said.

I pondered, 'But if Force is going around asking millions for it, is it worth millions?'

Sombrely, Lawson-Young said, 'We don't know.'

Adam Force had said the same thing, 'I don't know.' Not a lie, it seemed, but a statement that the process hadn't yet been extensively tested. The tape was a record of a possibility, or of an almost certainty whose worth was still a gamble.

I said, 'But you do have back-up copies of everything that's on that tape, don't you? Even if the tape itself should now show horse racing?'

Almost as if he were surrendering to an inevitable execution, the professor calmly stated the guillotine news.

'Before he left with the videotape, Adam destroyed all our at present irreplaceable records. We *need* that tape, and I hope to God you're right that he's lying. It's two years' work. Others are working along these lines, and we would be beaten to the breakthrough. We'd more likely *lose* the millions we might have earned.'

Into a short silence the telephone buzzed. George Lawson-Young picked up the receiver, listened, and mutely handed it to me. The caller was Jim in a high state of fuss.

He said with lively alarm, 'That medic you saw yesterday, the one with the white beard?'

'Yes?'

'He's here in the street.'

'Bugger . . . what's he doing?'

'Waiting. He's in a car parked fifty yards up the road, facing towards you, and there's a big bruiser sitting next to him. He's got another car waiting and facing towards you, but coming the other way. It's classic squeeze setup, with you in the middle. So, what do you want me to do?'

'Where exactly are you?' I asked. 'To reach you, do I turn left or right?'

'Left. I'm four cars in front of White-Beard, pointing towards the door you went in at. I'm parked there, but there's a traffic warden creeping about. I'm on double yellow lines here, which White-Beard isn't, and I can't afford any more parking tickets, it's not good for my business.'

'Stay on the yellow lines,' I said. 'Move only if you have to, because of the warden. Dr Force saw you and your car yesterday. It can't be helped.'

Jim's voice rose, 'White-Beard's got out of his car. What shall I do? *He's coming this way* . . .'

'Jim,' I said flatly, 'don't panic. Also don't look at Dr Force if he comes near you, and don't open the window. Keep on talking to me, and if you have anything near you that you can read, read it aloud to me now.'

'Jeez.'

Lawson-Young's eyebrows were up by his hairline.

I said to him, 'Adam Force is in the road outside here, alarming my driver.' And I didn't say that on our last encounter the doctor had seen me off with a poisonous-looking syringe.

Jim's voice wobbled in my ear with the opening paragraphs of the Rover's instruction manual and then rose again an octave as he said, 'He's outside my window, he's rapping on it. Mr Logan, what shall I do?'

'Keep on reading.'

I gave the receiver to the professor and asked him to continue listening, and without wasting time I hurried from the part of the laboratory where we'd been standing, along the hallway and out into the street. Along to my left, Adam Force stood in the roadway tapping hard on the window of the grey Rover on the driver's side and clearly getting agitated at the lack of response from Jim.

I walked fast along the pavement, and then, strolling the last part, crossed the road and came up quietly behind

Dr White-Beard and, as I'd done to Victor on Taunton station, said, 'Hello,' at his shoulder.

Worthington and Tom Pigeon wouldn't have approved. Adam Force spun round in astonishment.

'Are you looking for me?' I asked.

Inside the car, Jim, in great agitation, was stabbing with his finger towards the lab's front door and the road beyond. Traffic in this secondary road was light, but one of the approaching cars, Jim was indicating to me, was ultra bad news.

'Adam Force,' I said loudly, 'is too well known in this street,' and with total lack of complicated advance planning, and with unadulterated instinct, I grabbed the charming doctor by the wrist, spun him round and ended with him standing facing the oncoming car with his arm twisted up behind him, held in the strongest grip resulting from years of manoeuvring heavy molten glass.

Adam Force yelled, at first with pain and then, also, with bargaining surrender. 'You're hurting me. Don't do it. I'll tell you everything. Don't do it . . . God . . . Let me go, *please*.'

In between the two phases, from defiance to entreaty, a small object fell from the hand I'd gripped. It lay in the gutter quite close to a storm-drain grating, and I'd have paid it no attention were it not for Force trying hard to kick it down through the grating into the sewer, to be forever lost.

I didn't know what he meant when he said 'everything',

but I didn't in the least mind learning. He screeched again under my jerking pressure and I wondered whatever Professor Lawson-Young was making of it, if he were still listening. The advancing car stopped at the sight of Adam Force's predicament and the four cars behind it exercised their horns, the drivers impatient, not knowing what was going on.

'Everything,' I prompted Force from behind his ear.

'Rose,' he began, and then thought better of it. Rose would frighten anyone.

I jerked his arm fiercely to encourage him and, with some dismay, I saw the big bruiser now lumbering out of his car to come to his aid, to be Norman Osprey, with his gorilla-type shoulder development. Over my shoulder I could see the second car of the classic squeeze moving towards me. In consequence of these unwelcome surprises I jerked my captive's arm yet again, then feared to break or dislocate his shoulder. There were tears of real pain in the doctor's eyes.

Imploring for release, he half said, half sobbed, desperately, 'I got the cyclopropane gas for Rose . . . I took it from the clinic's pharmacy . . . I can't see red from green, but I'm sure of orange . . . now let me go.'

It was hard to hear him distinctly because of the street noises and the blaring horns, and his 'everything' only confirmed what had already seemed likely, but I kept the pressure on just long enough for him to shriek out the answer I badly wanted to the question, 'How come you know Rose?'

179

To him it seemed unimportant. He answered impatiently, 'Her sister Gina came with her mother-in-law to my clinic. I met Rose at Gina's house.'

Satisfied, I was faced with a fast, unharmed disengagement. The cars had advanced until they were radiator to radiator and going nowhere and blocking the street. The driver of the second was hurriedly disembarking, and to my horror, I saw that it was Rose. Uninvolved cars made a constant cacophony. The busy traffic warden, notebook to the ready, spotted the fracas from a distance and veered back towards Jim and his yellow lines infringement.

Norman Osprey, a mountain on the move, charged towards Force and myself to release the doctor and maybe continue with the entertainment Tom Pigeon and his dogs had interrupted in Broadway.

Not seeing anything except straight ahead, the traffic warden and Norman the bookmaker bumped into each other violently which slowed their pace and purpose while they cursed their mutual carelessness.

Jim unhelpfully kept his eyes fixed faithfully down on his instruction manual, as I'd told him, and went on steadfastly reading.

I tried screaming at him to gain his attention, but uselessly, and in the end I let out the loudest possible London-rain taxi whistle, which pierced even Jim's concentration.

'Window,' I shouted.

He at last understood, but it took him aeons to switch on the ignition and press the window-lowering button.

Rose started running. The traffic warden unwound herself from Norman Osprey. Car horns deafened because of the blockage of the highway.

I shouted at my driver, 'Jim, get the car out of here. I'll phone you.'

Jim suddenly proved his stunt-driving skills weren't a rumour. With not much more than two hand spans' clearance, he locked the wheels of his Rover and circled like a circus horse, bumping over the pavement, brushing me and my captive strongly out of the way with the rear wing and leaving us standing where the car had been, with the white-bearded doctor no longer in agony but still not going anywhere while I held him gripped. Jim's tail-light flashed briefly at the first corner as he slid round it and left the scene.

Everyone else seemed to be running and shouting to no real purpose. I let go of Force's wrist while at the same time shoving him heavily into the joint arms of the warden and Osprey, with a bounce-off weight that unbalanced them all.

In that disorganized few seconds I bent down, scooped up the small object Force had dropped and *ran*, ran as if sprinting off the starting blocks on an athletics track. It was only the unexpectedness of my speed, I thought, that made the difference. I ran, dodging cars and irate drivers, swerving round Rose's grasp like a player evading tackles in a rugby match, and believing – making myself believe – that I was fit enough to out-run them all, so long as no busybody stranger tripped me up.

I didn't have to test fate too much. The front door of the laboratory house swung open ahead of me, with George Lawson-Young, still with the telephone clutched in his hand, coming out under the pillared porch, looking my way and beckoning me to safety. I fairly bolted through the heavy shining black-painted door, and ended breathless and laughing in his hall.

He closed the door. 'I can't see what there is to laugh about,' he said.

'Life's a toss-up.'

'And today it came up heads?'

I *liked* the professor. I grinned and held out to him the small object I'd salvaged from the gutter, asking him with moderate urgency, 'Can you find out what this contains?'

He looked with shock at what I'd brought him, and I nodded as if in confirmation that I'd got it right. He asked a shade austerely if I knew what he was with great care holding.

'Yes. It's a sort of syringe. You can put the needle into any liquid drug and suck it into the bubble,' I said. 'Then you push the needle into the patient and squeeze the bubble to deliver the drug. Vets sometimes use them on horses that are upset by the sight of an ordinary hypodermic syringe.'

He said, 'You're right. You seem to know a lot about it.'

'I was with Martin once . . .' I broke off. So much of my life seemed to have touched Martin's.

Lawson-Young made no comment about Martin but

said, 'These little syringes can be used too on manic patients, to make them manageable and calm them down.'

Phoenix House treated patients with mental illnesses. Adam Force had access to a well-stocked pharmacy.

George Lawson-Young turned away from me and, holding the tiny balloon with great care, led the way back to that part of the laboratory that held the gas chromatograph.

The thumb-nail sized balloon was still full of liquid, and was also wet outside from lying in the gutter. George Lawson-Young laid it carefully in a dish and asked one of his young doctors to identify the baby balloon's contents as soon as possible.

'Should it be one of several forms of poison,' he warned me, 'it might be impossible to find out what it is.'

'It surely had to be something already in the Phoenix House pharmacy,' I said. 'It was only yesterday afternoon that I met Force. He hadn't much time to mobilize anything too fancy.'

The balloon's contents raised little but smiles.

It took the young research doctor barely ten minutes to come back with an identification. 'It's insulin,' he said confidently. 'Plain ordinary insulin, as used by diabetics.'

'Insulin!' I exclaimed, disappointed. 'Is that all?'

Both the young research doctor and the professor smiled indulgently. The professor said, 'If you have diabetes, the amount of insulin in that syringe might send you into a permanent coma. If you *don't* have diabetes, there's enough to kill you.'

'To *kill*?'

'Yes, certainly,' Lawson-Young nodded. 'That amount is a lethal dose. It's reasonable to suppose it was intended for you, not your chauffeur; but I can hardly believe it of Adam.' He sounded shattered. 'We knew he'd steal, but to kill . . .' He shook his head. 'Are you *sure* that syringe came from him? You didn't just find it lying in the road?'

'I'm positive he was holding it in his hand and I dislodged it.'

The professor and I by that time were sitting on swivelling chairs in the professor's personal office-like room section of the laboratory.

'Actually,' I murmured, 'the big question is *why*?'

George Lawson-Young couldn't say.

'Do me a favour,' he finally begged. 'Start from the beginning.'

'I will phone my driver first.'

I used my mobile. When Jim answered his car-phone he sounded, first, relieved that I was free and talking to him, and second, anxious that he was going to be late home for his wife's risotto, and third, worried about where he was going to find me safe and on my own. I was glad enough that he proposed to wait for me. The professor, taking my mobile, gave Jim pin-pointing instructions for one hour's time, and suggested to me that I waste none of it.

'It's a tale of two tapes,' I tentatively began.

'Two?' said the professor.

'Yes, two,' I replied, but then hesitated.

'Do go on, then.' The professor was in a natural hurry.

'One was filmed here and stolen by Adam Force,' I said. 'He persuaded Martin Stukely to keep it safe for him, so that it couldn't be found.'

'We obtained a Search and Seizure Order from the Courts, and had already started searching everywhere for it,' said Lawson-Young, 'including in Adam's own home, but we didn't ever think of it being in the care of a jockey.'

'That must be why he did it,' I said. 'But as I understand it, Martin thought Force's tape would be safer still with me, a friend who hasn't four inquisitive children.' And no talkative or quarrelsome wife, I could have added. But, I thought, would Martin have really given me the tape if he knew the contents were stolen?

The professor smiled.

I continued, 'Martin Stukely received the stolen tape from Force at Cheltenham races and gave it into the temporary care of his valet while he went out to ride a horse called Tallahassee in the race from which he didn't return.'

Lawson-Young nodded. 'When Martin Stukely died, his valet, Eddie, gave the tape to you, as he knew that's what Martin intended.'

'Eddie, the valet,' the professor went on, 'was eventually one of the people that our investigators talked to and he said he didn't know anything about any stolen laboratory tape. He said he thought he was handling a tape that you yourself had made, a tape which explained how to copy an ancient and priceless necklace.'

'That's the second tape,' I said. 'It's also missing.'

'Eddie had seen your duplicate of the necklace in the jockeys' changing room. And, incidentally . . .' George Lawson-Young's smile illuminated his little office . . . 'he said your copy of the necklace was stunning. Perhaps you will show it to me one day, when all this is over.'

I asked him what he would consider 'over', and his smile disappeared. 'For me, it will be over when we find the tape of our work.'

He was aware, I supposed, that it was comparatively easy to make duplicates of videotapes. And that the knowledge recorded on them was like the contents of Pandora's box; once out, it couldn't be put back. The stolen tape itself might now show racing. The records of the cancer research might already be free in the world, and would never again be under the professor's control. For him, perhaps, it was already over.

For me, I thought, it would be over when Rose and Adam Force left me alone – but, abruptly, out of nowhere, the spectre of the fourth black-mask floated into my consciousness. It wouldn't be over for me until his mask came off.

As casually as I could, I mentioned Number Four to the professor, fearing he would discount my belief, but instead he took it seriously.

'Add your Number Four into all equations,' he instructed, 'and what do you get in the way of answers? Do you get a reason for Force to want you dead? Do you get a reason for anyone to attack you? Think about it.'

I thought that that method must be what he used in nearly all research: if I added in an x factor, an 'unknown' into all I'd seen and heard and hadn't wholly understood, what would I get?

Before I could really learn the technique, one of the young doctors came to tell me and the professor that Adam Force was standing on the pavement opposite with a thin woman with brown hair – my friend Rose. Dr Force was staring at the entrance of his former workplace as if deciding how best to storm the Bastille. The young doctor, on the other hand, seemed to enjoy devising an escape from the fortress.

The professor said thoughtfully, 'Adam knows his way round this house and its environs at least as well as any of us. He'll have stationed the other man, the one we can't see now, at the rear door into the mews. So how do we get Mr Logan out of here without Adam Force being aware of it?'

The brilliant researchers came up with several solutions that required Tarzan-like swinging over an abyss, but with civil regard for each others' brains, they voted unanimously for the exit I actually took.

The glowingly pretty female doctor whose idea I followed gave me life-threatening directions. 'Go up the stairs. Beside the top of the staircase, on the sixth floor, there's a bolted door. Unbolt it. Open it. You'll find yourself on the roof. Slide down the tiles until you meet a parapet. Crawl along behind the parapet there, so that the man in the mews doesn't see you. Crawl to the right. Keep your head down. There are seven houses joined together. Go along behind their parapets until you come to the fire escape at the end. Go down it. There's a bolt mechanism that lets the last part of the iron ladder slide down to the pavement. When you're down, shove the last part of the ladder up again until it clicks. My car is parked in the mews. I'll drive out in half an hour. You should be on the ground there by then, out of sight of Dr Force. I'll pick you up and go to meet your driver. When I pick you up, lie on the floor, so that my car looks empty except for me.'

Everyone nodded.

I shook hands with George Lawson-Young. He gave me multiple contact numbers and mentioned with a grin that I already had the phone number of the lab. He would expect me to find the stolen tape. Deduction and intuition would do it.

I said, 'What a hope!'

'Our only hope,' he added soberly.

The author of my escape and a couple of her colleagues came up to the top floor with me in high good spirits and unbolted the door to the roof.

Cheerfully, but in whispers because of the man in the mews far below, the researchers helped me slide down the gently sloping roof tiles to reach the parapet along the edge. Seeing me safely on my knees there, they happily waved goodbye and bolted the top floor door behind me.

It was true I could have crawled along on my hands and knees, but I would have been visible to Norman Osprey waiting below. She, my saviour, being tiny, hadn't realized that I was almost double her body size. To be invisible I would have to go on my stomach, as the height of the parapet was barely the length of a forearm.

I sweated and trembled along on my stomach within the parapet's scanty cover and had to freeze my nerves and imagination to zero in order to cross crumbling bits of old mortar. It was a long way down to the ground.

Dusk gathered in unwary corners and made matters worse.

The seven houses seemed like fifty.

When at last I reached the fire escape I'd begun to think that falling over the parapet would be less terrifying than inching along so precariously behind it.

At least, I thought grimly, if Adam Force had ever been up on the laboratory house's roof, he wouldn't expect me to have gone up there myself.

My dear pretty saviour, on picking up my shaky self, remarked critically that I'd taken my time on the journey. My dry mouth found it impossible to reply. She apologized that the recent rain had drenched the roof and wet my clothes. Think nothing of it, I croaked. She switched on the headlights and the heater. I gradually stopped shivering – both from cold and from fear.

We found Jim at the rendezvous in his usual state of agitation. My saviour, handing me over, reported that the fun escape had been a great success. She wouldn't accept anything for petrol. She did accept an absolutely heartfelt hug of gratitude, and a long, long kiss.

CHAPTER NINE

I made a detour to talk to Bon-Bon on my way home and found her tears fewer and her memory recovering. When I asked her questions, she sweetly answered. When I suggested a course of action, she willingly agreed.

By the time Jim decanted me yawning to my hill house we were both very tired and he still had a few miles to go. Far and away the most orthodox of my three self-appointed minders, he also lived nearest. His wife, he said, had told him to apply to drive me regularly until I got my licence back. I was considering the cost, and he was considering a ban on radio and music. We had agreed to let each other know.

On that Wednesday, Catherine's transport stood on its frame outside the kitchen door. Inside the kitchen, when Jim had driven away, the warm welcoming smell of cooking seemed as natural as in the past with other girls it had been contrived.

'Sorry about this.' She pointed with her elbow at half-scrambled eggs. 'I didn't know when you were coming back, and I was hungry.'

I wondered how much care had gone into saying 'back' instead of 'home'.

She gave me a careful look, her eyebrows rising.

'I got a bit wet,' I said.

'Tell me later.' She cooked more eggs while I changed, and we ate in companionable peace.

I made coffee for us both and drank mine looking at her neat face, her blonde curving hair and her close-textured skin; and I wondered without confidence what I looked like to her.

I said, 'I saw Dr Force again today . . .'

Catherine smiled. 'And was he still charming and good-looking and filling everyone with belief in humanity?'

I said, 'Well, not exactly. He quite likely meant to bump me off, if he got a chance.' I yawned, and bit by bit, without exaggeration, told her about my day.

She listened with concentration and horror.

I collected her coffee mug and put it in the sink. We were still in the kitchen, which thanks to my mother had a pair of large comfortable chairs near an efficient heater.

We sat together, squashed into one of the chairs, as much for support for the spirits as for physical pleasure.

I told her about the professor and his x-factor method of research. 'So now,' I finished, 'I go over everything that anyone has said and done, add in x and see what I get.'

'It sounds difficult.'

'Different, anyway.'

'And when you find him? Black-mask Number Four?'

'He gives me nightmares,' I said.

I smoothed her hair. She felt right in my arms, curling there comfortably.

If I added Black-mask Four into the picture when he'd first blown into my awareness of his existence I had to remember every separate blow of that encounter on the Broadway pavement and, I realized with distaste, that I had to go back and listen again in my mind to every word of Rose's.

She'd shouted, 'Break his wrists . . .'

Catherine stirred in my arms and cuddled closer, and I discarded Rose in favour of bed.

Catherine woke early and went off before dawn to her morning shift, and I walked down in the dark to Logan Glass thinking of the past two days in Lynton and Bristol and wondering, like Professor Lawson-Young, if Dr Force still possessed and could produce for sale the irreplaceable data he'd stolen.

Strictly speaking, none of it was truly the business of a provincial glass-blower, but my fast-mending skin reminded me still that not everyone agreed.

Also, strictly speaking, none of it was truly the business of a dead steeplechase jockey, but his wife and children had been assaulted by gas and comprehensively robbed of their video machines.

The dedicated professor depended, he'd hopefully said,

on my deductive abilities, but to my mind he was staking his shirt on a non-runner, as Martin would have put it.

I had come to see the hunt for the videotape as sorties up a series of roads leading nowhere: as a star-burst of cul-de-sacs. The professor believed that one of the roads would eventually lead to his treasure, and I thought of Lloyd Baxter and Ed Payne and Victor and Rose and Norman Osprey and Bon-Bon and Adam Force, all as blind alley. I thought of all they'd said and done, and the professor was right, if I could discard the lies, I'd be left with the truth.

Far more absorbing of my time and mental energy was his assertion that if I included factor x (Black-mask Four) in all my insoluble sums, I would find them adding up.

Although I arrived at work half an hour before the normal starting time, Hickory was there before me, obstinately trying again to make a perfect sailing boat. He'd made the boat itself much larger and had put in red and blue streaks up the mast and the whole thing looked lighter and more fun.

I congratulated him and got a scornful grunt in return, and I thought how quickly his sunny temperament could blow up a thunderstorm, and hoped for his sake as well as for our competent little team's that it would blow over just as fast. Meanwhile I tidied the shelves in the stock room end of the furnace room, where Hickory had set the melted glass at the working temperature of 1,800 degrees

Fahrenheit. To give Hickory his due, he handled semi-liquid glass with a good deal of the panache he would need on the way to general recognition. I privately thought, though, that he would get stuck on 'pretty good' and never reach 'marvellous', and because he understood deep down where his limit lay, and knew I could do better, his present feeling of mild resentment needed patience and friendly laughter if he were either to stay or to leave on good terms.

Irish and Pamela Jane arrived together, as they often did, and this time were arguing about a film they'd seen that had a bad glass-blower in it. They asked Hickory what he thought and embroiled him so intensely in the argument that with a fatally noisy bang Hickory's precious new sailing boat cracked apart into five or six pieces. It had been standing free on the marver table, the outer surface cooling more rapidly than the super-hot core. The stresses due to unequal rates of contraction had become too great for the fragile glass. The pieces had blown away from each other and lay on the floor.

All three of my helpers looked horrified. Hickory himself glanced at his watch and said bleakly, 'Three minutes, that's all it took. I was going to put it in the oven . . . Goddam that *stupid* film.'

No one touched or tried to pick up the fallen pieces. They were still near to their liquid heat and would incinerate one's fingers.

'Never mind,' I said shrugging and looking at the sad

bits, 'it happens.' And I didn't need to remind them that practice glass was cheap. It did happen to everyone. It happened to the best.

We worked conscientiously all morning, making swooping birds for mobiles, which always sold fast. Pamela Jane, loving them particularly, was the one who fixed their strings the following morning early and who at noon would carefully pack them in boxes in such a way that they would pull out easily to fly.

Hickory, who could make neat little birds, had recovered his good humour by the time Worthington drew up outside in Marigold's Rolls. Marigold herself, in a dramatic black and white striped kaftan, issued from her glossy car with mascara-laden eyelashes batting hugely up and down like a giraffe's. She had come, she announced, to take me to lunch in the Wychwood Dragon. She had a favour to ask, she said.

Worthington, always a step behind Marigold when on active bodyguard duty, looked the more richly sun-tanned from the skiing trip. He had spent most of the time on the slopes, he said with satisfaction, while Marigold's wardrobe had swelled by three enormous suitcases. And a good time had clearly been had by both.

Her intense vitality as usual stirred anyone in Marigold's vicinity to giggles and, as on other days, she and Hickory were soon indulging in batting a sexual ball to each other with gleeful freedom.

Marigold, with enjoyment, stayed for half an hour – a century for her – during which time Worthington drifted

me with a gentle tug on the arm into the furnace end of
the room, and told me with the unhappiest of expressions
that the underground fraternity of bookmakers were fore-
casting my destruction, if not death.

'Rose is still actively prowling round here, looking for
vengeance, because she can't understand why you aren't
on your knees to her. They are *laughing* at her because
you and Tom and I have walked away from two of her
best-planned smasheroos, and there's no way she's going
to put up with such a loss of face. So you just look out,
because I hear that someone in Broadway has binocs on
you now, reporting every twitch you make straight back
to Rose.'

'Binocs?'

'Bins. Where have you been all your life? Binoculars.
Race-glasses. But seriously, Gerard, Tom Pigeon says it's
no joke.'

I promised to be careful, but who could live for ever
in a state of alarm? I said, 'I suppose I'd better tell you,
then, that Adam Force and Rose did try to do me in
yesterday. At least, I think so.'

He listened grimly and asked the unanswerable,
'Where's Rose now?'

Marigold and Hickory, having enjoyed their flirting as
much because of their twenty-year age difference as in
spite of it, gave each other a pecking kiss on the cheek
in farewell, and Marigold and I made a head-turning
entrance into the Wychwood Dragon dining room. The
Dragon herself swept in full sail between the tables to

fetch up by Marigold's side, two splendid ladies eyeing each other for supremacy.

I counted it a draw for outrageous clothes and an easy win for Marigold in the mascara stakes, and nearly two hours slid by before Marigold, tiring of the underlying contest, told me the reason for her invitation to me for lunch.

She declaimed to start with (unnecessarily), 'I am Bon-Bon's mother!'

'Ah,' I said. I knew.

'At Christmas,' Marigold continued, 'Martin gave his wife a video camera from the children, and he was going to give her a necklace from himself as well.'

I nodded. 'But she preferred warm winter boots.'

'The silly girl has no taste.'

'But she gets cold feet.'

Marigold considered fashion far more important than comfort. 'Martin said you had made a spectacular necklace once, and that you could make the same one again. So . . . for Bon-Bon, will you do it now? As a present from me, of course. And I'd like to see it first.'

She waited an uncharacteristically long time for my answer, gazing hopefully into my face. I didn't know in fact what to say. I couldn't insult her by telling her it would cost more than the woolly boots and the video camera combined, though she would need to know, but the videotape describing how to make it and listing the detailed ingredients in grams, was not only missing but might have come into Rose's field of things to die for.

When I said I would make a necklace for Bon-Bon, I hadn't known Rose.

After too long a pause Marigold asked, 'What's the problem? Can't you do it?'

When an answer of some sort became essential I said, 'Does Bon-Bon give the necklace idea her blessing?'

'She doesn't know about it. I want her to have a lovely surprise to cheer her up. I thought of buying her something in Paris, but then I remembered what Martin wanted you to do, so will you?'

She was so seldom presented with a negative that she couldn't understand my hesitation. I put together my most persuasive smile and begged for a little time. She began to pout, and I remembered Martin, laughing, saying that the Marigold pout meant the knives were out.

Hell, I thought, I wished he were alive. He'd been dead twenty-one days and I'd found each one a quandary without him.

I said to Marigold, 'The necklace I made is in a strong box in the bank down the road here. I do agree that you should see it before we go any further.'

The pout cleared away to a broad smile of understanding, and although we could easily have walked the distance, Marigold grandly summoned Worthington, equally grandly paid for our lunch, and outshone the poor Dragon all the way to the Rolls.

In the bank Marigold had the manager bowing to the floor while minions were sent scurrying to bring my locked box into the private room where contents could be checked. I opened the metal box and laid the flat blue velvet folder containing the copy of the Cretan Sunrise onto the bench-shelf, opening it for her opinion.

I hadn't seen the antique original except lit behind glass, so I couldn't completely compare them, but in the chill light of the bank's viewing room the duplicate I'd made gleamed as if with inner life, and I gave way to such a bout of self-regard as would have caused my Uncle Ron to bury his head in his hands in shame.

Marigold exclaimed 'Oh!' in astonishment, then drew in a breath and said, 'Oh, my dear,' and couldn't decide whether or not she liked it.

The necklace designed 3,500 years ago was a matter of twenty flat pieces, each made of aquamarine-coloured and dark-blue glass streaked together with melted gold. About two inches, or five centimetres, long, by a thumb-nail wide, each flat shining piece bore the imprint of a flower. When worn, the long pieces, strung loosely together round the neck by their short sides, spread out in rays like a sunrise, the imprinted flowers, outermost, lying flat on the skin. In a way barbaric, the whole thing was antiquely magnificent, and definitely heavy. I didn't blame delicate Bon-Bon for not wanting to wear it.

Marigold, regaining her breath, asked if Martin had seen it.

'Yes.' I nodded. 'He thought it would suit Bon-Bon, but she wanted the boots more.' I'd lent the necklace to him without conditions, and he'd shown it around in the jockeys' changing room. Dozens of people had seen it.

Marigold, incredibly brought again to speechlessness, said nothing at all while I re-enclosed the necklace into darkness and put the velvet folder back in the metal strong box. There were the other papers there that I checked yet again – will, insurance policy, deeds of the hill house, all the conventional paper-trail of living, but of an instructional videotape, still not a sign.

I searched carefully once more through the pile of envelopes.

There was no tape. Nothing. I reflected with irony that even if one followed the instruction tape, it wouldn't be enormously easy to fabricate. I kept it partly because of the difficult hours it had cost me.

The bank minions re-locked everything and gave me back my key, and Marigold grandly commanded Worthington to drive us all back to Logan Glass. Apart from her instruction to her chauffeur she remained exceptionally quiet on the very short journey, and also, as I'd noticed in the Wychwood dining room, her gin intake had dropped to scraping zero.

Back at Logan Glass she paraded up and down the brightly lit gallery as if she'd never been in there before, and halted finally in front of Catherine's wings before addressing all of us, Worthington, Irish, Hickory, Pamela Jane and myself, as if we'd been a junior class in prep school. She said we were lucky to be in a studio which stood so high already in the world's estimation. She was going to give us all a huge jump forward in reputation because, 'Gerard . . .' she blew me a kiss . . . 'with the

help of all of you, of course, is going to make a marvellous necklace for me, which I'm going to call the
Marigold Knight Trophy, and I'm going to present it each
year to the winner of a steeplechase run at Cheltenham
on every New Year's Eve in memory of my son-in-law,
Martin Stukely . . . and *there*,' she spread her arms wide,
'what do you think of *that*?'

Whatever we thought, we gazed silently in awe.

'Well, Gerard,' she demanded, 'what do you say?'

I didn't say, 'Over the top. In fact, out of sight,' but I
thought it.

'You see,' Marigold went on triumphantly, 'everyone
benefits. People will flock to your door, here.'

Apart from terrible trouble with insurance the one dire
probability ahead in her scheme was that someone somewhere would try to exchange the modern for the antique,
with Marigold embroiled in legal pincers.

'I think it's a *beautiful* idea,' Pamela Jane told Marigold, and the others, smiling, agreed. Even Worthington
raised no security alarms.

Marigold, delighted with the scheme she had thought
up within ten minutes, filled in the details rapidly. She
would consult the Cheltenham Race Trophy Committee
immediately . . . Gerard could start work at once . . . the
Press should be alerted . . .

I hardly listened to those plans. Almost anything would
be a better trophy than a copy of a jewel worth a million.
The obituary for Martin that I hadn't yet fashioned would
be more suitable. Glass trophies were common in racing

and I would be elated in general to be commissioned to make one.

Irish with enthusiasm clasped Marigold's hand and shook it vigorously, to the lady's surprise. Hickory beamed. The trophy necklace idea swept the polls at Logan Glass, but the Cheltenham committee might not like it.

The Cheltenham committee was given little time more to remain unconsulted. Marigold used my telephone to get through to an influential high-up whom she galvanized into visiting Logan Glass at once.

An hour later, Marigold, irresistible to many a powerful man, greeted the man from Cheltenham, Kenneth Trubshaw, with a familiar kiss and explained her intention even before introducing Irish, Hickory and Pamela Jane.

I got a nod from the smoothly urbane member of the racecourse's upper echelon. He knew me by sight, but we hadn't until then talked. Marigold with arms raised put that right.

'Darling, you know Gerard Logan, of course?'

'Er . . . yes, of course.'

'And it's Gerard who's made the *fabulous* necklace which you *must see*, which is down in the bank here . . .'

Everyone looked at a watch, or the clock on the showroom wall. The bank had closed its doors five minutes before and Marigold looked frustrated. Time had ticked away too quickly.

I suggested diffidently that Mr Trubshaw, so not to have wasted entirely his short journey, might care to see a few other things I'd made and although Marigold protested, 'Darling, there's more *gold* in the necklace and it's going to be a gold trophy race . . .'

Kenneth Trubshaw, though perhaps more courteous than interested, took the first few brisk uncommitted steps into the gallery. Then, to my great relief, he paused, and stopped, and went back a pace, and finished thoughtfully in front of Catherine's wings.

'How much is this one?' he asked. 'There's no price on it.'

'It's sold,' I said.

My assistants all showed astonishment.

'Pity,' commented Trubshaw.

'There isn't enough gold,' Marigold complained.

'Um,' I said, 'I did a horse jumping a fence, once. The fence was solid gold, so were the horse's hooves. The rest of the horse was crystal, and the ground, the base of the piece, was black glass, with tiny gold flecks.'

'Where is it now?' Kenneth asked.

'Dubai.'

He smiled.

'What about the necklace?' Marigold demanded, cross.

Her Kenneth appeased her gently. 'I'll come over and see it tomorrow, but this young man has more than a necklace to show us. These wings, for instance . . .' He stood in front of them, his head on one side. He asked me, 'Couldn't you make that again? If this one's sold?'

'Part of what I sell is a guarantee of one-of-a-kind,' I apologized. I wasn't sure I could, even if I wanted to, repeat the wings. The climbing powerful splendour of their construction had come from the subconscious. I hadn't even written up my notes.

Could I instead, then, he asked, make a tribute to Martin Stukely?

I said, 'I could make a leaping horse with golden streaks. I could make it worthy of Cheltenham.'

'I'll come tomorrow,' the trophy chairman said and embraced Marigold in farewell with smiling enthusiasm.

Marigold, having agreed earlier with her daughter to take me back to Bon-Bon's house, she, Worthington and I made tracks to the Stukely gravel, arriving at the same moment as Priam Jones, who was carefully nursing the expensive tyres he'd bought to replace those wrecked on New Year's Eve. Priam, Bon-Bon had reported, had after all decided not to sue the council for erecting sharp-toothed barriers overnight, but had already transferred his disgust to Lloyd Baxter, who'd ordered his horses, including Tallahassee, to be sent north to a training stable nearer his home.

Bon-Bon came out of the house in welcoming mood, and I had no trouble, thanks to her manoeuvring it privately on my behalf, in talking to Priam Jones as if our meeting were accidental. Priam looked like being the last of the cul-de-sacs.

'Bon-Bon invited me to an early supper,' Priam announced with a touch of pomposity.

'How splendid!' I said warmly. 'Me too.'

Priam's face said he didn't care to have me there too,

and things weren't improved from his point of view when Bon-Bon swept her mother into the house on a wardrobe expedition and said over her departing shoulder, 'Gerard, pour Priam a drink, will you? I think there's everything in the cupboard.'

Bon-Bon's grief for Martin had settled in her like an anchor steadying a ship. She was more in charge of the children and had begun to cope more easily with managing her house. I'd asked her whether she could face inviting Priam to dinner, but I hadn't expected the skill with which she'd delivered him to me in secondary guest capacity.

The children poured out of the house at that moment, addressing me unusually as 'Uncle Gerard' and Priam as 'sir'. They then bunched round Worthington and carried him off to play 'make believe' in the garage block. Priam and I, left alone, made our way, with me leading him through the house, to Martin's den. Here I acted as instructed as host and persuaded Priam with my very best flattery to tell me how his other horses had prospered, as I'd seen one of his winners praised in the newspapers.

Priam, with his old boastfulness re-emerging, explained how no one else but he could have brought those runners out at the right moment. No one, he claimed, knew more about readying a horse for a particular race than he did.

He smoothed the thin white hair that covered his scalp but showed pink skin beneath and conceded that Martin had contributed a little now and then to his training success.

Priam at my invitation relaxed on the sofa and sipped weak Scotch and water while I sat in Martin's chair and fiddled with small objects on his desk. I remembered Priam's spontaneous tears at Cheltenham and not for the first time wondered if on a deeper level Priam was less sure of himself than he acted. There were truths he might tell if I got down to that tear-duct level, and this time I'd meet no garden hose on the way.

'How well,' I asked conversationally, 'do you know Eddie Payne, Martin's old valet?'

Surprised, Priam answered, 'I don't know him intimately, if that's what you mean, but some days I give him the colours the jockeys will be wearing, so yes, I talk to Eddie then.'

'And Rose?' I suggested.

'Who?'

'Eddie Payne's daughter. Do you know her?'

'Why ever do you ask?' Priam's voice was mystified, but he hadn't answered the question. Eddie and his daughter had worn black masks, I thought, but could Priam have been Number Four?

I said with gratitude, 'You were so kind, Priam, on that wretched day of Martin's death, to take back to Broadway that tape I so stupidly left in my raincoat pocket in Martin's car. I haven't thanked you properly again since then.' I paused and then added as if one thought had nothing to do with the other. 'I've heard a crazy rumour that you swapped two tapes. That you took the one from my pocket and left another.'

'Rubbish!'

'I agree.' I smiled and nodded. 'I'm sure you took back to my place in Broadway the tape I'd been given at Cheltenham.'

'Well, then.' He sounded relieved. 'Why mention it?'

'Because, of course, in Martin's den, in this very room, in fact, you will have found tapes all over the place. Out of curiosity you may have slotted the tape I had left in the car into Martin's VCR and had a look at it, and maybe you found it so boring and unintelligible that you wound it back, stuck the parcel shut again, and took it back to me at Broadway.'

'You're just guessing,' Priam complained.

'Oh, sure. Do I guess right?'

Priam didn't want to admit to his curiosity. I pointed out that it was to his advantage if it were known for a certainty what tape had vanished from Logan Glass.

He took my word for it and looked smug, but I upset him again profoundly by asking him *who* that evening, or early next morning, had he assured that the tape he'd delivered to Broadway had nothing to do with an antique necklace, whether worth a million or not.

Priam's face stiffened. It was definitely a question he didn't want to answer.

I said without pressure, 'Was it Rose Payne?'

He simply stared, not ready to loosen his long-tight tongue.

'If you say *who*,' I went on in the same undemanding tone, 'we can smother the rumours about you swapping any tapes.'

'There's never any harm in speaking the truth,' Priam protested, but of course he was wrong, the truth could be disbelieved, and the truth could hurt.

'Who?' I repeated, and I suppose my lack of emphasis went some way towards persuading him to give the facts daylight.

'When Martin died,' he said, 'I drove his things back here, as you know, and then as my own car was in dock having the ... er ... the tyres, you see, needed replacing ...'

I nodded without judgement or a smile.

Priam, encouraged, went on. 'Well, Bon-Bon said I could take Martin's car, she would have said yes to anything, she was terribly distraught, so I just drove Martin's car on to my home and then back to Broadway, with Baxter's bag and your raincoat, and then I drove myself home again in it. In the morning, when I came in from morning exercise with the first lot, my phone was ringing, and it was Eddie Payne ...' Priam took a breath, but seemed committed to finishing. 'Well ... Eddie asked me then if I was sure the tape I'd taken back to your shop was without doubt the one he'd given you at Cheltenham, and I said I was absolutely certain, and as that was that, he rang off.'

209

Priam's tale had ended. He took a deep swallow of whisky, and I poured him a stronger refill, a pick-you-up from the confessional.

Eddie himself had been to confession. Eddie hadn't been able to face Martin's funeral. Eddie was afraid of his daughter Rose, and Eddie had put on a black mask to do me a good deal of damage. If Tom and the Dobermanns hadn't been passing, Eddie's sins would have involved a good deal more of deep-soul shriving.

It had taken such a lot of angst for Priam to answer a fairly simple question that I dug around in what I'd heard to see if he knew consequences that I didn't.

Could he have been Black-mask Four? Unknown factor x?

Ed Payne had probably told Rose that the tape stolen from Logan Glass at the turnover of the new century was to do with a necklace. Rose had not necessarily believed him. Rose, knowing that such a necklace existed, but not realizing that the tape, if found, wasn't itself worth much and certainly not a million, may have hungered for it fiercely enough to anaesthetize everyone around at Bon-Bon's house with cyclopropane, and gather up every videotape in sight.

I had thought at the time that it had been a man who had sprung out from behind the door and hit me unconscious, but on reflection it could have been Rose herself. Rose, agile, strong and determined, would without question lash out when it came to attacking a man. I knew all about that.

Thoughtfully I asked Priam, as if I'd forgotten I'd asked him before, 'How well do you know Rose Payne?'

'I don't know her,' he replied at once, and then, more slowly, revised the assertion and watered it down. 'I've seen her around.'

'How well does she know Adam Force, would you say? Do you think Dr Force would be foolish enough to provide her with a cylinder of gas from a nursing home he visits?'

Priam looked as shocked as if I'd run him through with swords, but unfortunately from my own point of view he didn't actually flag-wave any signs of guilt. He didn't feel guilty; almost no one did.

Bon-Bon's 'early supper' proved to be just that, slightly to Priam's disappointment. He preferred grandeur, but everyone sat round the big kitchen table, Marigold, Worthington, the children, Bon-Bon, me and Priam himself. I also acted as waiter, as I often did in that house, though Daniel, the elder boy, carried empty dishes sometimes.

'Gerard,' he said, standing solidly in front of me between courses, to gain my attention, 'who's Victor?'

I paid attention very fast and said, 'He's a boy. Tell me what you've heard.'

'Is it still the same?' Daniel asked. 'Do we get the gold coins?'

'No, of course not,' Bon-Bon scolded. 'That was a game.'

'So is this,' I promised her, 'so do let's play the same way.'

211

I dug in a pocket and found some loose change, surprised I had any left after the twenty or more coins they'd won several days earlier.

'What about Victor?' I asked. I put a coin flat on the table and Daniel said, 'There are two things,' so I put down a second coin.

'You're teaching these children all wrong,' Marigold berated me.

Theoretically I might agree with her but Daniel unexpectedly spoke up. 'Gerard told Worthington and a friend of his that you have to pay for what you get.'

Marigold's disfavour spread to her chauffeur, but Daniel, not understanding, simply waited for me to listen.

'Go on,' I said. 'Two pieces of treasure. And they'd better be worth it.' I grinned at him.

He put his chubby hand flat over the coins and said directly to me, 'He wants to tell you a secret.'

'When did he say that?' I took him seriously, but the other adults laughed.

Daniel picked up one of the gold coins. Mercenary little devil, I thought.

Daniel said, 'He phoned here. Mummy was out in the garden, so I answered it. He said he was Victor. He didn't want to talk to Mummy, but only to you. You weren't here, but I told him you were coming for supper so he said to tell you he would try again, if he could.'

Daniel's hand hovered in the air over the second coin. I nodded philosophically and he whisked it away in a flash.

'That's disgraceful!' Marigold told me severely. 'You're teaching my grandson all sorts of bad habits.'

'It's a game,' I repeated; and one for eleven-year-olds. Bright though he was, I thought Daniel had done a good piece of work.

'Early supper' ended at seven-thirty, an hour before the younger children's bed time. Marigold, her mercurial spirits restored, gave Daniel a forgiving goodnight hug that swalllowed him in kaftan, and after coffee, three large slugs of Grand Marnier, and a giggly chat on the telephone with Kenneth Trubshaw involving the sponsorship of gold trophies, Marigold floated out to the Rolls in clouds of good will and let Worthington solicitously install her in the back seat and drive off to her home.

Priam Jones felt less than decently treated. He let Bon-Bon know, while thanking her for her hospitality, that as a racehorse trainer of prestige, and especially as her husband's ex-chief employer, he would have enjoyed more attention and consideration. He bestowed an even cooler farewell nod to me and in irritation gave his new tyres a harsh workout in his departure across the gravel. Poor Priam, I thought. It couldn't be much fun being *him*.

Victor kept me waiting a long time. Bon-Bon, going upstairs to read stories to the children, gave me a kiss goodnight and waved me to the den for the evening, but it was after eleven o'clock when the fifth caller on the line spoke with the familiar cracked voice of Taunton.

'Gerard? I'm in a public phone box. Mum thinks I'm in bed. She threw away your mobile number and I can't use the e-mail . . . Auntie Rose has taken my computer. I'm absolutely sick of things. I want to see you. Tell me where. I'm running out of money.'

There were indeed many time-over warning clicks. He was feeding small coins, I supposed, because he hadn't any others. In a short period of peace I said, 'I'll come to Taunton station, same train, on Sunday.'

'No. Tomorrow. *Please*, tomorrow.'

I agreed, and the line went dead.

'You're raving mad, that's what you are,' Tom Pigeon said at seven in the morning, when I rang and told him, 'Today's Friday. The boy should be in school.'

'That's probably why he was so insistent. He could skip school without his mother knowing.'

'You're not going,' Tom said positively, and then, a few seconds later, 'We'll get Jim to drive us. He's got an estate car for the dogs. Where are you?'

'At the Stukelys. Can you pick me up here?'

'Last Sunday, five days ago,' Tom said with mock patience, 'dear Rose tore your face open in Taunton with the tap end of a garden hose.'

'Mm,' I agreed.

'And the day before yesterday, I hear, you nearly got yourself killed.'

'Well . . .'

'How about staying at home?'

I smiled at the silly idea.

CHAPTER TEN

By Friday Jim's wife had told him I was accursed by demons and he should no longer drive me. Our lateness on Wednesday had burned her risotto.

Jim and I however came to a mutual understanding and shook hands on it. He would drive when I needed him in bodyguard status, there would be no radio, and I would pay him double.

Despite this slightly crabby start, Jim drove Tom, me and the dogs cheerfully to Taunton and stopped in the no-parking zone outside the station. I remembered too late that the weekday timetable was different from Sunday and the expected train had come and gone, leaving Victor stranded.

He wasn't on the platform.

Giving Tom the news and receiving a promise to sit and wait, I hurried along the road until 19 Lorna Terrace was in sight. No Victor. Back to the station – and I found him there, cold and anxious, in the waiting-room.

He stood up, looking thin and stressed, my arrival not enough to bring out smiles. I'd spent part of the journey adding Victor into every event that Black-mask Four could have attended without disguise, and feeling I was nowhere near as good as George Lawson-Young at this factor x stuff, I couldn't make x fit Victor anywhere.

'I'm late because I didn't come on the train,' I briefly explained. 'What's the matter?'

'I want . . .' He sounded as desperate as he looked. He began again. 'Auntie Rose has moved into our house . . . I hate her. I can't bear her, and Mum won't speak to me unless I do what Auntie Rose says, because Mum's that scared of her. And my dad, when he gets out, won't come home while she's there. I know he won't, so where can I go? What can I do? I don't know anyone except you to ask, and that's a laugh really, considering your face . . .'

'Did you try your grandfather?'

Victor said hopelessly, 'He's shit scared of Auntie Rose. Worse than Mum.'

I said, 'Last Sunday – ' and he interrupted.

'I'm sorry. I'm really sorry about your face. I thought you wouldn't come today . . . I thought you hadn't come.'

'Forget about last Sunday,' I said. 'Concentrate on Adam Force instead.'

'He's great,' Victor said without fervour, and then with a frown, added, 'Everyone says so. He sometimes used my computer. That's how I got his letter. He thought he had deleted the file but I found it in the cache memory.'

It explained a lot.

I asked, 'How long has he known your Auntie Rose?' and this time I got an answer.

'About as long as he's known Mum. Months, that is. Mum went on the coach trip to his clinic, and he got hooked on her. He was a real cool guy, I thought. He came round for her when Dad was at work. So when Auntie Rose finds out, she goes round to the hotel where Dad's working and says if he comes home quick he'll catch them at it in Dad's own bed. So Dad goes round and Dr Force has gone by then, but Dad gives Mum a hell of a beating, breaking her nose and about six of her ribs and things, and Auntie Rose goes round to the nick and tells on Dad. So they put him away for twelve months. Then, last Sunday,' he said miserably, 'Auntie Rose takes Adam Force off Mum, which she meant to do all along, I reckon, and now he does what she tells him, and it's queer, but I'd say she *hits* him pretty hard most days, and then I've seen them kissing after that.'

He spoke in puzzlement, and Worthington, I thought, could explain a thing or two to Victor. Fatherly, steady and worldly, Worthington, a great fellow, simply *couldn't* be Black-mask Four. And Victor? Surely not Victor, though Black-mask Four hadn't been bodily substantial, like Worthington, but lithe, like Victor. But Victor *couldn't* have bashed me about then, and asked me for help now.

Not Victor, not Worthington, but what about Gina?

Was she muscular enough? I didn't know for sure and,

I decided reluctantly, I would have to find out. I'd been through almost the whole register of cul-de-sacs and failed to find anyone that fitted a factor x. Yet there had indeed been a fourth black-masked attacker. I had felt the hands. I'd felt the blows. I'd seen the eyes within the mask. Black-mask Four was real.

According to the professor, there was a question I wasn't asking, and if I didn't ask the right question, how could I expect to be told the right answer? But *what* was the right question? And whom should I ask?

With a mental sigh I took Victor out of the station and, to his obvious pleasure, reunited him with Tom and his three black canine companions. He told Tom that that day, the Sunday that we'd spent on the moor, had been one of his happiest ever. Happiest, that was, until his Auntie Rose had ruined it.

He played with the dogs, plainly in their good graces, and spoke to them instead of us. The black ears heard him say, 'I'll bet people can still run away to sea.'

After a while I said to Tom, 'I'll go round to Victor's house, and if his mother's in I'll ask her if he can spend the weekend with us.'

Tom protested, 'I'll go.'

'We'll both go,' I said, and in spite of Victor's fears we left him with Jim and, taking the dogs with us, knocked on the door of the roughly repaired entrance to 19 Lorna Terrace.

Gina Verity came to our summons and failed to close

her mended door against us fast enough. Tom's heavy shoe was quicker.

In the five days since the previous Sunday, Gina had lost her looks, her serenity and her confidence. She stared at my slashed and mending jaw as if it were one straw too many. She said helplessly, 'You'd better come in,' and with sagging shoulders led me down the now familiar passage to the kitchen. We sat, as before, at the table.

Tom and the dogs stood on guard outside the house because Gina didn't know when either her sister or Adam Force would return.

'I would like to invite Victor to stay for the weekend,' I said.

Gina lit cigarette from cigarette, as before. 'All right,' she agreed in a dull sort of way. 'Pick him up from school.' She thought it over. 'Better not let Rose find out, she wouldn't let him go with you.'

Gina's left-hand fingers were stained nearly orange with nicotine. The right-hand fingers were white. I stretched forward and lifted first her right hand and then her left, putting them down again gently. The muscles were flabby, with no tone. Too apathetic to complain, she merely looked at her own hands one by one, and said, 'What?'

I didn't reply. Black-mask Four's left hand hadn't been as intensely yellow as this one, even seen under the street lights and even while actively punching. With those strongly muscled arms, Black-mask Four had been male.

Gina had not been Black-mask Four. The certainty was unarguable.

Time to go.

Out in front of the house Tom's equivalent of my alarm whistle set up a howling, growling, barking clamour which the dogs only ever did at their owner's prompting.

Gina immediately stood and shrank away from the table, her eyes wide with unmistakable fear. 'It's Rose,' Gina said. 'She's come back. She always makes dogs bark. They don't like her. She makes their hair stand on end.'

Mine too, I thought. The deep-throated Dobermanns went on proving Gina right.

'Go,' Gina said to me, her tongue sticking on the words. 'Go out. Out through the backyard . . . and out through the gate and down the lane. Go, go. Hurry.' Her urgency was for my own safety as much as hers.

It might have been prudent to go, but I'd never been a wise devotee of the 'He who fights and runs away lives to fight another day' school of thought. Running away from Rose . . . I supposed that I'd already escaped three times from her traps, and once from Adam Force. With that amount of good luck, I thought, I might remain a bit longer undestroyed.

I stayed sitting at the table, though with chair pushed back and one knee over the other, while the front door creaked open and the purposeful footsteps came along the passage.

Not only Rose had come, but Adam Force with her. Rose had recognized Tom and his sidekicks, but the doctor was pinning his negative emotions entirely on me. He'd set me up two days ago as an insulin-dosed car crash hit-and-run victim – a scheme that had gone wrong. My presence in that house shook him.

Rose, interestingly, had bloomed as fast as Gina had faded. Her dry skin and frizzy hair seemed lubricated, and she was alight with what (thanks to Victor's run-through) I could only interpret as satisfied sex.

Adam Force, good-looking and charming though he still might be, was to my mind a con man sliding towards self-inflicted destruction. If he'd kept anywhere a copy of what he'd stolen from Professor Lawson-Young's laboratory, Rose in the end would have it. Rose would acquire whatever she set out to get, man, tape or power.

Rose had definitely worn one of the black masks, but Adam Force hadn't. He hadn't known who I was when I turned up at Phoenix House.

I said lazily, rising to my feet, 'We'll not have a repeat of last Sunday. I came to see Gina principally, but I came also to leave a message for Rose.'

They listened attentively, to my amazement.

I said, 'The fourth of your band of black-masked thugs has whispered in my ear.'

The possibility of my untruth being accurate froze Rose long enough for me to go forwards along the passage and into the Dobermanns' territory of safe keeping. Tom, eyebrows up, joined in step beside me once we were out in the road and, unpursued, we walked along and round the bend towards the station, the dogs following in silence.

'However did you manage to get out of there unharmed?' Tom asked. 'I was sure you would whistle.'

'I told them a lie.'

He laughed. But it hadn't been funny. Adam Force's sharply focused calculating assessment of me from neck to ankles had been too much like a matter of adding up the amount of deadly substance needed per kilo of body weight to finish me off. A lethal amount of insulin . . . a syringeful of 'goodbye' threat, a cylinder of cyclopropane gas, a prelude to any sort of injected extinction. Rose would inflict instant damage, but Adam Force would more deliberately kill.

In a normal kitchen, although Rose could always slash with knives, Adam Force wouldn't have to hand any poison, his weapon of choice. He would need more time than he had.

I had kept a good distance from Rose on my way out, but it was the white beard and orange socks, the gracious manners and the Phoenix House pharmacy, the hunger for a million and the belief of infallibility, these were the long-term dangers that I had most to fear.

There were two particular videotapes missing, and both had at some time been in my care. Did Rose have the one detailing the necklace? Did Force after all retain the cancer-research tape he'd stolen? I might believe the answers to be yes and no, but how the hell could I find out for sure?

On the way back to Broadway we veered into Cheltenham to call on Kenneth Trubshaw, the trophy committee man, who'd said on Jim's car phone that he would be at home. Slightly surprised by our numbers, he nevertheless generously offered the warmth of the kitchen stove to my travelling companions, plus a large tin of biscuits, and shepherded me alone into his much colder drawing room. It was a large room facing north, its daylight grey and its carpet green, a combination I found depressing.

I gave him the book I'd taken along for the purpose, which contained a series of glossy coloured eight-by-ten photographs, a long record of the work I'd done over maybe twelve years.

I explained that I couldn't in good faith repeat any of the items exactly, but I could make something similar, if he liked.

He laid the book flat on a big table and turned the pages slowly. It mattered to me quite a lot, I discovered, that he would like some at least of the pieces, even if half of them weren't suitable for racing trophies. Vases of odd shapes had recently been blown for trophies of all sorts, though. There was no ban these days on anything surreal.

Trubshaw finished turning the pages. Then he closed

the book, to my severe disappointment, and with too serious a tightening of his mouth gave me his verdict.

'If you can lend me this book I'll put it before the committee when they meet tomorrow morning. I know dear Marigold wants action. I will telephone her when the decision's made.'

I'll be damned, I thought. How did he look when he was altogether turning things down?

He said, 'The leaping horse is the one I'd choose. Can you do anything like it? And I'll need to know how high it would be overall, and how heavy. The one in the photograph looks too big.'

'Any size you like,' I promised, and told him that the leaping horse in the picture belonged to one of the Leicester Stewards and his wife.

While Kenneth Trubshaw exclaimed with surprise, I recalled minute by minute as best I could the conversation I'd had on the Stewards' guests' viewing balcony, where Lloyd Baxter had first told me about a white-bearded man stealing my money along with the much travelled video-tape.

Lloyd Baxter, with his epilepsy, couldn't be factor x. His body hadn't the shape or the agility of Black-mask Four.

Kenneth Trubshaw put his hand down on the book of photos and said thoughtfully, 'Could you include enough gold to satisfy Marigold?'

'Yes. Any amount.'

'Er . . . how? And would it be . . . well . . . enormously expensive?'

'Not very expensive.'

Kenneth Trubshaw held definite reasons for concerning himself and his committee members with the subject of cost, but he hesitated for a measurable time before he waved me to a chair and, sitting himself, said, 'I don't know if you follow the background ins and outs of racing politics at all? I don't mean the form of horses or speculations about their fitness. I mean the question about whether the cost of a winner's trophy should be deducted from the prize money, as it usually has been until recently. Many owners refuse to take the trophy, preferring the whole prize to be given as money. It's being suggested that we give the whole prize *and* the trophy in every case. Ask Marigold if she is giving the trophy herself outright, or if she expects the racecourse to pay for it. Warn her the debate exists.' He stopped slowly, not proud of his shunting of his dilemma onto me.

'Well, all right,' I said, 'but don't expect Marigold to decide. She's terrific, but she leaves life's really serious decisions to her chauffeur.'

'You don't mean it!'

'Of course, I do. Her chauffeur, Worthington, is worth his weight in cut crystal ten times over.'

Kenneth Trubshaw absorbed the news manfully and then with relief went back to straight expense, saying, 'The necklace Marigold wants is very expensive, isn't it?'

I nodded. 'Very. And that necklace, if on public show, is inviting thieves. The gold is genuinely solid in that case.'

'Isn't solid gold always the real thing?' He looked quizzical.

I explained, 'Well, you can paint hot glass with molten 18 carat gold, that's seventy-five per cent mixed with other metals. You paint what you want to look gold when it's finished. Then you anneal the work for a second time, but only at 450 degrees Fahrenheit, and when it cools the second time the gold you painted on will have adhered completely to the glass, and it will look like solid gold, even if it isn't.'

Kenneth Trubshaw was fascinated, but didn't want to be considered cheap. 'Gold has to be gold,' he said. 'I want Marigold to like it, of course. That is, if we decide on this sort of thing for her trophy.'

I made murmuring agreeing noises.

He asked curiously, 'Which of all those sculptures in the book was the hardest for you to make?'

'The most difficult was the gypsy's crystal ball.'

It surprised him, as it did most people. He thought a crystal ball was blown up like a child's balloon.

'No,' I said. 'It's solid glass. And it's extremely difficult to make a perfectly round large ball of glass without air bubbles forming in it as it cools in an annealing oven.'

He wanted me to enlighten him about annealing, and

when I told him, he said, 'Could you make a leaping horse taking off from a crystal ball?'

Nodding, I said, 'It would be heavy . . . and difficult . . . but I could make sure it was unique.'

He pondered for a while, walking to his tall sash window and looking out into his sleeping winter garden.

'If we decide on giving you the commission, can you make drawings for us to choose from?'

'Yes,' I said, 'I could. But actually I'll probably make examples in glass. I'm more at home that way. Glass itself isn't expensive, and if you don't like the things I make, I can sell them in the shop.'

He smiled with irony at my frugal business sense. My chances, I judged, weren't much more than fifty:fifty.

Kenneth Trubshaw collected my crew from his kitchen and lined them up in an elegant striped nineteenth-century hall. Carefully then he looked them over. I followed his gaze and also his mind: a tubby driver in a wrinkled grey suit, a thin anxious boy, a piratical-looking vigorous man with a little black pointed Elizabethan beard, and three large black Dobermanns with watchful eyes and uncertain moods.

I said to Kenneth Trubshaw with a smile, 'They're my barbed-wire fence. Don't expect them to be pretty as well.'

He glanced my way, then said, 'It isn't enough for you and Marigold to make, pay for and give a splendid trophy to the winning owner of a race in memory of Martin

Stukely.' He stopped for reconsideration. 'At least, it's enough for that great lady Marigold, but not for you.'

He opened his front door for my guys to leave. Tom Pigeon bowed to him with ceremony, his glimmering smile making a mockery of solemnity. His dogs crowded his ankles to give him honour, and Kenneth earned Tom's allegiance for evermore by bowing back to him in return.

Then Trubshaw, hand on my arm again, made me stay while the others trooped out to the car. He said, 'Martin Stukely's darling widow may not realize that his good name is in doubt just now. Marigold certainly doesn't, nor does the racing public, nor, thank God, does the racing press. But you do, don't you? I saw it in your reaction to Marigold's enthusiasm for a race in his memory. You need, don't you, to scrub clean his honourable reputation first?'

I felt a chilled moment of disbelief that anyone else beside myself had perceived the possibility that Martin could have been knowingly dishonest.

There had been the moment when, reading through the contents of the slim hard-to-find drawer in his desk, I'd had to face the unwelcome photocopy of the letter he had written to Force. Parts of that short note had reverberated in my awareness ever since.

'. . . your formulae and methods . . . record them onto a videotape . . . and give it to me at Cheltenham races.'

Martin had known precisely what was on that tape. Had he after all known all along that the formulae and methods had been stolen? Kind George Lawson-Young had given his assured conviction that Martin had been one hundred per cent innocent in his dealings with Force. Terrible doubts all the same remained, and I didn't like finding them alive in the Cheltenham hierarchy.

I said to the racecourse trophy chairman, with a lightness I wasn't altogether feeling, 'Could you tell me what you mean?'

With disillusion, he did. 'As I understand it, on the day he died, Martin had possession of a videotape on which were recorded medical secrets of practically unlimited value. Medical secrets stolen by a Dr Force who had been known to Martin Stukely for some time. You yourself were to keep that tape hidden.'

I took a steadying breath and asked who had told him all that. 'Private investigators working for the laboratory from where the secrets were stolen interviewed all sorts of people at Cheltenham.' He looked at me curiously. 'I also heard from Marigold that you had been attacked by a pack of thugs outside your shop. The bookmakers had all heard it was the doing of Rose Payne, the racecourse valet's daughter, and she has a bit of a reputation for being violent. One of the bookmakers, a man called Norman Osprey, who looks a bit like Elvis Presley, he was boasting about the hammering they gave you. But it seems you didn't give them any tapes anyway.'

He waited for me to comment, but I didn't have much to say.

He smiled. 'Apparently, the valet thought that what he'd given you was a tape you yourself had filmed, explaining how to make a striking necklace, a copy of an antique. It seems that all the jockeys, and Ed Payne as well, had seen both the necklace and its how-to-make-it instruction tape in the changing room. Ed Payne told his daughter, Rose, that he had given you a tape and so she tried to find it by stealing every tape she could lay her hands on, including by attacking Martin Stukely's family with knock-out gas.'

'Rose herself?' I asked.

Kenneth Trubshaw didn't know. That was also the end of his up-to-dateness, except that, in the Cheltenham Stewards' opinion, Martin Stukely had very likely known that the scientific knowledge he'd promised to hide had been stolen from a research lab.

'And at present,' I said with regret, 'all those tapes are still missing. Whoever has them isn't telling.'

'I'm told you yourself are looking for them.'

'Who tells you all these things?' I really wanted to hear, but it seemed to be a matter of general supposition and logic.

'I'll tell you something myself,' I said, and I gave him Victor's latest purple homelife news.

'Dr Force and Rose deserve each other.' He laughed in his throat. 'That will do nicely for tomorrow morning's committee.' He walked with me to Jim's car. 'Give my warmest regards to Marigold. I'll be in touch.'

He shook my hand with sincerity.

He said, 'Find those tapes and clear Stukely's name.'

So simple, I thought.

When I disembarked at Bon-Bon's house, she herself with Daniel by her side came out to meet us.

'There's a message from Catherine Dodd for you,' Bon-Bon said to me. 'She has the evening free. She wants you to go to your house, if you can.'

I thanked her but she, like me and also Tom, was watching with fascination the flash of understanding between Victor, fifteen, and the four years younger Daniel. Alienation seemed more normal for that age bracket, but those two discovered immediately that they spoke computer language with a depth that none of the rest of us could reach. Victor climbed out of Jim's car and went indoors with Daniel as if the two of them were twins. Cyber twins, perhaps.

Bon-Bon would keep Victor for the night, instead of Tom, she said, amused, following the boys into the house, and Jim drove Tom, the dogs and myself back to Tom's house first, and then on to mine.

'I never thought we'd come back in one piece.' Tom left me with that bright thought and a positively jaunty wave, and I would have cast *him* as Black-mask Four if I hadn't twice owed him a rescue from crippling injury, and perhaps my life.

231

Catherine's motor cycle graced its customary spot outside the kitchen door, and she herself came out when she heard Jim's car arrive. There was no difficulty in interpreting her reaction to my return, and Jim drove away with a vast smile (and double cash), promising his service again, 'day or night'.

Coming home to Catherine had become an event to look forward to. I'd never asked her to take me to see her own living space, and when I did, that evening, she laughed and said, 'I'll take you there tomorrow. It's better by daylight.'

She asked me how my day had been, and I asked about hers. She frowned over Victor's troubles and was encouraging about a glass trophy horse. It was all very *married*, I thought, and we'd only known each other for three weeks.

'Tell me about the police,' I said, as we squashed companionably into one of the oversize chairs.

'What about them?' She was slightly defensive always about her job, but this time I especially wanted to know.

'The priorities,' I said. 'For instance, on that New Year's Day, you in your plainish clothes and the hobo lying on the doorstep, you were both there to frighten thieves off, weren't you, not to arrest them?'

She shifted in my arms. 'Not really,' she replied. 'We like to get our man.'

I knew better than to tease her. 'Tell me abour your partner, the hobo.'

'He's not really a hobo,' she replied smiling. 'His name is Paul Cratchet. He's a big guy but misleadingly gentle. Paul's a good detective. Many a villain has been surprised by his hand on their collar. He's known as Pernickety Paul at the station because he is so fussy over his reports.'

Smiling, I enquired plainly, 'What events get most police attention?'

'Accidental deaths, and murder, of course. Especially murder of a police officer. The murder of a fellow police officer, I'd say, gets people going most.'

'But after that?'

'Any physical assault.'

'Especially of a police officer?'

She twisted her neck and searched my purposefully straight face for levity. Satisfied, she nodded. 'Especially of a police officer.'

'And next?'

'Aggravated theft. That's when a weapon is used, or a severe physical threat, or violence as a means to achieve theft. It's called robbery.'

'And then?'

'Actually, and in general,' Catherine said, 'if someone's bleeding, then police officers will come at once. If goods are stolen, but no one's hurt, the officers will probably come in the morning after the 999 call. If cars are stolen, the police will take the registration number and promise to inform the owner if the car is found.'

'And that's that? That's all for cars?'

'More or less. It depends. They're usually found burnt out.'

'And who,' I asked mildly, 'would I go to if I found some stolen property?'

'Are you talking about those old videotapes again?'

'Yup. Those old tapes.'

'Well . . .' She let a good few seconds pass, then said, 'I did enquire about this . . .'

'It sounds bad news,' I said.

Catherine sighed. 'The tapes themselves are worth practically nothing. You said they hadn't even any covers. The information recorded on them, on both of them, even if they're totally different from each other, is called intellectual property. It has very little priority in police thinking. How to make a copy of an antique necklace? You must be joking! Industrial secrets, even medical secrets? Too bad. No one is going to waste much police time looking for them. There would be slightly more interest in your bag of cash, *if* you could identify a single note of it for sure. It would be much more likely, after three weeks, that it's been spent and dispersed. It was a fair amount to you personally, but not much in world terms, do you see?' She stopped as an entirely opposite thought struck her, then said, 'Does this dreadful Rose still believe you know where to find the tapes?'

'Don't worry about it.'

'But does she?' Catherine was insistent. 'Does she, Gerard?'

I told her, smiling, 'I now think she's had the necklace

tape almost from the beginning, and if she has, she knows I haven't got it.' And Rose knows, I thought, that I could repeat it any day.

'But the other one?' Catherine begged. 'The one stolen from the lab?'

'Yes.' I felt light-hearted. 'I could make a guess. Let's go to bed.'

I awoke first in the morning, and lay for a while watching Catherine's calm gentle breathing. At that moment, it filled me with total contentment . . . but would I feel the same in ten years? . . . and would she? When she stirred and opened her eyes and smiled, ten years didn't matter. One lived *now*, and now went along as a constant companion, present and changing minute by minute. It was *now*, always, that mattered.

'What are you thinking about?' she asked.

'Same as you, I dare say.'

She smiled again, and asked simply if I had plans for us both on her free Saturday? Relaxed, I offered the comfortable new chair in Logan Glass, and accepted a pillion ride to get there.

Hickory had again arrived before me and was again intent on a perfect sailing boat. He greeted me like the good friend of time gone by, tentatively asking if I could assist him, as he was finding it difficult on his own.

With uncomplicated pleasure I stripped down to a working singlet and helped Hickory, bringing a gather out of the tank when he needed it and holding the hot glass ready for his use. Hickory typically kept a running commentary for Catherine's sake and flirted with her mildly, and seldom, I thought, had I more enjoyed a frivolous start to the morning.

Hickory this time remembered to put the finished boat in the annealing oven, and if he accepted Catherine's unstinted praise with smugness, he had at least taken a satisfactory step forward in his training.

Irish arrived and brewed tea. Pamela Jane tidied and refilled the tubs of coloured powder that we would use during the session, to restock the shelves. The rest of the regular Saturday morning unwound in work from nine to twelve o'clock.

At a few minutes past noon, the shop embraced first Bon-Bon and the two boys, Daniel and Victor, for whom glass-blowing had temporarily become a greater draw than e-mail.

Not long after them, Marigold swooped in, batting the eyelashes, grinning at Hickory, smothering Daniel in a bright pink gold-smocked cloud-like dress and telling Bon-Bon at the top of her voice that 'Darling Trubby' would be with them right away.

'Darling Trubby', Kenneth Trubshaw, swam through the bright pink experience and emerged with lipstick on his cheek. The trophy chairman of Cheltenham races was carrying my book of photographs, and besides being apparently unnerved by the chattering din, he eyed my half-undress with a degree of disbelief and suggested that the Wychwood Dragon might be better for a business meeting.

'Darling Trubby, what a *great* idea!' Marigold's immediate enthusiasm resulted in herself, Kenneth Trubshaw,
Bon-Bon, Catherine, myself and, of course, Worthington
(Marigold insisted) occupying a quiet corner of the dining
room to listen to the opinions of that morning's meeting
of the Cheltenham Racecourse Company's trophy committee.

Irish was dispatched down the hill to fill the two boys
with hamburgers and Cokes, and Hickory and Pamela
Jane were left in peace to deal with that less demanding
breed, the January tourist.

When six of us were neatly seated and listening,
Kenneth Trubshaw began his spiel. 'First of all, dear
Marigold,' he said, 'everyone on the committee wants me
to thank you for your splendid generosity . . .' He gave
flattery a good name. Marigold glowed. Worthington
caught my eye and winked.

'The committee voted . . .' the chairman came at last
to the point. 'We decided unanimously to ask you, Gerard
Logan, to design and make a Martin Stukely memorial of
a horse rearing on a crystal ball, like the one in the book.
If it pleases Marigold and the committee – ' His final
words got temporarily lost in a bright pink Marigold hug,
but came out the other side with provisos about cost. To
Marigold, cost was a bore. Worthington bargained, and I
telephoned a jeweller who promised enough gold.

'Can you make it today, darling Gerard?' Marigold
enthused. 'It's barely three o'clock.'

'Tomorrow would be difficult,' I said, 'next week would

be better. Today, I'm sorry, is impossible.' Sooner rather than later, I thought, to keep Marigold happy.

The Marigold pout appeared, but I wasn't going to help it. I needed time for thinking if it were to be a good job; and a good job was what I needed to do for Bon-Bon, for Marigold, for Cheltenham racecourse and for Martin himself.

'I'll do them tomorrow,' I said. 'The crystal ball and the rearing horse. I'll do them on my own, alone except for one assistant. They will be ready on Monday for the gold to be added, and on Tuesday afternoon I'll join them together onto a plinth. By Wednesday the trophy will be finished.'

'Not until then?' Marigold protested, and urged me to think again.

'I want to get it right for you,' I said.

And also I wanted to give my enemies time.

CHAPTER ELEVEN

Marigold objected to my wanting no audience to the making of the rearing horse and the crystal ball. Kenneth Trubshaw understood, he said.

'Darling Trubby', substantial, grey-haired and very much a businessman, mentioned to me the one quiet word, 'Fees?'

'Worthington and I,' I said, 'will fix a price with Marigold, then you can haggle if you like.'

He shook my hand wryly. 'The Leicester Steward whose wife owns several of your things is also a Steward of Cheltenham, and he told our committee this morning that five years ago we could have bought this trophy for peanuts.'

'Five years ago,' I agreed, 'yes, you could.'

'And he said,' Trubshaw added, 'five years from now works by Gerard Logan will at least cost double again.'

Uncle Ron would have loved it. Well . . . so did I. It was surviving the next five *days* that caught my attention.

By mid-afternoon everyone had collected and split apart again. Bon-Bon and Marigold left the boys in my

care while they browsed the antique shops, and Worthington and Kenneth Trubshaw developed a strong mutual
regard in a stroll.

In the workshop, Victor, utterly impressed, watched
Hickory show off with two gathers of red-hot glass that
he rolled competently in white powder and then coloured
powder and tweaked into a small wavy-edged one-flower
vase. Pamela Jane expertly assisted in snapping the vase
off the punty iron and Hickory with false modesty lifted
it into an annealing oven as if it were the Holy Grail.

Daniel, for whom the workshop was a familiar stamping ground, mooned around looking at the shelves of
bright little animals, pointing out to me the scarlet giraffe
his father had promised him the day before he died. That
story was most unlikely, I thought, remembering Martin's
absent-mindedness towards all his children, but I gave
Daniel the giraffe anyway, a gift that would have dis-
pleased his grandmother.

Giving to Daniel, though, always reaped a worthwhile
crop. This time he wanted me to go outside with him and,
seeing the stretched size of his eyes, I went casually, but
at once.

'What is it?' I asked.

'There's a shoe shop down the road,' he said.

'Yes, I know.'

'Come and look.'

He set off, and I followed.

'Victor and I came down here with Irish, looking for

hamburgers,' he said, 'but we came to the shoe shop first.'

The shoe shop duly appeared on our left, a small affair mostly stocked with walking shoes for tourists. Daniel came to an abrupt halt by its uninspiring window.

'I should think it might be worth two gold coins,' he said.

'For two gold coins it had better be good.'

'See those trainers?' he said. 'Those up there at the back with green and white striped laces? The man with that gas, those are his laces.'

I stared disbelievingly at the shoes. They were large with thick rubber-like soles, triangular white-flashed canvas sections and, threaded in precision through two rows of eyeholes, the fat bunched laces of Daniel's certainty.

He said again, 'The man who gassed us wore those shoes.'

'Come into the shop, then,' I said, 'and we'll ask who bought some like them.'

He agreed. 'OK,' and then nodded, 'It might cost two more gold coins, to go into the shop.'

'You're an extortionist.'

'What's that?'

'Greedy. And I've no more coins.'

Daniel grinned and shrugged, accepting fate.

The shop had a doorbell that jingled when we went in, and contained a grandfatherly salesman who proved useless from our point of view as he was standing in for his daughter whose baby was sick. She might be back some day next week, he vaguely thought, and he knew nothing about previous sales.

When we went back into the street, Bon-Bon, further up the hill, was beckoning Daniel to her car, to go home. Only the fact that she had already loaded Victor, having offered him another night's computer hacking, persuaded her son to join her, and presently, when Marigold and 'Darling Trubby' had gone their separate ways, only Catherine and my little team were left, and those three, as it was Saturday afternoon, were setting things straight as if for a normal winter Sunday of no action. They departed with my blessing at four-thirty, leaving only myself and Catherine to lock up: and I gave her a bunch of keys for the future.

I also told police officer Dodd about the laces, which sent her on a brief reconnaissance only, as first of all she said she needed another officer with her if she were to question the shop owner, and second, the grandfather salesman had shut up shop and left it dark.

Catherine, like Martin before her, grew minute by minute more interested in the technical details and the chemical complexities of bright modern glass. Old glass could look grey or yellow, fine to my eyes but dingy on racecourses.

Catherine asked which I would make first, the horse or the ball, and I told her the horse. I asked her whether, even though they would not be on duty the next day, she could persuade her Pernickety Paul hobo partner to come and walk up and down Broadway with her a couple of times? She naturally asked why.

'To mind my back,' I joked, and she said she thought he might come if she asked him.

'He might be busy,' I said.

'I doubt it,' she replied. 'He seems rather lonely since his wife left him.'

We rode her motor bike to a hotel deep in the country and ate there and slept there: and I avoided Black-mask Four and explained to my increasingly loved police officer, before I kissed her, that she and the hobo might find handcuffs a good idea on the morrow. 'He always carries them,' Catherine said.

In the morning she said, 'All this walking up and down Broadway . . . is it because of the tapes?'

'Sort of.' I nodded. I didn't mention life or death. One couldn't somehow.

All the same, I woke Tom Pigeon, who woke his dogs, who all growled (Tom included) that Sunday was a day of rest.

I phoned Jim. At my service all day, he said. His wife was going to church.

Worthington was already awake, he said, and had I noticed that Sundays weren't always healthy for Gerard Logan?

'Mm. What's Marigold doing today?'

'I've got the day free, if that's what you're asking.

Where do you want me to turn up when? And most of all, why?'

I hesitated over the last answer but replied in order: 'Wychwood Dragon lobby, soon as possible, on account of fear.'

'Whose fear?'

'Mine.'

'Oh yeah?' His laugh travelled with bass reverberation. 'You'll be alone in that workshop of yours, is that it? In that case, I'll be with you soon.'

'I won't exactly be alone. Catherine and her partner officer will probably be in the town, and in the workshop there will be Pamela Jane, who's going to assist.'

'The girl? Why not that bright young man, what's his name . . . Hickory?'

'Pamela Jane doesn't argue.'

Worthington's deep voice arrived as a chuckle. 'I'm on my way.'

I made one more phone call, this time to the home of George Lawson-Young, apologizing for the eight-thirty wake-up.

'The hour doesn't matter,' he yawned, 'if you bring good news.'

'It depends,' I said, and told him what he might expect.

He said, 'Well done.'

'More to do.'

'I wouldn't miss it.' His smile came across the air. 'I'll see you later.'

Catherine and her motor cycle took me to Logan Glass,

where local inhabitants could have seen a display of affection to wag tongues for a week. I unlocked the doors, being there intentionally before Pamela Jane, and again read the notes I'd made (and filed in the locked bookcase) last time I'd tried my hand at a rearing horse.

This one would take me about an hour to complete, if I made the whole trophy, including plinth and ball. At a little less than half a metre high it would weigh roughly twenty kilos; heavy because solid glass itself weighed a good deal, let alone the added gold. Marigold had, with wide-sweeping arms, insisted on magnificence. It was to be Martin's memorial, she proclaimed, and she had been exceedingly fond of her son-in-law. Both Bon-Bon and Worthington thought this much-to-be-publicized admiration a little retrospective, but 'Darling Trubby' might think the trophy handsome in the sun.

I had filled the tank with clear crystal and put ready to hand the punty irons I'd need, also the small tools for shaping muscles, legs and head. Tweezers, too, essential always. I set the furnace temperature to the necessary 1,800 degrees Fahrenheit.

By then I 'saw' the sculpture complete. A pity they hadn't wanted Martin himself on the rearing horse's back. I saw him there clearly now, at last. Perhaps I would repeat the horse with Martin riding. Perhaps one night . . . for Bon-Bon, and for the friend I'd lost and still trusted.

While I waited for Pamela Jane to arrive, I thought about the wandering videotape that had raised so many savage feelings and, like curtains parting, the deductive faculty Professor Lawson-Young had put his faith in continued to open vistas in my mind. I had at last added in his factor x, and the mask had dropped from Black-mask Four.

Out of doors it started raining.

I stood looking at the furnace and listening to its heart of flame, looking at the raisable trap-door that kept 1,800 degrees Fahrenheit at bay. Irish, Hickory, Pamela Jane and myself were so accustomed to the danger of the extreme heat roaring within the fire-bricks that taking care was automatic; was second nature.

I knew at last the sequence of the roads in the cul-de-sacs. I listened in my mind to Catherine's list of punish-able crimes and their penalties, and reckoned that Rose and Adam Force should, if they had any sense at all, just leave the videotapes where they rested and save them-selves the grief of prosecution.

Thieves never had any sense.

I'd surrounded myself with as many bodyguards as I could muster that Sunday simply because neither Rose nor Adam Force had shown any sense or restraint so far, and because the making of the trophy horse left me wide open to any mayhem they might invent. I could have filled the workshop with a crowd of onlookers and been safe . . . safe for how long?

I knew now where the danger lay. I couldn't for ever look over my shoulder fearfully and, however rash it might seem, I saw a confrontation as the quickest path to resolution.

If I were disastrously wrong, Professor Lawson-Young could say goodbye to his millions. The breakthrough that would save the world in the cure for cancer would be published under someone else's name.

When my enemies came, I found it wasn't just time I had given them as much as an opportunity to out-think me.

I was still listening to the furnace when sounds behind me announced the arrival of Pamela Jane. She had entered through the side door, though usually she came in through the front.

'Mr Logan . . .' Her voice quavered high with fright, and besides, she normally called me Gerard.

I turned at once to see how bad things were, and found that in many unforeseen ways they were extremely bad indeed.

Pamela Jane, dressed for work in her usual white overalls cinched around the waist, was coming to a standstill in the centre of the workshop, trembling from a situation far beyond her capabilities. Her raincoat lay dropped in a bundle on the floor and her wrists were fastened together in front of her by sticky brown packing tape. Simpler and cheaper than handcuffs, the tape was equally immobilizing, and more effective still in Pamela Jane's case as the charming Adam Force held a full syringe in one hand and, with the other, had dragged down a clutch of female overalls to reveal a patch of bare skin inches from the needle. Thin and frightened, she began to cry.

A step or two behind Pamela Jane came Rose, every muscle triumphant, her whole face a sneer. She too came quietly, in soft shoes, and fast.

Rose, strong, determined and full of spite aimed powerfully my way, held in a pincer grip the upper arm of Hickory. My bright assistant stood helplessly swaying, his eyes and his mouth stuck out of action by strips of brown packing tape. The same tape had been used to bind his hands behind his back and also to form a makeshift hobble between his ankles.

Roughly steadying Hickory's balance loomed the bookmaker Norman Osprey, more bully beef than beauty, but arithmetically as fast as a computer chip. Just inside the side door, keeping guard and shifting uncomfortably from foot to foot was, of all people, Eddie Payne. He wouldn't meet my eyes. He took instructions steadfastly from Rose.

The actions of all four intruders had been whirlwind fast, and I had arranged little in any way of retaliation. All my bodyguards were simply to roam the street outside. Catherine and her hobo were to patrol their normal disjoined beat. Rose and her cohorts had somehow slid past them in the rain.

I was wearing, as usual, a white singlet which left my arms, neck and much of my shoulder area bare. The heat from the furnace roared almost unbearably beyond the trapdoor, if one weren't used to it. I put my foot and my weight sideways on the treadle, which duly opened the trap and let a huge gust of Sahara heat blow out over Norman Osprey's wool suit and reddening face. Furious, he made a snatch towards me, hurling me onto the trapdoor itself, but I side-stepped and tripped him, and unbalanced him onto his knees.

Rose yelled to Norman, 'Stop it, you stupid asshole, we don't want him damaged this time. You know bloody well we'll get nowhere if he can't talk.'

I watched as Rose tugged my blindfolded assistant across a good length of floor, with Norman Osprey holding him upright in a fierce grip. Hickory stumbled and fell tentatively forwards step by step until he reached the chair I'd bought for Catherine. At that point Rose revolved Hickory roughly until he fell into the chair on his side and had to struggle to turn and sit upright.

Behind me now I could hear the distressed breathing of Pamela Jane, and also the unmistakable heavy wheeze of Adam Force's asthma. He said nothing at all about his near miss with insulin at Bristol. He definitely needed an inhaler but had no free hands.

Rose said to Hickory with malignant satisfaction, 'Now you sit there, buddy boy, and it will teach you not to put your nose in where it isn't wanted.' She redirected the pleased venom back my way while Hickory tried hard to talk but produced only a throttled tenor protest.

'Now you,' she told me, 'will hand over everything I want. Or your friend here will get holes burned in him.'

Pamela Jane cried out, 'Oh no, you *can't*!'

'You shut up, you silly little bitch,' Rose acidly told her, 'or I'll spoil your soppy looks instead.'

Whether or not he was aware of Rose's speed in standing on the treadle part of the floor that raised the flap of the furnace, Hickory was unable to protest more vigorously than to shrink ever deeper into the chair. He did understand, though, the diabolical choice she was thrusting under my nose.

As if she could read his mind, she said in the same sharp tone, 'You, what's your name, Hickory? You'd better pray that this boss of yours won't let you burn. Because I'm not fooling: this time he's going to give me what I want.'

She picked up one of the long punty irons and pushed it into the tank of molten glass. Her movement was ungraceful rather than smooth with constant practice, but somewhere, sometime, she had watched a glass-blower collect a gather from a tank. She withdrew the iron with a small blob of red-hot glass on the end of it, and revolved the rod so that the glass stayed adhered to it and didn't fall off.

Pamela Jane moaned at the sight and all but fell onto the doctor's needle.

'Gerard Logan,' Rose said to me with emphasis. 'This time you will do what I tell you, now, at once.'

Extraordinarily, she sounded less sure of herself than screaming 'Break his wrists' into the Broadway night, and I remembered Worthington's judgement that as I would beat her at the tennis match of life, so she would never again face me on the actual court. Yet here she was, visibly pulling together the sinews and nerves of resolution.

I'd seen Martin summon his mental vigour when going out to race on a difficult horse, and I'd seen actors breathe deeply in the wings when the play ahead dug deep into the psyche. I understood a good deal about courage in others and about the deficiencies in myself, but on that Sunday in January it was Rose's own mushrooming determination that pumped up in me the inner resources I needed.

I watched her as she in turn watched me, and it wasn't what she said that mattered at all, it was which of us would win the desperate battle for pride.

She plunged the small, cooling ball of glass into the tank again and drew it out, larger. She swung the iron round until the molten red-hot lump and advanced it to a too-close spot under Hickory's chin. He could feel the heat. He shrank frantically away and tried to scream behind the adhering tape.

'Look out, for God's sake,' I shouted automatically and, as if surprised, Rose swung the iron away from Hickory's face until he wasn't for the minute threatened.

'You see!' Rose sounded all of a sudden victorious. 'If you don't like him burned you'll tell me where you've hidden the videotapes I want.'

I said urgently, 'You'll disfigure Hickory if you're not careful. Glass burns are terrible. You can get a hand burned so badly that it needs amputating. An arm, a foot

251

... you can smell flesh burning ... you can lose your mouth, your nose.'

'Shut up,' Rose yelled, and again, at the top of her voice, 'Shut up!'

'You can burn out an eye,' I said, 'you can sear and cauterize your guts.'

Pamela Jane, who lived with the danger, was affected least of all in spite of her fluttery manner, and it was big Norman Osprey of the great muscular shoulders who sweated and looked ready to vomit.

Rose looked at her red-hot iron. She looked at Hickory and she glanced at me. I could more or less read her rapid mind. She had come to threaten me through my regard for Hickory and now here I was, a target again myself.

Beside Rose's powerful identity her companions' egos were pale. Even Adam Force's good looks and persuasive smile faded to second rate in her presence and I began to realize fully that her reputation in inspiring real abject terror, in men particularly, was in no way a myth. I felt the fringes myself, try though I might to counteract it. Her effect on her father sent him to the confessional at the best of times, and this being Sunday again I could barely imagine the turmoil churning in his good Catholic conscience.

To Norman Osprey no doubt one day was as good or bad as the next. His days were judged by the amount of muscle needed to achieve his own way, coupled with the fizzing ability to add, divide or multiply as if by instinct.

Adam Force's finger seemed to itch on the plunger set to activate the syringe's undisclosed contents. I wished to heaven that poor Pamela Jane would sniff back the tears and swallow the sobs, both of which seemed increasingly to irritate Dr White-Beard, and as for Hickory, stuck with wide brown bands into silence and sightlessness, and deep in the soft armchair, I thought he would be staying exactly where Rose had put him until someone pulled him out.

Impressions flashed and passed. Rose stared at me with calculation, enjoying her certainty that she would defeat me pretty soon. I couldn't swear she wouldn't. This time there were no black masks or baseball bats. But to be faced bare-armed with molten glass was worse.

Suddenly and unexpectedly Rose said, 'You came here this morning to make a trophy horse of glass and gold. I want the gold.'

Wow! I thought. No one had brought gold into the equation before. Gold for the trophy hadn't been mentioned in Rose's hearing as far as I knew. I had ordered enough for the trophy, and a little over for stock, but a quantity worth holding up the stage-coach for, it was not.

Someone had misled Rose, or she had misunderstood, and her acquisitive imagination had done the rest.

Rose was still sure that, one way or another, I could make her rich.

Adam Force was admiring her with a smile and applauding her with his eyes.

If I could use this, well . . . *golden* . . . opportunity, I could but try . . . I did need time now, and if I made the trophy horse I could slow things nicely.

I said, 'The gold isn't here yet. I'm fed up with the delay.' The carefree but complaining tone I used non-plussed Rose into lowering the tip of the punty iron for the moment.

'If I don't get the glass-horse trophy ready on time,' I said, 'the one that's ordered, that is, well . . .' I stopped abruptly, as if I'd teetered on the brink of a monster mistake. 'Never mind,' I said as if nervously, and Rose demanded I finish the sentence.

'Well . . .' I said.

'Get on with it.'

'Gold . . .' I said. 'I have to use it on the horse.'

Pamela Jane, to her eternal credit, dried her tears in mid-sniffle and in horrified disgust told me frankly across the workroom that I should be thinking of freeing Hickory, not making a trophy for Cheltenham races.

'How can you?' she exclaimed. 'It's *despicable*.'

'A car from the jewellers is bringing the gold for the hooves, mane and tail,' I said.

Rose wavered, and then demanded, 'When?'

I said I wouldn't tell her.

'Yes, you will,' she said, and advanced the hot iron in menace.

'Eleven o'clock,' I said hastily. A good lie. 'Let me make the horse,' I suggested, and made it sound on the verge of pleading. 'Then, when I've made the horse, I'll tell you where to look where I think the tape might be, and then you must promise to set Hickory free as soon as you have the gold.'

Pamela Jane said helplessly, 'I don't believe this.'

She couldn't understand how easily I had crumbled. She couldn't see that her scorn was the measure of my success.

Rose looked at her watch, discovered she would have to wait an hour for the gold to arrive and did the unwise calculation that she could afford to wait for it.

'Get on and make the trophy,' she instructed. 'When the gold comes, you'll sign for it in the normal way, or your Hickory's for the slow burn, understand?'

I nodded.

'Get on with it, then.' She looked round the workshop, assessing the state of things, and told Pamela Jane to sit deep in the other soft chair. There, while Adam Force held his threatening needle at her neck, Norman Osprey taped her ankles together.

Pamela Jane glared at me and said she wouldn't be assisting me with the horse, or ever again.

Rose consolidated this decision by telling her I'd always been a coward. I looked expressionlessly at Pamela Jane and saw the shade of doubt creep in, even while she listened to Rose pour on the disdain.

I hadn't meant to shape the trophy horse under the threat of Rose's hand on the punty irons. I had in fact mobilized the bodyguards to prevent it, and they hadn't. On the other hand a confrontation with Rose some day had been inevitable, and if it were to be *now* then I'd need to think a bit faster. I stood flat-footed, without drive.

Rose taunted, 'I thought you were supposed to be good at glass.'

'Too many people,' I complained.

She peremptorily ordered Norman Osprey and Eddie Payne to go round the half-wall into the showroom, and with more politeness shifted Adam Force round after them. All three leaned on the half-wall, watching. Having pulled out one of the punty irons that I'd put to heat beside the active part of the furnace, Rose thrust it into the crucible – the tank – holding now white-hot glass, and drew it out, a reasonably sized gather, revolving it just speedily enough for it not to fall off onto the floor.

'Go on,' she said. She shoved her lump of burning devastation towards my right arm and I retreated far enough for it not to char my skin.

It was no way to make a trophy of any sort. I needed to start the horse's body with several gathers of clear crystal and Rose, with irons loaded with plum-sized tips that would destroy whatever they touched, hovered over Hickory's and Pamela Jane's heads and threatened to melt off their ears, to make their roasting flesh smell like meat cooking if I gave her the slightest cause. I was to tell her all the time what I proposed to do next. There were to be no sudden unforeseen moves on my part. Hickory and Pamela Jane would suffer. Did I understand? Rose demanded.

I did.

I understood. So did Pamela Jane, and so did Hickory, who could hear.

I told Rose I would need to take four or five gathers from the tank, and while she had her own lump of destruction close to Pamela Jane's ear I harvested enough glass to make a horse standing on his hind legs a third of a metre high.

Pamela Jane closed her eyes.

I told Rose in advance that it was almost, if not totally impossible, to make a horse of that size without an assistant, which was partly because the body of the horse had to be kept at working heat after one had sculpted the muscles of the neck and the upper legs while one added two pieces of glass for each lower leg and foot, and others for the tail.

'Get on with it and don't whinge,' she said. She was smiling to herself.

People in circuses could keep a dozen plates spinning in the air by twiddling sticks under them. Making that rearing horse in Broadway felt much the same: keep the body and legs hot while you sculpted the head. The resulting head wouldn't have won in a pre-school contest.

Rose was enjoying herself. The less I blocked and opposed her the more certain she grew that I was on the way to capitulation. She liked it. She smiled again, a secretive dirty-little-girl underhand twist of the lips.

I looked at that smile and abruptly I personally understood what Worthington had described. Victory for Rose was never complete without the physical humiliation of a male adversary.

Victory over Gerard Logan, which Rose now saw as gloriously her own, wouldn't be sufficient for her in that place unless it included her inflicting some depth of burn.

I might shudder at such a prospect but Rose wouldn't. I might use plain muscle power in an all-out attempt to defeat her, but I wouldn't try to wreak havoc of molten glass on Rose. Nor on anybody. I lacked the brutality.

Neither, though, could I desert my team and run.

With tweezers I pulled the horse's front legs up and its rear legs down and held the whole body on an iron within the furnace to keep it hot enough to mould.

There were still things I could do, I thought.

Honourable exits.

Exits that were more or less honourable, anyway.

I managed to juggle body and leg pieces into a headless racer.

Exits, hell, I thought. Exit wasn't enough. Defeatism never got anyone anywhere.

I held two punty irons with difficulty and transferred enough glass from one to the other to attach and shape a mane, but it hadn't the elegance necessary for Cheltenham.

Worthington opened the gallery door and began to come in from the street. His eyes widened as fast as his comprehension as he spun a fast one-eighty degree turn and was on his way down the hill before Rose could decide which had priority, chasing Worthington or keeping me penned.

When Worthington was out of anything but whistling distance she told Force and her father to lock the gallery door immediately and was furious because neither of them could find a key. I hoped to hell and back that Pamela Jane wouldn't report obligingly that she herself had a key to everywhere.

She gave me another uncertain stare and shut her teeth.

Rose stopped smiling, loaded her punty iron with a white hot golf-ball sized end of glass and held it close to Hickory.

I did my best to make and fix a tail to my increasingly non-thoroughbred creation. The tail and two hind feet formed a triangle to support the rearing horse. When I wanted a great result, this stage often went wrong. That day it all balanced like perfection.

Hickory wriggled desperately to get away from Rose's white-hot threat.

Pamela Jane saw me doing nothing to help Hickory while constructing only a toy, and went back to despising me.

I stuck the head on the neck and tweaked the ears forward. Finished, the object had four legs, head, mane and tail, and no grace whatever. I stood it upright on the marver table, where rearing, it was ready to start leaping into the future from a crystal ball.

In spite of the faults, Rose seemed impressed. Not

impressed enough, however, to lower her guard, or her punty iron beside Hickory's head.

I glanced at the workshop clock.

A minute – tick tock, tick tock – was a very long time.

I said, 'The gold will cover the hooves and the mane and the tail.'

Tick tock, tick tock.

Rose thrust her cooling punty iron back into the furnace and brought out a new white-hot gather which she again held near Hickory's head.

'How long,' she demanded, 'until that gold gets here?'

Hickory wriggled violently, trying desperately to free himself from the sticky strips on his mouth and his eyes.

Pamela Jane, eyes closed, seemed to be praying.

Two minutes. Tick tock.

'The gold,' I said, 'will come in small bars. It has to be melted, then it has to cover the hooves and the mane and the tail . . .'

Hickory threw himself forward, trying to get out of his embracing chair. Rose didn't move her punty iron far enough away fast enough to avoid him, and one of his ears did touch her waving white-hot blob of glass.

Under the parcel tape, he couldn't scream. His body arched. Rose jumped back, but Hickory's ear sizzled and now smelled of fried meat, and would never be perfect again.

Three minutes. Eternity. Tick tock.

Hickory's horror, plain and agonizing, had everyone staring. Rose should have jettisoned her iron and gone to his help, but she didn't.

Three minutes, ten seconds since I stood the rearing horse on the marver table.

Dangerous to wait any longer.

I picked up the big tweezers I'd used to form the horse's mane, and with them tore the parcel tape securing Pamela Jane's ankles. I pulled her up by her still tied wrists, and Rose turned towards me from Hickory and yelled at me to leave her alone.

Pamela Jane had no idea what she should do, and to dither could be fatal. I said to her urgently, '*Run*' and she didn't, but hesitated, looking back to Hickory. No time left. I lifted her up bodily and carried her.

Pamela Jane objected. Rose ordered me to put her down. I didn't, but aimed a bit unsteadily for the way into the showroom and shouted at the trio there leaning on the half-wall to get down behind it.

Rose came fast across the workshop after me, and drove at me, holding her hot glass-laden punty iron like a sword.

Half seeing her, half sensing the searing future, I twisted both myself and Pamela Jane roughly to let the iron miss us, like a bullfighter, but Rose in her fury dragged and stabbed and burned a long black slit through my white singlet.

No more time.

I lugged Pamela Jane round the half-wall to the show-room and threw her, screaming protests, to the ground, and I fell on top of her to pin her down.

The rearing horse had stood unannealed at maximum heat on the marver table for three minutes forty seconds when it exploded.

CHAPTER TWELVE

The horse exploded into scorching fragments that flew like angry transparent wasps throughout the workshop and over the half-wall into the showroom beyond.

Adam Force, refusing to get down because it had been I who suggested it, had been hit twice, once in the upper arm, and once, more seriously, across the top of the cheekbone below the eye, taking away a chunk of surface flesh. Half fainting from shock, the doctor dropped his syringe. Blood reddened his sleeve, but there was no spurting arterial flood.

It was the wreck of his good looks though, I thought, that would in the end grieve him most, and if he had peered into a looking glass at that moment, he would probably have collapsed altogether. The speed and sharpness of the flying glass fragment had opened a furrow that was bound to leave an untreatable scar, and like many facial cuts this one was bleeding copiously. Adam Force bled into his white beard, which was fast turning red.

Dr Bright-Scarlet-Beard Force. Serve him right, I

thought. A pity it would wash clean. Wash clean ... other things would wash out, too ... an idea.

Glass cooled rapidly if it expanded and thinned. One could gently blow down an iron into semi-liquid glass so that it would expand until it looked like a soap bubble: a dollop of red-hot glass would cool to the cold shell of a brittle bubble in the few seconds it took to blow it from one state to the other.

The trophy horse though, hadn't been blown on purpose from the inside. It had split violently apart along the internal stress lines caused by the pulling and stretching as the glass cooled, the outer regions cooling faster than the inner core. The splinters had still been fiercely hot when they'd dug into the first thing they met. Adam Force had been lucky not to lose an eye.

Norman Osprey, kneeling in spite of his antipathy towards the source of good advice, had survived the shattering of the horse with his skin intact, if not his temper.

Although pale and slightly shaking, the Elvis lookalike still clung to the doctrine of 'get Logan'. In consequence he'd risen from his knees and planted his gorilla shoulders close inside the gallery-to-street door, making an exit that way a matter of hand to hand fighting and a toss up whether I won or lost. A hand-to-hand fight against that visibly dramatic strength would have been daunting always but in my tottery state at that moment, even if I'd wanted to quit the scene, which I didn't, a win would have been impossible. As long as Norman Osprey thought he was usefully stationed where he was doing me no good, however, I could count him one less trouble to deal with, and be grateful.

Eddie, who seemed not to understand what had happened, was still on his knees beside the wall. Martin's valet who, with his stubborn misconceptions, had accompanied Rose on this whole unholy tape-hunt, now looked as though he were begging absolution. To my mind he certainly failed to deserve it.

Pamela Jane heaved herself from under me in a troubled dilemma as she couldn't decide whether to thank me for saving her from razor-sharp damage since, in the chair, she'd been in a direct line to be peppered, or to revile me for leaving Hickory to take whatever came his way in the blast.

Pamela Jane, of course, had understood the physics of stress and strain in super-heated glass, and she would now be sure I'd intended to shatter the horse from the moment I'd started to make it. She would be puzzling over the nonsense of the gold delivery, both the amount and the timing because, as she confessed to me much later, it had all been so *unlike* me. She had believed every word I'd said to Rose, and now she felt a fool. 'Dear Pam J,' I contentedly said, 'you were sincerely a great help.'

That was afterwards. At the time, during the immediate aftermath of the destruction of the trophy horse, she still worried over the outcome for Hickory.

When I stood up and looked over the half-wall to see what shape Rose and Hickory were in, I found Rose bleeding down one leg but still shaking with determined fury while she shoved a clean punty iron into the tank and drew out a second one already tipped with white-hot hate.

Hickory, who had finally succeeded in flinging himself out of the chair altogether, lay face down on the smooth brick floor trying to rub the adhesive off his mouth. Tears from the pain of his damaged ear seemed to be running helplessly down inside his nose, and he was trying to deal with that by sniffing.

Sharply aware that at some point somewhere Rose had succeeded in drawing a line of fire across my own lower back ribs, I felt I'd already had enough for one morning of the unequal combat.

Rose hadn't. Rose, it seemed, had energy in stock for a third world war. As she drew her loaded iron with speed from the fire, she told me that if I didn't get back at once into the workshop the burn to Hickory's ear would be only the beginning. She could have freed him. She could at least have helped him, but she didn't.

I went round the half-wall. Hickory still lay face down on the floor, but instead of rubbing his face raw without results, he was now threshing his legs instead. Hurting and helpless, he was in no immediate danger from Rose who chose to advance on me, holding the silvery black five-foot long punty iron loaded ready to strike if I didn't dodge fast enough.

'Adam Force's videotape,' she demanded. 'Where is it?'

Short of breath from evading deep burns so long, I

managed dry-mouthed to reply, 'He said he'd re-recorded it with horse races.'

'Rubbish.' Rose advanced towards me with the white-hot ball of glass inexorably leading the way. Had we been armed the other way round I could with two cuts of heavy scissors have sliced the ball into a pointed spear. The spear, if one thrust it fiercely, would burn a path right through a body, searing, cauterizing and killing. Rose had no spear but a ball was bad enough. Its effect would be the same.

With at least some sort of plan I backed away from Rose and her deadly fire, cursing that I couldn't reach the five or six punty irons lying idle to one side – irons I could at least have used to fence with – because Hickory with his shocking wound lay suffering in my way.

Rose began again to enjoy compelling me to retreat step by backward step. Backwards past the furnace, its trapdoor shut. Backwards across the workshop, faster as she increased her pace.

'The videotape,' she repeated. 'Where is it?'

At last, *at last*, I saw Worthington again outside the gallery door, Worthington this time flanked by Tom Pigeon, Jim, Catherine and her hobo partner, Pernickety Paul.

Norman Osprey, suddenly not liking the odds, stood back to let them in and dived fast round them out into the street. I had a last glimpse of him as he set off down the hill with Tom and his three four-legged companions in pursuit.

The two plain-clothes officers, with Worthington and Jim, filled the doorway he'd left. Furiously seeing the advent of my friends as her last chance to make me remember her for life, Rose rushed recklessly at my abdomen. I side-stepped and dodged yet again and ran and swerved, and ended where I'd aimed for, beside the wide round pots of coloured powders on the stock shelves.

It was the white colour I wanted, the dust the Germans called *emaill weiss*. I snatched off the lid and plunged my hand into the open pot, grabbed as much dust as I could in one handful and threw it at Rose's eyes.

Emaill weiss – white enamel ground to dust – contained arsenic . . . and arsenic dust made eyes blur and water and go temporarily and effectively blind. Rose, her eyes streaming, her sight gone, went on sweeping around with her petrifying length of death-bearing punty iron.

Eddie seemingly rose from his prayers and walked around the half-wall pleading with her to be still. 'Rose, dear girl, it's over . . .'

But nothing would stop her. Blinded for a while she might be, but she lashed out with the killing iron at where she'd last seen me, trying still to penetrate my stomach or chest, then wildly slashing at where my head had been.

Missing me didn't stop her being more dangerous blundering about than if she could see me and finally, disastrously, the unimaginably hot glass connected twice with living flesh.

There were screams chokingly cut off.

It was Eddie, her father, that incredibly she had hit first. She had seared the skin from his fingers as he had held them in front of his face to defend himself. There were crashes of iron against walls and a fearful soft sizzling as the worst of all calamities happened.

Pamela Jane hysterically threw herself into my arms and hid her face, but it wasn't she who had burned. From across the workshop, where the air again smelled of funeral pyre, Paul folded to the ground and lay motionless, his limbs sprawling in the haphazardness of death.

Catherine in a state of shock and anger stared hollow-eyed in disbelief. I stretched an arm towards her and hugged both girls as if I could never let them go.

Adam Force came to stand against the safe side of the workshop wall and begged Rose to stand still and let someone – like himself – come to help her and her father, with the only result that she changed direction towards his voice, lashing through the air in great sweeps of the punty iron.

Catherine, a police officer to the bone, stiffened after her first need for comfort and, with Rose following the sound of her voice, walked away from me and called her station urgently for back-up. Stifling human terror she spoke tightly on her personal radio, pushing the transit button, 'Officer down,' she said. 'Red call. Red call. Officer in need of immediate assistance.'

She reported the address of Logan Glass, and then and with less formality, and genuine, extreme emotion, added, 'Come at once. Dear God.'

She dodged Rose's rushing speed and with incredible bravery knelt down beside her silent hobo partner. The plain-clothes inhabitant of doorways, whose name to me had never been more than 'Pernickety Paul', would catch no more villains. Pernickety Paul had taken a long white-hot direct hit through his neck.

I disentangled myself from Pamela Jane and half ran across the room away from Catherine and called to Rose, 'I'm here, Rose. I'm over here and you'll never catch me.'

Rose turned half circle my way and pivoted once more when I jumped past her again and yelled at her. She turned again and again and finally began to tire enough with her blurring eyes for Worthington and Jim to reach my side and for Catherine to come up behind us, and for the four of us to grab Rose at high speed and immobilize her still slashing punty-iron arm. I wrestled the iron a good safe way away from her, feeling the heat of it near my legs, but not on my skin, and *still* she went on struggling in Worthington's and Jim's grasp.

The police side of Catherine flowed in her like a strong tide. She sought and found the handcuffs carried by Pernickety Paul on a belt round his waist. She clicked them roughly onto Rose's wrists behind her back, the metal bands squeezed tight against her skin.

Rose kicked.

'Take my belt,' Worthington shouted, and I unbuckled his pliable woven-leather belt and tied it round one ankle and knotted it to the other, until Rose overbalanced and lay on her side on the floor, still threshing her legs and cursing.

There was nothing about 'going quietly' in the arrest of Rose Payne. An ambulance with paramedics and two cars full of bristling young police officers drew up outside the gallery and filled Logan Glass, crunching the fragments of the shattered horse to dust under their heavy boots. They talked with Catherine and fetched a blanket in which they rolled Rose like a baby in swaddling clothes and, with her struggling to the end, manhandled her out through the showroom and gallery door and shoved her into the back of one of the police cars.

Spitting fury, Rose was soon joined there by the burly Norman Osprey whose muscles had been no match for three sets of canine fangs. Tom told me later that the big man had sat in the road quivering with fear, his head and hands between his legs, begging for the police to rescue him from the black snarls circling around him.

In the workshop I watched as Catherine, dry eyed, brought another blanket in from a police car to cover the silence of Paul.

More police arrived, some in uniform and others in plain clothes more suitable for a Sunday in front of the television than a trip to a fiery hell on earth. Off duty or not, some things demanded attendance. White overalls and grey plastic shoe covers were produced and soon the workshop took on the look of unreal science fiction.

I watched a policeman wearing surgical rubber gloves carefully lift the fallen syringe and place it gingerly in a clear plastic bag which he sealed.

Methodically the police began to sort and list names, and it was the Dragon across the road who offered solace and recovery with a warm heart. One of the police officers removed the tape from Pamela Jane's wrists, took her personal details, and then with a solicitous arm helped her to the hotel.

I knelt beside Hickory. I told him I was going to remove the sticky strips from his eyes and mouth. I asked him if he understood.

Hickory nodded and stopped struggling against the floor.

As humanely as possible I pulled the tape from his eyes. It came off painfully with eyelashes attached and it was several minutes before his long obstructed sight cleared and he was staring straight at me beside him.

'I'm going to take the tape off your mouth,' I said.

He nodded.

One of the young police officers stretched a hand down over my shoulder and with a lack of sensitivity simply ripped the strong tape off. Hickory yelled and went on yelling, telling the police officer to free his taped-together hands, and to hurry up.

I left them for a moment and brought the first-aid box from the stock shelves to put a dressing on Hickory's ear, and after a good deal of chat, the paramedics and the police decided together that he should go to hospital along with Eddie who was now deep in shock with hands that had already blistered badly.

Catherine stood by the ambulance's open door watching Eddie being helped aboard for treatment.

I told her other things she ought to know, extra things about Black-mask Four that had come to me during the night, that I hadn't mentioned in the dawn.

She said thoughtfully, 'Our superintendent is that man standing beside Paul. You'd better talk to him. I have to go to the station. I'll come back here when I can.'

She took me across the room, introduced me as the owner of the place and left me to deepen the frown of the top brass.

I shook hands with Superintendent Shepherd of the West Mercia police.

First of all he looked with disenchantment at my singlet, now no longer white and clean but grubby from constant contact with workshop clutter. He took in the singed piece of cloth hanging loose in the lower ribs area where Rose's relentless attentions had connected. He asked if the reddened skin beneath was painful and I tiredly said yes, it was, but I'd had worse burns in the past and would prefer to ignore it: but, I added to myself, the burns had always before been accidentally self-inflicted.

I looked down at the blanket over Pernickety Paul, the fuss-pot who had cared like a father for Catherine's safety in the violent streets.

'He was a good policeman,' I said.

The superintendent let a small silence ride by before mentioning come-uppance for the perpetrator. He would need me to proceed to the police station to make a statement which would be videotaped and in every way recorded. Judiciously he agreed I could cover the burns with dressings and restore my shirt on top, and then, reluctantly, he also agreed I could hang my coat over my shoulders so as not to freeze out of doors.

During this display of humanity George Lawson-Young arrived, and with his presence, transformed the general police atmosphere from suspicion to common sense. He was the sort of deeply respected man that other men in authority instinctively trusted. When he greeted and treated me with noticeably high levels of deference, my standing with the super took a slow drift upwards. I thought he went so far after a while as to believe what I said.

George Lawson-Young asked me as if expecting the answer 'Yes', 'Did you work out the identity of the fourth man who assaulted you outside here on the pavement two weeks ago?'

'Yes.'

He knew that answer in advance as I had told him that morning on the telephone. I had used his search-and-discard method to sort out truth from lies, and to go carefully down the cul-de-sacs, but however flatly I said the name, it would cause consternation.

The professor, tall, tidy and short-sighted, made a slow visual inspection of the damage to the most familiar of faces turned his way. No one tried to hurry him, not even the superintendent.

Adam Force, his facial bleeding down from Niagara to a trickle, had wandered dizzily into the workshop from the showroom and was standing beside Hickory, looking down on him as, on his knees, Hickory cradled his mutilated ear.

When Adam Force saw the professor, he looked as if he would prefer to evaporate rather than be in the same room as his one-time boss, and George, usually the most forgiving of men, produced a thoroughly baleful glare with no pity component for his expert practitioner of treason.

One of the policemen in white overalls asked Dr Force his name and address while another took his photograph. The flash seemed to startle him and, with a blood red rivulet still meandering down his cheek into his beard, he looked far from the assured physician I had first met on the hill at Lynton.

A spent Force, I thought ironically.

The photographer moved on, snapping under the direction of the Scene Of Crime Officer. Nothing was to be missed. Pernickety Paul would have been proud.

It was George Lawson-Young, saying he was hoping I'd done enough for him for the next thousand years, who related to the superintendent step by step how the data stolen from his research laboratory had caused me so much pain and trouble.

Naming each person in turn to identify them for the policeman's sake, and referring back to me for confirmation when he needed it, George quietly threaded his way through the complexities of January 2000.

'Adam Force,' he said pointing at Doctor Bright-Scarlet-Beard, 'worked for me but jumped ship and stole the cancer research that just may be worth millions and would certainly be to the advantage of the whole world.'

I could see the superintendent begin to be sceptical but I nodded and he focused back on the professor.

'We knew,' George went on, 'that he had stolen the information, had transferred it to a videotape and had destroyed all other records of our research. Understandably, we searched everywhere for it, even engaging private investigators, after the police had shown little interest.'

Superintendent Shepherd flinched not at all but continued listening intently.

'All our searches were in vain. We did not expect him to have entrusted the tape to the safekeeping of a jockey. Dr Force had passed it to Martin Stukely but Stukely preferred to hand it on to his friend Gerard Logan here, away from the fingers of his own children. As perhaps you know, Martin Stukely was killed at Cheltenham races on New Year's Eve. But the tape had already begun its tortuous journey by then. Adam Force tried to steal it back. Tapes were stolen from here, from Gerard's home and from the home of Martin Stukely.'

'Were we informed of those thefts?' asked the police-man.

'Yes,' I replied, 'but the theft of a few videotapes for no apparent reason hardly brought the law out like today.'

'Hmm,' replied the superintendent, knowing it was true.

'One of your officers did come round here the following morning,' I said, 'but there was far more interest in the money stolen with the tape.'

'Did Dr Force steal the money as well?' asked the super, looking at Force.

'Yes,' I replied, 'but I think that was just an opportunist theft which he might have thought would somehow smoke-screen the removal of the tape.'

Dr Force listened impassionately, his bloodied face giving away nothing.

'Anyway,' went on the professor, who did not welcome the interruption, 'somehow all the thefts failed to get back the tape they wanted and Dr Force, with assistance from Rose Payne and others, has been trying here to coerce Mr Logan to reveal its whereabouts. But he tells me he hasn't got it.'

'And have you?' asked the voice of authority.

'No,' I replied, 'but I think I know who has.'

They all looked at me. Adam Force, Lawson-Young, the superintendent and even Hickory, who had been listening with his good ear, they all waited expectantly.

Into this tableau swept Marigold, floating in emerald

silk with gold tassels and brushing aside the young constable who tried to stand in her way. In her wake came Bon-Bon, Victor, Daniel and the other children like the tail of a kite.

Marigold demanded to see how her trophy was getting along but was brought up sharply by the sight of the blanket-covered form in the workshop and the mass of evidence gatherers crawling cautiously around it on their hands and knees. Bon-Bon, realizing the enormity of the situation, swept her brood back out of the door, leaving just her mother and Victor inside, both of them stock-still, transfixed, living through their eyes.

'Gerard, darling,' Marigold exclaimed, 'what *is* going on? And where is Worthington?'

'Marigold my dear,' I said wearily, 'there's been a disaster. Please go across the road to the hotel and wait for me there.'

She seemed not to hear, her eyes steadfastly on the blanket. 'Where is Worthington?' Her voice began to rise. 'Where's Worthington? Oh my God.'

I took her in my arms. 'Marigold, Marigold, he's all right. I promise. That's not Worthington.'

She sobbed on my shoulder near to collapse.

Victor turned to me and said, his voice barely more than a whisper, 'It's not a game any more, is it?'

The question needed no answer, and presently the young constable led him and Marigold across to the Wychwood Dragon.

'So who is Black-mask Four?' asked Lawson-Young into the silence when they had gone.

'Who?' said the superintendent. 'What are you talking about?'

The professor told him. 'Gerard was attacked by four people in black masks outside his shop here. Three of them were Rose Payne, her father Eddie Payne and Norman Osprey. Gerard told me earlier today that he had worked out the identity of the fourth, so,' he turned to me and said with faith, 'who is it and where is my research?'

'I don't think Black-mask Four has the tape,' I replied.

'What!' exclaimed the professor. His shoulders dropped, his expectations had been so high and he took it now that I was leading him only to another cul-de-sac, another dead-end.

I put him right, 'My fourth assailant, Black-mask Four, was just a hired help and I'm not sure he even knew exactly what he was looking for.' But he knew, I thought, how to inflict maximum damage to my wrists. 'He is, however, a dab hand with a baseball bat and anaesthetic gas.'

'Who is it, for God's sake?' The professor was finding it difficult to stifle his impatience, as was the superintendent, yet it wasn't the easiest disclosure I'd ever made. Still . . .

'Who was the fourth man, Hickory?' I asked.

Hickory looked up from where he was kneeling on the floor still holding a dressing to his ear.

'Why are you asking me?' he said.

'You bunched my fingers.'

'Of course I didn't.'

'I'm afraid you did,' I said. 'You held my hand against a wall ready for a baseball bat to smash my wrist.'

'You must be crazy. Why would I attack you? Why you of all people?'

It was a piercing question and one with a complex answer. He didn't answer it, but we both knew what he had intended.

'Did you do it for money?' I asked.

I suspected that it was for more convoluted reasons than that. Something to do with my ability with glass-blowing and his comparative lack of it. Envy was a strong emotion and, I reckoned, he wouldn't have needed a whole lot of persuasion to oppose me.

He still refused to admit it. 'You're crazy, you are,' he said getting to his feet and turning away as if looking for some quick escape.

'The green and white laces,' I said.

He stopped dead and turned back.

I went on, 'You wore them here the day Martin Stukely was killed, and you wore them again the following day when you stole the tapes from his house, the day you hit me with the orange cylinder. Martin's eldest son Daniel saw the laces and told the police about them.'

Hickory advanced a step or two, his ear clearly hurting. His poise cracked.

'You're so fucking clever,' he said. 'I wish we *had* broken your wrists.'

The superintendent stopped leaning on the half-wall and stood up straight.

But Hickory had only just started.

'You and your fancy ways and your condescending comments about my work. I hate you and this workshop. I'm a damn good glass-blower and I deserve more recognition.' He raised his chin and sneered.

'One day,' he went on, 'John Hickory will be a name worth knowing and people will smash Fucking Logan glass to get to mine.'

Such a shame, I thought. He really did have some talent but, I suspected, it would never be allowed to develop as it should. Arrogance and a belief in skills he didn't have would smother those he did.

'And Rose?' I asked.

'Stupid bitch,' he said holding his hand to his throbbing head, 'bloody mad she is. Tie you up, she said. Use you as a hostage, she said. Nothing about frying my effing ear. Hope she rots in hell.'

I hoped she'd rot on earth.

'She promised me my own place,' Hickory said. 'Claimed she'd close you down. Her and that stupid father of hers.' He began to realize the hole he was digging for himself. 'They put me up to it. It was their fault, not mine.'

He looked wretchedly at the rapt faces around him.

'It wasn't my fault. It was their idea.'

No one believed him. It had been Hickory who had reported all to Rose. Hickory had been the 'Binocs' in Broadway.

'So where is the tape?' asked George Lawson-Young.

'I don't know,' replied Hickory. 'Rose said that it must have been in Stukely's house or in Logan's but I've sat through hours of bloody horse racing and glass-blowing and I'm telling you, there was no tape of medical stuff.'

I believed him. Otherwise, I thought ruefully, I might have been saved a couple of beatings and Pernickety Paul would still be lying around in shop doorways.

A paramedic appeared and said that it was time to take Hickory to the hospital to dress his burn. The superintendent, roused into action, arrested Hickory, 'You do not have to say anything . . .'

'Too bloody late,' retorted Hickory, as he was led off to the ambulance by a white-overalled police officer and the paramedic.

The super turned his attention to Dr Red-Beard Force who had listened in silence throughout.

He said, his speech always in the pattern of officialese, 'Well, Dr Force, can you enlighten us as to the whereabouts of a videotape containing medical research results stolen from the professor here.'

Force said nothing. It seemed that he had at least learnt one lesson from our discussion under the fir trees in Lynton.

282

'Come on, Adam, tell us.' The professor, I saw, still had some vestige of friendship for the man before him dripping blood from his beard onto my smooth brick floor.

Force looked at him with disdain and kept silent.

In his turn, he too was arrested and taken away for wound-stitching and fingerprinting. 'You do not have to say anything . . .' So he didn't.

In time, the gallery, showroom and workshop began to clear. The coroner's representative arrived and supervised the relocation of Paul to the local morgue. The other officers stopped work to stand and watch the sorry procession of undertakers and their highly regarded and valued burden move through the gallery to the door. There were tears in my eyes as well as in theirs. He had been a good man as well as a good policeman.

A few more photographs were taken and a few more pieces of evidence were collected. Blue and white 'Do Not Cross' tape was strung about, doors were locked and guarded, and the professor and I were gently eased out to the street into the grey appropriate drizzle.

The superintendent again asked me to accompany him to the police station to make a full statement although, this time, there was more warmth in his manner. I agreed, but first, I asked, could we all go over to the Wychwood Dragon as I was thirsty and needed a jug of tea. I looked at my cheap watch. Amazingly it was still morning though it felt to me more as if teatime must have come and gone.

They were in the residents' downstairs sitting room. Bon-Bon and her four children sat tightly side by side on the wide sofa in descending height from the right. Coca-Colas had been bought and a line of empty bottles with straws sat on a coffee table. Marigold occupied a deep squashy armchair while Worthington perched on its arm by her side. The manner in which Marigold clung to Worthington's hand reminded me of his fly-trap warning. He didn't appear to protest.

The Dragon poured tea into large millennium souvenir mugs and told us that Pamela Jane, still badly shocked, had been given a pill by the police doctor and dispatched to bed upstairs.

Victor stood by the window unable to remove his eyes from Logan Glass opposite. I took my tea over and joined him.

Without turning his head, he said, 'I suppose my Aunt Rose will be inside for a long time?'

'Yes,' I said, 'a very long time.' For life, I thought, either in prison or a secure mental hospital. Police killers didn't get early parole.

He stood in silence a moment longer, then turned and looked me straight in the eye. 'Good,' he said, 'it might give me and Mum a chance.'

I turned and took Bon-Bon out into the hotel lobby. I

needed her to do me a favour. Certainly, she said, and trotted off to the telephone booth beneath the stairs.

I went back into the sitting room to finish my tea and soon after Bon-Bon returned with a smiling nod.

I thought about the events of the morning, and wondered if there had been another way.

Punty irons in anyone's hand had to be swung around carefully. In Rose's hands a punty iron tipped with semi-liquid glass had literally been a lethal weapon, and it had seemed to me that as it was me she was after, however weird and mistaken her beliefs, it was I who ought to stop her.

I'd tried to stop her with the shattering horse and I hadn't succeeded. It had torn a hole in her lover and stoked her own anger, and I'd thought then, if I could blind her she would stop, so I'd thrown the powder, but blinding her had made her worse.

Paul had died.

If I hadn't tried to stop her, if instead I had surrendered at once to her as she'd demanded, then Paul would be alive. But, I reflected, searching for comfort, I couldn't have given her the tape she demanded as I hadn't known exactly where it was.

I'd done my best, and my best had killed.

The voice of the superintendent brought me back to the present. He said he was eager to get to the police station to interview his prisoners and also that he was less eager, but duty demanded it, to visit DC Paul Cratchet's family. 'Would the professor and Mr Logan come with me now, please, sirs,' he said.

'Another cup of tea?' I replied.

The super was not happy. 'Contrary to popular belief, the tea at the nick is quite drinkable. So, if you please.'

I needed more time.

Settling into another deep armchair, I said, 'Just a moment to sit down? I'm exhausted. How about something to eat before we go?'

'We have a canteen at the station. You can have something there.' The voice of authority had spoken and there seemed little else to do but comply.

I rose slowly to my feet and with relief found my expected guest hurrying at last through the door.

'Hello, Priam,' I said.

He looked past me towards the tall elegantly suited George Lawson-Young. He flicked a glance at Bon-Bon as much to say, 'Is this the one?'

'Priam,' I repeated, 'it's so good of you to come. Priam Jones, can I introduce Superintendent Shepherd of the West Mercia police.'

Priam turned slowly my way and instinctively shook an offered hand.

'I'm sorry?' he said, puzzled, 'I don't quite understand. Bon-Bon called me to say that she was with a potential racehorse owner and I should get down here pronto if I wanted the business. Interrupted a good lunch too, I can tell you.'

He looked around him still searching for the elusive owner.

'Priam,' I regained his attention, 'that wasn't quite the truth. I asked Bon-Bon to make that call because I needed to talk to you.' He wasn't pleased. Far from it.

'What's wrong with the bloody telephone if you needed a chat, although about what I can't imagine.' He looked down at four sets of childhood eyes staring up at him. 'Hmp . . . sorry.'

I said, 'I needed a chat about a videotape.'

'Not that bl— er . . . er . . . videotape business again,' he said. 'I have told you already, I don't have any videotape.'

Daniel said distinctly, 'I know where there's a videotape.'

'Shhhh, darling,' said Bon-Bon.

'But I *do* know where a tape is,' Daniel persisted.

I had learnt to take Daniel very seriously indeed.

I squatted down to his level on the sofa. 'Where is the videotape, Daniel?' I said.

'I think it must be worth at least three or four gold coins,' he replied.

'What *does* he mean?' asked Professor Lawson-Young.

'It's a game we've been playing,' I said. 'I give Daniel treasure if he gives or finds me information.' I turned back to Daniel. 'I think it might indeed be worth three or four gold coins.'

'A whole bagful of treasure,' said the professor, 'if it's the right tape.'

Daniel looked positively delighted at the prospect.

'It's in Daddy's car,' he said. 'It's in the pocket on the back of Daddy's seat. I saw it there yesterday when Mummy brought us to your shop.'

He looked at me questioningly and beamed when I told him, 'Ten gold coins this time if the professor agrees.'

George Lawson-Young, speechless, nodded his head until it seemed it might fall off.

Daniel said, 'I like finding things for Gerard. I'll always look for things for him.'

Priam shuffled uneasily beside me.

I said to him, 'Why did you switch the tapes?'

'I told you—' he started.

'I know what you told me,' I interrupted. 'It was a lie.' Discard the lies, the professor had told me in Bristol and I would be left with the truth. I asked again, 'Why did you switch the tapes?'

He shrugged his shoulders. 'I thought,' he said, 'that the tape Eddie Payne passed to you was one showing the hiding place of an antique necklace. Worth millions, I'd heard from someone. I found it in your raincoat that night and I thought, with Martin dead, no one would know if I kept it.'

Half truths and misconceptions had woven a path to death and destruction.

Priam went on, 'I took another tape from Martin's den, one with racing on it, and wrapped it in the same piece of paper and put it back in your raincoat pocket. When I played the original tape at home that night I discovered that it was all unintelligible mumbo jumbo with nothing about a necklace. So I just put it back in Martin's car when I drove it back to Bon-Bon's the next day.'

He looked around him. 'No harm done. You have the tape back. No need for the police.'

No harm done. Oh God, how wrong he was.

It was four days before the police would allow me back into Logan Glass.

Broadway had been the centre of a media circus. The Dragon from over the road had previously said, 'You were always news in this town, lover' and, for filling her rooms, she allowed me use of her best suite and paraded her little glass animals along a shelf in the lobby with a notice offering duplicates for sale.

Marigold, her natural competitor in the matter of saris, kaftans, eyelashes and 'Darlings', wandered in and out waiting for me to start again on her trophy. Worthington, who had been upgraded from her chauffeur to her arm-in-arm companion, was dispatched with me to collect the necklace from the bank. Marigold secured total victory over the Dragon by wearing it day and night and finally buying it from me outright at huge expense.

Rose, Norman Osprey, Dr Force and Hickory had been

remanded in custody while Eddie had been remanded in hospital, his hands a mess.

Priam, not understanding the fuss, had been given police bail, which meant that his passport had been confiscated. 'Most inconvenient,' he had declared. 'Why have I been treated like a common criminal?' Because he was one, Worthington had told him and anyone else who'd listen.

Professor George Lawson-Young had been given the tape from Martin's car. There had been a few ugly moments when the superintendent had tried to hang onto it as evidence. Having once lost the information it contained, Lawson-Young had no intention of allowing it out of his sight again. The police had reluctantly consented to him taking it away briefly to make a copy.

Catherine, cuddling in my arms every night, kept me up to date with the news from the police station.

Rose did little else but scream abuse, most of it in my direction, it seemed.

Hickory blamed, me, Rose and the world in general.

Dr Force had said a little but denied most. He had revealed, however, that Martin Stukely had not been aware that the information on the tape had been stolen. Indeed, the doctor had told Martin that he was protecting the research from others trying to steal his own work.

I was glad of that. Had I doubted it?

On Thursday we re-opened. The showroom was busier than it had ever been on a weekday in January and sales boomed. But, in truth, there was far greater interest in the bloodstains, which had proved difficult to remove from between the bricks on the floor, than in the stock.

Pamela Jane had recovered sufficiently to return in time for the weekend although she preferred to work in the showroom and made rapid transits across the workshop to her locker only when she couldn't avoid it.

On Sunday, one week after the mayhem, I set out again to make the trophy horse.

Dependable Irish had agreed to act as my assistant and this time we had an audience of one. Catherine sat in her now familiar chair and watched as I again readied my tools and stripped down to my singlet.

I stood on the treadle to lift the door to the furnace and let the heat flood into the room.

Catherine took off her coat.

'Hang it in my locker,' I said, tossing her the locker keys.

She walked to the far end of the workshop and opened a door to the tall grey cabinet.

'What's on this?' she said holding up a videotape. 'It has a label "How to make the Cretan Sunrise".'

I moved swiftly to her side. She had by mistake opened Hickory's locker and there inside we found not just the necklace instruction tape but also, tucked into a brown paper bag, a pair of bright laces, green and white striped.

I laughed. 'A tale of three tapes and one of them was under my nose all the time.'

'Three tapes?' she asked. 'Two were bad enough.'

'There were three,' I replied. 'The only really important, valuable and perhaps unique tape was the one Force
made of the stolen cancer-research results. He gave it to
Martin who via Eddie gave it to me. Priam swapped it,
mistakenly thinking it a treasure finder's dream to millions. When he found that it wasn't, he simply left it
hidden in Martin's car. That was the tape that Rose and
Dr Force were trying so hard to find.'

'And the necklace tape?' Catherine asked. 'This one?'

I said, 'I had lent the necklace instruction tape to
Martin and it remained in his den at his house until
Hickory stole it along with all the others. Hickory kept it
because, to him, the tape had some value. He thought he
could make a copy of the necklace. He obviously kept
the tape in his locker.'

'What's the third tape then?' she said.

'The tape,' I went on, 'that Priam took from Martin's
den before Hickory's theft. He put it in my raincoat
pocket and it's that tape that Force stole at midnight on
New Year's Eve thinking it was his cancer tape. I would
have loved to have seen his face when he played it and
found horse racing instead.'

I made the trophy horse. With Irish's help I gathered the
glass from the furnace and again formed the horse's body,
its legs and tail. But this time I took time and care and
applied the knowledge and talent both learnt and inherited

from my Uncle Ron. I moulded the neck and head of an intelligent animal, prominent cheekbones and a firm mouth. I gave it a mane flowing as if in full gallop and then applied it seamlessly to the body.

I had started out to make a commercial work for Marigold and Kenneth Trubshaw and his Cheltenham Trophy Committee. In the event I made a memorial to a trusted and much missed friend. A memorial worthy of his skill and his courage.

The leaping horse finally stood on the marver table and Irish and I lifted it quickly but carefully into one of the annealing ovens. There it would cool slowly and safely allowing the strains and stresses to ease gradually. This one was not for shattering.

I went with Catherine to the funeral of Pernickety Paul, but I abandoned her at the church door to her colleagues, uniformed and not. A small bunch of plain-clothes police-men enveloped her and mourned with her and it was a thoughtful and subdued police officer who, an hour later, mounted her motor cycle, paused before starting the engine, and said blankly to her future passenger, 'The private cremation's tomorrow and there are drinks in his memory in the pub this evening. I've been given leave for the rest of the day, so where do you want to go now?'

'To bed,' I said without hesitation, and added that surely Pernickety Paul would have approved.

Catherine shed sorrow like melting snow.

I said, 'I haven't seen where you live, remember? So how about now, then?'

She smiled with a touch of mischief and then kicked down on the starter and invited me to step aboard.

Her home was maybe five minutes' walk or less than one minute's motor-cycle ride along a straight grey road from the district police station. She stopped outside a single-storeyed semi-detached bungalow in a row of identical stuccoed boxes, and I knew within a second blink that this was not the place for me. Going there had been a mistake but, as Catherine was my transport, I would smile and pretend to like it.

I actually did both, and not from politeness's sake.

Inside, the plain clothes's one-floor living space had been allied to *Alice's Adventures in Wonderland*, where a more than life-size March Hare and a same-size Mad Hatter sat at the kitchen table and stuffed a dormouse into a teapot. A white rabbit consulted a watch by the bathroom door, and a red queen and a cook and a walrus and a carpenter danced a quadrille around the sitting room. All the walls, everywhere, were painted with rioting greenery and flowers.

Catherine laughed at my expression, a mixture no doubt of amusement and horror.

'All these people,' she said, 'came to me from a closing down fun-fair when I was six. I've always loved them. I know they're silly but they're company.' She suddenly swallowed. 'They have helped me come to terms with losing Paul. He liked them. They made him laugh. They're not the same now, without him. I think I've been growing up.'

In keeping with the rest of the house, Catherine's bedroom was a fantasy land of living playing cards painting rose bushes white and strong pink against puffball clouds and vivid green leaves.

Brought to a standstill, I said weakly, 'Lovely,' and Catherine laughed.

'You hate it, I can see.'

'I can shut my eyes,' I said, but we pulled the curtains closed.

We made love there in Pernickety Paul's honour but, in the evening, after the party in the pub, when Detective Constable Dodd and her pillion rider climbed back on the saddle, it was to the big quiet house on the hill that they went.

It was like coming familiarly home.